Sometimes we forge our own path.

Sometimes the path is created for us,
and we can only follow.

Chapter 1

Rachel

There has to be a corollary scientific relationship between being genetically blessed and acting like an asshole.

I looked again at the reason for my friend's inebriation standing outside the men's room. Of course, the line for the ladies' room was five deep, because only men should be allowed to relieve themselves at their leisure. Married Guy was standing there, texting away on his phone—probably lying to some other unsuspecting woman. I studied his left ring finger as his fingers worked furiously. No ring. *Shocker*. I'm sure a shiny metal band that symbolizes eternally committing yourself to another person tends to make selling that you're single and *looking for the woman of your dreams* more difficult.

Ugh. What an asshole.

I loved Ava, but I think I'd be suspicious of any thirty-year-old guy who said that type of crap on a first date.

My eyes lifted from Married Guy's hand to his face, just as he looked up. If only eyes could really shoot daggers. I scowled at the bastard. I'm not sure why I was surprised when he smiled at me.

Jerk.

Probably thought I was checking him out.

I took my own phone from my pocket to distract myself and cast my eyes down to catch up on texts while I waited. Only...I couldn't see the damn letters without my glasses. I put the phone away and felt eyes on me as I patiently waited, but frowning uses more facial muscles than smiling, and this jerk wasn't worth a wrinkle.

After I used the ladies' room and almost scalded my hands washing them—the sink at O'Leary's only has one temperature: hotter than shit—I was ready to go home. My shift was over an hour ago, and Ava had been miserable since the cheater walked in, so I doubted she would object to calling it an early night.

A rich baritone voice stopped me on the way out of the ladies' room. "Do I know you from somewhere?"

I turned to find Married Guy pushing off the wall as if he'd been waiting for me. *Ignore him, Rachel. He's not worth your time.* I looked him in the eyes to make certain he knew I'd heard him, then turned my back and headed down the long hallway to the bar.

He didn't take the hint. Falling in stride next to me, he started to say something when I stopped abruptly. I turned to face him. "You're a total asshole. You know that?"

He had the nerve to look shocked. "Me? I guess we do know each other?"

"I know your *kind*."

"What the hell does that mean?"

I rolled my eyes. "You think just because you're gorgeous you can go shitting all over people, that you can smile your way out of anything. Well, I really hope karma bites you in the ass someday, that your pretty little wife winds up fucking half of New York and passes you an STD that makes your big dick fall off."

He held up his hands. "Listen, sweetheart, I don't know who you think I am or what you think my *big dick* has done wrong, but I'm pretty sure you're confusing me with someone else."

My face told him to save his bullshit. "I'm here with *Ava*."

"*Oh. Ava.* That explains it."

I growled at him—literally. "*Grrrrrrr*...Well, it should."

The jerk flashed a mega-watt smile. "You're cute when you growl like that."

My eyes nearly bulged from my head. "Are you actually *hitting on me*?"

"That would be wrong, wouldn't it? Considering...you know...me and Ava and all."

"You're a piece of work." I turned to walk away.

"Wait." He grabbed my arm, stopping me again. "Can I just ask you one thing?"

"What?"

"Who's Ava?"

Unreal. A guy like him—it was possible he didn't remember the names of the women he screwed over. I mean, it had been a whole *two weeks* since the last time they'd slept together. "Go home to your wife, *Owen*."

I left married Owen standing in the hallway and went back to the table where Ava was quietly drinking away her pain.

"You wanna get out of here? I'm sort of tired, and I need to be up early in the morning."

I figured there was no use in mentioning my little run-in with Owen. It would only make things worse. Unfortunately, Ava had really started to fall for the asshole. In the month they were seeing each other, he'd made her swoon—feeding her crap about how he saw their future with two kids and a pug.

Ironically, he was right. Their future did entail two kids and a pug. Because he'd been holding a leash while walking with his two, tow-headed little girls when she ran into him in the park. Only he'd failed to mention that in this version of his future, his *wife* would also be holding their month-old son as they strolled.

Ava wobbled a bit as she hopped from the barstool. "I should climb up on this bar and tell every woman to watch out for that asshole."

Normally, I would've agreed. But tonight I was pretty sure her climbing up on the bar would end in a trip to the emergency room.

"He's not worth your breath." I slipped her sweater from the back of the stool and held it up for her to put on. She sighed and missed putting her arm into the hole the first two times.

Behind the bar, Charlie—who had been listening to us for most of the night—was pouring a beer. "That's it. From now on I want names." He slammed the full mug on the wooden bar, causing beer to slosh all over. "I'm runnin' any assholes either of you go out with." Charlie O'Leary owned the Brooklyn pub where Ava and I worked. He was also a retired cop.

I smiled. "Okay. But you know that makes me want to give you the names of suspected serial killers—just to watch your ears turn that lovely shade of purple they turn when you're pissed off." I leaned over the bar and kissed him on the cheek. "'Night, Charlie-o."

He grumbled something about being grateful he didn't have daughters and waved me off.

"Can we go out the back door?" Ava asked. "I don't want to pass him on the way out."

"Sure. Of course."

I hooked my arm with hers to make sure she stayed steady as we walked. After a few steps, I looked up and saw Married Guy standing next to the back door.

"Ummm, Ava, we should go out the front. He's standing at the back door now."

She looked around the room. "No, he's at the front door talking to Sal, the new waiter."

She was more wasted than I thought. I lifted my chin toward the rear exit, a straight line to Owen. "That's the back door, Ava."

"I know. Owen's at the front door."

I furrowed my brow. "Isn't that Owen? With the blue button-up shirt?"

She drunk-snorted. "I said he was the good-looking guy in the blue shirt, not the Greek god modeling one."

My head whipped to the front of the bar. There was only one guy near the front door who I didn't know, and he was talking to Sal. "Owen is talking to the new waiter right now?"

She looked again and then sighed and nodded. "I should tell Sal to punch him."

"Ava—the guy talking to Sal right now, right at this moment, is Owen?"

"Yes."

"His shirt is *brown*, Ava. Not blue."

She turned again toward the front door, squinted, and shrugged. "Maybe. I can't see so good. My contacts are all smudgy from my makeup and crying."

When she'd said her ex had just walked into the bar and pointed in the general direction of the front door, there'd been only one guy with a blue button-up on.

Shit.

I'd told off the wrong guy.

Since I couldn't very well make Ava leave through the front door where the *real* Owen was standing, I sucked it up. Of course, Not Owen had his eye on me, with a smirk, the entire way to the back door.

He nodded at my friend as we passed. "Have a good night, Ava. 'Night, Feisty."

I took the cowardly way out and kept my head straight, not making eye contact with the guy, until we were out the door.

Ava wasn't so strong willed. Her head turned as she kept her eyes fixed on Not Owen, even as we made our way into the alley. She might have been drunk with smudgy contacts, but she wasn't blind.

"Holy shit. Did you see that guy? And did he just say my name?"

I glanced back just as the bar door was closing. Not Owen waved with a cheeky grin.

"You're hearing things."

———

God, I was going to be late.

As if Monday classes weren't bad enough after working a double shift on Sunday, I had a stain on my blouse from spilling my coffee when I had to jam on the brakes for an old man driving an enormous Cadillac. He'd decided he needed to make a left...from the right lane.

The first day of school was always a nightmare. People wandered around campus, standing in the middle of the road while giving fellow classmates directions to various buildings. I honked my horn at two underclassmen doing just that. They looked at me like I was the annoying one.

Come on. Move it, people.

After circling the parking lot three times, I parked in a reserved spot in front of Nordic Hall. Leaning over, I rummaged through the glove compartment, half of the contents falling to the floor as I searched for what I needed.

Got it.

I tucked an old ticket under my windshield wiper and took off for lecture hall 208. I really needed to pee, but was going to have to hold it until after class. I knew three things about Professor West, other than that he was in the music composition department. One: He'd gotten rid of his last TA because she refused to grade as hard as he wanted her to. Two: For the last week, whenever I told anyone I'd been reassigned to Professor West, they made a face—not an encouraging one—and said he was an asshole who almost got fired a few years back. And, three: He hated when students were late. He was known to lock the door as class started so latecomers couldn't interrupt his lecture.

None of those boded well for me. But what choice did I have? My TA position with Professor Clarence had been eliminated when he died suddenly three weeks ago from an aneurysm. I was lucky to secure anything, at this point. And without a teaching assistant position, there was no way I'd be able to afford the tuition at the Music Conservatory. I was already waitressing full time at O'Leary's just to pay my rent and partially reduced tuition.

Beads of sweat trickled into my cleavage as I arrived at the classroom. The door was closed, so I took a minute in an attempt to make myself presentable, smoothing down my dark, wild curls as best I could, considering the humidity. It was hopeless to try to fix the stain that pretty much covered my right breast, so instead I switched hands and hid it with the leather portfolio I was carrying. Taking a deep breath, I reached for the door handle.

Locked.

Shit.

Now what? I checked the time on my phone. I was only eight minutes late, and it was the first day of the fall semester, yet I heard the professor already lecturing inside. Did I knock and interrupt the class, knowing it was his pet peeve? Or did I pull a no-show on day one of my new position?

Lateness was the lesser of two evils.

Or so I thought.

Rapping my knuckles lightly on the door a few times, I hoped a student at the back of the classroom would hear it, and I could slip in unnoticed.

The professor's booming voice silenced just as the door opened. It was a stadium-seating lecture hall, so I was entering at the top row, while the professor was down at the bottom. Luckily for me, he was facing the other way and writing on the board when I tiptoed in. "Thanks," I whispered as I settled into the closest seat in the back and let out a relieved breath.

But perhaps that feeling of reprieve was premature.

The professor continued to write as he spoke. "Who arrived late?"

Ugh.

I wanted to sink down into my seat and pretend it wasn't me. But I was the TA, not a student. I needed them to respect me, as I'd be teaching this class on occasion.

I cleared my throat. "I was late, Professor."

He capped the dry erase marker and turned around.

I blinked a few times. My eyes had to be screwing with me. Reaching into my purse, I pulled out my glasses and slipped them on—even though my distance vision was perfectly fine—as if by some miracle putting on my reading glasses would make the man standing in front of the room someone other than who he was.

But he wasn't someone else.

There was no mistaking that. He had a face people didn't forget.

A damn gorgeous one.

It was *him*.

Holy shit.

It was really *him*.

Screwed.

 I was royally screwed.

The professor scanned the room of more than two hundred students, unable to ascertain where the voice had come from. I prayed he'd drop it and give the class a general warning on his intolerance for lateness.

No such luck. I never had any.

"Stand up. Whoever was late, please stand up."

Oh, God.

I felt the weight of the twenty-five-thousand-dollar tuition discount I had as a TA sink in my stomach like lead. It made it hard to get up from the chair. But he was waiting. There was no avoiding it. This was going to be a problem.

Hesitantly, I stood, holding my breath that he wouldn't recognize me.

Maybe he'd had too much to drink and wouldn't even remember our short exchange at the bar last night.

"I will not tolerate student lateness. It interrupts my class."

"I understand."

The overhead lighting reflected into his face as if he were an actor on a stage, making it difficult for him to see up to the top rows of the classroom. He held a hand up, shielding his eyes. Now, I was elevated twenty rows above him—we had to have been more than fifty yards apart—yet when our eyes met, they locked like we were the only two people in an empty room.

I knew it the minute he recognized me. I watched it play out in slow motion. A lazy smile spread across his handsome face, though not a happy one. I'd say it was more reminiscent of a dog who'd just backed a kitten into a corner and was about to have his fun playing with the poor little pussy.

I swallowed. "It won't happen again. I'm Rachel Martin, Professor. Your TA."

Chapter 2

Rachel

The class was completely empty. I wasn't even sure he knew I was still in my seat. If he did, he was good at ignoring me as he packed up his laptop.

"Contrary to the rumors you've probably heard, I don't bite."

I jumped when he spoke. Now that the lecture hall was no longer filled with students, the acoustics of the large space bounced his deep voice all over the walls.

I stood and began my walk of shame down to the front of the classroom. There was no doubt I owed the man an apology, even if he wasn't a professor—a professor who would be my new boss for at least the next fifteen weeks. I wanted to kick myself in the ass for not apologizing last night before I left the bar. Now it would seem like I was only doing it because of the situation I was in.

Which was true, don't get me wrong, but I didn't want it to *seem* that way.

I took a deep breath. "I'm so sorry about last night."

His face was unreadable. "I figured you might be, right about now."

"I obviously thought you were someone else."

"So I assumed. You thought I was the asshole. The one with the big dick, was it?"

I shut my eyes. For the last ninety minutes, I'd replayed the entire exchange from last night over and over in my head. I thought I'd remembered everything I said, but apparently I hadn't. When I reopened my eyes, Professor West was still watching me. His stare was pretty damn intense.

I started to babble. "My friend Ava went out with this guy Owen for a month or so. He was full of shit from day one, but she didn't see it. Actually walked up to her when she was leaving work one night and said, 'Do you mind if I walk you home? My mother always told me to follow my dreams.' She fell for it, the entire act, from the first day. Then one Saturday, he was supposedly out of town on business, and she was across town running errands for her mother. She took a shortcut through Madison Square Park on her way back from the grocery store and ran into him. He was with his wife and kids."

"And you thought I was him, apparently?"

I nodded. "She came in during my shift and started drinking Long Island iced teas. When Owen walked in, she pointed to where he was standing and said he was the one in the blue shirt."

"And we were both wearing blue shirts, I take it?"

I couldn't help but smile, thinking of Ava last night. "Actually, no. Ava's not much of a drinker. Turned out she was more sloshed than I thought. Owen's shirt was brown—not even black that could be mistaken as navy or something."

I saw Professor West's lip twitch.

"Anyway, I'm really sorry. I barely gave you a chance to speak, and then when I realized what had happened, I was so mortified I didn't even stop to apologize."

"I accept your apology for last night. Even though you shouldn't be approaching a man in the hallway to tell him off alone, your intentions were admirable."

I should have shut up and been grateful he'd accepted my apology. *Should have.* "Why can't I approach a man in the hallway?"

He leveled me with a stare. "Because you're five foot nothing in a loud bar, and no one would have heard you if I'd dragged you into the men's room and locked the door."

I folded my arms over my chest. "I can take care of myself."

"I didn't say you couldn't. I said you shouldn't put yourself in those situations."

"But you insinuated that I couldn't by making that statement."

He zipped his leather bag closed. "Ms. Martin, I just accepted your apology for calling me an asshole last night. Would you like me to retract that acceptance?"

God, I really was an idiot. Being around this man seemed to turn me into a psychopath. "No. I'm sorry. I acted like a jerk, and I'd like to start over, if that's possible."

He nodded. "Everything prior to this morning is forgotten."

"Thank you."

"But this morning is not. I won't accept lateness. Don't let it happen again."

I swallowed. "It won't."

He lifted his worn, brown leather laptop bag over one shoulder. "Meet me here at five tomorrow. We'll go over the syllabus and the classes you'll teach, as well as my grading rubric."

That was smack in the middle of my shift, but I'd figure something out. "Okay."

"Are you done for the day?"

"I am. I actually have to get to work. I'm covering Ava's shift because she isn't feeling too well after last night. We both work at O'Leary's."

"You waitress there?"

"Waitress, bartend, occasionally tell off patrons."

That earned me a full smile from Professor West. *God, he should do that more often.* No, forget that. He definitely shouldn't.

"I'll walk out with you."

We walked through the halls together and out to the parking lot. When we arrived at my car, I stopped. "This is me. So...five o'clock tomorrow?"

Professor West looked at my beat-up old Subaru. "You're parked in a spot reserved for the Provost. You got a parking ticket." He squinted. "Actually, it looks like you have *two* parking tickets. Was your inspection expired or something?"

Crap. "Umm...no. I keep an extra ticket in the glove compartment and stick it on my windshield when I'm forced to park illegally."

His brows shot up. "Inventive."

"Obviously it doesn't always work."

"Obviously."

"They need more parking. When you're late, it's impossible to find a spot."

He studied me. "Lateness is a frequent occurrence for you, I take it?"

"Unfortunately, it is."

"Then I should clarify something I said earlier."

"Oh, no, that's not necessary. I won't be late for your class."

He took a step closer and leaned in. "I'm glad to hear that, Ms. Martin. But that's not what needs clarification."

I swallowed. *God, he smells good.*

"Earlier I told you I didn't bite students." He smiled, and I felt the wickedness from it shoot down to some interesting places. "I don't. But I make no promises about not biting feisty TAs."

Some girls had dads who cleaned their shotguns when boys came to pick their daughters up at the house. I had Charlie.

Even though the City of New York had banned smoking in eating establishments at least ten years earlier, Charlie still lit up behind the bar. Filterless Benson & Hedges. Who was going to tell a burly ex-cop otherwise?

"So who's this man you're meeting tonight?" He pulled out the bat he kept behind the bar and placed it on top. "I'm gonna leave this right here for when he comes in."

I laughed as I lifted my drink tray. "I'm good, Charlie. He's a thirty-two-year-old accountant from the Upper East Side."

"Don't let that fool you. Looks can be deceiving. Salt looks a hell of a lot like sugar, sweetheart."

I wasn't even sure why I was attempting to date now. Ever since things ended with Davis eight months ago, I'd been on a self-imposed dating hiatus. I didn't have the time or energy to put into a relationship. Not to mention I didn't have a great track record with men, in general. I'd mostly done it to cheer up Ava. Last winter, she and her boyfriend of seven years broke up on her twenty-fifth birthday. They'd been together since their senior year in high school. After months of watching her pout, I finally talked her into signing up for one of those dating websites. I'd signed up in solidarity, too, although I never really had intentions of going out with anyone. Great job I'd done— the dating website was where she met married Owen. With friends like me to cheer her up, she'd be on Prozac in no time.

I delivered the drinks to my table and took an order from table eight, even though my shift was over. Basically, I was stalling to avoid going to change and get ready for my date. Table service at O'Leary's ended any time we felt like it after eight, and Charlie's motto was '*There's a burger joint down the street. Don't let the door hit you on the ass on the way out*', for anyone who didn't like it.

After I changed out of my uniform, I washed up in the bathroom, swiped some mascara on my lashes, glossed my full lips, and looked in the mirror. I was lucky I had my mother's naturally clear porcelain skin, so I never had to wear much makeup. I considered highlighting my green eyes with some black liner, but then changed my mind. *Good enough*, I thought. Which was probably not the effort I should have been putting into a first date.

After our initial email exchange, Mason had seemed nice enough that I continued to chat with him over the last few weeks. He checked all the boxes of the right guy for me to go out with: Gainfully employed—check. Polite—check. Over thirty, but not knocking on forty's door—check. Didn't use phrases like *fo-shizzle* and *my bad* in our message exchanges—check. Nice looking. Well groomed. Check, check. I should have been more excited. It had been a long time since Davis—time to move on.

I noticed him before he noticed me. I'd gone to the stock room to grab a few bottles of tequila for Charlie and saw Mason looking around. He looked like his pictures, so that was a plus. Maybe a little thinner than I'd expected, but nothing drastic enough to surprise me. He was medium height, medium build, and handsome, but not quite the type of looks you felt in your belly. Mason was also wearing a blue shirt. Which reminded me of Professor West last night. Oddly, *that* made me feel a little fire in my belly.

"I make no promises about not biting feisty TAs."

I shook my head to physically shake some sense into my brain and took a deep breath before heading to meet Mason.

You know that feeling you get when you think you're going to taste one thing and it turns out to be another? Maybe water and soda? It's not that you don't like either of them, but you were prepared for something tasteless and non-carbonated and instead you get unexpected fizz—a lot of fizz.

Mason was fizz when I expected tap water. Perhaps it was *accountant* that had led me to preconceived notions that he would be a certain way in person. But he was way more confident and forward than I expected.

"You're really gorgeous. Not that I thought otherwise from your profile picture, but you only had a head shot. I guess I didn't expect Megan Fox to continue from the neck down."

"Thank you...I think." While it was a compliment, I didn't like the way he eyed me. We had gone to dinner a few doors down and then come back to O'Leary's for a drink. His eyes roamed my body as he sipped his fourth Jack and Coke—which was another red flag—three hard liquor drinks during dinner on a first date? Each one made him bolder in a way I liked less and less.

"You said you were a hundred-percent Italian, right?"

"No. I have a little German in me, too."

He leaned in, putting one hand on my knee. "How'd you like a little more German in you tonight?"

Ugh. I was just about to tell the idiot he'd be playing with himself tonight, when Charlie interrupted. *With the bat.* He tossed it on the bar right between us, causing Mason to jump back.

"Everything okay over here?" My girl doesn't look too happy."

I didn't want to cause a scene. Just wanted my bad date to be over.

"That's your father?" Mason asked.

I ignored him and spoke to Charlie. "Everything's fine here. We were going to call it a night anyway."

Mason misunderstood. After he gulped back the remnants of his drink, he stood. "My place or yours?"

"You're going to yours. I'm going to mine."

He reached for me, and I stepped back. "Go home, Mason. Before you go home with Charlie's bat up your ass."

Realizing he wasn't getting laid, Mason paid the tab and took off. I smiled at Charlie after he was gone. "Did you double the price of Jack and Coke?"

"Asshole surcharge."

I laughed. Not wanting to walk out right after Mason, I sat at the bar with Charlie for a while.

"Dating sucks," I huffed. "No wonder I don't do it that often."

"I'm glad dating wasn't what it is today back in my day. I'd never have met my Audrey."

Charlie's wife had been gone at least ten years—heart attack in her early fifties.

"How did you two meet anyway?"

"The old-fashioned way, in the grocery store."

"That's sweet. Did your carts crash into each other like in the movies?"

"Something like that. Audrey was in the fruit and vegetable aisle picking out some eggplant, and she put her things in the wrong cart. She was halfway down the aisle before she realized. When she went back to find her cart, she noticed the cart she'd taken had a handwritten grocery list in it."

"She'd taken your cart?"

"Yep. She handed the list back and said, 'I took the wrong cart. Wouldn't want you to forget some of the important items on your list'."

"What was on your list?"

Charlie shrugged. "It said 'cheese and other shit'."

I furrowed my brow. "Literally? It said *cheese and other shit*? Not a list of the other shit?"

"I only cared about remembering the cheese. I like a slice of cheddar at night before I go to bed. The *other shit* covered the rest and wasn't as important." Charlie stared into space. "Anyway, Audrey smiled at me, and my heart did this weird double pump that it had never done before. Thought I was having a heart attack. Had to sit down right there next to the eggplants to catch my breath. Turned out it wasn't just cheese and shit I picked up in the supermarket that day."

"Maybe I should try the supermarket. I don't think online dating is for me."

"I never tried it, but seems dumb. Causes you to make this mental checklist of what you're looking for in a mate and then try to find people who can check all the boxes. But the reality is, doesn't matter which boxes are checked. When you meet the right person, your heart will let you know." He winked. "And other parts of your body."

Chapter 3

Rachel

I wasn't late. I was *really* freakin' late.

I also needed a shower, a mechanic, a bottle of wine, and quite possibly a new job—not necessarily in that order. And to think, I'd been running a half hour early just four blocks from the college. Plenty of time to find a parking spot and still walk in fifteen minutes before I was supposed to meet him, showing Professor Punctuality that I could be on time. But then...a blowout. A loud *boom* followed by a long *whoosh*. I tried to ignore it and kept on driving, but eventually the repeated flopping and tug of my car to the right made me pull over.

It sucked. But I had time, and my ex-roommate, ex-whatever he was for a little while, Davis, had taught me how to change a tire. All was good...at first. I whipped out my jack, lifted the car like a pro, and went to work on the flat. Everything was moving along nicely until I got to the very last lug nut. The damn thing was stuck. *Really stuck.*

At one point, since the lug nut was at the three o'clock position, I had the wrench on it and used my foot to try to bear down—it still wouldn't budge. Then I had the bright idea that maybe I should put *all* of my weight on it. So I jumped up on to the long handle of the lug-nut wrench, hoping the sudden force would pry the sucker loose. But instead, the wrench slipped off and somehow snapped back to smack me right in the shin.

Now I was twenty minutes late, my leg was killing me, and I'd just limped to school in ninety-degree heat, smelling like tire grease. My only hope was that maybe Professor West had also gotten a flat and was late himself. It was a long shot, but I had to hold on to something in order to keep from having a total breakdown as I rushed through the hallways.

Arriving at the lecture hall, I peeked in before opening the door. Of course, Professor West was sitting at his desk.

I took a deep breath and went inside to face the wrath.

"Before you say anything—I was a half hour early. I swear."

He'd been writing in a planner, and when his head came up, I saw he was wearing glasses for the first time. *Damn. They make him even sexier.* Was I insane for even finding his scowl kind of hot?

"And what happened today, Ms. Martin? Did you get distracted somewhere between parking illegally a half hour ago and finding my classroom? Stop to play in the dirt, perhaps?"

"What?"

He looked me up and down. "You have dirt all over your face and clothes."

My hand rose to my face, where I began to rub at my cheek. "Oh. This isn't dirt. It's grease."

"That makes it much better."

"I got a flat tire on the way over here." I had no idea where the dirt was on my face, but I was nervous and rubbed at random spots all over as I spoke. "The lug nut was stuck, and I couldn't get it off. I tried to—"

"Ms. Martin," he interrupted. "Stop doing that."

"But it's true. I really tried to get here early. I built in all this extra time and then boom—a flat tire. It wasn't my fault this time."

"I wasn't referring to your elaborate story. Stop rubbing your face. Look at your hands."

I examined my palms. *Shit.* They were full of grease. "Did I get it all over my face."

He pulled some napkins from inside his desk, stood, and walked to me. "Your face is covered in grease. Why don't you go to the ladies' room and wash up."

I nodded. Turning, I took a few steps toward the door and then thought of something. "You'll be here when I get back?"

Professor West smiled. "Yes, Rachel. I'll be here waiting. It seems to be our thing."

After I scrubbed the grease from my hands and face, I considered trying to wash the big spot from my shirt, but it was no use. So far I'd met my new boss three times. The first time I told him off, the second time I interrupted his class wearing a shirt stained with coffee, and the third time I made him wait almost a half hour and walked in covered in grease, looking like a disaster. It just kept getting better and better.

When I arrived back at the classroom, Professor West was already packed up.

"I'm sorry. Do you have a class now?"

"No. But it's going to start to get dark soon so we better get going."

Dark? "Ummm...okay. Can we reschedule? Maybe I can come before class tomorrow, and we can quickly go over what you'd like me to do?"

"No. We'll do it tonight." He put his hand on the small of my back, guiding me to start back up the stairs of the lecture hall with him. "You don't have to work your other job, do you?"

"No. I took the evening off."

"There aren't any other classes in here tonight, so we can come back after we're done."

"After we're done?"

"With your car. I'll get your spare on and follow you to the tire shop. Then we can come back and go over what we need to discuss."

"You're going to change my tire?"

"I'm not going to leave you stranded, Rachel."

"You don't have to do that, Professor West."

"Of course I do. And call me Caine."

Caine had some muscles to match that perfect face. He'd been wearing a white dress shirt, but removed it before starting to change my tire. Wearing only a thin, white undershirt, he worked the lug nut wrench while I fixated on the way his muscles bulged every time he flexed. He was able to dislodge the jammed lug nut, although it took a little elbow grease. He had the most incredible biceps, carved and tanned, with a vein that popped from the middle and ran all the way down to his forearms. If there was a such thing as arm porn, I was watching my very own channel. It felt wrong to look, but God, was I enjoying the view.

At one point, after he removed the tire, he lifted it to put into my trunk and his T-shirt rose, exposing two, deep-set indents that formed a V at the bottom of his chiseled abs. I had the strongest urge to reach out and touch his stomach, run my fingers through the thin trails of hair that ran down from his belly button and dipped into the black band of his underwear, which was slightly exposed.

He placed the deflated tire in my trunk and went to work installing the donut.

"You really should have a full-size spare," he said as he tightened the new tire. "These little donuts aren't safe. They throw the balance of the car off, and if you get into an accident driving on it, you're more likely to flip."

Every once in a while he looked up at me, and I almost got caught checking him out. I really needed to distract myself, so I went into the car and grabbed my phone to look up the nearest tire shop.

The sun was setting as he loaded the jack back into the trunk and slammed it shut. Even though it had cooled off a bit, it was still so humid. Caine was sweaty, and his T-shirt was definitely ruined.

"I think I owe you a T-shirt," I said, eyeing the grease all over it.

He looked down. "As long as it's ruined, might as well make good use of it." Caine wiped both his greasy hands on his chest, streaking lines across the remaining white of his shirt. He then proceeded to reach back and tug the dirty T-shirt over his head.

Getting the full view of his incredible body, I think my jaw nearly reached the ground. I had no idea if he noticed my staring, because I was unable to lift my eyes from feasting on the sight. He used the shirt to wipe the sweat from his face and then cleaned off his hands some more. I was beginning to sweat myself, even though I hadn't exerted an ounce of physical energy.

"Do you know where the nearest tire shop is?"

"Umm...it's only about three blocks from here."

"Give me a minute to throw my shirt back on and I'll follow you."

What a shame. "Okay. Thank you."

I sat inside my car for a minute, glad for a chance to collect my thoughts before I had to drive. How long had it been since I'd had sex? Eight months? God, I probably should've done the deed with Mason last night just to satisfy my libido. A little show of abs and muscle, and my panties were wet. I felt like a horny seventeen year old.

By the time we dropped the car at Tire Express, it was almost seven-thirty, and they told me I'd have to pick it up in the morning. Caine stayed by my side the entire time and even dealt with picking out a tire that was affordable when the salesperson tried to sell me one that cost more than I earned in tips in a week at O'Leary's.

"I feel like a broken record," I said once we were settled inside Caine's car. "I'm either apologizing or thanking you."

"No problem. You still feel up to going over the curriculum and working on a game plan for the semester?" He looked at his watch. "It's getting late. I can drop you at home if you're tired."

"I'm a night owl. Mornings are my issue."

He nodded. "Okay, then."

Just before he started the car, my stomach let out the most horrific growl. It was a loud, rumbling, gurgly sound that echoed through the quiet car. There was no trying to pretend it didn't happen.

Caine grinned. "How about we work on our planning over something to eat?"

I was clearly starving. I'd planned to eat something before I left work, but then we got busy, and I didn't want to stop somewhere and chance being late. Today was just filled with great planning.

"I'd love that."

He started the car. "What are you in the mood for?"

"I'm easy. Whatever you want is fine with me."

"How about a burger? Do you eat meat?"

Thankfully it was dark enough to hide my blush. "Umm...yes. I eat meat." And apparently that's exactly what my body and brain were in the mood for.

Chapter 4

Rachel

"**F**or the record, I wasn't feeding you a line the first time I saw you. You do look familiar." Caine sipped his beer.

The fact that he'd ordered a beer struck me as odd. I'd have taken him for something fancier—expensive wine or aged scotch, perhaps. Seeing him relaxed with a beer in his hand had me viewing the uptight professor in a whole different light. Or perhaps it was his abs that had adjusted my thinking.

"We've probably seen each other around campus," I said. Although I was pretty sure I hadn't seen him before. I'd remember a man who looked like him.

"Maybe."

"Do you go to O'Leary's often?" I asked.

"The other night was the first time I was ever there. Stopped on the way home from a friend's who just moved in a few blocks away."

"Well, basically, I'm either at O'Leary's, on campus, or home sleeping, or studying. Not much time for anything else these days." I pointed a mozzarella stick at him and smirked. "And that's not due to change. According to *People* magazine, this is going to be a year of all work and no play."

"Oh yeah? *People* magazine? Sounds like a solid source to set your expectations for the future."

"I think so. I did answer five questions to get that prophecy, so it's pretty reliable. One wrong answer and I could have been doomed for a year of adventure or soothing self discovery."

Caine chuckled. "Well, try to squeeze in a little playtime. You know the old saying—too much work and no play can make life dull."

"I'm good with dull. I've retired from being exciting."

"Retired from excitement? How old are you? Twenty-two, twenty-three?"

"Twenty-five." I shrugged. "I got my adventure quota in during my teen years, which were out of control. I'm playing catch-up with my adult life. Busy is good. Adulting is good."

Caine scratched his chin. "Out of control, huh? Like what?"

"No way, Professor. I've made enough bad impressions on you to last a while. I'll save some of those stories for after I've shown you how smart and talented I am."

Caine smiled. It was the first unrestrained smile he'd let slip past his guard. Leaning back into his seat, he slung one arm casually over the back of the booth. "Alright. Then tell me about you and music. I'll get to hear a little bit about your smarts and talent, and it'll help me plan which lessons you should teach."

"What would you like to know?"

"Why music?"

"You mean, why did I pick music for a major?"

"No. You obviously picked the major because you love music. But why do you love music?"

"That's a really broad question and kind of hard to capture in a few sentences."

"Give it a shot. There's no wrong or right answer."

"Okay." I thought for a few long moments. "Because music expresses all the things people can't say, but are impossible to keep quiet."

He didn't immediately respond. "Sing or play an instrument?" he asked after letting it sink in.

I smiled. Having been a music major for undergraduate, I knew my answer always confused people. "Neither. I can hold a tune, but I don't sing exceptionally well, and there isn't a particular instrument I excel at, like most music majors."

Basically, eighty-five percent of all music majors either sang or played guitar or piano. The remaining fifteen percent were the random drummers or saxophonists.

"Can't say I hear that often."

"I know. I learned to play a few instruments decently during my undergraduate work, but I don't want to be a musician or a rock star. My master's degree will be in musical therapy."

The waitress came and delivered plates with giant burgers. I'd hoped it would transition some of the attention away from me, but Caine must have been busy piecing the little bits I'd already shared together.

"I'm guessing whatever music helped you express that couldn't be said might be the same thing that caused you to have those out-of-control years."

"Am I that transparent, or are you that good at reading people?"

His eyes studied mine. "Neither. Let's just say I can relate well."

I nodded. "What about you? Did you want to be a rock star?"

"Something like that."

I grinned before shoving the burger into my mouth. "Wow. Thanks for sharing. You're an open book."

Caine chuckled. "Are you always such a wiseass?"

"Are you always so vague and dodgy when asked a direct question?"

He stared at me while he chewed and swallowed. "Alright. I wanted to be a rock star when I was younger. Is that a straightforward enough answer for you?"

I grinned. "Do you sing or play an instrument?"

"I played the drums."

"Play or played?"

"You ask a lot of questions."

"Does that bother you?"

He chuckled. "And there's another one. Eat your burger, Ms. Martin."

After that, we ate in relative quiet. But it was a comfortable kind of quiet. Caine cleared his plate, and I was still picking at my French fries when his cell phone rang. Looking at the name on the screen, he excused himself, saying he needed to take the call, and he left the table to speak in private. We weren't on a date or anything, but it made me wonder if he was married and didn't want his wife to know he was with someone. Cheater Owen was still fresh in my head.

When he came back, Caine apologized. "Sorry about that."

"No problem." Yet for some completely unwarranted reason, I was annoyed. "I'm done eating. We can get started. I've taken up enough of your time."

Once the busboy cleared the table, Caine took a folder out of his bag, and we began to go through the syllabus. We did some rough lesson planning for my first lectures and talked about meeting after the next class to finish going through the rest of the planning we needed to do. I'd be sitting in on three of his five classes and teaching one of my own. Caine asked about my work schedule and scheduled the extra-help sessions I would hold around my hours at O'Leary's, which was thoughtful. When we were done, he ordered a coffee.

"So, what rumors have you heard about me?" he asked, leaning back in the booth.

"Do you really want to know?"

"I'm sure I've heard most of them. But let's lay them on the table, and I'll tell you if they're true or not."

"Okay. Well, for starters I heard you were a stickler for punctuality. I guess I don't really need to ask if that one's true."

"I guess not." He smiled. "Anything else?"

"You fired your last TA because she wouldn't grade hard enough."

He nodded. "That's true, too. Although you're missing part of the story. She wasn't grading *her boyfriend* hard enough. Unless she was grading the things he wanted to do to her...because those were pretty well thought out. I'd know since that's what I found he was writing on his tests. No actual music answers, yet he was getting all As."

"Oh."

"Anything else?"

I have no idea why, but I decided to embellish the last rumor to satisfy my own curiosity. "You're married and you almost got fired for sleeping with your students."

The look on his face told me I'd hit a sore spot. Caine's jaw clenched, and his full lips thinned as they drew into a line. "Not married and stopped sleeping with my students after the first year."

I crinkled my nose. "So you used to sleep with your students?"

"I was young and stupid. The first year I taught, I spent almost all of my time on campus. It was the only place I met people."

"Ever hear of match.com?"

"Of course, wiseass. But people are rarely what they seem online."

36

I scoffed. "Tell me about it."

Caine raised an eyebrow. "Sounds like you know from experience."

"Just last night in fact."

"And..."

"And he only had one thing on his mind."

"Sex?"

I nodded. "Men can be such assholes. No offense."

That damn lip twitched again. "No offense taken. Unless of course you're calling me an asshole—clearly it wouldn't be the first time."

"Do you spend weeks talking to a woman and telling her you're looking for a relationship and then show up on the first date wanting nothing but sex?"

Caine's gaze shifted between my eyes. "I'm not looking for a relationship. But I'm upfront about that to try and avoid any expectations. Although I can tell you that even putting it out there from the get go—women don't always hear what I'm telling them. They hear what they want to hear." He paused. "Guess you could say women can be assholes, too. *No offense.*"

I laughed. "None taken."

His eyes roamed my face. "Can I offer you some advice?"

"Sure."

"You're beautiful. Any man who tells you he doesn't have thoughts of having sex with you running through his brain the moment he meets you is full of shit. But a man who can't tell that isn't what you're looking for isn't paying attention. Chances are that translates into a lack of attention in the sack anyway, and he isn't worth your time."

He was absolutely right, and there would be time to analyze his theory later, but in that moment, I was wondering one thing...*is* he *thinking about having sex with me right now?*

Chapter 5

Rachel

O ral perception.

Okay, so maybe the class was Aural Perception. Whatever. My mind was definitely all over the place as I sat in the back, watching Professor West teach about how different people—philosophers, composers, medical professionals, teenagers—conceptualize the act of listening. I remembered taking the course in my first year of undergrad school. I wasn't sure if I had matured and could appreciate a lecture like this more at twenty-five than at barely twenty-one. At least now the particular professor lecturing was able to hold my rapt attention.

While I was busy listening, the beanie-wearing guy next to me was drawing nudes. He'd sketched a page of faceless bodies that were actually pretty amazing, even if they were sort of lewd and graphic. He shrugged when he caught me looking, smiled and whispered, "Gotta do something while this full-of-himself jerk drones on."

Caine wasn't a professor who sat at his desk to lecture. He wandered around the room and interacted with the students. "Listening can be broken down into categories: informative, appreciative, critical, relationship, perceptive, discriminative. The method and timing of delivery can affect what we hear. Tell me, where do you listen to music, how is it delivered, and who was the last musician you listened to?"

A bunch of hands flew up. A woman in the front answered, "On the train, delivered from my iPhone, and Adele."

A male student responded, "I work at Madison Square Garden, so I get a lot of live music delivered at work. Last jam was Maroon 5 warming up."

The lecture hall had two sets of stairs, one on either side of the wide middle row of seats. I was sitting at the top, in an aisle seat next to the left staircase. Caine walked up a few steps at a time, taking responses from different students as he went.

A few rows ahead of me, a guy with a long beard said, "In the truck. I work for UPS and listen through an aux cord. Last night was an old Slayer album."

A woman on the opposite side of the stairs said, "At work. It's piped in at the doctor's office where I work as a receptionist. And it's the same instrumental music over and over."

"Seems like most people are getting their music delivered while traveling or at work. Anyone listen while doing anything else?" Caine walked up a few more stairs and stopped two below where I was seated. It gave me the perfect excuse to look at him, without overtly appearing to check him out. He spoke to another nearby student as I ogled.

Today he wore a dark suit vest buttoned over a white, textured dress shirt, sans tie. I wasn't exactly a fashionista, but I knew expensive clothing when I saw it, and Caine shelled out more for his dress shirts than I did for most of my complete outfits. He had a rich elegance about him, even though he'd paired the shirt and vest with a pair of jeans and black chucks. His skin was naturally sun-kissed, so I was reasonably certain he was European in descent— perhaps Greek or Italian. I couldn't quite place which, but whatever it was, it produced one hell of a chiseled man. His nose was straight and masculine, and from a profile view was as damn close to perfect as I'd ever seen. From the side, his dark lashes were magnificent. Any woman would pay a small fortune for the lushness that framed those chocolate-colored eyes. His jaw line was peppered with fresh stubble, and I found myself wondering what that might feel like against my skin. I was lost in that thought when I realized he was now looking right at me. He squinted, and I saw a hint of amusement in his eyes, even though he didn't smile.

When he took another step up, I tried to seem nonchalant, as if I hadn't been worshiping his ancestors, and looked forward—only to realize I was now perfectly aligned to stare at his crotch. I attempted to find somewhere else to put my eyes, but—was that...was that something in his pocket...or...? By the outline, I was pretty sure it wasn't something. Or actually it *was* something—something damn impressive.

Caine twisted at the waist to call on a woman on the other side of the stairs, and his jeans pulled more snugly, confirming exactly what I was looking at. Figures the gorgeous man also had a big dick. I turned my head, needing to look away from his thick bulge, and beanie artist gave me a flirty smile. I smiled back...right before Caine called on him.

Beanie artist was the first student the professor called on who hadn't volunteered by holding up his hand. Maybe he'd caught what the guy was doing and decided to bring him back into the fold of the class.

"What about you?" Caine's voice was curt. "What was the last song you listened to, and how was it delivered?"

The guy smirked. "Some Pharrell, delivered from my Bose speakers in my bedroom while I was getting it on."

The class snickered.

"Thank you, Mr...."

Caine held out his hand to invite the man to fill in the blank, and he did. "Ludwig."

Caine nodded and turned to head back to the front of the class. "All the examples today are appreciative listening. Before the next class, I want each of you to download Jason Derulo's 'Trumpets'." Listen to it using whatever method you last appreciatively listened to music—with your headset on, while commuting on the train, in the truck while you're working delivering packages, or, in

Mr. Ludwig's case, listening on his Bose at home while masturbating."

The class cracked up.

"When you're done, I want you to answer the questions on this page." Caine began to hand out papers for the students in the first row to pass back. "This isn't a test of any kind, so your answers should be honest. Don't read the questions on the paper until after you've listened to the song once. Otherwise, your brain will be searching for the answers as you listen instead of truly appreciatively listening. In our next class, we're going to compare the results you get with the results you'll get while doing other types of listening."

A few minutes later, the hour and a half class was over, and students piled out the door. I waited until the room had emptied and went down the stairs to the front to talk to Caine.

"On time and no stains on your clothing," he said as he packed his laptop without looking up. "Impressive."

"I've always considered fourth impressions the most important, you know." I smiled.

Caine zipped his bag. While I'd thought our conversation was playful, apparently I was wrong. His tone was stern, and he leveled me with a look that matched. "You shouldn't fraternize with students."

"Fraternize?"

"Whatever you want to call it."

"I don't understand."

He huffed. "Fuck. You shouldn't fuck the students. Is that clearer, Rachel?"

"Well, yes, it's clear what you meant now. But I'm not sure what would give you the impression I was screwing a student. I don't sleep with college guys."

"Does Mr. Ludwig know that?"

I had a feeling that's what this was about. "You don't need to worry about me giving anyone a preferential grade like your last TA. I promise."

Caine held my gaze for a few seconds, possibly assessing my sincerity, then gave me a curt nod. "So, which princess is it?"

I furrowed my brows. Then I realized he must've caught the quiz I was doing in the back of *In Style* magazine before class began—*Which Disney Princess are you?* I'd tossed it on top of my book bag on the floor once class began.

"Jasmine from Aladdin." I smiled.

"They get it right?"

"I like to think so. Jasmine is logical and skeptical."

"You know those things are a bunch of crap, right?"

"God, I hope so. Last month I took one in *Men's Health* called *How healthy are your testicles?,* and it wasn't looking very good for me."

Caine's lip twitched. "Wiseass. You ready to finish going through the syllabus?"

"I have about an hour before I have to get to work."

He lifted his bag from the desk. "Everything go okay with picking up your car?"

"Actually...no."

"What happened?"

"When they took off the tire, they found my ball joints were bad—whatever they are. They're replacing those, too, today."

"You need a ride to work?"

"I can take the bus. There's one right on campus that drops off two blocks from O'Leary's."

"I was going to suggest grabbing a bite while we finish up planning. I have a department meeting tonight and need to eat before then. Why don't we grab a bite at O'Leary's? Then you'll already be at work when it's time to start your shift."

"That would be great. And I'll treat." I grinned. "Since our food will be free and all."

"Looks like someone went to the supermarket?" Charlie looked over my shoulder at Caine standing behind me.

"Umm...no. This is Professor Caine West. I'm his teaching assistant at the music conservatory. Caine, this is Charlie. He owns O'Leary's."

Caine reached out his hand. "Nice to meet you, Charlie."

Charlie shook. "You got a record, Professor?"

"A record?"

"Yeah. I don't like my girl hanging out with trouble."

I piped in. "Charlie—he's my *professor*. I don't think an interrogation is necessary."

Charlie shot me a look. "Fine. But I'll be keeping my eye on you."

Caine didn't seem bothered in the slightest by Charlie's threat. If anything, he seemed amused. "Good to hear."

Finally releasing their handshake, Charlie lightened up a bit. "What can I get you, Professor?"

"I'll take whatever beer you have on tap. I was in here the other night. A friend of mine just moved in around the corner and said you made the best wings. But the kitchen had already closed for the night, so I didn't get to try them. How about an order of wings?"

Charlie was old school. Two things made him like a man: A firm handshake and complimenting his wife's wings. His face lit up proudly. "That's my Audrey's own secret recipe on those wings. Two orders coming right up. By the way, if you're ever here after the kitchen closes, just let someone know you're a friend of Charlie's. My crew is pretty friendly."

"Yes, they are. Rachel was very welcoming when we first met." He glanced over at me with a wicked gleam in his eye. "I should have asked her to make me a batch. I'm sure she would have been happy to."

None the wiser, Charlie poured Caine a beer and me a Diet Coke, and then headed to the kitchen to make our wings himself. It was that in-between time of the afternoon where the day crowd had gone home, but the evening crowd hadn't started to trickle in yet, so there were only a few regulars sitting at the bar—most of whom were retired cops.

"Cute. Very cute, Professor."

"I thought so."

46

Caine and I went to sit at a quiet table in the corner where there was room for us to spread out and work while we ate. Since I was teaching the next lesson, he talked about what he wanted the students to take away from the assignment he'd given them today.

"The locked closet in the corner of the classroom has two hundred pair of Bose noise-cancelling headphones. Teach them about how appreciative listening can become critical listening just by changing the mode of delivery. Have them listen to the song I assigned again in the same place—on the train, or at work—only cutting out the background noise. Then have them answer the same questions I gave out today. At least half the class will notice things they didn't the first time. The trumpets are synthesized."

"They are?"

"It's a good lesson on understanding the method of delivery and leads perfectly into the upcoming lessons on synthesized music."

"Wow. Okay." I furrowed my brow. "So, you let the students take home two hundred pair of Bose headphones? The professor didn't do that when I took the class a few years back. The college has certainly upgraded from the crappy headphones they used to give out in music-recording class."

"They're mine, personally. Not the college's."

I did the math. That was at least five thousand dollars for one lesson. "What if you don't get them back?"

"It's never been an issue."

I smirked. "Because all the students are afraid of you."

"Unlike the smartass TA," Caine muttered.

Charlie had his hands full with trays of wings, so he used his ass to push open the door that led from the kitchen. I slipped out of the booth to grab them from him.

"You should have whistled for me like you usually do. You shouldn't be carrying trays with your back."

"I didn't want to interrupt your date."

"It's not a date."

He looked over at Caine and shrugged. "Looks like a date to me."

"It's not," I said flatly. "We're working on lesson plans for class."

"Whatever you say," Charlie trailed off as he headed back to the bar.

I set the trays down at our table and noticed Caine's beer mug was empty. "Want another beer?"

"If you're joining me."

"I don't drink."

Caine's brows furrowed, but then an understanding crossed his face, and I realized what he'd thought.

"I'm not an alcoholic, if that's what you're thinking."

"Okay."

I really didn't want to elaborate, but he was waiting for me to speak again.

"I grew up around alcoholism. At one point, I found myself drinking a little too much when my life was spinning out of control. I didn't check myself into rehab or anything—I'm not a formal friend of Bill with a lifetime membership card or fancy sobriety chips—but I try to limit my drinking to celebrations and special occasions."

The reason I didn't normally elaborate was because people looked at me with sympathy in their eyes when I made such a statement. *Oh. She had a bad childhood.* Oddly, that wasn't what I found on Caine's face. His seemed to have admiration for what I'd just said, and I wasn't sure what to do with that. It made me uncomfortable.

"So...I'll grab you another beer, and I'll have an O'Doul's to join you."

He smiled warmly. "Sounds good."

When I returned to the table, I redirected the conversation back to work. "I was thinking—when it's time to collect the Bose headphones from the class, I'm not touching Mr. Ludwig's set. They need to be disinfected first."

Caine's beer was at his lips. "He was drawing you today, you know."

"Drawing me? He was sketching headless women with great bodies."

He sipped his beer. "And your point?"

"He wasn't drawing me."

Caine narrowed his eyes, and I got the feeling he was weighing whether or not to say whatever was on his mind. Apparently, he decided to go for it.

"You have two freckles on the left side of your neck."

My hand flew to my neck. He was absolutely right, but my hair was covering them. "What are you talking about?"

"You have a tendency to push your hair to one side—the right side. I noticed them the other day when we were in my car."

"Okay..."

Caine caught my eyes. "The sketches your friend was drawing. They had necks, but no heads."

"Yes. I noticed them. They weren't exactly appropriate to be drawing during class. But he's a really good artist."

"Yes, he pays attention to detail. All of the women had one thing in common."

My eyes widened. "No."

Caine nodded. "Two freckles on the left side of the neck. He was sketching you."

"But he's never seen me naked."

"He has an imagination." Caine's eyes dipped down for a glance at my cleavage. They gleamed with wickedness when they returned to meet mine. "Pretty damn good one, I'd say."

That caused a flutter in my belly that quickly traveled south.

Oh, God.

I tried to shake it off with a joke. "And this is why I don't date frat boys. Needless to say, I won't be collecting beanie boy's headphones or sitting next to him anymore."

"Good call." Caine smiled. "Stick to men."

He was right. Although I was starting to question whether my sticking to men meant getting stuck on one in particular.

Chapter 6

Rachel

It was that time of the month. Not the dreaded time, but the time I actually looked forward to. Davis's monthly texts came in like clockwork. I looked down at my phone.

Davis: *Next Wednesday 7pm? Miss you.*

On the first Wednesday of every month, my three old college roommates and I got together for dinner. Davis had been one of the roommates for the last two years of college. We'd had a thing for a short period—but the timing wasn't right for him.

I typed back.

Rachel: *Can't wait.*

Just as I hit send, Ava walked in. She worked the early-evening shift waiting tables, which meant I moved to behind the bar, and Charlie went home.

"Hey, Rach."

"Hey. Davis just texted. He's going to be at dinner next week."

Ava wiggled her brows. "It's about time. He's missed the last three. Maybe you can liquor him up and break that dry spell finally."

"Shut up."

Ava was the only person who knew about me and Davis. I threw the towel I'd been using to wipe the bar down at her. "I should never have told you."

"Told me?" she said, then proceeded to caress her torso with her hands as she groaned, "Oh, Davis. *Oh, Davis.*"

I laughed. "God, I can't stand you."

While Ava went to change for her shift, I thought about my old roommate. Davis wasn't the typical college student—not by any means. He was southern, full of *yes, ma'am* and *no, ma'am* polite manners, and had spent eight years in the military before coming to Brooklyn to study business. When he'd first moved in, he was also going through a divorce, having married his high school sweetheart at eighteen in a romantic gesture before leaving for his first tour in Iraq. As Davis told the story, their marriage had seemed to work for a long time. He'd occasionally visit and sent her home his paychecks. It stopped working when he left the military and his wife realized it was difficult to sleep around without getting caught when her husband wasn't halfway around the world.

Over the two years we lived together, Davis had become one of my best friends—until the night we celebrated his graduation. We both had too much to drink. One thing led to another, and before the night was over...*Oh, Davis.*

Even though I'd never honestly thought of him in that way before, the next day I was like, *Huh. Great guy. Nice looking. Giving in bed.* Suddenly I saw him in a new light.

It lasted a little over a month. While I'd been growing into the idea of coupledom, Davis apparently was not. He ended things, saying it was too soon after his divorce to be in a new relationship, especially with someone he already cared deeply about. I understood—well, sort of. Shortly thereafter, when our lease was up, we parted as friends... with promises to take some time and maybe explore things in the future. Between his years in the military and being married, he'd earned his freedom.

Although my dating hiatus since then could have had something to do with hoping his promise to explore things in the future might come to fruition, after eight months, I was finally taking the hint.

My phone buzzed with another text.

Davis: *What? No miss you back?*

Smiling, my fingers hovered over the keys as I tried to decide what to text. Ava emerged from the ladies' room in her server polo and ponytail. She tied an apron around her waist as she spoke.

"I almost forgot. You're never going to believe what I watched today."

"What?"

"Come on, guess."

"Okay. Porn. You watched porn."

"Nope," she smirked.

"You finally finished your *Walking Dead* marathon?"

"Nope."

"I'm going to need a little hint here. You're giving me nothing to go on."

"Okay." She tapped her nails on the bar deep in thought, then grinned from ear to ear. "It rhymes with *undress her best*."

I laughed. "I think you've lost your mind."

A couple I'd seated a little while ago at table two motioned they were ready to order. I lifted my chin to my crazy friend and pointed with my cell phone.

"It rhymes with *cable glue*."

She repeated what I'd just said out loud a few times. "Cable glue, cable glue, cable glue..." Then her eyes lit up. "Table two!"

I took an ordering pad and pen from the box under the bar and slid them over to her. "Go take the order, crazy lady."

I was still staring down at Davis's text, trying to figure out my response, when I figured out her riddle. Decoding it, I suddenly lost interest in my phone and tucked it under the bar where I kept it while I was working.

Ava took the order from table two and dropped it in the kitchen before returning to where I was pouring a beer.

"Undress her best—Professor West?" I asked.

"Very good! Although his name wasn't Caine West in what I was watching. It was Able Arsen."

"What are you talking about?"

"I was in a TA meeting today, and I met a guy who used to be the TA for Dr. Anderson."

"The music department chair?"

"That's the one. By the way, the TA's name is Norman—really bad name for a guy in his twenties, but he's cute. He asked me to get drinks with him and a bunch of other TAs this Friday, so you're going with me."

"Okay..." I was glad to see Ava had found something to cheer herself up with after the way she'd been feeling about Owen. Although I still didn't make the connection to how this guy related to Caine or who the hell Able Arsen was. "But what does this have to do with Professor West?"

"Dr. Anderson told him Professor West used to be in a band. Had a contract with a major music label, too." She pulled out her phone and began to swipe. Landing on what she was looking for, she pushed some keys and turned the phone to face me. "Meet Able Arsen."

The video was grainy, and the sound quality was horrible—probably shot on a first-generation flip phone. All I could make out was four guys playing onstage at a distance.

"Keep watching," Ava said.

Eventually, toward the end of the video, the person recording zoomed in on the drummer, who was also singing. His head was down as he banged away on the drums, bobbing along to the beat. There was something so sexy about the assertive way he gripped the sticks and the way his muscles flexed with each wail of the drum pad—what stamina must be required to move like that for hours on end.

The little flutter in my belly confirmed it, even before the musician looked up. But when that face met the camera, my breath caught.

Professor West had been just as gorgeous as a teenager as he was now. Only back then, he'd had that whole bad-boy-musician thing going on. Now, if I didn't know him and had to guess, I would have taken him for a jazz musician or maybe even classical of some kind. Somehow, sexy bad boy had grown into a sexy maturity.

When the song ended, Caine lifted his head and gave the crowd a crooked smile. His shoulder-length hair was wet from the workout, and he tossed a stick in the air, catching it with the other. Then he used his free hand to reach back over his head and tug off his sweaty shirt. The girls went crazy at his eight-pack abs. Rock star, Beatles-type crazy.

Wow.

That smile.

That body.

Just wow.

There were apparently many layers of Caine West, and I'd barely scratched the surface.

By the time I got home that night, it was after two in the morning. My feet were killing me, and all I wanted to do was soak in a tub and get some sleep. For a change, I didn't have to be at school or work until the afternoon. The tub was warm, and I let the water from the faucet sluice over my feet as I settled back to relax.

Although my brain had ideas other than relaxing. The minute I shut my eyes, a vision of a young Caine West up on stage infiltrated my thoughts. I'd forwarded myself the videos and watched them more times than I cared to admit between serving drinks tonight.

Giving in, I reached up for my phone and allowed myself one more replay. Finally in private instead of being caught by a smirking Ava as I tried to discreetly look down at my phone, I searched the grainy face for Caine's mannerisms. There were a few I recognized—the way his lip twitched and he shook his head when women started to scream his name while he played his solo. The way he walked around the stage like he owned it. Today his arena was a classroom, but the confidence he strutted with was the same. Yet it was his arms that really nailed it home. Each time he banged on the drum, the vein that ran from his bicep to his forearm bulged. I'd never thought a vein could be so sexy.

After I finished watching, the tub was nearing full so I used my toes to turn off the water. I knew I wouldn't be able to relax enough to fall asleep tonight if I didn't satisfy my curiosity, so I Googled Caine's old stage name.

Able Arsen.

I was shocked when thousands of hits came back. Scrolling through like a fiend, I found picture after picture of Caine. He wasn't the front man for the band, but apparently the media adored him—and who could blame them? I noticed the same girl in quite a few photos. She had long, dark hair and was thin—almost too thin. The hollow of her cheeks made her beautiful, high cheekbones jut out just a little too much. In most of the photos, she wore sunglasses and seemed to shun the attention of the camera. There were various pictures of her with the band, some with Caine's arm around her in an almost protective way. She was definitely younger than him—seventeen or eighteen, at best—and I couldn't quite tell if she was his girlfriend or perhaps a little sister.

When I sorted the photos and articles into date order, with the oldest ones first, I realized the pictures seemed to have stopped abruptly nine years ago. Three or four pages down in the search results, there was an article about the death of the lead singer, Liam Marshal. Able Arsen had disappeared after that.

What happened to you, Able Arsen?

Better yet, how did you wind up *Professor* Caine West?

Chapter 7

Caine - Fifteen Years Ago

"**B**less me, Father, for I have sinned." Looking up at the cross in the tiny, dimly lit room, I inhaled, sucking deep until the red ember tip burned through to the end of the rolling paper, heating my thumb and forefinger.

"You can't ask forgiveness for shit when you're in the middle of sinning again. You're supposed to be repentful, dickwad."

"Show some respect with your language. We're in a church, for Christ's sake."

Liam laughed from the other side of the dark booth. "Yeah, right. You just smoked a fatty in a confessional, and it's my language that's disrespectful."

He had a point. And since my half-baked brain was transitioning nicely into full-on mellow mode, I ditched out the tiny remnant of my smoke on the floor and slipped it into my pocket while it was still warm.

"I'm outta here," Liam said.

"We're supposed to work until noon."

"Screw that shit. Tell Father Frank I went home to spank one out if he looks for me." The sliding wooden window we'd been talking through, the one that separated the two sides of the confessional and covered the confidentiality screen, slammed shut. The door followed right behind as Liam took off.

There was still a half hour until I could go sign out with Father Frank, so I settled in, leaning my back against the cushioned red fabric, hoping to catch a few z's. The chair was pretty damn comfortable on the priest's side, must have been because they got stuck listening to other people's bullshit for hours every Saturday afternoon. I had no idea how these guys spent their entire lives in this place. Just being here for the last few Saturdays had been enough to freak me out.

Three weeks ago, my mother caught Liam and me ditching school again. It was our senior year, my mom was normally pretty cool, and parents expected a few cuts. That wasn't what sent God-fearing Grace West off the deep end. It wasn't even finding a half-naked and fully-stoned Emily Willis on her knees about to give me a blowjob in the yard that had freaked Mom out. Nope. What had gotten me involuntarily signed up for a month of cleaning St. Killian's on Saturday mornings was my music. Both of my parents hated that I had no intention of going to college or becoming part of the upstanding, family-owned investment firm that bore the West name.

So, I was sentenced to community service for wanting to play my drums and sing. After Father Frank's long talk with my mother, he also took every chance to remind Liam and me that playing music was no way for a man to make a living. Thank God, I only had one more week left here.

I'd just started to zone out with my eyes shut when the confessional door squeaked open. I had assumed it was Liam again.

"Sin again so soon, loser?" I said.

It sure as hell wasn't Liam who responded. The voice was tiny and shook with nerves as she spoke. "Bless me, Father, for I have sinned."

Shit.

A little girl was on the other side and had assumed I was a priest. From the sound of her voice, I figured she couldn't have been older than ten or eleven. *What the hell could she have to confess?*

I probably should have opened the door and walked out before she started to let me in on her darkest secrets. No, not probably. I *definitely* should have walked out. But...maybe it was the good weed. Maybe it was the sound of her shaky little voice that had me curious. Maybe I was just fucked up in the head. But instead of literally opening the door, I opened a figurative one instead. One that I had no idea would change my life forever when I opened my mouth.

"Go on," I told her. "Tell me your sins."

Chapter 8

Rachel

Caine had slipped in halfway through the class.

Suddenly I could understand why he found lateness distracting. For the last twenty minutes, *I'd* been distracted by the man sitting in the seat I'd sat in during the last class. Next to him, Mr. Ludwig, the beanie-wearing artist of nudes, looked as nervous as I felt. Although his nervousness probably had more to do with the fact that the professor had just quietly slipped the notebook he'd been drawing in again today from his desk, and it was now closed and sitting in Caine's bag.

I tried not to look up to where they were sitting, yet I could feel Caine's eyes watching me. How is it that I had two hundred pairs of eyes focused on me, and I only sensed two?

I cleared my throat. "Since we have a few minutes before the end of class, I'm going to hand out the headphones we spoke about earlier." I went to the supply closet in the corner of the classroom and pulled out a box. Handing it to the first row, I asked the student in the corner to take one and pass the box down as I delivered a full box to each row. Caine got up and quietly grabbed a few boxes to help me distribute to the rows at the back of the lecture hall before taking his seat again. As I distributed, I reminded the class of the exercise that built on Professor's West first assignment, and then I gave them one of my own.

"Along with the exercise we already discussed, I'd like you all to do a second listening assignment. We all have songs that remind us of good times in our early teens. Pick out the one that has the strongest memory for you. Tonight, when you're alone at home, I want you to shut the blinds, turn off all of the lights, and get the room as dark as you can. Then lie flat on your back somewhere comfortable, preferably in your bed, and listen to the song that holds those memories for you using the Bose headphones. Listen to it twice. That's it. Nice and simple. We'll use what you hear in an upcoming class."

After the class had emptied, Caine walked to the front. "Nice job."

"Thank you. I didn't think you'd be sitting in. It kind of threw me when you walked in late." I smirked. "I don't like lateness. I find it disrupts my class."

Caine raised a brow. "I'll keep that in mind."

I packed my laptop into my bag. "Mr. Ludwig didn't look happy to see you."

"Mr. Ludwig is lucky he's still sitting in my class at all."

Caine helped me collect the leftover headphones from each row, and then we consolidated the stragglers to make one box of headphones and nested the empty boxes inside each other.

"So, what's your song?" he asked.

My brows drew down. "Hmmm?"

"The assignment you gave. What's the song that reminds you of your childhood?" What immediately came to mind was an old Lynyrd Skynyrd song, "Devil in a Bottle," but that was a little more honesty than I could handle.

"I don't know. Probably anything from Maroon 5." Since I was a crappy liar, I avoided his eyes. But when I glanced up at him, I caught him doing that squinting thing. "What?" I asked.

"You're full of shit."

"What are you talking about?" I attempted to play dumb. Unfortunately, I felt my cheeks heat under his stare.

"There's a song you thought of right away. And it wasn't a damn Maroon 5 song." He scratched at his chin. "I bet there's more than one, too."

Rather than continue to lie, I decided to turn the table. "What's your song, Professor Know-It-All?"

He held my eyes. "'Going, Going, Gone'."

"Bob Dylan?"

"That's the one."

Hmm... Off the top of my head, I couldn't think of the words, but I knew it was a heavy and heartfelt song. I'd definitely be listening to that later on tonight with my borrowed Bose headphones. No better way to hone my critical-listening skills than trying to figure out the mystery of Caine West. Since he'd shared, I felt compelled to give him something. "'Hurt'."

He nodded. "The original Johnny Cash or Nine Inch Nails?"

I smiled. "Johnny. Always. He was my mom's favorite."

There was a tension between us as we looked at each other. Every time we were together I'd felt it. Each time it was a little different than the last, but the tension was always there—a crackle in the air. Today's wasn't so much sexual in nature as it was a feeling of understanding and acceptance. We'd both have depressing titles in our lives as narrated by song. Which reminded me...

"I heard another rumor about you."

"Oh yeah?"

"Well, actually, it was a rumor, but I know it to be true now. So I'm not sure it's a rumor anymore."

"You've figured out the rumors about me being an arrogant asshole are true, huh?" Caine teased. "That wasn't a hard one."

"Actually, this one was more along the lines of you being a closet rock star signed to a label."

I knew the second the words came out of my mouth that I'd made a mistake. Caine's face, which had been warm and playful, morphed into cold and serious. I'd crossed a line and overstepped somewhere he didn't want me. He was more than a little pissed off.

"Keep out of my personal life, Rachel."

I opened my mouth to apologize, but he cut me off.

"You should get to your other job. It might be the only one you have soon." With that, he grabbed his leather bag and was up the stairs and out of the classroom before I could even shut my big mouth, which had been hanging open.

He punctuated his exit with a slam of the classroom door that left the walls shaking in his wake.

"You sure everything is okay?"

It was the third time Charlie had asked. The first time was when I dropped a full tray of drinks on the floor. Two of the glasses shattered, and I was so dazed cleaning it up that I sliced open my finger. The second time, I was lost in my head and over poured a beer from the tap. Now he was getting ready to leave, and his face was etched with concern.

"I'm fine, Charlie. Just a little tired," I lied. "I stayed up working on my thesis, and I have a bit of a headache. But I'm fine. I'm sorry about earlier."

"I could give two shits about the glasses as long as you're okay." He looked me in the eyes. "You're sure? I can stay and you could take off."

I smiled. "I'm good. But thank you."

Wednesday night was the slowest night of the week anyway. It was just Al and me tonight, an old retired cop friend of Charlie's who worked the bar a few nights a week. I was glad Ava wasn't working so I wouldn't be grilled about my mood. All evening, my emotions had jumped back and forth between feeling bad that I'd pried into Caine's life and feeling pissed that he'd been such an asshole when I mentioned his past.

There were only a few customers in the small, open dining area that adjoined the bar, which left me ample time to overanalyze what had transpired between me and Caine this afternoon. Clearly I'd ventured into territory where I wasn't welcome, but it didn't feel like it was because of our pseudo employee-employer relationship. He led the way poking into my personal life, so it wasn't as if having a personal-ish relationship was out of bounds for him. This felt more like I'd touched a nerve than pushed the boundaries too far. He'd said, "Keep out of my personal life," yet for reasons that didn't make any sense, I was certain he meant *Keep out of* this *area of my personal life*.

But that wasn't what was bugging me. Don't get me wrong, I felt bad that I'd upset him. I would have felt bad for intruding on anyone's life in an area where they didn't want a flashlight shined. What was confusing was the degree to which it bothered me. I was attracted to Caine on a physical level, that I couldn't deny—who wouldn't be? But him being so curt and upset made me realize my attraction to him was more than physical. I was crushing on my damn professor. Since that first day after class, I'd been drawn to him on another level.

Just before nine, I came out of the ladies' room and checked on my one remaining couple who lingered at their table having coffee. Out of my peripheral vision, I spotted someone who had seated himself at one of the pub tables and went over to make sure he knew the kitchen was already closed for the day. I was shocked to find it was Caine sitting alone at the table.

"Professor? What are you doing here?"

His eyes answered for him. There was trouble lurking in the background. "Can you sit for a few minutes?"

"Ummm...sure. Let me just drop off the bill at my last table, and I'll let Al know they'll bring it up to him when they're ready."

Caine nodded. "Thank you."

When I returned, there was already a Diet Coke on my side of the table and a beer in front of Caine. Untying my apron, I sat down and waited for him to speak.

"I want to apologize for this afternoon," he said.

"I should be the one to apologize. I shouldn't have been poking around in your personal life."

"That's true." He smiled. "But I was wrong for the way I reacted."

I shook my head. "If there's anyone who should know there are things in people's pasts they might not want brought up, it's me."

Caine nodded. He rubbed one finger around the top of his beer bottle. "I listened to some Johnny Cash tonight."

"You did?"

He held my eyes. "I think we both have parts of our lives we'd rather not shake for fear of waking them up."

That described perfectly the way I felt about my past. For the most part, I'd moved on and didn't think about it on a daily basis. But it was always with me, and I worked hard to keep it locked away.

"Yes. I'm sorry. I really wasn't thinking. I'm sure there's a reason you don't mention your history in your classes."

Caine drank his beer, watching me over the rim. When he set it down, he asked, "How did you find out?"

I didn't want to get anyone in trouble. "A friend of a friend."

He nodded.

I thought it was best to come clean all the way. I took a deep breath before confessing. "And I might have Googled you. Well, not you. Adam's other son."

Caine shook his head, but there was a sad smile on his face. "I needed a haircut."

"You were in style. I liked it. You had the whole sexy-bad-boy thing going on."

"I'll keep that in mind next time I go to the barber."

"Can I just ask you one thing?"

"Will it help put this shit to bed?"

I smiled. "It will."

"What's your question?"

"The last article I read said you'd signed a record deal. But I couldn't find an album. What happened?"

Caine was quiet for a while. His thumb rubbed at the label of his beer bottle when he spoke. "The lifestyle was tough. Partying, staying up all night, sleeping away half the day. It made me lose track of reality and my priorities." He looked up at me. "After we signed with the label, we missed honoring the deadlines a few times. Album kept getting pushed back. Then I lost someone close to me."

"I'm sorry."

He nodded. "I took some time off. My parents pushed me to go back to college. I needed something to focus on. They wanted me to study finance and work in the family business. We settled on a degree in music because I couldn't imagine not having it be a big part of my life. Later realized I was good at teaching musical composition, so kept going until I finished my doctorate." He lifted the beer bottle and tilted it to me before bringing it to his lips. "And here I am."

"And here you are." I smiled. "Thank you for sharing that with me."

The moment was interrupted when Al yelled from the bar. "You're all closed out, Rachel."

I turned and waved. "Thanks, Al."

"You're done for the night?" Caine asked.

"Yep. Do you want me to get you another beer?"

"No, thanks. I should get going."

I was disappointed, even after a long day of teaching and working a full shift on my feet.

After I said goodnight to Al, Caine walked me to my car. He opened the door so I could get in and held on to the top.

"By the way, Professor Clarence was the topic of my faculty meeting today."

We'd never spoken about it, and I wasn't sure if he knew I'd been his teaching assistant last year.

"He was such a good person. I worked for him last year."

"I heard that. Your name was mentioned, actually, along with another student's. You both had him as faculty advisor for your thesis."

I nodded. "He helped me pick my topic. It was a subject near to his heart."

"You haven't found a faculty member to replace him as your advisor yet?"

"No. Not yet. I need to get on that."

"I'll take you on, if you want."

The surprises kept coming tonight. "You will?"

"Think about it."

"Okay. Thank you."

Caine shut my door and waited for me to start the car. As I pulled away from the curb, I waved one last time and thought to myself, *I have a new advisor.*

Chapter 9

Caine - Fifteen Years Ago

What the fuck am I thinking?

I sat waiting in the quiet confessional, not even stoned this week. It was almost one o'clock, and Liam was long gone—like I should've been. We'd finished our last day of volunteering an hour ago and yet...here I was, waiting for a little girl who had enough trouble at home and sure as shit didn't need my ass pretending to be a priest to add to her problems.

But I couldn't not show up.

I had no idea why I'd told the little girl to come back this week to begin with.

Actually, that's a crock of shit. The reason had played over and over in my mind every night before I went to bed. I couldn't get her little voice out of my head.

Sometimes he falls asleep on the couch with a cigarette in his hand, and I think about not putting it out and letting the house go on fire. That was her confession.

I wasn't even positive if thinking about letting someone hurt himself was a sin. But I wasn't going to let this poor little girl feel guilty over wanting someone who I suspected wasn't a good guy to get hurt. Fuck that shit.

I also needed to know what the asshole was doing to make an innocent little girl have those types of thoughts. She should've been thinking about ponies and unicorns, not her house catching on fire. My mind automatically thought the worst.

I was just about to give up—and light up on the way home to clear my head of the shit running through it—when the door creaked open on the other side.

"Bless me, Father, for I have sinned," she whispered.

"Didn't we talk about this last week? You aren't sinning by thinking bad thoughts. You'd have to act on them to sin."

Of course, that wasn't true necessarily—the Catholic Church had some screwy rules—but it was the only thing I could do to take some of the weight off her shoulders right now.

"Alright."

I knew from last week that she was skittish on sharing. I'd need to gain her trust if she was going to let me in on whatever was going on at home. So, I started her talking about the first thing I could think of.

"How was school this week? Do you like your teacher?"

"It was okay. I don't mind my teacher so much, but Tommy, who sits next to me, is gross. He always has his hand down his pants."

Somehow I managed not to laugh. *Don't we all.* "You should keep away from him. He sounds like trouble."

"He always smiles at me."

"Yeah. He's no good. What grade are you in?"

"Fourth."

I'd guessed right. She had to be about ten.

"Did you tell your mother about him?"

She was quiet for a long time before responding. "My mother died last year."

Shit. I'd been afraid there was no woman in the picture, for some reason. "I'm very sorry to hear that." I paused then added, "She's in Heaven now. It's a nice place."

"Does the pain stop when you die?"

"Was your mom sick?"

I saw the outline of her head through the square-latticed screen opening and knew she was nodding.

"She's not in pain anymore."

"Is Yoda there, too?"

I furrowed my brows. "The little green guy from *Star Wars*?"

She giggled. The sound was better than music. "No. Yoda was my dog. He had ears that stuck out of his head weird. He died, too."

"Oh. Yeah, Yoda is in Heaven with your mom. They're hanging out."

"That's good."

"Is it just you and your dad now?"

"He's not my dad." She answered that question really damn quick. *Too quick.*

"Who do you live with?"

"My stepfather. He doesn't like me very much, most of the time. But sometimes he likes my sister."

"You have a sister? Is it just the two of you?"

"Yes."

"Is your sister older?"

"She's fifteen."

I had a gnawing feeling in the pit of my stomach. "How do you know he doesn't like you very much? And what makes you say he likes your sister sometimes?"

She was quiet. "I should go. Benny is going to come home from work soon. He gets mad easy."

"Benny? Is that your stepfather?"

"Yes."

I wanted to know more, but I definitely didn't want to be the cause of her getting in trouble.

"Come back next week. Okay?"

"Okay."

Chapter 10

Rachel

On Friday afternoon, I took more time than usual getting ready. I'd always liked school. It gave me things to focus on when I was feeling unsteady. But these days, it definitely wasn't my studies that I looked forward to.

Caine's office door was open when I dropped by unannounced. We made eye contact, and he used the hand not holding the cell to his ear to point to a chair opposite him in front of his desk. I listened to one side of his conversation while I looked around his office.

"Yes. I'll be there."

He listened and then rolled his eyes. "I would prefer you didn't do that."

There was a woman on the other end of the phone. I could hear the pitch of her voice even if I couldn't make out her words. I tried to act like I wasn't paying attention, checking out the art on his walls and the books on his shelf, but I was definitely listening.

"Ellen Werman and I are not going to be a couple no matter what table you seat her at."

Pause.

"Because I have a penis, and Ellen doesn't care for them, Mother."

Pause.

"Okay. I have to go now. Someone just came into my office. I'll see you soon."

After he hung up, Caine let out a deep breath and tossed his phone on the desk.

"Is it just *your* penis Ellen doesn't like, or penises, in general?"

He smirked. "Ellen has been out since eighth grade. My mother is the only person on the planet who still doesn't get it. She's my father's business partner's daughter. We're good friends, but my mother's had her heart set on us getting married for the last thirty-three years. She's called me four times to talk about the seating chart at some charity event my parents host every year, and it's not for two months. I should have just told her I couldn't wait to sit next to Ellen and left it at that." His phone started to buzz again, and he swiped to ignore it. "Do you have an extra-help session this afternoon? I thought that was on Thursdays."

"It is. I just wanted to come by and tell you, if the offer is still open, I'd really appreciate if you would take over as my thesis advisor."

Caine leaned back in his chair. "It's about time. I was starting to think you were going to turn me down."

More like I didn't want to look desperate. "Well," I teased. "I did have to consider my other offers."

"Is that so? Guess I should consider myself lucky then."

I grinned. "Guess so."

"Why don't you email me what you've done so far. I'll take a look at it, and we can sit down and go over it one day next week."

"Okay." I dug my iPhone out of my purse. "What's your email?"

He slid his phone over to me on the desk. "Put your number in. I'll text you my contact information to save."

After we exchanged details, I caught the time on my phone. "I better run."

Caine eyed me suspiciously. "Date?"

"No. They're having a TA get-together tonight, and I told Ava I'd go with her."

He nodded. "Have fun. Be safe."

The next morning, I'd just gotten out of the shower when my phone buzzed, indicating a new text. I finished towel-drying my hair and grabbed my glasses. I was surprised to find it was from Caine. It was the first text we'd ever exchanged, and my body stirred as I read it.

Caine: *Do you still visit Umberto on Sundays?*

Even though I'd emailed him my thesis-in-progress last night before going out, I hadn't expected him to read it so soon. It made me excited and nervous at the same time. I was proud of my work with Umberto, but my rough draft contained a lot of personal thoughts and notes. Having Caine read it made me feel vulnerable.

Rachel: *Yes, every Sunday.*

Caine: *I'd like to join you, see the study you've been working on first hand.*

My pulse increased. *Get a hold of yourself, Rachel.* It's Professor West working on a thesis with a graduate student, not a sexy man asking you on a date. He didn't even find it proper for me to fraternize with undergraduate students. Yet any contact from him made me feel like an excited teenager whose phone finally rang after hours of waiting for the cute boy to call. *God, I'm pathetic.*

Rachel: *That would be great. You're welcome any time.*

The dots jumped around as I waited for his response.

Caine: *How about tomorrow?*

Rachel: *Sure. I usually try to arrive at ten so I don't interrupt his daily activities.*

Caine: *Try to arrive at ten...is that code for somewhere between ten and noon?*

Maybe. I grinned down at my phone.

Rachel: *Lucky for me, Umberto isn't such a stickler for punctuality.*

Caine: *I'll pick you up at nine-thirty.*

Rachel: *At my apartment?*

Caine: *Unless that's a problem. If you prefer to take two cars, I can meet you there.*

Rachel: *No. One car is great. I'd like that.*

I gave Caine my address and then got dressed and ready for work. Though the day seemed to drag on forever, the smile I wore didn't leave my face at all.

I wasn't sure of the proper protocol for your boss picking you up at home. Did I go outside at nine-thirty or wait for him to ring the bell and invite him up? The answer was decided for me at twenty after nine when my buzzer sounded, and I wasn't finished getting ready yet.

I pressed the intercom. "Caine?"

"Yes."

"Third floor. I'll buzz you up."

I hit the button that unlocked the main door to my building and opened the door to my apartment. When Caine stepped off the elevator, I took a deep breath to try to hide my reaction to his appearance. He was dressed more casually than I'd ever seen, but even in a simple, fitted navy polo and jeans, he still managed to look sexy as hell. I realized it wasn't the clothes he wore, but the way he wore them that seemed to work for me. He had a quiet confidence and casual elegance that I found extremely attractive. The stubble he tended to sport by mid afternoon was clean-shaven, and even though I really liked the scruff, his tanned skin and the strong lines of his jaw were just as hot.

He looked at my wet hair. "I can see you're ready on time, as usual."

"You're early."

Checking his watch, he raised a brow. "It's nine twenty-four. You're going to be ready in six minutes?"

I opened the door and stepped aside, rolling my eyes. "Just come in."

Caine grinned and stepped inside. Of course, the man always smelled amazing, too. I wasn't sure if it was aftershave or cologne, but he had a masculine scent that was distinct and woodsy. It sparked a desire I hadn't felt in a really long time, and for a second, I considered sticking my nose in a can of coffee beans to stop the assault on my body. *That* would have been interesting to explain my way out of.

My apartment wasn't very big, but it was clean and decorated in a shabby chic way that I loved. Caine looked around, taking in the crazy different patterns all over the place. Each chair at my small kitchen table was different. Two of the walls in the living room were painted deep red and lined with art or photos framed in matte black, while the other walls were nude and stark.

After a minute, he nodded.

"What?"

"This fits you." His tone didn't indicate whether that was a good thing or bad.

"What does that mean?"

"I don't know. It just feels like you should live here."

"Because it's a little crazy?"

His lip twitched. "Maybe."

My hands went to my hips. "What exactly does your apartment look like?"

Still surveying everything around him, he seemed to give my question some thought. "It looks like anyone could live in the place. Lots of white, black, and stainless steel. I've lived in my house for five years and never realized it says nothing about me until I walked in here."

Hmm. No idea what to make of that. "I'm going to take that as a compliment."

Caine smiled. "You should. It was meant that way."

I had been just about to get dressed when the bell rang, and I completely forgot what I was wearing until Caine's eyes reminded me. He wasn't leering or anything, but I watched as his eyes did a sweep up and down my body, and I felt exactly where they lingered. The sheer T-shirt I was wearing left little to the imagination, and my nipples had hardened as he stepped off the elevator. Watching him check me out, I could feel them saluting through the fabric.

"Okay...I'll...uh...go finish getting ready. There's coffee brewed in the kitchen, if you want."

I disappeared into my bedroom. The outfit I'd planned on wearing seemed suddenly not good enough for Caine West to appreciate, and I wound up changing three times before I even started to dry my hair and swipe on some makeup. When I was finally ready, it was close to ten o'clock. I thought I'd find Caine tapping his foot, but instead he still seemed intrigued by my apartment. I found him studying the framed pictures on the wall.

"I'm so sorry. I lost track of time."

"It's fine. I helped myself to two cups of coffee."

"Oh, good."

As I dumped my thesis files and notes into an old leather tote, I noticed Caine had stopped in front of a framed black and white photo.

"Is this your mother?"

I'd looked at it so often that I knew every nuance in the photo, even without looking. She was sitting on a swing in the yard of the house I grew up in, a white daisy tucked behind her ear. Her smile sparkled so wide, I sometimes used it to brighten my day.

"Yes."

"She's beautiful."

"Thank you. She was."

He turned to me and studied my face. "You look just like her."

"Cancer," I blurted out.

I had no idea what possessed me to say it. To this day, I don't think I've spoken about her to anyone but my sister. I've been friends with Ava since we started undergraduate school five years ago, she was my roommate for years, and she has no idea what my mother died from. It wasn't a secret; I just kept a lot of things bottled up.

I stared at the photo. "Ovarian."

Caine put his hand on my back and gently rubbed. "I'm sorry."

"Thank you." I cleared my throat and pointed to a different picture. "This is my Aunt Rose and Uncle Nate—my mom's sister and her husband. They raised me and my sister after...well, they raised us as their own after Mom died. My father wasn't in the picture from the time I was an infant." Even though I'd opened the bottle voluntarily, I wanted to cork it. "You ready? They serve lunch at twelve-thirty, and I don't like to interrupt Umberto's routine."

"Just waiting on you. *As usual.*"

"Do you need to be back at any specific time? Sometimes I take a break and write my notes while he has lunch and does an activity or two. Then I go back and finish up."

"Nope. I'm yours for the entire day."

I liked the sound of that.

Chapter 11

Rachel

Caine drove a stick shift, a little old Porsche that had been meticulously maintained. I don't know anything about cars, but I suspected it was a classic and had more value than a new one. It seemed to fit him—expensive, yet sexy and understated.

I'd never been so happy to be stuck in traffic. Caine had to constantly change gears, and something about the way his large hand gripped the shifter just worked for me. Not to mention his forearm...and that damn vein. God help me. I was still finding a vein attractive.

Caine noticed me watching him. "Do you know how to drive a manual?"

"No. I tried once, and I hurt my nose."

His brows drew down. "You hurt your nose?"

"I kept stalling, and the car would jerk. On the fifth or sixth time, I was letting off the clutch and starting to move, and then the damn tires screeched to an abrupt halt, and I lurched forward and hit the steering wheel. I thought I broke my nose."

Caine chuckled. "I think you might be a little too tightly wound to drive a stick."

"Me? You're more tightly wound than I am."

He side-glanced at me. "Did you forget how we first met?"

"That was different. I thought you hurt my friend."

"So rather than determine if I was the person you thought I was, you jumped down my throat. You're wound tight."

My first reaction was to argue the point with him, which I realized would only prove his conclusion further. "Maybe you're *a little* right."

"Just a little."

"You know, that's how I became interested in musical therapy. Growing up I learned to use music to relax."

"Did you have music on when you tried to drive the stick shift?"

I thought back. "You know what? I didn't. I was nervous and didn't want to be distracted, so I turned off the radio."

"Maybe you should have left it on."

"Hmmm...I never thought of that. Maybe you should let me drive yours and see if that works."

Caine laughed. "I like my clutch too much."

The drive to Umberto's in New Jersey was normally about forty-five minutes on Sunday mornings, but today it was more like an hour and a half. The GW Bridge was closed except for one lane, and we crawled to cross. Once traffic opened up on the other side, we started to talk about my research.

"Tell me about Umberto."

"Well, you read the basics in my summary, I'm sure. He's seventy-three, late stage or stage six Alzheimer's, has spent his entire life living in the home he grew up in—even had his medical practice in the house. He was a general practitioner who still made house calls up until ten years ago. He's been married to Lydia for fifty-one years, and she visits him every single day. They have one son who lives on the West Coast and comes to see them a few times a year. Most days Umberto doesn't remember Lydia anymore. He went through a two-year period of depression and found some happiness with a fellow patient, Carol. Sometimes Umberto and Carol sit and hold hands while Lydia visits him. I've never seen the kind of love his wife has for him. The man she spent her entire life with thinks he's in love with another woman, and she's happy for him. It's the most selfless thing I've experienced. She wants him to truly be happy, even if he finds that happiness with someone else."

"Wow."

"Yeah. It's something beautiful in an otherwise tragic disease."

"And the music he's responding to, it's in Italian?"

"Yes. When I first started to visit the center, I was working with a larger group, trying to find a few candidates to study individually. Umberto didn't have much interest, even though his wife has control of his medical decisions and had signed him up for the study. I'd interviewed the families to learn about some music from the individual patients' histories, and each week we'd play music and do exercises to see if I could get a response. Umberto had never reacted to anything one way or the other. He seemed to enjoy music, but neither his wedding song nor anything from other memorable times in his life sparked any type of special interest."

"So what made you try Italian music?"

"It was just a whim, really. The week before, I'd heard Umberto respond to something the nurse asked him in Italian. I hadn't even known he spoke it fluently. Apparently he slipped into speaking it every once in a while. So the next week, when I came, I thought I'd try an opera. People tend to really respond to the music at a show, so I figured, why not play one?"

"And Umberto responded?"

I clutched my chest. "He started to sob. It was heartbreaking. But it was the first reaction at all I'd gotten from him with music—negative or positive. That day was the most lucid he'd been in years. He started to tell old stories about his mother that his wife didn't even remember. I wasn't sure if it was the opera itself or the music that brought back a memory."

"What do you have planned for today?"

I'd been alternating weeks between English and Italian music. This was actually an English week, but I'd decided to change things up a bit. Maybe a little part of me wanted to show off for the sexy professor.

"*Le Nozze di Figaro.*"

"Ah. Mozart."

"You're an opera fan?" I asked.

"I'm a music fan. Doesn't matter what kind. I actually saw *Figaro's Wedding* in undergraduate school—Composition Two. The whole class went as part of the course."

"I've never been to an opera." We approached the turn to Regency Village, the assisted-living community where Umberto lived, so I pointed up ahead. "Make your next left. You can't really see it until you're almost past it. It sneaks up on you because it's hidden behind those trees."

After we pulled into the parking lot, I started to get a bit nervous. I'd worked on my thesis for over a year. What if Caine found my research flawed or didn't believe it was the music that brought Umberto's memories back to the forefront? While he always enjoyed listening, not every session brought the same reaction.

Caine killed the engine and turned to face me with one arm casually slung over the wheel. "I've read your research. Your arguments are strong. You're going to do fine."

I hadn't mentioned my nerves out loud. He must have read the confusion on my face.

His eyes pointed down to my wrist. "You play with your watch when you're nervous."

I'd been fidgeting with my watch. I immediately stopped. "When else did I mess with my watch that you noticed it?"

"The first day of class after it emptied out and you had to come down the stairs to talk to me." We stared into each other's eyes. "Earlier in your apartment, when I noticed you weren't wearing a bra."

Embarrassed, I looked around the car to avoid his stare. To my surprise, when my eyes returned to his, he was focused on my lips. Which caused me to jump from one nervous habit to another.

I bit my lower lip as the sleeping butterflies in my belly woke to a flutter.

Caine cleared his throat, but his voice was still gravelly. "You have nothing to be nervous about. Now come on, I'm looking forward to watching you kick ass."

Umberto was with his ladies, Lydia and Carol. He was smiling and laughing as we walked to their table in the visitor's lounge.

I whispered who was who to Caine as we approached. "His wife's across and his girlfriend is next to him."

Caine whispered back. "Umberto's got some racket going on."

I elbowed him in the abs to *shh*.

"Hi, Umberto."

"Hi."

Every week was like starting all over. One thing I'd learned is that Umberto was good at pretending he knew who people were.

"Did Max go?" he asked.

"Umm. Yes." I whispered to Caine. "Max was his dog—a black lab. For some reason, he frequently asks people if Max went to the bathroom. He thinks we were out walking him or something."

I turned to the ladies. "Hi, Lydia. Hi, Carol."

Lydia stood and kissed my cheek. We'd become good friends over the last year. I was just about to introduce Caine when Carol took it upon herself.

"Who's the handsome fella? You a new doctor here?"

I laughed. "This is Caine West, Carol. He's a music professor at Brooklyn College, where I'm a graduate student."

Caine delivered a dazzling smile as he extended his hand. "It's very nice to meet you, Carol."

We joined the three of them as they chatted about the movie that had been shown last night. Carol's Alzheimer's was less advanced than Umberto's, so she tended to remember more.

She put her hand on Umberto's arm. "*The Hunt for Red October*. Remember, honey? It had that Sean Connery in it."

"Oh, yeah. Yeah."

I was certain Umberto didn't recollect anything about the movie.

Throughout our conversation, Caine was mostly quiet, just observing. I caught his eyes moving back and forth between Lydia's face and where Carol's hand touched Umberto a few times. I'd grown used to the unusual trio, but it was definitely something interesting to watch the first time. A woman who didn't want to claw another woman's eyes out when she caught her touching the man she loved—a man she had spent fifty-one years being faithful to. Caine was definitely watching for a reaction. But the only one he'd see from Lydia was contentment. She'd come to terms with whatever allowed her husband to feel some happiness.

Eventually, the nurse came to collect Carol for an activity. Lydia had insisted we never begin therapy while Carol was present. She didn't want her husband to have a memory that made him reach for her and upset Carol. There was a special place in Heaven for Lydia someday.

After Umberto hugged Carol goodbye, he sat back down with us, but seemed agitated.

Lydia reached across the table and covered her husband's hand. "Umberto, Rachel is going to play you some music. Do you remember that Rachel plays you music sometimes?"

"Oh, yeah. Yeah."

That was Umberto's way of saying, *I have no idea, but I'm not telling you that.*

She squeezed. "Rachel's going to put some headphones on you. Okay?"

"Yeah. Sure."

I placed a set of wireless headphones over Umberto's ears while Lydia dug into her purse and took out a small case of earbuds she'd started to carry. It wasn't necessary for her to listen, but she liked to keep in tune with her husband. Realizing for the first time that I hadn't brought an extra set of wireless buds, I offered to share mine with Caine. It wasn't necessarily a hardship having to inch up directly next to him so we could each listen through one bud.

I started the music, and Umberto immediately closed his eyes. Within seconds, the tension etched in his face seemed to flee. I glanced over at Caine, who was watching Umberto, and he nodded his head and smiled. At some point during the song, Umberto reached out and took his wife's hand. It was such a small gesture, but those tiny moments of recognition made a world of difference to a family dealing with advanced Alzheimer's.

We played two songs, and then I removed the headset from Umberto's head.

"How are you feeling today, Umberto?"

"Good. Good." I wasn't sure if he felt any different than before, but the agitation from ten minutes earlier was gone.

Lydia tried to build on the effect of the music. "Umberto? Do you remember when Francesca used to play this song?"

"Sure." He nodded. Then he pursed all five of his fingers together in the universal Italian grandmother hand language and said, "*Belle parole non pascon I gatti.*"

Lydia laughed. She looked to me. "It means *Fine words don't feed cats.* My mother-in-law, Francesca, used to say it all the time. I never really understood what it meant."

We stayed for a few hours, even breaking for lunch and then coming back afterward. But that was the extent of Umberto's brief burst of memories that day. A second round of music in the afternoon didn't bring back any specific recollections, but I hoped the music had something to do with the smiles everyone wore.

Lydia looked at her watch. "Umberto, it's almost time for mass. Do you want to get washed up before the service?"

"Okay."

She turned to Caine and me. "Would you like to join us?"

Even though I was definitely not a Sunday mass person, I'd joined them on a few occasions to observe Umberto's reactions to the music.

"I think we're going to head out," I told her. "It's getting late."

As we were saying our goodbyes, Umberto looked to Caine. "You going to take Max out now?"

Caine went along with it. "Yeah. I'll take good care of Max."

After the nurse took Umberto back to his room to get ready, Lydia walked us to the lobby. "Somehow I don't get offended that my husband has fallen in love with another woman and doesn't remember me, but every time he remembers Max, I can't help but be insulted." She laughed, but seemed only half kidding. "So, I hope our Rachel scored an A today. The musical therapy really seems to be working."

I smiled. "It's not like that. Professor West doesn't give me a grade. He sort of oversees the research I'm doing and the writing of my paper."

"Oh. Okay. Well, I hope you were impressed."

Caine looked at me with warmth in his eyes. "I was. Very."

Lydia gave me a hug. "See you next week?"

"I'll be here."

"Will I be seeing you again, Professor?"

"If Rachel will have me."

Umm. Are we talking literally or figuratively here?

Back in the car on the drive home, I could tell something was on Caine's mind. He was quieter than usual.

"Did you want to go to mass? I didn't even think to ask you before I declined, and I've monopolized your entire Sunday."

Caine glanced at me and back to the road. "Haven't gone to church in fifteen years. Wouldn't step back inside if you paid me."

Chapter 12

Caine - Fifteen Years Ago

W*hat the hell is she doing?*
I ducked behind a wide marble column to watch. I was later than usual because Liam had been screwing around at band practice, and we all lost track of time trying to learn a new song he'd written while drunk last night. Half of what he'd chicken-scratched down on a brown paper bag was smeared and unreadable. But the other half was pretty damn good. So we riffed and riffed, trying to get the jackass to remember the words he'd written.

I normally showed up at twelve-thirty and set myself up in the confessional to wait. My little friend generally wandered in sometime before one. But today I was late, and she was early. At least I thought she was early. I hadn't really ever seen her clearly enough to be positive it was her. For all I knew, I could be hiding from some other random little girl who'd wandered into church on Saturday afternoon.

The old wooden confessional was dark to begin with, and the latticed grate that separated us made it even more difficult to make out any detail other than her ponytail. I knew she had dark hair and was tiny—just like the little girl currently peeking into the priest's side of the confessional. I watched curiously from a distance as she looked around and then opened the door. She stepped inside for a half a second and then darted back out and into the parishioner's side—the sinner's side.

Five minutes passed, and she hadn't opened the door back up, so when the coast was clear, I made my way over and slipped inside for my priestly duty. The booth looked as it normally did, except for two coins on the floor. I figured maybe she was trying to get a peek at the priest.

"Bless me, Father, for I have sinned."

It had to have been at least six weeks now we'd been doing this, yet every time she said those words, I felt an ache in my chest. She was carrying too much baggage for a kid. Lately, we didn't even talk about the sins she thought she was committing. She just showed up and we shot the shit for a half hour or so. I got the feeling I was the only adult she trusted. Which was pretty fucking ironic considering I wasn't even really an adult yet, and I'd been lying to her since the first minute she stepped into the booth.

"How was your week?"

"I got in trouble at school."

I smiled to myself. "Oh yeah? What did you do?"

"It was also a sin."

"Tell me about it."

"Well, you know the boy who sits next to me that I told you about? Tommy?"

"The one who always has his hand down his pants?"

"That's him. He made me say a bad word, and I got detention. We both got detention."

"How did he make you say a bad word?"

"We were reviewing shapes in class for some state test. The teacher drew a diamond on the board and asked what shape it was. We'd learned rhombus a few years earlier, but when she called on me to answer, I forgot the word. The teacher gave me a hint to try and help me. She said it started with an R. I got excited because I thought I remembered, and I yelled out the wrong R word."

"What did you yell?"

"I yelled *rectum*."

I had to stifle my laugh. "Do you know what that means?"

"I do now. Tommy explained it to me by yelling that I was an A-hole." She paused. "He said the whole word, too."

I tried to provide some priestly guidance. "Your mistake was honest. It sounds more like Tommy is the one who sinned by using the bad word intentionally. Not you."

"Well...I used it, too."

"Oh?"

"At recess, some of the kids were still making fun of me, calling me an A-hole lover. So I told the kids I learned the word *rectum* from Tommy...because when he has his hands down his pants he sometimes sticks his thumb up his rectum during class. Only I didn't use the word *rectum* when I said it."

What I wanted to say was *Atta girl*, but instead I stuck to my priestly ways. "You'll say three Hail Marys for using the bad word. But, between us, it sounds like Tommy's a jerk and deserved it."

My little lamb giggled.

"Anything else?"

Last week she hadn't mentioned home, and I was anxious to find out how things were going. The only thing I'd been able to draw out of her, other than her own admission that she had bad thoughts about her stepfather, was that he drank too much and yelled.

"How are things at home?" I prompted. "Did anything happen to make you have bad thoughts?"

"I wore the headphones you gave me." Two weeks ago, she'd told me she got scared when her stepfather yelled at night. She had trouble falling asleep sometimes. I'd suggested she put on headphones and listen to her favorite song to drown out the sound. But she didn't own headphones. So last week I put my extra set in the booth before she arrived and told her to take them home. I explained how shutting her eyes and singing quietly along with the music would help ease her into sleep.

"Did it help?"

"Yes. I fell asleep after the fourth time."

I was probably delusional, but I felt like I was helping this kid in some screwed-up way. "That's good."

"I told my sister to try it, but she said she couldn't."

"Does she not have headphones?"

She didn't respond for a few minutes. I'd begun to learn that her silence often spoke louder than her voice did.

"She has headphones. She got them for Christmas the year before our mom died. They were in her stocking."

That feeling of dread hit the pit of my stomach. "So why does your sister think she can't wear them? Does she not like music?"

"She has to listen for Benny."

"What does that mean?"

"Sometimes when he's drinking and mad, he comes into her room at night."

Chapter 13

Rachel

"**A**re you hungry?"

I'd debated asking the question in my head for the last five minutes. Even though I'd spent all day with Caine, I wasn't ready for it to end. But I wanted my suggestion to have dinner to come off casual. He'd asked me to grab a bite to eat before, yet for some reason when it was me doing the asking, I felt like I was asking him out on a date.

Caine glanced over and then back to the road. He was quiet, and I got the feeling he was debating the appropriateness of our situation before answering. I was surprised when he said, "Starving. What did you have in mind?"

"I'm easy. There's a Greek restaurant a few blocks from my place that's good. Or there's Chinese on Grand Street. Or we could go to O'Leary's and then it'll be my treat again." I smirked at that last part.

"How about Greek, and my treat this time?"

"Sounds good. Take a left on Elwyn Street. It's up on the right if we can find parking—Greek Delight."

Inside the restaurant, the hostess sat us in a quiet booth in the back and brought us hummus and pita chips to snack on while we looked at the menu. I knew what I wanted, but Caine took out glasses from his pocket to read the menu. Those *really* worked on him, although I couldn't help myself.

"How old are you that you need reading glasses?"

He looked up over the rim of his studious Burberry frames. "You wear glasses. Why does my needing reading glasses mean I'm old?"

"I have an astigmatism. I've needed them to read since I was in a training bra."

Caine's eyes dropped to my cleavage before returning to the menu. He grumbled something I didn't catch. When I continued to stare at him, he took his glasses off and looked up at me. "What?"

"You didn't answer my question. How old are you?"

"Old enough to be your professor."

I dipped a piece of pita in the hummus and popped it in my mouth. "So, what? About sixty then?"

"I'm thirty-two, wiseass. Are you happy?"

I smiled. "I am, actually."

Caine slipped his glasses back on and returned to the menu.

I leaned in. "You don't look a day over thirty-one."

He shook his head and continued reading, but I caught the corner of his lip twitch.

Why did I love that lip twitch? It felt like a little reward of some sort. I seriously needed my head examined when it came to this man.

After he seemed to have decided, he leaned back in the booth. "You're doing a great job with your research."

"Thank you."

"It's one hell of an interesting dynamic going on there."

I remembered how awkward I'd felt sitting with the trio the first time. "I know. It was weird at the beginning, but I've gotten used to it now. Lydia is a pretty amazing person, isn't she?"

"She is. Not sure I could do what she's doing."

"What do you mean?"

"Watch my wife sit there with another man and smile."

"True love is selfless. She wants the best for him, even if that doesn't include her anymore."

The waitress brought our drinks and took our order. Caine had ordered a Greek beer, and I'd ordered my usual diet soda. I had to look away when his lips wrapped around the bottle. I was way too attracted to him to hide it very well.

"You sound like an expert on the subject. I take it you've been in love like that?" he asked.

"Not with a man."

Caine's brows jumped, and I realized what that must've sounded like—what he thought.

"I meant...I felt that way about my mother. Not that I'm a lesbian or anything. I like men. Not that I have anything against lesbians. I just prefer...you know...men when it comes to sex. Not that I have much of a sex life at the moment." I was definitely babbling.

Caine chuckled. "You're fucking adorable when you get embarrassed."

I drank my cold soda to occupy my mouth and hopefully keep my skin from turning noticeably pink. "Anyway, when my mother was really sick, I wanted her to die so she wouldn't be in pain anymore. I was going to be without a mother, but I didn't care. I just wanted her to be at peace. That's what Lydia and Umberto remind me of." I set my glass down on the table. "How about you? Ever been in love like that?"

Caine shook his head. "Not sure I'm capable of selfless. Spent most of my life on the -ish side of self, rather than the -less."

"No girlfriends?"

"Plenty of those. None that I wasn't a selfish bastard with."

I stared at him. "That'll change when you meet the right woman."

He brought the beer bottle to his lips. "Maybe. Or maybe I'm just destined for a life of selfish screwing. I could think of worse things."

I couldn't see Caine as selfish—he'd changed my tire after I told him off and interrupted his class. And I couldn't imagine he wasn't attentive in bed. He was so observant that it was often distracting, not to mention how intense he could be. Then there was the musician thing...skilled hands and good rhythm. No. There was no way Caine West was selfish in bed. Of *that* I was certain.

He squinted. "What's going on in that head of yours?"

"What do you mean?"

"You got quiet after I said there were worse things in life than selfish screwing."

And there was the observant thing again. He paid attention to women. Men who paid attention were good in bed.

"I was just thinking about what you said. You don't seem selfish to me."

"We're not in that kind of a relationship."

"Maybe." I shrugged. "But you seem too attentive to be selfish in that way, too."

A look of understanding crossed Caine's handsome face, as if he'd just realized what I was thinking. He leaned in to me with a wicked grin that made my heart palpitate.

"I didn't mean I was selfish in bed." His eyes dropped to my neck and slowly rose to focus on my mouth—which parted for his gaze. "A woman's needs always come before my own. And I enjoy every minute of taking care of those needs." His eyes returned to mine, and he leaned in even closer. "She comes before me...multiple times."

I swallowed. My whole body reacted, and Caine knew it. He leaned back with a cocky smile and a gleam in his eyes.

When I finally attempted to speak, my hoarse voice croaked. "Then what are you selfish about?"

"The stuff that comes after we get out of bed. The relationship part."

"Oh."

"Not everyone has the ability to be Lydia."

"I'm not sure I agree. I think we all have the ability to be Lydia. It's a choice not to try and find your Umberto. And usually there's a reason for that choice."

The muscle in Caine's jaw ticked, but he stayed silent. Luckily our food came shortly after that. Caine had ordered a falafel, and I'd ordered a gyro. We dug in and gave our full attention to eating, for the moment.

In no time, my meal had turned into a big mess. The pita had torn, and half of my gyro was leaking out. I didn't realize, but white tzatziki sauce had dripped down the back of my hand.

"You have some sauce..." Caine pointed.

Still holding the gyro, I turned my wrist to look. The sauce had trailed down my hand, past my wrist, and was making its way steadily down my arm, about to drip onto my shirt. If I put down the disaster of a gyro, there was no way I'd be able to pick it back up without it falling apart. So, I licked a line from my arm up over my wrist to my finger, cleaning the mess in one long stroke. Not very ladylike, but it was better than wearing it on my nice shirt.

When I looked up, Caine was staring at me. "Christ. Are you *trying* to get me fired?"

"What?"

His eyes moved back and forth between mine. "You really have no goddamn clue, do you?"

"I don't understand."

Caine looked down at his food, shaking his head. "Just finish eating. We should go."

The ride back to my apartment was awkward. Neither of us said a word. Honestly, I had no idea what to say. I'd realized Caine's comments had to mean he was turned on by my inadvertent lick show, but it was also a reminder that I needed to stop fantasizing about something that was never going to happen.

When we arrived at my apartment building, Caine double parked and turned off the ignition. "I'm going to walk you up."

"You don't have to do that. I'm fine."

"I'm not leaving you at the curb." He opened his door, effectively closing the discussion.

"Okay then," I mumbled to myself.

The awkwardness continued as we rode the elevator up to my apartment. I fumbled for my keys in front of my door. "Thank you again for taking me on and coming with me today."

"Of course. I'd do it for any student."

Another reminder. One that hurt.

I unlocked the door and opened it. "Would you like to come in? I could make you some coffee or something?" I really wasn't propositioning him to come in for the proverbial night cap. It just seemed like the polite thing to say.

Caine was quiet for a very long moment. "I think it's best we don't spend time together outside of class anymore. Your research is solid, and I think we have the semester schedule planned out well enough. If you need to discuss your thesis, the department secretary has access to my calendar and can set up an appointment."

Maybe we had gotten a little too friendly, but... "Did I do something to upset you?"

"No." He lifted his chin toward the inside of my apartment. "Lock up behind you."

I took a quick shower, changed into an old concert T-shirt to sleep, and climbed into bed feeling confused and sad. My feelings for Caine had grown despite the fact that I knew it was stupid to fall for a man who had no interest in a relationship, even if he hadn't been my professor. I tried to fall asleep, but it was no use.

Plucking my phone from the charger, I thought I might type my notes from today into an email to add to my research later. But when I powered my cell on, it opened to my last text from Davis. I'd completely forgotten to respond to his comment regarding me not texting that I missed him, too.

Even though the timing was off for us, Davis never gave me mixed signals. He didn't play hot and cold. He owned up to his feelings and was honest with me. I sighed and texted back.

Rachel: *I miss you, too.*

Chapter 14

Rachel

C aine had successfully avoided me for four days.
Until today. There would be no way to avoid seeing me unless he skipped the once-per-semester, mandatory faculty meeting TAs were required to attend, as well as professors.

I was sitting alone in the back of the large conference room with a seat open next to me—not that I was saving it for anyone in particular. Caine hadn't shown up yet. Each time someone walked in, my eyes darted to the door. The music department chair had taken his place at the front of the room, readying to begin, when Caine finally showed up.

Stopping in the doorway, his eyes scanned the room, falling on me before quickly looking anywhere else. He couldn't have taken a seat farther away from me.

I was surprised his hair didn't catch fire during the forty-five minute meeting with the way my eyes were burning into the back of his head. After it was over, I stayed in my seat to see if he would walk back out the door without a single word.

Caine stood and glanced over at me, but was quickly joined by a woman who walked over to greet him with a big smile. She wore a bright pink suit that screamed for attention, but aside from that, she was actually rather pretty—though I hated to admit that. I'd seen her around the halls and knew she was an adjunct professor, although I didn't know her name.

Professor Pink was also the complete opposite of me—she had unnaturally blonde, Marilyn Monroe-type hair, stood only a few inches shorter than Caine, and her suit, even being a tacky color, was definitely designer. She was very touchy-feely with Professor West, and there was a definite familiarity in the way she rested her hands on his arms as they spoke. After the second or third time she tossed her hair back and laughed, I was done watching. Standing up, I headed for the door but got stuck behind two professors who were talking while they walked and moving as slow as shit.

Caine and Professor Pink were a few people ahead of me in line to exit the room, and he made a point not to look in my direction. When his hand went to the small of her back to usher her out the door, I realized I was a total idiot. Obviously the mighty professor didn't have an issue with fraternization—unless it was with me.

Screw him. I couldn't believe how full of shit he was.

As soon as I was out of the conference room, I bolted down the hall. My legs couldn't get me off campus fast enough. I was annoyed for thinking it was possible Caine was interested in me but held back because I was his assistant. Even more so, I was pissed at him for pretending that was the case. I hadn't been imagining the signals he gave the other night at dinner.

I'd nearly made it out of the building when I abruptly stopped, causing a student to crash right into me.

"What the hell?" he barked.

"Sorry."

I started walking again. I should get the hell out of this building, but I knew myself—certain things ate at me. If I didn't get this off my chest, I was going to be miserable all day. I needed to go give Caine a piece of my mind. *Screw it.*

Turning around, I crashed into the same student again.

"Seriously?" he said.

"Jeez. You'll live. Don't walk so close behind people!"

I took off for Caine's office. I might lose my job for telling him off, but at least I would be able to sleep tonight. So what if I was proving his point that I was *tightly wound*?

The door to Caine's office was cracked open. I paused to collect my thoughts for a moment, then reached for the door handle. *Screw knocking.* But a woman's voice stopped me from busting in. Her laughter hit my skin, sparking a fire that burned its way up to my cheeks. I hadn't heard Professor Pink's voice earlier, yet somehow I was certain it was her.

"Remember that little Italian place?" the woman said. "The one with the fireplace in the back?"

"Giordano's."

"Yes, that's the one. We should go there again sometime. The dessert cart looked incredible." She paused. "Although we didn't make it to dessert that night, did we?"

I'd heard enough. I didn't stay for Caine's response. I couldn't. As pissed off as I was when I'd marched my ass to his office, hearing him with another woman had turned that into hurt and embarrassed—something I preferred not to let others see. So, I prescribed myself my own therapy and instead of barging into his office, I popped my earbuds in and headed home.

I had zero desire to go out to our monthly friends' dinner tonight. I preferred to stay at home and wallow in self-pity. But when I attempted to cancel, Ava guilted me into showing up. So, I forced myself to get ready. Screw it. If I didn't feel good, I might as well look good. Plus, blow-drying my hair was oddly therapeutic for me. I found the constant, repetitive brushing and smoothing very calming.

Needless to say, my thick, naturally curly hair was pin straight by the time I was done—I'd needed a lot of calming. Since I'd taken the time to make my locks look good, I went all out with a full face of makeup and even put on a cute outfit and high-heeled sandals.

Davis's expression told me he, at least, appreciated the extra effort when I arrived at O'Leary's. Tonight it was only me, him, and Ava since our other former roommate was away with her new boyfriend on a cruise. Once the three of us sat down, I was glad I'd come. I really did enjoy my time with these guys. We laughed as we caught up, mostly at the crazy stories Ava told. But then just a half hour into our night, Sal, the new waiter, came over and said he was sick and needed to leave. He asked if one of us could call Charlie to come in and take over his shift.

Since there were only a few hours until the kitchen closed anyway, Ava and I both volunteered to cover for him. Plus, his complexion was slightly green, and I was pretty sure he wouldn't make it hanging around until Charlie drove in from Queens.

"You look too nice to work tonight," Ava said, pointing to my feet. "And those are not waitressing shoes. I got this. There aren't many tables left, so you two hang out, and I'll come join you in between serving."

Although Davis and I had ended things in a good way, we really hadn't hung out just the two of us since whatever we had ended and he'd moved out. Since I was dressed up, and awkwardness set in as soon as Ava left, it felt sort of like a first date.

"So..." Davis said. "This feels weird."

I laughed. "I know. Why? It shouldn't. It's just us. We've hung out a million times."

Davis shot me a sheepish look. "Because you look really hot tonight."

"Are you saying I didn't look really hot when we lived together and I rolled out of bed every morning?" I'd said it joking around, but Davis's answer was serious.

"Actually, I think you look beautiful all the time."

I blushed. "Such a southern charmer."

Davis and Ava had ordered a bottle of wine, and he lifted it to refill his glass, then held the bottle over my empty one. "Have one with me?"

I hesitated, thinking back to the last time we'd had drinks together—I'd wound up in Davis's room.

With a devious grin that told me he was thinking the exact same thing, he filled my glass...to the brim and said, "Just one."

The wine definitely helped. Now that the bottle was empty, the strain between Davis and me was gone. We'd gorged on pasta and wine and caught up on the last few months. Things were feeling back to normal.

"How are Umberto and Lydia?" he asked.

It was just like him to remember their names because they were important to me. He was always very thoughtful and attentive.

"They're doing really well. Still the happy threesome."

"And your thesis?"

"Good. Caine seemed happy with my progress. Although who knows." I finished off my glass of wine. "He could hate it tomorrow."

"Caine?"

"My new thesis advisor."

Davis nodded.

"He's kind of a giant ass," I added. *Not that he'd asked.*

"When are you finished?"

"Another few months and I'll be done with my thesis and graduating."

"Then what?"

"I'm not sure yet. My minor was elementary education, so I was thinking of applying to some local school districts that have musical therapy programs for autistic children."

Davis smiled. "That suits you. I could definitely see you doing that."

I sipped my wine. I was now on glass two and already feeling a buzz. "What about you? Are you happy here in New York? Do you think you'll stay forever?"

"Maybe."

I wasn't sure if I'd imagined it, but I could have sworn his eyes had dropped to my lips.

"What about you? Are you happy? Seeing anyone?"

My good mood took a nose dive. I wasn't seeing anyone, but that didn't mean I was happy about it. I'd managed to forget about Caine for the sum total of an hour tonight.

I sighed. "No. I'm single. You?"

Davis must've taken my downturn of spirit as a general statement about my single status.

"Not seeing anyone. But I'd like to be."

Yeah. Me, too.

I sipped more wine. "Oh yeah? Tell me about the lucky girl."

Davis grinned. "She's short, kind of quirky, beautiful, smart."

I rested my head on my hands. "Sounds perfect. Does she have a brother for me?"

Instead of answering, Davis reached over the table and took my hand in his. "I've really missed you."

"I've missed you, too."

"Have dinner with me this weekend? Just me and you."

Huh?

Seeing the confusion on my face, Davis continued. "I wasn't ready to date last year. I didn't want to jump into something with you when my head wasn't screwed on straight. I'm in a better place now."

The wine must've totally gotten to me. I seriously hadn't realized he was talking about asking *me* out. I'd waited for this for almost a year, yet now I felt unsure. Luckily, Ava came to my rescue. She scooted into the booth next to me, playfully bumping my hip with hers, and took over the conversation. I was grateful for the reprieve.

After another hour of sitting around and talking, we decided to move to the pub tables in the bar area since the dining room was empty.

Davis looked at his watch. "I have to be at the airport at five a.m. for work, so I'm going to take off."

The three of us made plans for next month's dinner, and he gave Ava a hug goodbye before turning to me. Only he didn't let go after my hug. Instead, he took both of my hands in his.

"Think about it. Okay?"

I had no idea what to say, so I simply nodded and smiled. Then he was gone.

The minute he was out the door, Ava turned to me. "What the hell was that all about?"

"He wants to take me out on a date."

"And how do you feel about that?"

"I have no idea. I'm so confused right now."

"You know what will make things clearer?" She smiled.

"What?"

"Let's get stinking drunk."

Chapter 15

Rachel

"He has the most amazing ass."

Well, that's what I intended to say, but what actually came out of my mouth was, "He has lemony lass."

Luckily, Ava had joined me in my binge, so my slur sounded perfectly fine to her.

"Who are we talking about? Davis or the professor."

I sighed. "The professor. Davis's is nice, but I never had the urge to bite it."

Ava quirked a brow. "You want to bite the pompous professor's ass?"

"I do. Is that strange?"

She smirked and lifted her drink to her lips. "Not at all. Well, the biting part isn't strange. I like a little biting during sex myself, but biting his ass when you're not sleeping with him might be a little strange. Especially if you do it during a class while he's lecturing."

"He's just so frustrating. So infuriating."

"So maybe you should give Davis another chance?"

I sucked back the remaining contents of my third drink and held the empty glass up, dangling it between my thumb and pointer. "Time for a refill, waitress."

Ava laughed. "I was done an hour ago...but I'll get your refill because I'm not sure you could make it the ten feet to the bar." She stood and took the glass from my hand. "You're cut off after this one, though."

While Ava was behind the bar, I dug my phone out of my purse. I had no idea why, but I wanted to scroll through Davis's Facebook account. I remembered he'd posted a few pictures with the same woman a few months back, and I wondered if he'd dated her since things ended with us.

When my phone illuminated, I was surprised to find I'd missed two texts from Caine.

Caine: *Could you possibly cover my afternoon class tomorrow at three?*

A few minutes later, another text came in.

Caine: *Sorry about the last-minute notice. Something important came up.*

What a jerk.

Of course, he wasn't really a jerk. He was just not interested in me the same way I was him and didn't want to lead me on, so that made him a jerk in my drunken, emotional head. I should have turned off my phone and ignored him, responded to my boss when I was in the right frame of mind, but the alcohol had other ideas. I typed back.

Rachel: *Sure. I'll do your job so you and Professor Pink can go back to your office and do whatever it is you do...again.*

I watched the dots start to jump around, then stop, then start again.

Caine: *What are you talking about?*

I rolled my eyes.

Rachel: *Your ass isn't that great anyway.*

In that moment, the text made complete sense to me. Caine typed back immediately.

Caine: *Excuse me?*

I snorted. Loud. *What a jerk.* And then, my texting went downhill.

Rachel: *I bet she doesn't come late.*

I was holding my phone, but I'd been expecting a text, so I jumped in my seat and dropped it on the table when the damn thing started to ring. Caine's name was flashing, and that just pissed me off even more.

I swiped to answer. "What?"

"Rachel?"

"That's me, your lowly TA."

Something dawned on me, and I thought it was a pretty clever pun. In fact, I was damn proud of myself for coming up with something so witty.

"I'm your lowly TA, who has great T&A, only you're too full of yourself to notice."

"Have you been drinking?"

"Have you?"

"No, Rachel, I haven't been drinking."

"Well, you don't know what you're missing. Because after the first one, everything that's been jumbled in your brain becomes so clear."

Ava returned with our drinks to find me on the phone. "Who are you talking to?"

I did a half-assed job of covering the receiver. "It's Professor Tight Buns."

Ava's eyes flared wide and then she shut them briefly. When she reopened them, she took the phone from my hand.

"Hi, Professor Tight...umm...Professor West. This is Rachel's friend, Ava."

She paused to listen.

"Yes. She's fine. I'll take care of her."

Another pause.

"Yes, I'm sure. We're at O'Leary's, and I'll take her home in a cab and make sure she gets inside safely."

After she swiped to end the call, she put the phone in her purse. "I'm keeping this so you don't do anything else stupid."

"What? All I did was answer the phone. It's not my fault he's a big, fat jerk."

"Please tell me you didn't call him that."

"I don't remember."

Ava let me ramble on for another forty minutes as I sipped my drink. Either I'd grown accustomed to the foul-tasting liquor, or the last Tanqueray and tonic tasted more like tonic than Tanqueray. Since I was still able to speak, I was guessing it was the latter. Ava had watered down my drink.

"So what are you going to do about Davis?"

"I don't know. He's a great guy. He really is."

Ava's eyes turned to saucers.

"What? Don't look so shocked. He's a nice guy. And God knows I haven't had sex in forever."

"Oh no. Professor West."

"Well, obviously I'd rather have sex with him. But maybe that's all it is. Maybe I'm just really sexually frustrated, and my attraction to Caine is only physical."

"No, Rachel. Professor West." She motioned to the other side of the bar. "He came for you."

Unfortunately, I was lost in my little alcohol-marinated brain and not paying attention. I hadn't even realized she was actually pointing to something...or *someone*. In fact, I thought we were still having the same conversation.

"He'd better come for me. It may have been almost a year, but I think I still know how to use my vagina." I paused. "Do you think my vagina is re-virginized from not having sex for so long?"

I brought my drink to my lips and closed my eyes as I tipped my head back to finish it. When I opened them, I thought I was dreaming. In fact, I was certain of it. I blinked a few times to snap myself out of it.

Caine did that stupid sexy lip twitch thing as he stood next to our table. "Still here."

———

Ava was a traitor. Caine asked her if he could have a few minutes alone with me, and I'd said no at the same exact time she said yes. She'd shot me a warning look before promptly slipping from our table to make room for Caine.

"What are you doing here?" I scowled.

"Making sure I'm the only man you talk to about *coming* while you're in this intoxicated state."

I folded my arms across my chest. "Davis wants me."

The muscle in Caine's jaw ticked. "That's nice. Who's Davis?"

"My ex. Well...sort of. We had dinner tonight. He wants me back."

"So that's what this is about?"

"Well, it's not about you," I lied.

"Really? He sat back with an arrogant smirk. "Because it sounded on the phone like it was about me. Well, about Professor Tight Buns anyway."

There was at least one good thing about alcohol; it kept me from flushing when I should have been embarrassed. In fact, it kept me from even realizing I should have been embarrassed.

"So what? You have a tight ass. That doesn't make you the be-all and end-all. I have a pretty nice ass myself. Only you're too much of a jackass to notice it."

Caine rubbed at his lip with his thumb. "Is that what you think?"

"That you're a jackass? Yes."

He leaned forward. "I meant you think I haven't noticed your *pretty nice ass*."

His voice had grown husky, and I felt the guttural sound of it between my legs. I swallowed and shifted in my seat, staring at him. He took it as license to continue speaking when I kept quiet.

"You have a tiny little waist. When you wear jeans, there's a gap in the back. When you lean over, I can see your G-string. You like to match it with your shirt. Wednesday you wore a blue shirt and had on a baby blue G-string. The day you taught class and were giving out headphones, you bent over nicely to distribute them to each row. It's why I got up to help you with the boxes. You didn't think I was being chivalrous, did you? That day, you had on a thin white blouse and a lacy white thong. I *really* liked the white lace."

My mouth was hanging open.

Caine leaned in a little closer. "So you're wrong if you think I haven't noticed your pretty nice ass. For two reasons: First, it's not a *pretty nice* ass. It's a fucking spectacular ass. And second, I've noticed it. Every damn day since you walked out of that bar bathroom. In fact, I watched it sway from side to side until you were out of sight that night—even though you'd just told me off."

"I had no idea."

"Clearly."

"Why didn't you say something?"

"What should I have said, Rachel? You're my teaching assistant, and I'm your thesis advisor. Plus, even if that weren't the case, I actually like you. You're not a casual fuck I'd stop calling when I was done with you."

That was harsh. I didn't want to think of Caine in that way. But then I remembered the faculty meeting. "Like Professor Pink?"

His brows drew together. "You mean Ginger Ashby? Professor Ashby who was wearing a pink suit today? What about her?"

"You two seemed cozy."

Caine looked away. "We're not sleeping together, if that's what you're asking."

If they weren't currently sleeping together, I knew they had a history. I could tell by the way she touched him, the way she looked up and batted her fake eyelashes.

"But you did sleep with her?"

"It was a long time ago. I don't make the same mistake twice."

I wasn't sure if he was referring to the professor specifically or sleeping with someone at work, in general—not that it mattered.

Ava came back to the table to check on me. "Everything okay, Rach?"

My smile was sad. "Everything's fine."

She put my phone on the table. "Your phone was ringing." Ava looked at Caine. "I put it in my purse so she wouldn't regret something she said to you. Guess that worked well." Caine smiled, and she turned her attention back to me. "I'll be at the bar if you need me."

The moment Ava walked away, my phone began to ring. Davis's name flashed on the screen. Caine saw it and looked up at me. "You need to get that?"

It stopped ringing, but when I scrolled, I saw Davis had texted, too. He wanted to make sure I got home safe.

"I'll just send him a quick text to let him know I'm okay."

I felt Caine's eyes on me as I typed.

When I was done, he said, "You want to talk about it?"

I wanted to see if I could get a rise out of the composed professor. "We used to have sex. Then we stopped. Now he wants to start again. Oh, and he wants to take me to dinner, too."

The clench in Caine's jaw was clear. "And how do you feel about that?"

"I don't know. I'm confused, I guess."

"About what?"

"He's a great guy. When we broke up, I was upset at first. But then I sort of got over it. At least I think I did. I didn't sit around and pine for him anyway. I feel like I would have if he was the right guy. You know?"

Caine looked into my eyes. "I think the right person would be difficult to move past, yes."

"But maybe I haven't actually moved past him yet. I haven't...you know...since we broke up."

"Had sex?"

"Yes."

Caine's eyes sparkled. "Hence the re-virginized vagina?"

Even in my drunken-ish state, I couldn't believe I was having this conversation. "You heard that?"

He nodded with a sly grin. "How long ago did you split up?"

"Close to nine months."

"So you haven't had sex in almost nine months?"

I sighed. "Maybe I should just pick someone up in a bar and do it. Then it'll be easier to decide if it's Davis I miss or just the sex."

The pupils in Caine's eyes dilated to the point where there was more black than brown iris. "That's not a good idea."

"Why? You've never picked someone up and brought them home just to satisfy your needs?"

"I didn't say that."

"Well, then why is it okay for you to do it, but not me?"

"Because I don't do it to try to solve a problem." His voice turned stern. "Fucking someone won't help you decide if you want to be with another man. Trust me on that one, Rachel."

"Sounds like you're speaking from experience."

Caine looked away. "I'm going to grab a beer. You want a soda?"

"I'll have another Tanqueray and tonic."

"I think you've had enough."

I huffed. "Fine. I'll take a Diet Coke."

We sat around and talked for another hour after Caine returned with our drinks. I had sobered up some, but still felt more daring than usual.

"Can I ask you something?"

"Will it stop you if I say no?"

I smiled. "Probably not."

"If you weren't my professor...and I wasn't looking for my Umberto..." I trailed off, but the rest of the sentence didn't even need to be said.

Caine brought the beer he'd been nursing to his lips and stared at me over the top while he finished it off. He set the empty bottle on the table and cleared his throat before leaning in. Then he curled one finger, motioning for me to come closer. I leaned in, and our noses were no more than a few inches apart.

"If I weren't your professor and you weren't a nice girl, your re-virginized pussy would be sore as hell right now."

Chapter 16

Rachel

I didn't feel half bad when my alarm went off. My eyes opened, and I braced myself for a pounding headache and nausea, expecting a hangover. Instead, I was tired, but the typical aftereffects didn't seem to hit me. After drinking a full glass of water without stopping to take a breath, I decided to climb back into bed for another fifteen minutes.

Caine had insisted on driving me home. Half way, he'd stopped and run into a twenty-four-hour convenience store, coming out with a brown paper bag that he'd handed me before leaving me at my apartment door.

"Take everything inside. It doesn't work unless you finish it all," he'd said.

The bag had two bottles of water, a banana, and a single packet of Motrin. Since he'd gone to the trouble of picking it all up, I followed his orders.

Unplugging my iPhone from the charger on the nightstand, I keyed in my password and decided to text him.

Rachel: *No hangover. Thank you. You're a miracle worker. Where were you when I was eighteen?*

Caine responded right away.

Caine: *You're welcome. Glad you're feeling better today.*

I was feeling better. The brash brushoff Caine had left me with last week had really been bothering me. Seeing him had helped. Don't get me wrong, I was more confused than ever—especially with what Davis sprung on me last night—but I no longer felt off balance, at least.

Rachel: *I owe you one. For everything. For showing up to make sure I was okay, for talking to me about Davis, taking me home and giving me your secret recipe for a hangover-free morning. Actually... maybe I owe you two. LOL*

Caine: *We'll call it one, and we're even. But can I cash that one in today, if you're feeling up to it?*

I'd forgotten Caine had asked me to cover his class this afternoon. I was working the day shift, but Charlie wouldn't mind if I left a little early. Late afternoon was always dead anyway.

Rachel: *I can cover your class. Sorry, I forgot that was what started my drunken rampage last night.*

Caine: *Thank you.*

Things between Caine and me had changed last night. Our attraction was out in the open now, so I figured cheeky was okay.

Rachel: *I'm not covering for you to have a nooner, am I?*

I visualized Caine's lip twitching as he shook his head.

Caine: *I do have a date with two pretty girls. But one is two and a half and the other is four, and they usually cry when they see me.*

Rachel: *?*

Caine: *Sister's kids. She's having a biopsy this afternoon and needs me to watch her little monsters.*

Rachel: *Oh. I'm sorry. I was just joking. I hope everything is okay. I'll cover the class no problem.*

Caine: *Thank you.*

After class was over, I sat in Caine's chair for a while, waiting for the students to empty out. Sitting in his spot at the front of his room somehow made me feel closer to him. Since I was thinking about the sexy professor, I figured I'd send him a text to see how he was making out babysitting. The thought of Caine wrangling two little girls made me smirk. I wondered if he changed diapers—I'd guess he'd have to in order to watch two girls under four.

Rachel: *Class was good. I think they like me better than you. ;)*
Caine: *That's good. You might be taking over my job when my sister kills me.*
That didn't sound like things were going well.
Rachel: *What happened?*
Caine: *I forgot Lizzy had a nut allergy. We're in the emergency room.*

I was pretty surprised that Caine had taken me up on my offer to come give him a hand at the hospital—until I got there. I'd lied and said I was family to get into the back treatment area, and I spotted Caine in a little open-curtained examination area on the other side of the nurse's station, looking uncharacteristically freaked out. He had what I assumed was the two year old dangling from one hip while she cried at the top of her lungs. The older girl was sprawled out on a stretcher, blowing up a latex glove like a balloon.

As I got closer, I got a better look at the little girl. *What the*? What the heck was she wearing? It looked like a backwards T-shirt and a strange diaper of some sort.

"Hi," I said.

Caine was definitely relieved to see me. "Hey. Thanks for coming."

"Is everything okay?"

"Lizzy is going to be okay. It's just a rash, luckily. They gave her some Benadryl, and the doc wants to keep an eye on her for a while."

I smiled at the little girl on his hip, and she quieted her screaming to check me out. "Hi, there. You must be Lizzy."

I'd assumed the older girl lying in the bed was the patient, but the niece Caine was holding had a rash on her face and neck.

The sweet little girl nodded while her bottom lip quivered. She had a crazy head full of red ringlet curls. I reached out and fingered one. "I love your curls. They remind me of Merida. Do you know who Merida is?"

She nodded.

"I bet you're brave just like the Disney princess."

I pushed a long curl that was plastered to her wet cheek back off her face. The bracelets on my wrist jingled and caught her attention.

"You like those?"

She nodded again.

"I'm Rachel—a friend of your Uncle Caine's. You want to wear one?"

He eyes lit up, and she nodded again, only faster this time.

I slipped two of the bracelets from my wrist and held them out. She smiled and let me put them on her. It was then that I got a closer look at what the poor thing was wearing.

"Ummm...Caine? Why is her diaper *duct taped*?"

"I couldn't get the damn thing to stay on."

I held back my laugh as best as I could. The poised picture of perfection was so out of his element and frazzled.

Extending my arms, I smiled warmly at Lizzy. "Can I hold you? Maybe I can fix your diaper and put your shirt on the right way."

Caine's brow furrowed as he looked at his niece. It was obviously news to him that her shirt wasn't on right. Lizzy was apprehensive, but eventually she leaned toward me, and I took her from her uncle's arms.

"Do you have a diaper bag?"

"No. I flew out the door so fast, I didn't even think about diapers." He looked at his niece's bare legs. "Or pants, apparently."

I smiled. "That's okay. I'm sure the nurse can give us one."

The other little girl sat up from the stretcher and was looking at me.

Caine did the introduction. "This is Alley. She's no help getting a diaper to stay on either."

Lizzy and I visited the nurse's station, and one of the aides was nice enough to go up to the pediatric unit and get us a few diapers and a small package of wipes. She also grabbed us kid-size pajama pants. After I straightened Lizzy out in the bathroom, I went back to Caine and Alley.

"All fixed." Lizzy was smiling now. "And I think her rash has started to fade already."

Caine examined his niece. "You're right." He raked his fingers through his hair. "Thank Christ. The last thing my sister needed today was to come home to one of her kids in the hospital. She had thyroid cancer at twenty and had her thyroid removed. Last week she found a swollen lymph node under her arm. Doctor doesn't think it's anything, but she's freaked out anyway. They're doing a biopsy as a precaution."

"Wow. I'm sorry to hear that. I hope everything turns out okay."

Caine nodded. "Thank you."

A doctor stopped by to check on Lizzy, who was still in my arms. He pulled the curtain along the track on the ceiling and converted the open nook to a private treatment room. "How's the little princess doing here?"

Caine answered. "It looks like the rash is starting to fade a little."

"Let's take a look." He examined Lizzy's face, belly, legs, and arms. "The Benadryl is kicking in. Let me just examine her one more time, in maybe a half hour, and then we can send you on your way. She's going to be getting sleepy from the medicine pretty quick." Before he walked out of the curtained area, he added, "Or not. Sometimes Benadryl can have the opposite effect on kids."

Less than an hour later, we were discharged with a handful of papers. I walked Caine to his car and helped him strap the girls into their car seats.

"My sister insisted I take these things in case I had to go somewhere in an emergency. I told her she was nuts, I wasn't planning on driving anywhere, but she stuck them in my car anyway."

"Sounds like your sister made the right call."

Caine grumbled. "She'll lord that over me until we're eighty, too."

After the girls were strapped in, Alley asked if I could come back to her Uncle Caine's to play with her. I'd started to say I couldn't when Caine interrupted.

"I make a mean macaroni and cheese, if you're hungry. You sure I can't persuade you? We might have another diaper incident, and I'm almost out of duct tape. I may need to resort to Krazy Glue."

I smiled. I was tempted, but when Caine's face turned serious and he looked me in the eyes and said, "Please?" there was no way I could say no.

"I'll follow you."

His face lit up, and my damn heart started to race in response.

Calm down in there. He isn't inviting you to a romantic dinner. He only wants you to help with his nieces. Put on a diaper, not take off your clothes.

The entire drive to Caine's house, I tried to reason with my heart. Talk it down from the perch of excitement his invitation had pushed it out onto. But there was no reasoning with it. My head knew the truth, yet my heart didn't really seem to give a shit.

Chapter 17

Rachel

A gigantic black lab ran full-speed to greet me and almost bowled me over. I kneeled to say hello. "Hi, big guy. You're so cute. What's your name?"

Caine answered. "That's Murphy." He attempted a stern voice. "Down, boy." The dog completely ignored him and attempted to burrow into my body.

I scratched behind Murphy's ears while he went crazy sniffing me. "He listens to you well."

"That's your fault. He's never going to listen with the way you smell."

"The way I smell?" I wasn't quite sure how to take that.

"A dog's sense of smell is 1,000 times greater than a human's."

"And what, exactly, do I smell like?"

Caine walked over to where the dog was still mauling me and gave his collar a firm tug. "Come on, Murph. Give her a break, buddy."

Eventually, the dog backed off enough for me to stand. Caine leaned in and took an exaggerated whiff of my neck with his eyes closed. "Summer. You always smell like summer." Then he stepped back and winked. "My favorite season."

And there went my damn pulse again. The talk I'd given myself in the car on the way over went out the window. Caine chuckled, probably at the expression on my face.

"Come on in. I'll give Murph a treat to distract him from how good you smell."

I followed Caine and quickly forgot everything else once I got a look at his place.

Totally not what I expected.

Caine's apartment was incredible. I'd assumed it would be nice, but not *this* nice. The girls had run down the hall to get a video they wanted to watch the minute we walked in, and I looked around in awe. His living room was bigger than my entire apartment. Not to mention, he had a foyer. *A foyer in Manhattan?* That entryway alone had to be worth five hundred bucks a month. Caine noticed my expression. "My great grandfather started an investment company. Every subsequent generation of the West family grew the fortune he'd made by another zero. Except me. But I did inherit twenty-five percent of the company from my grandfather. It pays slightly better dividends than a teacher's salary."

"Uhh...slightly? I'd say. You have a view of the damn park." I walked to the wall of glass. "This place is amazing."

When I turned back, Caine was standing in the kitchen, which was open to the living room, and staring at me.

"Thank you for coming today," he said.

"I owed you one, remember?"

"You would have come whether you owed me one, or I owed you ten."

"What makes you say that?"

"Because that's the kind of person you are."

The girls came running back to the living room with a backpack. They jumped up and down. "Can we play tea?" they asked us.

"I guess she's having that opposite effect from the Benadryl," Caine grumbled.

"Sure. I love tea," I said.

Alley unzipped the backpack, lifted it by the bottom, and dumped the entire contents onto Caine's couch. It looked like she had enough ceramic teacups and saucers for a party of twenty.

The girls started to set the coffee table, and I walked to Caine's stainless steel kitchen. "Do you have herbal tea?"

"I think so."

It was amusing to see him sit on the floor and sip tea out of a little cup. Watching the way the girls interacted with him, I could tell he spent a fair amount of time with them, even if he was inept at changing a diaper.

"I take it this isn't your first time playing tea?"

"I'm forced to play it twice a month when I go to my sister's for dinner."

"Do the girls live here in the city?"

"No. They live up in Chappaqua. That's where I grew up. My sister stayed there to be near my mom."

"I lived in Westchester growing up, too. Pleasantville."

"You go to Pleasantville High School?"

"Umm...no. I moved to the city long before I got to high school."

During our two cups of tea, I loved watching Caine jump at the commands of a four year old. *Lift your pinky when you hold your teacup, Uncle Caine. You're slurping. The spoon goes on the saucer, not the table.*

Finally, it seemed the girls had mellowed out a bit. Lizzy was actually yawning.

"You tired, Lizzy?" Caine asked.

She yawned again in response.

He stood and lifted the sleepy girl into his arms. "Come on. How about you lie down, and I'll put the TV on for you?"

"Can I sleep in your bed?"

"Sure. Come on." Lizzy leaned from Caine's arms, reaching out to me. "Can you come put me to sleep, too, Rachel?"

I looked to Caine, and he shrugged. "Sure, let's make it a party."

Of course he was being sarcastic, but the girls didn't catch it and were excited anyway. The four of us walked down the hall to his bedroom.

An unexpected blush rose on my cheeks as we entered the room. Caine's bed was huge, definitely a king size. The four-post, carved-mahogany frame made it look even larger. It was also extremely high off the ground. The masculine feel of it really seemed to fit him. I could easily imagine him sleeping naked in it. Face down. With that tight ass I wanted to bite so badly peeking out from underneath a sheet.

I hadn't even realized I'd stopped in the doorway of the room, lost in my thoughts as I stared at the bed, until Caine spoke.

"You can come in. I won't bite."

Bite. That did it. That's all it took for the light blush on my face to heat to what I'm sure was a lovely shade of crimson. Caine took one look at me and a wicked grin beamed from his handsome face. He set Lizzy down, helped Alley up onto the bed, and walked back to the door, where I was still standing, twisting my watch back and forth on my wrist.

His hot breath tickled my neck as he whispered, "I know what you're thinking."

My entire body tingled from only his breath touching my skin. I could only imagine what would happen if his hands were on me. *Oh, God. Now I'm thinking of him, in that bed, with his hands on me.* I swallowed and took a deep breath, only to find Caine's scent still lingering as he walked back to the bed. Why couldn't he at least smell bad?

He fiddled with the TV in his bedroom, connecting wires to a DVR.

"I take it you don't watch movies in bed very often?"

"Pretty much the only time this thing turns on is when these two are here."

Conversation about TV and little girls was good—I was starting to feel calmer.

"I can't fall asleep without watching TV for a while," I told him. "I guess you're one of those people who falls asleep the second your head hits the pillow?"

Caine finished hooking up the wires, and the screen illuminated with the preview of some Disney movie.

Again, he walked back to me. "I didn't say that. There are *other things* to do before you fall asleep at night that I prefer over television."

I must've looked like a deer in the headlights, because Caine chuckled. "Relax, I'm just screwing with you. You looked uncomfortable, so I thought I'd help you out and make it worse."

"I'm going to go clean up the tea mess." I waved to the girls from the door and backed out of the room.

Five minutes later, Caine returned to the living room. I'd just finished washing the tea set and was drying the little dishes before packing them back into the girls' backpack.

"They're really sweet girls," I said.

"Luckily they take after their uncle and not their mom."

I laughed. "Yeah, right."

Caine took the dishtowel from my hand. "What, you don't think I'm sweet?"

"That's definitely not a word I'd use to describe you."

"Oh yeah?" He dried a tiny saucer and handed it to me to pack up. "And what word would you use?"

"I don't know. *Enigma*, maybe?"

Caine thought about it for a moment. "Not sure I can argue with that one."

After we finished packing up the tea set, we heard a phone buzzing.

"Is that mine or yours?" I asked.

"Mine's in my pocket. Must be yours."

I walked to the couch and dug for my cell in my purse, but it stopped making noise before I got to it. Reading Davis's name on the screen, I sighed audibly.

"Everything okay?"

"Yeah."

Caine waited for more.

"It was Davis. He texted me earlier, and I forgot to text him back."

He nodded. "You make a decision on that?"

"No."

"Want my help?"

My brows lifted. "You're going to help me decide if I should give my ex another shot?"

"Sure. Why not? Tell me about him."

"What do you want to know?"

"What's he do? How old is he? Ever married? The basics."

"Okay. Well, he's twenty-nine, divorced, and a regional sales manager for a nuclear medicine durable equipment company."

Caine deadpanned, "Sounds like a dick. You shouldn't give it another shot."

"What? Why?"

He held up three fingers on one hand and began to tick them off as he spoke. "Three reasons: One, he's twenty-nine and divorced. Something's wrong there. Bad track record. Two, salesman. That right there is a red flag. He sells crap for a living. It's only a matter of time before he's selling you a line of crap, too. And three, name's Davis." He shrugged. "It's a stupid name."

I stared at him incredulously. Feeling the need to defend my previous choices, I reminded him how ironic his assessment was. "One, you're thirty-two and don't have serious relationships. That right there says more than making a mistake when you're young and marrying your high school sweetheart. Two, you're a musician. Everyone knows musicians are notorious playboys. I'd venture to say the cheater ratio is double for a musician over a salesperson. And three, have you read the Bible? Cain wasn't exactly the good son."

Caine nodded. "Exactly. So I know the type. You should keep away from him."

I'd apparently misunderstood his point.

"I think you're a little insane. You don't know Davis's *type* just from his age and occupation. He's a great guy. He works hard, wants to have a family some day, calls his mother every Sunday. He even has a romantic side—took me on a picnic in the park once."

Caine scoffed. "That's not romantic. He sounds like a wimp."

My hands went to my hips. "What are you talking about? Of course that's romantic. What's your idea of romance, if you're such an expert."

Caine walked from the kitchen to the couch where I was standing. He stepped into my personal space, and I refused to move. When he leaned down, putting us eye to eye, our noses were practically touching.

"I don't do romance," he said. "I prefer fucking like animals to picnics in the park."

God, why was he being such a jerk?

More importantly, why did I like it so much? Goosebumps prickled all over my skin and a shiver ran through my body, causing a tingle between my legs. Not to mention, my nipples had grown so swollen I was going to need to step back in a minute if he didn't give me some room. And while he'd turned me on, he'd also pissed me off. I rolled with the latter.

"Maybe that's why you're still single."

Caine's eyes narrowed. "If everything about this guy is so great, what's taking you so long to answer his question?"

He had a point. It should have been a no-brainer. But if I was being honest with myself, the reason had nothing to do with how great Davis was or wasn't. The only thing keeping me from giving the man another chance is that he wasn't Caine.

I felt defeated. "You're right. There's really no reason not to have dinner with him tomorrow night. Who knows, maybe the spark will light again. I'll never know until I try."

Caine retreated with a stiff, blank mask. It didn't matter that we had chemistry like I'd never experienced or more in common than most happily married couples. He wasn't interested in me. The more I got to know him, the more I realized the professor-student thing was just an excuse. Caine West was not a man who'd let anything get in his way if he really wanted something.

With a little distance back between us, my thoughts were clearer. "I should go."

He was silent as I tucked my cell into the side pocket of my purse and took out my keys before slinging it over my shoulder. He didn't move when I brushed past him but then grabbed my elbow to stop me.

"I'm the last person who should be giving relationship advice. But if it's not there, you can't force it. No different than when it is there and you try to make it not be."

Again, I wanted to read something more into his comment than he'd meant. I needed to stop doing that. "Thanks, Caine."

He nodded, looking sad and resigned to stay that way. "Thank you for covering my class today and coming to my rescue tonight."

"Of course. That seems to be our thing. We rescue each other."

Chapter 18

Caine - Fifteen Years Ago

A little thing like her shouldn't be out riding a bicycle all by herself.

I'd waited outside the church this week, on the little bench hidden in front of the statue of Mary—most likely so people could pray in peace, not stalk ten-year-old girls. If anyone caught wind of the crazy shit I was up to on Saturdays, they'd probably think I was a goddamn child molester.

My little friend locked up her bike on the other side of the church and looked around to see if anyone was watching before running inside. I ducked but wasn't sure if she saw me or not. I wasn't even sure what the hell I was looking for—but at least I knew how she got here and that she came alone.

I waited a few minutes before going inside, figuring I'd let her settle in on her side of the booth. But when I slipped into the church, I found her kneeling in a pew near the confessional. Her head was bowed to her steepled hands.

She must have felt someone watching her, because after a minute her head came up and she looked around. Luckily she looked the other way before turning in my direction, giving me a chance to pull my head back behind the column. *What the fuck am I even doing?* I was hiding from a little girl I was reasonably sure lived in some sort of an abusive home and pretending to be a priest so I could what...*rescue her*?

Finding the coast was clear, the little girl got up from the pew and went to the confessional. Just like last week, she opened the priest side instead of the parishioner side. Although this time, she didn't go in. Partially blocked by the door she was holding open, I couldn't make out exactly what she was doing. But from the way her body folded at the waist and her arm came up and then right back down, I thought she might have tossed something inside. Then she opened the other door and disappeared inside.

What the hell was she up to?

Curious, I headed straight for the booth, only to find it just like each of the last six weeks I'd sat inside. There was the red velvet chair, the makeshift wooden pew with its worn-leather kneeling bench, a gold cross on the wall... and that was about it. Then I noticed a small coin sitting directly behind the front leg of the chair. I'd almost missed it. Leaning down, I picked it up. She spoke before I could even take my seat.

"Bless me, Father, for I have sinned."

I flipped the dulled copper penny over and over between my thumb and pointer as we got started. "Tell me your sins."

Her mood was melancholy this week. She didn't have any funny stories to share about Tommy, and even though she'd been on the other side for a solid twenty minutes, she hadn't actually said much at all.

"How was school this week?"

"I didn't go for three days."

"Why not? Were you sick?"

"No."

"Then why didn't you go to school?"

"Is it a sin to skip school?"

"Not really. But you should go. Education is really important." Apparently today I was channeling my mother instead of a priest. "And you can get in trouble for not going. Do you know what truancy is?"

"No."

"It's when you're absent from school illegally."

"So something can be illegal but not a sin?"

What was she getting at? "Well, breaking the law set by the state of New York is different than breaking God's law. Why were you absent from school?"

"Because I was waiting for my sister."

"Where was she that you were waiting for her?"

"I don't know. She ran away last week. But before she left, she told me she'd come back and get me once she found a new place for us to live."

"So you skipped school?"

"I pretended to go in the morning and then I came back to the house after Benny left. I didn't want to miss her if she came back for me while I was at school."

"Do you know why your sister ran away?"

She was quiet for a long time. Then she finally said, "I think it was because of Benny."

That sounded like the fucking understatement of the year. "Did Benny go looking for your sister?"

"No. He yells a lot about her after he gets home from work. But then he falls asleep on the couch that smells like him."

"You need to go to school. Talk to a teacher. Tell them what's going on at home."

"No. I don't want to get my sister in trouble."

"You won't."

"I don't know..."

I was thinking it was time I went to the police. But what would I say? *Hi. I'm a fake priest, and you need to look for a guy named Benny and a skinny little girl who rides a blue bicycle?*

"What's your name?"

She was quiet again. "I have to go."

"Wait!" I'd been flipping the penny around the entire time we were talking and suddenly stopped. "Did you drop some change on the floor?"

Her voice was low and almost melodic. "Find a penny, pick it up, and all day long you'll have good luck." Then the door creaked open and closed behind her.

With whatever shit was going on in this little girl's life, she was sneaking in to drop coins on the floor for the priest to find and have good luck. *Unbelievable.*

Chapter 19

Rachel

I agreed to have dinner with Davis in spite of the glum feeling I'd been walking around with for a few days. Or, maybe I hadn't done it *in spite* of myself, but more like *to spite* someone else. Because I made sure *that someone* knew I had plans for this evening. I'd blown my naturally curly hair straight, slipped on a sexy, little summer dress, and laced-up, high-heeled sandals that tied with ribbons wrapping up my legs. The ensemble made my legs look long and the skirt look extra short. *Perfect.*

The additional effort getting ready was worth the response. Caine had trouble keeping his eyes off me during the entire class. I'd chosen to sit in the front row today, an end seat, so I could casually dangle my legs. The way his eyes heated, I could feel their caress on my skin. But by the end of class, I realized I was getting hot and bothered by one man before my date with another. It was disrespectful to Davis, even if he had no idea.

So, when class was over, I decided not to stick around and chat with Caine like I normally did. There was no rule that the TA had to stay after class unless she was teaching an extra-help session. I'd made it about three steps up toward the exit when Caine's voice stopped me.

"Ms. Martin, can I see you for a minute, please?"

I couldn't very well ignore him. Taking a deep breath, I turned around and headed back down to the front of the lecture hall. A few students were lingering to turn in papers that had been due last class. I waited dutifully off to the side. Caine spoke briefly with each student and then began to pack away the papers in his bag, ignoring me while he did so.

Eventually, I grew impatient. "Did you want to speak to me?"

He looked up and watched the last of the students as they exited the classroom. Once the door closed, he finally acknowledged me.

"What are you doing?"

I acted innocent, pretending I was oblivious. "I'm standing here waiting for you to tell me what you wanted to talk to me about. Isn't that obvious?"

Caine frowned. "You know what I mean, Rachel."

"I don't think I do."

His response was not verbal. Instead, his eyes started at my feet and raked up my body. It was a slow, intense, heated gaze that made me want to squirm. But I didn't. Somehow I managed to stand tall and even pulled my shoulders back so my breasts were more prominent. When his eyes finally made their way up to mine, I returned his stare, not giving an inch. I was pretty damn proud of myself.

"You can't come to class dressed like that."

I looked down. "What's wrong with what I'm wearing?"

"It's distracting for the male students."

I arched a brow. "For the male students?"

He folded his arms across his chest. "Is there an echo in here?"

My hands went to my hips in full *don't screw with me* mode. "There is nothing wrong with what I'm wearing. It's a sundress and sandals. I'm not even showing any cleavage."

Caine's eyes dropped to my chest. I might not have been showing any cleavage, but the dress was thin, and I felt my pebbled nipples protruding.

"I can see the outline of your nipples."

"It's cold in here." My initial reaction was to want to cover myself, but...*fuck him*. I thrust my chest forward a little more. "You know what? *Your* pants were so snug a few weeks ago, I could see *your* outline. Why is that okay, but seeing my outline isn't?"

Caine's eyes rose to mine. His voice was hoarse. "You were staring at the outline of my cock?"

"It was right in front of my face. I couldn't help but look."

He took a step closer, his nostrils flaring. "Did you like what you saw, Ms. Martin?"

I have no idea where it was coming from, but I wanted to keep dangling a red cape in front of the raging bull. Rather than reply, I ran my tongue across my top lip. *Slowly*. His eyes followed in pursuit.

The way his chest was heaving up and down, I thought he might blow. It made me feel fearless and empowered. *You don't want to be with me? Good. But here's what you're missing,* Professor West.

"Don't ask for something you don't want, Rachel. I'm warning you." He took a step closer, invading my private space.

His pupils were dilated, and he looked angry as hell, but there was something lurking just beneath his dark gaze—desire.

I tilted my head coyly and leaned in. "Who says I don't want it? I've seen the outline."

Caine's jaw flexed while I waited with my heart hammering inside my chest. I held my breath as he reached for me, the blood swirling around inside my ears so loudly I couldn't even hear my own gasp as his hand gripped my hip.

I braced for it...waiting for a string of frustrated curses I would have sworn were coming before his mouth crashed down on mine.

But instead, it wasn't Caine's voice I heard.

"Professor West?"

Oddly, I'd heard the door creak open at the top of the lecture hall, it just didn't register in my brain until a few seconds later when reality smacked me in the head.

Caine stepped back. He walked to his desk and cleared his throat. "Ginger—Professor Ashby. Can I help you with something?"

She looked back and forth between us. "I was hoping I could speak to you in private—about a student. But if I've come at a bad time?" She pointed to the door that was now behind her. "I can come back later."

"No. It's fine." He looked at me sternly. "Ms. Martin and I are finished."

For a moment I was still in shock from the rapid change of events. But that didn't take long to morph into anger. I looked at him with disgust and spoke under my breath so Professor Pink wouldn't be able to hear me.

"Are you *serious*?"

He lifted his bag. The desire so openly on display just two minutes ago had been quickly shuttered over. He spoke under his breath. "We're done here, Rachel."

The bastard had dismissed me already. *Well, screw you, Caine West.*

I walked up the stairs with Caine a safe distance behind me as we made our way to Professor Pink—only today she had on an aqua suit. Apparently *Ginger* liked color. My guess was she liked to stand out in a sea of black-wearing New York women.

As I reached the top of the stairs, she smiled at me. "I love your sandals. But must be tough walking through campus in those heels."

I offered a broad, phony smile in return. "Thank you. But I only had the one class today. I wore them for my date." I turned to Caine, spread my lips wide, and gave him a chance to check out my teeth. "See you Friday, Professor West. I don't want to keep Davis waiting."

I didn't give him the satisfaction of a second glance before I was out the door.

Chapter 20

Rachel

My mood was effectively ruined. *Screw you, Caine West, I'm going to have a good time with Davis even if it physically hurts.* I took a few minutes in the car to settle myself before going into the restaurant. Looking up at the sign, I realized Davis had picked a place we'd been to together during our short period as a couple. Roberto's had incredible food and was romantic, with an olden-days type of feel. I wondered if he'd picked a spot with those memories on purpose.

Inside, I looked around and spotted him sitting at a table in the back corner. It was exactly where we'd sat the last time we were here. If there was any doubt that Davis was trying to rekindle the mood we'd once experienced, the table he'd arrived early to secure confirmed his intentions. It was actually sort of sweet of him to put so much thought into where we had dinner. That was Davis—

sweet and thoughtful. He was the polar opposite of Caine's bitter and thoughtless.

I had no idea why I was even comparing the two men. It didn't feel fair to Davis, even though he'd win in pretty much any category I could scribble down on paper and analyze. The problem was, Caine made me feel something that couldn't be categorized—something I couldn't even really describe. And for a reason I didn't quite understand, that stupid feeling trumped all of the awesomeness of Davis.

But this afternoon had been a real eye-opener. I'd practically thrown myself at a man who was attracted to me physically, but hated that he was. No good could come of tempting a man to act who had no interest in anything more than sex and would also immediately regret giving in to his temptation.

I sighed and vowed to enjoy my evening and focus on the man sitting across from me.

As I approached the table, Davis' smile brought back all the good times we'd had over the years. He stood as I approached and pulled me into a giant hug. It felt so good. His arms wrapped tight around my waist as he buried his face in my hair and inhaled deeply.

"I missed you," he said. "You always smell so good."

I didn't realize how much I'd missed being held. Yes, I missed the sexual gratification of being with a man...but being held and feeling wanted felt pretty damn amazing. Down deep, I knew I was needy after Caine's rejection, but I buried that and allowed myself to enjoy Davis holding me anyway. He took a long time before he released me, and when he did, he stepped back, holding my hands so he could look at me.

"Wow. You look incredible, Rach."

"Thank you."

We sat, and Davis just kept staring.

A nervous giggle snuck out. "You're staring at me like I have two heads."

His eyes had such a tenderness as he smiled. "I was just thinking...remember that picture we took at my graduation? The one where I had on the gown and you were wearing my cap crooked with a goofy smile?"

"I think so."

"Well, I printed it out, and I have it on my dresser, and..." He trailed off.

"What?"

"Nothing. I don't want to scare you off before the appetizers even come."

I laughed. "Don't be silly. What were you going to say?"

Davis looked me in the eyes. "I was going to say sometimes I wake up and look at it, but it doesn't hold a candle to seeing you in person." His eyes flickered to my lips. "I miss your goofy grin. That's all."

There was so much warmth in his gaze. It seemed to be contagious because I felt my insides turn a little mushy. Why had I thought tonight was a bad idea? In that moment, I couldn't think of a single reason.

The waitress interrupted to take our drink order. Davis ordered his usual Tanqueray and tonic, and he looked to me. "Diet Coke?"

I was feeling rebellious tonight. "I'll have a Tanqueray and tonic, too."

Once the waitress disappeared, Davis lifted a brow. He knew my stance on drinking. He also had to remember that the one night we drank too much together, we wound up in bed.

"Is tonight a special occasion?"

"I think it is. We haven't seen each other in a while."

"It's been way too long."

By the time I finished half of my drink, my shoulders had dropped, and the muscles in my neck were a lot looser. We'd started to settle into the old Davis-and-Rachel comfortableness. I gave him an update about my classes, and he asked how my sister was. Never liking to talk about myself too much, I steered the conversation back to him.

"So what's new with you? How's your job?"

"Good. Got a little promotion—a bigger territory."

"Wow. Congratulations. I knew you'd do great. Do you get a big fancy corner office now?"

"Nah, I spend three-quarters of my time on the road. But they did give me a better car allowance, so I got myself a fun new car to enjoy while I'm doing all that driving."

"What did you get?"

"The Audi A4. It's a manual transmission. Makes for a fun drive on long hauls with hills."

My brain was being unfair. It immediately conjured up the memory of Caine driving his little car—the way his hand gripped that gear shifter. Such an odd thing to have gotten me all hot and bothered, even odder that I shifted in my seat remembering it.

I sipped my drink. "You'll have to take me for a ride sometime."

"I'd like that. You can even take it for a spin, if you want."

"Thank you," I scoffed. "Caine wouldn't let me drive his car. Thought I'd ruin his precious clutch."

"Caine?"

"Professor West. My thesis advisor."

Davis seemed contemplative for a few seconds and then nodded. "That's right. You mentioned him the other night at O'Leary's. You still working six days a week over there?"

"Actually, not the last few weeks. Between teaching and student extra-help sessions, faculty meetings, and writing lesson plans, I've had to cut down a bit."

Over dinner, we chatted away like long-lost friends. Davis was good company, and our familiarity gave me a sense of comfort—*Davis* had always given me a sense of comfort. When our conversation came to a lull, I could see he was thinking. It looked like he was debating saying something.

"Spit it out," I said.

He chuckled. "You could always tell when something was on my mind."

"What's going on? Is everything okay?"

He stopped eating and put down his fork. "You said you weren't seeing anyone?"

"No, I'm not."

"Is there a reason for that?"

"Other than that I barely have time to breathe and most of the men at O'Leary's are sixty-year-old retired cops, no. Not really."

"Have you dated anyone since...you know...we were together?"

"Does one guy who was a total jerk and Charlie almost hit with a baseball bat count?"

We laughed, but Davis remained serious. "I went out with a woman for a while—Stacey. We had a lot in common and got along great."

I felt a pang of jealousy. "Are you still together?"

"No. We broke up."

"What happened?"

Davis looked away for a few seconds, then returned to meet my gaze. "She wasn't you."

I opened my mouth to respond three times, but each time I shut it, realizing I wasn't sure what to say. Davis caught my bewildered expression and seemed amused.

"You don't have to say anything. In fact, don't. Let me just finish, if that's okay?"

"Okay..." I managed to get a word out—a single one, but it counted.

"First of all, this wasn't how I planned to talk to you about this. My plan was to have dinner tonight, charm you into remembering how great things were between us, and then take you out a few more times before I laid it all out there."

"I'd say you went off script."

"Yeah...sorry about that. I got a little jealous and stepped on the gas."

"Jealous. About what?"

"Nothing. It was stupid."

"Tell me."

"You mentioned that professor a few times at dinner the other night, and then when you mentioned being in his car a little while ago, I visualized you... My mind just started to race a bit. I thought maybe you were seeing him or something."

I scoffed in denial. "Definitely not." Although the emphatic tone in my voice made even me not believe it. Obstinate denial is often the loudest confession. But Davis didn't seem to notice.

"Anyway, my plan was, after I got you to remember how good we were together, I would tell you I've never stopped thinking about you." He paused, looking up at me with a shy and vulnerable expression. "I've tried to move on, but every person I start to date—no matter how great they are—has one flaw I can't seem to move past. They're not you."

Wow. Just. Wow. I was caught *so* off guard by his seriousness. I was also a bit confused.

"I don't understand, though. When we stopped seeing each other, you said you weren't ready for a relationship. I completely understood that because of everything you'd just come out of. You needed time and space. Yet you started dating someone not long after that. So you didn't really need time? You just needed time not with me?"

Davis ran his fingers over his short hair. It was slightly longer than a military cut, but still neat and cropped close to his head. Again I thought of Caine. He'd frequently dragged his fingers through his thick, unruly hair when I'd done my best to frustrate him.

"You're sort of right. I needed time not with you—because I didn't know how to do slow. I could see a future with you, and that scared the shit out of me because I was just climbing out of a relationship I'd seen as my future at one time. When I dated Stacey for those few months, I couldn't see things long-term—didn't see a future—so I felt comfortable with her."

"So you stayed with a woman for a few months because you couldn't see a future with her. But walked away from one after only a few weeks because you *could* see a future?"

Davis's laugh was mocking. "Pretty stupid. I know."

It actually wasn't. It sounded like a protective mechanism. If you know you can't stop yourself from eating the whole cake, you don't buy it at the store.

"It's not stupid. I get it. Our timing was just off."

When Davis and I stopped seeing each other, I was upset—even though the logical part of me understood he was right. But I'd always believed he was honest with me, that he needed his freedom. I figured if it was meant to be, it was meant to be, and someday we'd find our way back to each other. And here we were.

That someday had come.

I hadn't had any relationship to speak of, so it should be easy to pick up where we left off.

Only...

It didn't feel easy.

But did love always come easy? Look at Umberto and Lydia...

"Say something."

My thoughts were so jumbled inside my head, I hadn't realized I'd been quiet for a few minutes.

"I have no idea what to say."

"Well, then I might as well finish and lay all my cards out on the table."

"Finish?"

He chuckled. "Don't worry. There's not much more." Davis reached for my hand. "I've made some big mistakes in my life, but the biggest mistake I've ever made was walking away from you. I know this might seem like it's coming out of nowhere, but I promise you it's not. Not one single day has gone by that you weren't in my thoughts. I just finally owned up to the truth."

Everything he said was exactly what I wanted to hear... almost nine months ago. Only now I wasn't sure Davis had ever been the right person for me. If he was, why hadn't I been more devastated when it ended? Why was I able to let go? My mind kept returning to Lydia and Umberto. She wouldn't even let go now—when he doesn't remember who she is and thinks he's in love with another woman.

But maybe not pining my days away with thoughts of Davis was my defense mechanism. Maybe I'd buried my feelings so as not to get hurt—who knows. I just felt overwhelmed and confused.

"I don't know what to say."

"You've mentioned that," he teased with a boyish smile. "How about saying you'll at least give it some thought? Don't say no. Not yet, at least. Take some time."

"Okay."

"Okay?" His eyes widened. "You mean you'll think about it."

"Yes. But I can't really think straight right now. Between the drink and everything you just said, I'm not in the right frame of mind to respond anyway."

"That's better than a no. I'll take it."

Somehow we managed to get back to regular conversation and enjoy the rest of our...date? Were we even on a date? I'd called it that to Professor Pink, but just in an attempt to rile up Caine. What were Davis and I doing, actually? I hadn't really thought of this as a *date* date—I was simply meeting him for dinner.

Although it definitely felt like a date toward the end of the evening.

When dinner was over, I was glad I'd driven to meet him at the restaurant instead of letting him pick me up like he'd suggested. It saved us from the awkward moment where I'd have felt rude for not inviting him up, but wary about what it might look like if I did invite him up. However, even though it prevented *that* awkward moment, it didn't make the one that came when he walked me to my car any easier.

Davis took both my hands. "Can I give you a call in a few days? Maybe we can make a plan to meet up for coffee or something?"

I smiled. "Sure. I'd like that."

He leaned in slowly, almost as if he wanted to give me a chance to move before he entered my space, and brushed his lips softly across mine. "'Night, Rach."

In a fog from the last two hours, I got into my car, and Davis closed the door. He waited for me to start it before walking to his. I needed a few minutes before I drove, so I fished my phone from my purse and checked for missed calls and text messages as my engine idled. The first thing that popped up was a text from Caine. It must've come in during dinner.

Caine: *Don't do something stupid to get even with me.*

What nerve! The man seriously thought the world revolved around him. The fog I'd been in suddenly lifted, and my anger from earlier was back, clear as day. I typed in a frenzy.

Rachel: *Screw you. Not everything is about you.*

The dots immediately started jumping around.

Caine: *This is.*

A hundred scathing responses ran through my head. But then I noticed Davis waiting for me to go before leaving the restaurant parking lot himself. God, I'm such an ass. Tossing my phone into my purse, I forced a smile and gave Davis another wave before putting my car in drive.

The restaurant was about twenty minutes from my apartment. I was on schedule to make it in about five when I had to jam on my brakes and narrowly averted smashing into the back of a Honda stopped at a stop sign. I was so angry, so unfocused, I hadn't seen the big, red reflective sign or the two tons of steel yielding to the law.

Between my emotions getting the best of me and the adrenaline that kicked in after a near-accident, my heart was palpitating like mad in my chest. I had to pull over for fear my next close call wouldn't just be close.

Of course, since I was stopped on the side of the road, I pulled my phone out of my purse.

Dumb move.

I should have just caught my breath, calmed down, and driven myself home at a normal speed. Instead, when I swiped, I found both a missed call and a text from Caine. There was no voicemail, but the text read '*We need to talk*'.

I was furious. Not only did he think everything was about him, he thought he could issue commands. *We need to talk.*

You know what? He was right. We did need to talk. But I was going to be the one doing all the talking, and it was going to happen on *my terms*.

My tires screeched as I pulled away from the curb and hung a U-turn to head toward Manhattan. That talk he wanted was going to happen now.

Chapter 21

Rachel

If you looked up *unstable* in the dictionary, I'm pretty sure my picture would be there.

In the span of five or six hours, I'd been aroused during a heated argument where I goaded Caine into touching me, angry and deflated when he dismissed me as if he hadn't been right there with me, and then confused yet flattered when Davis told me he wanted to get back together. Then, the minute dinner was over and Caine started barking at me over texts again, I rounded the circle back to angry.

Now it was almost eleven o'clock at night, and I was parked two buildings away from Caine's apartment. Suddenly all the angry nerve I'd harnessed on the drive over had disappeared, and I debated why I'd even come. Talk about emotionally unstable.

Why was I here? To tell off Caine, give him a piece of my mind for his hot-and-cold dismissive behavior. Sure, I wanted to tell him off. But I knew that's not what I really wanted. Sitting in the still-warm car, I took out my phone and swiped to re-read Caine's texts.

Don't do something stupid to get even with me.

He wasn't off base. My choices today—getting dressed up hours before dinner to go to class, showing up in something sexy, even deciding to go to dinner with Davis alone in the first place—they all had to do with Caine...and most of them *were* stupid.

I let out an exaggerated, heavy sigh. This visit was a bad idea. I tapped my forehead against the steering wheel a few times, mock knocking some sense into my brain. All of this emotional instability had taken its toll at once, and I was tired. *Really tired.* Taking one final look up at Caine's building, I started my car and headed back home to Brooklyn.

Finding a parking spot in my neighborhood after eight o'clock was next to impossible. I was too tired to search and decided to head directly over to the overpriced parking garage five blocks away rather than get aggravated circling for an hour. I'd had my fill of aggravation for today.

By the time I reached my block, I was cursing my high heels, along with the city's maintenance department for the crappy, broken sidewalks I had to walk on. I almost tripped three times. Finally arriving at my building, I winced up every step of the tall stairs. I grumbled to myself as I opened the outer door to the vestibule, finding it unlocked once again. Anyone could wander inside.

I jumped when I stepped in and found a man standing there. Instinctively, I started to scream.

Caine looked just as freaked out as I was. He held up his hands. "Rachel, it's just me."

I clutched at my chest. "What the hell are you doing? Trying to scare the living shit out of me?"

"I'm sorry. I didn't mean to scare you. But the door was open, so I let myself in. I was just about to leave since you didn't answer the buzzer."

My heart hammered in my chest. This was the absolute day from hell. "What are you doing here?"

"I came to speak to you."

My fright easily transformed into anger. "That's right. *We need to talk*. You barked that to me in a text earlier." I stretched the truth. "While I was saying goodnight to my date."

Caine's jaw flexed. "I'm glad you at least came home."

I wanted to hurt him the way he'd hurt me. "Yes. I prefer a *quick fuck* and then to come home and sleep in my own bed."

He spoke between gritted teeth. "Let's go upstairs and talk, Rachel. I don't want to have this conversation in the lobby of your building."

"What conversation? I get it, Caine. You're not interested. Well, your dick might be, but you're not."

He glared at me. "Five minutes. Can we please go upstairs and talk like adults?"

I glared right back. "Fine."

The air crackled in the small elevator as we rode up to the third floor. I sensed Caine's eyes on me, but refused to look anywhere but forward. When the elevator dinged on level three, it was reminiscent of a bell to start the next round of boxing. *Round nine, coming up.*

My apartment was small, but it suddenly felt like a shoebox. I dropped my purse in the kitchen and was about to relieve my throbbing feet from their torturous high heels when I thought better of it. I needed to stand taller, as close to eye to eye as I could come with Caine.

The tension grew each second as neither of us uttered a word. Finally, it was Caine who cracked under the pressure.

"I didn't want you to make a mistake you'd regret because of the way we left things. But since I'm too late, maybe I should go."

"You're such an asshole!" I shouted.

Caine glared at me. His jaw was clenched so tight, I thought it possible he might crack a tooth. Seeing him pissed off made me feel stronger, fueled me. I was like a drug addict, and each burst of his anger was my fix. I wanted more.

"The world does not revolve around you. There are plenty of reasons to sleep with Davis that have nothing to do with you being an asshole. Let's see..." I counted with my fingers. "One, he's honest with himself. He doesn't make up excuses to avoid the truth. Two, he admits when he's wrong. Like tonight when he told me how much he misses me and wants me back."

Caine's nostrils were flaring, so I thought I'd help the explosion along.

"Three, he's good in bed. Attentive and generous. You know, now that I think about it, there's probably a relationship between being honest with yourself and your feelings and being a *good fuck*."

Caine stood still, though I caught his fist clenching and unclenching by his side as he maintained control. The man was so frustrating and unbreakable. Infuriated, I went toward the kitchen to get something to drink. When he didn't move out of my way, I brushed past him intentionally.

"Move, asshole."

My breath caught as he grabbed my elbow from behind and spun me around. "You think honesty and being a good fuck go hand in hand? Here's one that will cement you being right in calling me an asshole. You're standing here telling me how you fucked another man, and all I can think about is how much would you hate me tomorrow if I showed you what it was like to be *really fucked*. Not nicely fucked. Pushed up against the wall and fucked while I suck on your skin hard enough to leave marks—so the next time you take your clothes off to get back at me, the asshole knows I've been there."

Caine used his grip on my elbow to pull me against his chest. We were eye to eye.

My voice shook when I spoke. "I didn't sleep with Davis to get back at you."

"Then why did you fuck him, Rachel?"

This was a moment of truth. Keeping my eyes on his, I swallowed my pride and whispered, "I didn't sleep with him. I just said that to piss you off."

His eyes darkened to almost black. We stared at each other for a long time, letting everything sink in, and then his grip on me released. At first, I thought he was rejecting me again. Then I saw his hand at his belt buckle.

"Turn around. Bend over, and put your hands against the wall."

I looked at him in question, too at a loss for words to make a sound.

He lifted his chin toward the wall a few feet behind me. "The wall." His buckle unfastened, he tugged his belt, and it made a sharp *whooshing* sound as he pulled it through all of the loops in one smooth motion. "Hold on tight."

It felt like I was having an out-of-body experience as I turned and walked to the wall. I could see myself bending and splaying my fingers wide as if I were floating somewhere above, watching it all unfold in slow motion. I felt the warmth of Caine's body behind me before he spoke.

"This little dress…" The fabric barely covered my ass in this position, but he lifted the skirt until it was up over my bent waist, exposing my entire ass. "You wanted to taunt me with this little fucking dress, didn't you?"

I didn't think he actually expected an answer—wasn't sure I was capable of one either. But I was wrong.

"Didn't you? Say it. Tell me you wanted to taunt me."

I nodded. "Yes. I wore it for you."

His hand connected with my ass with a loud smack. He'd slapped me. *Hard.*

"That's for being evil when I was trying to be so good."

175

Oh, God. I felt a surge of wetness between my legs and gasped. He leaned over, covering my body with his, and pushed my hair to one side to kiss the back of my neck. I could feel his arousal at my ass, even through the jeans he still wore. His hot breath sent a shiver through my body.

"You liked that, didn't you? I'll remember that."

Then suddenly he straightened, and cool air hit my body. His fingers slipped under my G-string, and he dragged it down my legs until he was kneeling with the material at my feet. "Spread wider."

He dipped down and came up with his mouth directly between my legs. I whimpered and hoped my knees didn't give way as he buried his entire face in my pussy. It wasn't gentle. It was desperate and rough. He sucked hard on my clit and lapped at my arousal like I was his last meal and he was starving. I felt my orgasm build faster than it'd ever happened before, and I thought I might not be able to maintain my balance.

"So fucking sweet..." Caine groaned. "*So fucking wet for me.*" He pushed two fingers inside, and my eyes rolled into the back of my head.

I moaned. "Caine."

He pushed in and out. "So fucking tight."

"*Caine.*" My cries grew desperate. "*God, Caine.*"

He answered by standing and leaning over me again. The hand that wasn't inside me pulled my face to the side, and his mouth crushed to mine. His fingers never stopping, his tongue joined in unison. It was all so fast—too much. His hard-on pushed against the hot spot his hand had left on my ass, his fingers moved inside of me, his mouth, his tongue, his smell—all of it. My orgasm hit me violently, a series of whimpers swallowed by Caine as he kept going and going until I could barely breathe.

We both panted wildly, him still bent over me. Every breath tickled the goosebumps that had formed under the sheen of sweat on my skin.

"You okay?" he asked.

I answered with a goofy smile. "Oh my God, yes. Never better."

He chuckled. "You want to finish against the wall or in your bed?"

"Finish? I thought I already did."

"No, Feisty." He stood and scooped me into his arms. "You're just getting started."

If that was the truth, I was a little scared, because what already happened had totally kicked my ass. He must've read my mind.

Caine kissed my lips as he cradled me in his arms. "Bed. We'll give your legs a rest."

I liked that choice. Leaning my head against his chest I let him know. "I can definitely use a rest."

"I said your legs were getting a rest—not the rest of you."

Chapter 22

Rachel

I leaned up on my elbows, enjoying the show.

Caine caught me watching and smirked. "You know, you could help me out a little and undress yourself while I'm getting undressed."

"But I'm enjoying myself just fine watching you."

He shook his head and continued to unbutton his shirt. His jeans were unfastened and had slipped down a bit on his narrow waist. My eyes were glued to the deeply carved V on display as he finished and tossed his shirt to the floor.

"You should teach with no shirt on."

"I'm sure administration would like that."

"They'd like the increase in enrollment from all the women who would transfer from colleges with ugly, old professors."

"Is that so?" Caine's lip twitched, and his hand went to the zipper of his pants. He tugged them down and stepped out. My eyes dropped to his boxer briefs—or rather to the thick bulge on full display. I knew he was watching me, but I couldn't tear my eyes away.

Since I was enjoying the show so much, Caine must've decided to really give me one. His hand wrapped around his thick arousal, and he stroked up and down through his underwear.

"If I'm going to teach shirtless, I might as well leave off the pants, too." He squeezed, and when I looked up at him, our eyes met.

I swallowed. "I think just no shirt would be better."

"Oh yeah. Why is that?"

I licked my lips. "Because that's *mine.*"

Caine's wicked smile said he liked that comment. He hooked two fingers into either side of his boxers and bent to step out of his underwear. His thick cock bobbed high onto his stomach.

"*Jesus Christ.*" I thought I'd only thought it, but apparently I said it out loud.

Using his teeth and one hand, Caine opened a condom I hadn't noticed he was holding onto and sheathed his length before raising one knee to climb onto the bed.

"Don't worry. We'll go slow. That re-virginized pussy will be sore tomorrow, but only from multiple rounds, not from me taking you too fast. Now, let's get you out of this dress."

Caine took the hem of my dress and pulled it up over my head. With my underwear long gone, I was left in only my bra and shoes. Reaching around, he unhooked the clasp with one hand. Tomorrow I'd probably obsess over the fact that he had more experience removing a bra than I did, but right now I was only grateful he didn't waste any time fumbling.

He leaned back to take me in. "You're beautiful." He cupped one of my breasts, stroking the nipple with his callused thumb. "These tits. They've been making me insane for weeks. I can't tell you how many times I lost track lecturing when I looked over at you and saw them poking through your shirt."

His mouth lowered to my breast, and he lashed it with his tongue before sucking my nipple deep into his hot mouth. He looked up at me as he licked and nibbled, our eyes locked while he took in exactly what caused different reactions. Caine's intense attentiveness was finally making me squirm for much more enjoyable reasons.

Cool air hit my hardened nipples as his mouth moved up to my neck. He sucked on the sensitive skin below my ear while my hands explored his body. When he bit down on my earlobe at the same time he pinched my excruciatingly hardened nipple, I dug my nails into his back.

Caine groaned. "We'll get to that later. Once I've broken you in, we'll explore how rough you like it. I bet you'll like your hair pulled while you're on all fours with a red ass and my cock filling this sweet little pussy." Caine's hand lowered, and he ran two fingers over my slick center before dipping them inside. "Soaked. You like the thought of that, don't you?"

When I didn't answer, couldn't answer, Caine crooked his fingers inside me and rubbed a spot I knew could set me off. Since I was incapable of replying verbally anymore, I reached down between us and wrapped my hand around the length of him, giving a good, hard squeeze. After a few pumps, Caine shifted fully on top of me and took my mouth. His tongue flicked against my lips, instructing me to open, then slipped inside to find mine. I was completely lost in the kiss, feeling it everywhere on my body. There was a hunger to it I'd never experienced before. I had no restraint. I wanted to give him everything he was about to take and more.

Caine lifted a bit, enough so he could look down at me, but our bodies were still touching. Our eyes locked as he rubbed the length of him up and down my entrance, coating himself with my wetness. Then he began to push inside. Just a few inches at first, before pulling almost all the way back out and repeating it slowly. Each thrust went a little deeper, stretched me a little wider.

When he finally gripped my hips and bore down, filling me completely, my eyes fluttered closed. It felt so good to be completely overwhelmed by this man. I'd been fighting it since the day we met, and giving in was such an emotional relief.

"Open your eyes, Rachel." Caine wiped a stray hair from my face and whispered, "I didn't think you could be any more beautiful to look at. But your face with me inside of you is...I have no words..."

Reaching down, he cupped a hand behind my thigh, prompting me to bend my leg at the knee and allow him to sink even deeper inside me.

"Caine..." My body began to tremble.

"I know..."

He took his time, but the intensity just kept building. Each thrust went deeper as we began to move in unison, rocking back and forth. I felt him inside me in so many ways.

I moaned through my orgasm, struggling to keep my eyes open but wanting to share how good he made me feel. When I'd started to come down, Caine sped up, driving into me faster and harder as if he were chasing my release with his own. I loved the way he said my name over and over as he climaxed inside of me. It was more therapeutic than any music had ever been for me.

We held each other as Caine continued to move in and out of me for a long time after—lazy, unhurried strokes as we caught our breath and shared easy smiles. Eventually, though, he had to stop to deal with the condom. When he lifted from the bed to go into the bathroom, a chill rushed over my damp skin.

I hoped it wasn't a sign that once the heat was over, things with Caine would be getting cold again.

Chapter 23

Rachel

Caine surprised me by returning to the bed with a warm facecloth and gently washing me up. No man had ever been so tender in aftercare with me. The way he took the cloth to my sensitive skin was so intimate and thoughtful, it made my shoulders—which had tensed when he'd gotten up—relax again.

"Good?" His voice was low and soft.

"Yes. Thank you."

He disappeared back into the bathroom, and I heard the sink run for a few minutes. Then he emerged again. He was quiet as he picked up his clothes, slipping on his boxers and then jeans. Perhaps I'd relaxed a bit too prematurely.

"What are you doing?" I tried not to sound too snarky, but didn't quite hit the mark.

He was looking down, zippering, and stopped to look up at me. "Getting dressed."

"I can see that. But is there a reason you're running out the door so fast?"

Caine's brows furrowed. I realized he hadn't even given any thought to what he was doing. He was on autopilot.

"This is what you do every time after...you're with a woman, isn't it?"

His jaw flexed. "It's late."

"Whatever. Go."

I looked away, not wanting to let him see the disappointment I knew was impossible to hide on my face. The rustle of clothing pissed me off more and more each second. Five minutes ago he'd been so sweet and tender, and now it was back to Professor Asshole.

I couldn't help myself. I was, after all, feisty. "You're really an asshole, you know that?"

Caine froze, buttoning his shirt. "I believe you've told me that before, so yes, I'm aware I'm really an asshole. What I'm surprised about, though, is that you don't seem to be as aware of it as I am, yet you're the one who likes to remind me of my asshole status."

The man could get me so damn angry. It was like a switch flipped inside of me and I turned into some psycho bitch I didn't recognize.

"Are you going to leave cash on the end table?"

His eyes blazed. He was silent as he glared at me. I braced, waiting for the response I saw coming.

"I don't think you're a whore, Rachel. In fact, I think you're just the opposite—a nice girl. That's the problem."

"What are you talking about?"

Caine finally looked me straight in the eyes to answer. "When things end, or better yet, when I fuck things up, I'm going to hurt you."

"You don't know that."

He scoffed. "Yes, I do, Rachel."

Deep down, a part of me knew he was right. But I couldn't let him see that. "You're so full of yourself, you've already decided you're going to break my heart. Did you ever stop to think maybe it's *me* who will break *your* heart someday? Maybe I'm just using you for your body."

Caine's brows rose. I was completely full of shit, of course, but he didn't need to know that. All he needed to do was *stay*. I wasn't ready for him to leave me. Not tonight...not yet.

When his eyes dropped to my breasts, I was reminded that the one thing Caine couldn't deny was his attraction to me. So, I'd have to capitalize on that until I could figure out the rest. Reaching up, I cupped my breasts and gave them a good squeeze. Unbridled lust flared in Caine's eyes, and the control in the room shifted. If sex was the way I could get that right now, so be it.

Moving one hand down my body as seductively as I could, I shut my eyes and reached between my legs. When I opened them and saw the way Caine was looking at me, I knew I'd won this round—even if it was only a small battle in what I guessed was going to be a long war.

"Is that a problem?" I asked. "If I use you for your body?"

He answered by unbuttoning the shirt he'd just put on. "Not at all."

While he was making quick work of his clothes, I knelt on the bed. He was fully aroused again, even though he'd come less than fifteen minutes ago. In fact, it seemed even bigger now. If I hadn't been so turned on, I might've been a little scared of that thing.

Caine was watching me, so I went for it—gave him actions to go with my bold words. Turning to face the headboard, I got up on all-fours and looked back over my shoulder at him. My voice was hoarse. "I believe you said something about my hair and wanting me on all-fours?"

It was two in the morning by the time we'd finished rounds two and three. Or was it three and four, since technically round one had started in the living room earlier? Either way, I learned something about Caine this evening—his fight to keep me out was weakened when he was physically exhausted. Considering the method for getting him physically exhausted was pretty damn spectacular, I'd say the discovery was a pleasurable one.

My head nuzzled his bare chest while he stroked my hair in the dark. When he spoke, his voice was low. "How did you get that scar on your back?"

"Fell out of a tree when I was a kid and took some branches with me on the way down." I'd told the same story for so long whenever anyone noticed my jagged, three-inch scar, I almost felt like it was true.

"Ouch."

"It wasn't so bad. It healed fast. How about you? Do you have any scars?"

"No visible ones," Caine said. "Although the invisible scars are the hardest to heal."

I understood that sentiment more than he knew. I placed a soft kiss on his chest, right above his heart. After that, we were both quiet for a while, and I wondered if he was thinking about his scars.

"Do you mind if I stay tonight?" Caine broke our silence. "I think you sucked the strength out of me. *Literally* on that last round."

I giggled. *When was the last time I giggled?* "Of course not. I want you to stay."

He squeezed my shoulder in response.

A few minutes passed, and I thought he might have drifted off, so I whispered, "Are you sleeping?"

"No."

"Can I ask you something, then?"

I wasn't looking at him, but knew he was smiling when he spoke. "Would it stop you if I said no?"

"Don't you miss this?"

"What?"

"This...snuggling with a warm body and companionship."

Caine was quiet for a moment. "That's not an easy question to answer, Rachel."

"How come? Isn't it just yes or no?"

"Very few things in life are that simple."

"I think you make things more difficult than they need to be."

He sighed. "I spent a year on academic probation for giving in to wanting a warm body. You're my TA, and I'm your thesis advisor. I've never had a relationship that didn't end badly. There is no simple yes or no."

It hurt to be reminded that I wasn't the first dip Caine had taken in the academic pool. I was quiet, and he must have sensed that I was feeling needy.

He kissed the top of my head. "I've never spent the night with anyone from the college." He paused. "And before you jump to any incorrect conclusions, I'm *never* too tired to get up and go home. Even now."

I took that as a victory, however small. "Okay... When was the last time you—"

Caine interrupted, snuggling me closer in his arms. "And *this warm body* feels really good. Now get some sleep. You can interrogate me more while you make me breakfast in the morning."

A few minutes later, Caine's breathing slowed as he drifted off to sleep. I kissed his chest and shut my eyes to follow him to dreamland. I smiled and thought to myself, *I can't wait for breakfast.*

My eyes fluttered open, and I immediately reached over to the other side of the bed. Instead of finding Caine, I was met with only a cold sheet. My stomach sank. Stretching for my phone on the nightstand, I squinted at the time and was shocked to find I'd slept until almost eleven-thirty.

The last time I'd slept that late...well, I couldn't remember the last time I'd slept that late. No wonder Caine was gone.

Yawning, I dragged myself to the bathroom to wash up and brush my teeth. I was still completely naked, and when I looked in the mirror and saw my wild hair and the faint red marks on my neck from Caine's incessant sucking, I couldn't help but smile. *God, did I have memories.* And not just etched into my brain—muscles I hadn't even realized I had ached, and between my legs was swollen and sore. Yet I felt better than I had in a long time. I actually *liked* the crazy way I looked, and I didn't bother to fix it, feeling some sort of odd connection to Caine through my disheveled appearance.

Grabbing the first thing I reached in my drawer filled with lazy wear, I slipped on a vintage Rolling Stones T-shirt and headed to the kitchen for some much-needed coffee. I halted in place upon finding Caine at my stove. His back was to me, and he didn't seem to have heard me, so I stood in the doorway watching him, half stunned at what I was seeing and half shocked at finding he was even still here.

Caine was...*dancing*? Well, not technically dancing, I guess. But he was definitely swaying to the beat of something as he flipped pancakes in one pan and rolled the sausage around in the other. *Yum.* And the food smelled pretty good, too.

I continued watching quietly, utterly amused at seeing Caine so disarmed.

"You want some coffee while you stand there?" he asked without turning around.

I jumped and then smiled. "I didn't think you knew I was here."

"I know." He went to the cabinet, pulled down a mug, and poured me a cup of coffee. It seemed Caine and my kitchen had gotten acquainted while I slept. "Do you take cream and sugar?"

"One Equal and half and half."

Caine finished making my coffee, and for some reason, I stayed in the doorway of the kitchen. He brought me the mug and kissed the tip of my nose before handing it to me. "Morning, sleepyhead."

"How long have you been up?"

"About an hour."

"I didn't know you were still here. Why didn't you wake me?"

Caine returned to the stove. "Figured you were tired after last night."

I smiled and brought the coffee to my lips. "I am. I feel like I got beat up."

Plating pancakes and a few sausages, he set breakfast on the table. "Sit."

"You're really bossy, you know? Borderline rude. I'm not a dog. Sit. Stand."

Caine walked back to where I was still leaning against the doorway and put one hand on either side of my head on the wall.

"You didn't seem to mind it last night."

"That's different."

"No, it's not."

He dropped his head, chuckling. "How about we have breakfast without a fight?"

"Fine. I'll sit. But only because it smells really good and not because you barked at me."

He shook his head. "Whatever it takes, Feisty."

As soon as the fork hit my mouth, I realized I was starving. I woofed an entire pancake in a few bites.

"Hungry?" Caine raised a brow.

"Shut up. So what did you do while I was sleeping?"

"Listened to music on my phone, checked out the pictures on your wall some more."

I pointed my fork at him. "You were snooping? Wouldn't have taken you for a snooper."

"I didn't go through your drawers. I looked at pictures hung on the wall. I don't think that's the same as snooping."

"Snooper." I smiled like an idiot.

We ate in silence for a while. I smiled too much, and Caine looked like he was trying to hide that he was a little terrified of my enthusiasm over breakfast. But it was so much more than I'd expected from him after how things started off last night.

While I was rinsing the plates, my cell phone rang. It was plugged into the charger on the kitchen counter, and Caine and I caught the name flashing at the same time. *Davis.*

Caine's eyes flickered up to mine. Ignoring it, I went back to finishing the dishes.

"Not going to get that?"

"I'll talk to him later."

While I wiped down the table, Caine went back to the living room wall with another cup of coffee. I joined him when I was done. He stood in front of a picture that had been taken just about a year ago. It was of my three roommates and me the week before we all moved out and went our separate ways. Our couch was six feet long, made of two, three-foot cushions, but the four of us were all sitting squished on one. There were a lot of smiles in that photo.

"Who's this with you and Ava?"

"That's Beth and Davis. Beth is the one with the cleavage."

"I gathered that much."

Caine sipped his coffee. After a moment, he turned and faced me. "Why didn't you sleep with him?"

"We just had dinner. He wanted to talk."

"But he wants to sleep with you?"

"He wants to give dating another try, yes."

Caine sipped again, studying me over the brim of the mug. "And what do you want?"

You, you idiot. I want you. I knew he was skittish enough about what had happened last night, so I treaded cautiously, trying to make light of the subject. "I wouldn't mind some more of what I had last night."

Caine slipped his hand under the hem of my T-shirt and discovered I had nothing on underneath. He grabbed a handful of my ass and squeezed. "You've had nothing on under here since you got up?"

"Nope."

He took the coffee I was holding out of my hands and walked to the kitchen, leaving both our mugs on the table. Returning to me, he leaned down and lifted me up and over his shoulder, fireman style. I squealed, but loved every minute of it. Especially what came after...

It was the middle of the afternoon before Caine made mention of leaving. I had to work at O'Leary's at five, and we'd just taken a shower together. He dressed while I was in the bathroom doing my usual routine. Still wearing just a towel, I leaned into the bathroom mirror to rub moisturizer into my skin. Caine came up behind me and watched in silence. We exchanged smiles and looks, but for the most part, neither of us said anything. He just watched as I finished with my face moisturizer, rubbed a different one into my legs and arms, then brushed my wet hair.

Eventually he spoke. "Ever hear a song for the first time and you don't know the words, but the music is really familiar?"

"Sure. Like 'All Summer Long' by Kid Rock where he uses parts from 'Sweet Home Alabama' and 'Werewolves of London'?"

"No. An all-original song that you hear for the first time, but you know the music anyway?"

I turned to face him. "I guess. I mean, all songs have commonality to them. A riff, a chord, a lick, a common register or timbre. Our brain seems to index all those little things so we hear something and have that familiar feeling, yet we can't figure out where it came from. Why?"

"You're that song. I don't know any of the words, but the tune is so damn familiar."

I understood what he meant. I'd felt a connection from the first time we met, too. I didn't want to scare him, but whatever was between us had always felt bigger than me—bigger than us.

Teasing, I wrapped my arms around his neck. "Well, my body probably reminds you of some supermodel. I'm guessing the one that football player is married to."

Caine smiled. "You mean Tom Brady?"

"That's the one. My body? Dead ringer for his wife. And my heart, probably a little Mother Teresa."

"Is that so?"

"Mmm-hmmm."

He leaned down and placed a soft kiss on my lips. "That must be it. I gotta run, Mother Teresa, and you need to get to work. I'll see you tomorrow in class. I'll be the one at the front of the room, ignoring you and trying not to stare at your rack."

"Okay." I pushed up on my tippy toes and kissed him this time. "And I'll be the one you'll know has no panties on."

Chapter 24

Caine - Fifteen Years Ago

She didn't show up last week. It should have made me happy that after eight weeks of sneaking off to church, I finally had my Saturday back. But it didn't. It made me anxious, and the goddamned week dragged.

I looked up at the cross above the church and grumbled to myself before going inside. *Sorry about the* goddamned, *big guy.*

The church was empty as usual, and I had a song to learn, so I went to my regular spot to take a load off rather than stalking outside. Liam had been on one of his drunk-songwriting binges again. But after the last fiasco where he could only remember half of a kick-ass song, we'd all chipped in and bought him a portable digital recorder. The thing was smaller than a phone and could record twenty hours of music with the press of a button. It worked great. When he showed up hungover at practice this morning after his typical Friday night drinking and songwriting session, he couldn't remember shit. But all we had to do was upload.

We were grateful Liam had remembered to turn the damn thing on. Only, unfortunately for us—and for him—he didn't remember to turn it off all night. We were definitely going to find a way to sample some of his midnight jerking-off grunts on a track in the future.

I sat in the dark confessional for almost a half hour with my earbuds in. Even though she hadn't shown, at least I'd learned the lyrics Liam had come up with. When I was done, I sank down into the red velvety plush seat, closed my eyes, and put on some Bob Dylan. The sound of "Blowin' in the Wind" blocked out everything else around me—including the sound of the door creaking open on the other side.

I wasn't sure how long she'd been there when I finally opened my eyes and noticed her. Pulling a bud from my ear, I slipped from priest mode and let my sixteen-year-old self show. "Hey. I didn't think you were going to come."

The music blared from my dangling earbud.

"What are you listening to?" she asked.

I couldn't very well tell her I'd been listening to Dylan. That wasn't very priestly. "Some new hymns."

"It sounds like Bob Dylan."

I grinned. The kid knew Dylan. No wonder I liked her so much. I lowered my voice. "Shh. Let's not let the other priests in on our little secret."

I couldn't see her, but I knew she was smiling. "Okay."

"Speaking of secrets, what do you have for me today? Have you been a good little lamb?"

"My sister came back home."

"To get you?"

"No. She got in trouble, and the police brought her home."

Good. The police needed to be at that house. "What happened?"

"She was staying at her friend's father's hunting cabin up north. She drank all his liquor one night and wandered out to find a store and got lost. The police brought her home after she threw up all over the back of their car."

"Did they talk to your parents?"

"They talked to Benny. I listened through my bedroom door. He lied to the police, told them she drinks all the time and runs away with boys. That she'd been that way for a while."

Shit. "They didn't ask any other questions?"

"Not really. There were two of them, and one knew Benny from the garage."

"The garage?"

"Where Benny works."

"Benny fixes cars? He's a mechanic?"

"Yes."

"How is your sister now?"

"She's sad."

"Why didn't you come last week?"

"I couldn't leave my sister alone. Benny was really mad at her after the police brought her home. He was drinking and yelling a lot for days."

"Did he hurt her?"

"I think so."

This wasn't a game anymore. "You need to tell me. Did he or didn't he?"

She was quiet for a long time. I'd decided that if she took off, either I was following her home or the two of us were going to finally meet face to face. The fact that I'd violated this poor little girl's trust didn't even matter. She could hate me and run away from the church for all I cared, so long as she was safe.

I pushed with a stern tone. "Talk to me. *Did he* or *didn't he* hurt your sister?"

"She won't tell me. But I saw him come out of her room in the morning, and she told me I had to lock my door at night, that he'd promised he wouldn't bother me if she was nice to him from now on."

Fuck. Fuck. FUCK! "We need to go to the police. I'll go with you."

"I need to go home now." I could see through the lattice that she had stood.

"Wait!" I yelled.

She stilled. "Why did you come today if you don't want my help?"

"Because it feels safe here with you."

"You trust me?"

"Yes."

"Then I need you to do something for me."

"Okay."

"Get your sister and come back here."

"I can't. Benny's going to be home soon."

"Then tomorrow. It's Sunday. What do you usually do on Sunday?"

"Benny usually goes to work in the morning. My sister and I play music. We're not allowed to play it when he's home."

"When he leaves for work, come here. I want to speak to you and your sister. Together."

She was quiet for a while. When she finally did speak, her voice wasn't convincing. "Okay."

"You'll come? And bring your sister?"

"I'll try."

I waited until I heard the door to the confessional and then the church open and close. It would probably take a few minutes to unlock her bike, and I knew the direction she came from.

The last thing I wanted to do was scare her when I followed her home. But if she didn't show tomorrow, I needed to know where I was going.

Chapter 25

Rachel

Mind-blowing sex had after effects. It was not even nine o'clock, barely halfway through my shift, and I was dragging my ass. Even that thought, though, made me smile to myself. *I'm dragging my ass.* The ass that Caine had his hands all over last night...and this morning.

Ava caught me daydreaming. "Oh my God. You had sex with Davis."

"What are you talking about?"

She tossed her tray on the bar next to some random guy who was immediately interested in our conversation. "I can see it in your face. You're normally all..." She waved at her face while she scrunched it up to look like she might be in pain. "...uptight looking. Now you're not." She slapped the back of her hand against the guy drinking his beer and asked his opinion. "Am I right? She definitely got laid."

The guy examined my face carefully.

"Please ignore her." I walked down to the other end of the bar where no patrons were sitting. Ava followed and took a seat on an empty bar stool.

Getting back to work, I wiped down the counter, attempting to ignore her, but she just kept staring at me with a goofy smile.

Sighing, I stopped. "What?"

"You're really not going to tell me anything?"

"It's not what you think."

"So something *did* happen with Davis. Spill it!"

"Davis and I went to dinner last night."

"I knew something happened. You have that look on your face like you're in love or lust."

I hoped it was the latter that gave me butterflies in my stomach every time I thought of Caine West, because I was certain the former was not a good idea. Ava took my starry-eyed, glazed-over face to mean the latter.

"Sex looks good on you."

Luckily a couple walked in and wanted to be seated, providing a temporary reprieve from Ava's grilling. Even though she had a big mouth, I knew she'd never tell any of my secrets—that wasn't what kept me from telling her the truth. As silly as it sounded, I just wanted to keep what had happened between Caine and me to myself. I wasn't ready to overanalyze what was going on. I chose to remain in my own private, ignorant bliss for as long as I could.

That wouldn't be very long, though.

Around nine o'clock, I was shaking up a Cosmo in a silver shaker, not paying attention, when Ava's voice surprised me. She spoke in that sing-songy way that most girls grow out of around the time they ditch their training bras.

"Hiiii," she lilted. "I wonder what brings you here tonight?"

I looked up to find Davis at the end of the bar, shrugging out of his jacket. Guilt smacked me in the face. *Damn it.* Why hadn't I responded to his texts this afternoon? He waved, and I motioned that I'd be a few minutes. There was nothing keeping me from walking down there, so I had to create some reasons. I filled a customer's beer and chatted with him for as long as I could, then offered to close out a tab for a guy who wasn't nearly ready to leave. That was the extent of my customers, so I was almost out of stalls when I saw Ava coming toward the bar. Hopefully she had a drink order.

"Go take a break. I'll cover for you." She winked. "And I don't have any reason to come into the stock room at all, if you happen to want some privacy."

Guilt fueled my panic. As I glanced down the bar, Davis smiled, none the wiser that my armpits were damp, and I felt slightly nauseous.

"Actually, can you help me with something in the kitchen?"

Ava's brows furrowed. "Sure."

"I'll meet you back there in a minute. Let me just get Davis a drink."

"Okay. But you're acting strange."

"Just go."

"Fine."

I took a deep breath and walked down to the end of the bar. Forcing a smile, I said, "Hey. This is a surprise. I didn't know you were coming."

"A good surprise, I hope."

Ummm. "Of course. I just need to take care of something in the back. What can I get you to drink? You want the usual?"

"That sounds good. Thanks."

Somehow I managed to mix Davis's Tanqueray and tonic without spilling it and serve it with a smile. "Be back in a bit."

Ava was waiting in the kitchen. "What's going on? You looked like you were on cloud nine ten minutes ago, and now you're miserable since Davis showed up? I take it you weren't expecting him."

I paced back and forth. "No, I wasn't."

"What's bothering you? Did you not have a great time last night?"

"No, I did."

"Okay..."

I rubbed my forehead. "Davis and I went to dinner. We had a nice time, but I was confused, so I called it an early night and went home."

"That's it? I could have sworn I was looking at post-coital haze before."

"You were."

"What am I missing?"

I stopped my pacing and looked at my friend. "I slept with Caine after dinner last night."

"What? Caine...as in Professor West?"

I nodded.

"I'm confused. I thought you had dinner with Davis?"

"I did. And then I went home. Earlier in the day Caine and I had an argument at school...sort of. When I got home from my date with Davis, Caine was waiting for me. He wanted to talk. We had another argument and—"

Ava grinned. "Pissed-off sex is the best. Fuck me like you hate me."

"What am I going to say to Davis now?"

"He doesn't know anything happened other than you went home and went to bed after dinner, right?"

"I guess."

"So just pretend it didn't happen."

Obviously she'd never had sex with Caine. Pretending it didn't happen was like trying to eat only one Pringle out of a full can. "I'm a terrible liar."

"So don't lie. If he tries to talk about anything between the two of you, just say you're at work and would rather not talk here. Postpone having the conversation until you're ready. And even then, if you only want to be friends with Davis, you don't need to tell him anything else."

I took a deep breath. "You're right. I'm acting like an idiot. I feel guilty, and that's what this is all about."

"You have nothing to feel guilty about. You're a grown woman who's single. Did you make any commitment to Davis during dinner?"

"No. I told him I needed to think about things."

"So." She put her hands on my shoulders to calm me. "You're fine. You didn't do anything wrong. Take a minute or two, and then go back out there and act like a woman who didn't do anything wrong."

"Okay."

"You good?"

"I think so."

Ava went back out to the bar while I took a minute more to compose myself. She was absolutely right. I had nothing to feel guilty over, and Davis had no idea what had happened last night. *I can do this.* Keeping Caine out of my mind for a little while wasn't so tough.

I took a deep breath and swung open the door, feeling much calmer.

Until...

I looked over where Davis was sitting and saw a man sitting next to him. That man was *Caine*.

Ava saw me standing frozen in the doorway and walked over. Her eyes were wide. "Did you know either of them was coming?"

"Nope. Guess both decided to surprise me. *Fuck.* What the hell am I going to do?"

"Okay. Let's think about this. You still haven't done anything wrong. Although clearly you're going to act like a weirdo when you go over there."

"Clearly."

"Does Davis know who Caine is?"

I shook my head. "No. I don't think so."

"How about Caine?"

"He knows who Davis is from the picture on the wall in my apartment. I'm assuming he'll recognize him, if he hasn't already."

"Okay. I have a plan."

"Thank God."

"You're going to have to go over there and act like nothing's wrong."

"That's your plan? What kind of a plan is that?"

"The only one you have. Go back behind the bar and say hello, and then I'll stick close if I need to intervene."

My eyes flicked over to where the two men sat at the same moment Caine looked over at me. His face was unreadable. My stomach felt sick. I wanted to go behind the bar, grab a bottle of *anything*, chug it, and retreat out the back door.

Ava smirked, knowing what I was thinking. "We can have a drink when it's over. Just rip the Band-Aid off and go over there. It might not be so bad."

She handed me a ticket with a drink order. "Table three wants some fru-fru drink. It will keep you busy back there for a few minutes anyway."

Swearing under my breath, I took the ticket. "Stay close."

Ava smiled. "I will. I can't wait to watch the show."

I wagged my finger at her. "This is all your fault, you know."

"My fault?"

"If you knew blue from brown, I wouldn't have told off the wrong guy that night. Caine and I might not have gotten off to the rocky start we did, and we might have kept things professional."

Ava hooked her arm with mine. "You're welcome then. Let's go."

Behind the bar, I busied myself making Ava's drink order at the opposite end from where Davis and Caine were sitting. I avoided looking over as long as I could, but eventually curiosity won out and I found both of them watching me mix the drink.

I waved nervously and shook the drink in the shaker for way too long. Then I wiped down the counter and asked the only other two patrons if I could get them anything else. With nothing left to do and four eyes on me, I had no choice but to face the inevitable.

I took a deep breath and headed to the other end of the bar. Since I'd already said hello to Davis, I looked to Caine first. "Hey. I didn't know you were stopping in."

He glanced sidelong at Davis and then stared me down. "Yes. Apparently I should have called ahead for a reservation."

Shit.

Davis, oblivious to Caine's identity and the meaning of his comment, laughed. "Yeah, this place is an old man's bar. It's empty at night. I only come for the pretty bartender."

The muscle in Caine's jaw flexed.

I pointed to Davis's empty glass. "Would you like another?"

"Sure." He pointed to Caine. "And I'll buy my friend here one, too."

Caine stared at me. "No, thanks. On second thought, I'm going to call it a night." He stood abruptly, and the legs of the stool screeched on the floor as he pushed it back out of his way. "Get home safe, Rachel."

And just like that, Caine was gone.

"What's up with that guy? I take it he's a regular?"

I took Davis's glass from the bar. "He stops in once in a while. Let me get you that refill."

Ava met me at the other end of the bar. "What the hell happened?"

"Nothing. Caine left."

"Because of something Davis said?"

"No. He just left."

"So he just left you to spend the evening with a guy he knows you had a relationship with once and who wants to try it a second time?"

I knew she didn't intend for it to be hurtful, but she was right, and the truth stung. That was exactly what had transpired. Caine had bowed out. He wasn't in it for a fight. He wasn't in it for anything other than what we'd had—sex. Anything else I'd built up in my head was just wishful thinking.

Chapter 26

Rachel

I had no right to be angry.

Although not having a right to feel a certain way and actually controlling how I felt were two different things. I tried in earnest to disguise my bitterness after class the next day. As usual, I'd waited for the room to empty before going down to speak to Caine. I'd held an extra-help session before class, and he liked to keep the sign-in sheet to see who was making an effort. I handed it to him.

"You were late."

"No, I wasn't. I got here right on time."

"I was referring to the extra-help session."

The session hadn't even been held in a building Caine taught in. And I was barely late.

"I was literally two minutes late. And you're checking up on me?"

He stared at me. "I don't like lateness. Maybe you should plan to start the sessions later if you have to work late or whatever."

It was the *or whatever* that let me see past the blank mask he wore.

I squinted. "Were you looking for me this morning for a reason or just checking up on me?"

"Just be on time, Rachel."

"Answer my question."

Caine had turned away from me as he packed up his bag, but he stopped to look at me. His eyes were dark. "Not here. I can tell this conversation is not going to be one I should have in my classroom."

"Fine. Then where would you like to have it?"

He lifted his bag off his desk. "I prefer not to at all."

I folded my arms across my chest and raised my voice. "So you're done with me, then? Is that what you're trying to tell me? Because I prefer direct. If we're done fucking, you can just say so."

We had a mini stare off, and I knew I was pushing his tolerance to the max. I also didn't give a flying shit.

"Seven o'clock," he said. "I'll come by your place after my last class."

"I work day shift until eight tonight. I'll come to your place after."

I had no idea what had possessed me to say that. Why would I want to drive from Manhattan back to Brooklyn upset in the middle of the night? But my emotions felt so uncontrollable, I'd grasped for anything to have some semblance of control.

"Fine. But I'll pick you up. I don't want you driving at night tired."

Surprisingly, the rest of the day flew by. O'Leary's was busy, and working with Charlie rather than Ava meant I didn't have to talk about my life all day long. A little before seven, I was in the rear of the adjoining dining room talking to a couple who were regulars when my attention was diverted. I spotted Caine walking in. My heart started to race.

I was fooling myself trying to pretend I wasn't going to be hurt when he reminded me what we'd had was purely sex. All the logic in the world couldn't stop my heart from falling.

After I checked in on my tables and let the last straggling customers know they'd need to settle up at the bar, I went over to Caine. Charlie was standing nearby.

"You remember Caine, Charlie, right?"

Charlie extended his hand. "The Professor. West, right?"

Caine shook. "That's right."

"Got a middle name?"

Caine's brows furrowed, but he answered anyway. "I do. Maxwell—my father's name. Why?"

Charlie eyed me. "No reason. Just like to know who my girl is spending time with."

I rolled my eyes. "Ignore Charlie. He was a cop for twenty years. Everyone's a suspect until they're proven innocent. I'm going to go change. I'll be right back."

The car ride to Caine's was quiet and awkward. Since the way he handled the stick shift stirred me in places I didn't want to be stirred, I spent most of the time looking out the window. When we arrived at Caine's building, he came around to open my door, but I was already halfway out. He frowned and took my elbow to help steady me as I lifted from the tiny, low car. More silence ensued on the elevator up to his apartment. It wasn't until we were inside that either of us spoke.

"Can I get you something to drink?"

"I'll take a water." I kneeled to greet Murphy, who seemed to sense the tension between us and actually listened when Caine snapped at him.

"Down, boy."

Caine brought me a bottle of water and himself a glass of red wine. Again, I was staring out the window. I'd had the entire day to think about what I was going to say, but since the time had come, all my pent-up anger and frustration had disappeared. I was just sad and felt defeated and tired.

I sighed and continued to stare off into the city lights. "I didn't invite Davis to come to O'Leary's. We didn't have plans or anything."

"I know."

My eyes moved to Caine in the reflection. He stood behind me. "How do you know?"

"Because you wouldn't do that. You're not the type of woman who hops out of bed with one man in the morning and goes out with another."

I turned to face him. He didn't back up or give me any room. "So why did you leave, if you knew that?"

He looked me straight in the eyes. "Because you're better off with him than me."

My slumped shoulders squared. "You have no say in who I'm with. You can't just pass me off to someone else when you're done."

"That's not what I'm saying, Rachel."

"You know what? *Screw you.*"

"Rachel—"

His tone was a warning. But I was the one who should've been warning him. Because suddenly, I was infuriated. My frustration had morphed into anger. It pissed me the hell off that he was standing there so calm. It wasn't fair that he wasn't upset. I *needed* him to be hurt like I was.

"Don't Rachel me! You're right. I am better off with Davis. At least he's honest with me about how he feels. And he was pretty good in bed, too."

Caine's jaw clenched. "Are you done?"

"No, I'm not done. I'm just getting started. I think I'll fuck beanie boy, too. Maybe he can draw some better nudes after seeing the real thing up close and personal."

His voice was tight. "Now are you done? Because if you'd shut the fuck up for a minute, I'd like to get a word in edgewise."

My eyes widened. "Did you just tell me to shut the fuck up?"

Caine's head lowered so we were eye to eye. He spoke through gritted teeth. "I don't want to hear about you fucking other men. So, yes, shut the fuck up for a minute already."

"I will not. I can—"

Caine cut me off with a growl and then...his mouth crushed to mine. My gasp of shock was swallowed up by his kiss. His hands came up to cup my cheeks, and he growled again as he tilted my head to where he wanted it, deepening the kiss. My gut reaction was to fight, push away from his grip and run in the opposite direction. But that thought fled the second his tongue scooped inside and found mine. Instead, I kissed him back with all the pent-up anger inside me.

My arms wrapped around his neck, and I tugged at his hair as I clung to him. Caine gripped my thighs, lifting me off the ground as he backed me against the cold glass window. He guided my legs around his waist and groaned when he pressed between them. The sound made everything else disappear.

There was no yelling.

There was no telling me I was better off with another man.

There was only me and him—and this kiss.

This kiss.

Us.

We couldn't get close enough. Our limbs entangled, his hard body keeping mine in place. We were hungry for each other. I had no fight left in me. My head was spinning, and I was unable to form a coherent thought when our wild kiss finally broke.

Caine was panting, his voice hoarse. "Can you keep quiet for just a minute now?"

I managed to nod.

"Good." His grip on me tightened, but he pulled back enough to look in my eyes. "I said you were better off with him than me. But you didn't let me finish."

I held my breath, waiting to hear the rest.

Caine looked away in thought. "I left last night, thinking it was the right thing to do. I've never had a relationship longer than a few months, and I fuck up everything good around me."

"But you don't—"

Caine covered my lips with two fingers, silencing me. He closed his eyes and shook his head. Opening them, he chuckled. "God, you really never shut the fuck up." Then he leaned his forehead against mine. "Let me finish."

I nodded.

"You might be better off with him than me, but I'm a selfish bastard. And I'm selfish enough to not walk away when I should and to ask you to be with me until I fuck it up so badly that you run the other way."

Looking into his eyes, I realized he believed every word he was saying. For whatever reason, he thought he wasn't worthy of a chance—that things would inevitably end badly. A gnawing feeling in the pit of my stomach warned me I was going to get hurt, but I tamped it down.

"Will you tell me why you think you're going to fuck things up?"

"It's just history, Rachel."

"So we'll learn from it. But I can't do that if I don't know what there is to avoid."

Caine looked back and forth between my eyes. "You'll tell that douchebag you're not interested?"

My brows drew. "Douchebag?"

"Your roomie. Davis."

I didn't bother to tell him I'd already planned on telling Davis I wasn't interested. Let him think it was his victory. "Yes."

"Fine. We'll talk later."

Of course, I immediately started to protest. "Later? Why can't—"

Caine silenced me with a kiss. Again.

Later works.

I listened to Caine's heartbeat as my head rested on his chest.

"In high school, I had a girlfriend for a few months. I cheated on her."

His voice was low, and I had to move my ear away from his heart to be able to hear. Turning my head, I rested my chin atop my hands. The room was dark, although my eyes had adjusted enough to see him as he spoke. We were both naked, and I was feeling pretty content.

"You were young."

"With her twenty-two-year-old sister."

"How old were you?"

"Seventeen."

"Well, that still sounds like you were young. She was older and should have known better."

"My first year of college, I met Abby. We'd been dating for about five months when I decided to take a semester off and go on tour with my band. We were opening for a band that wasn't much bigger than us, but we thought we were going to be rock stars. That was my first experience with groupies. I didn't technically cheat on her, I guess. After seven weeks on the road, I called her and said we should see other people. She thought I was just lonely, so a few nights later, she flew out to Seattle to surprise me and see our show. She caught a show alright, but it was backstage and involved me and two women."

I wrinkled my nose. "You had a threesome?"

"I hadn't even known Abby was there. Apparently when she walked in, one of the girls invited her to join us, but I was too busy to notice."

"That's kind of gross."

"Abby got pissed, drank too much, and apparently fell walking up a flight of concrete stairs at her hotel. She rolled her ankle and broke her nose on the way down. Spent the night in the ER, and her parents had to fly out and get her the next morning. I didn't even know she'd been in town until the following week."

"That's horrible. Although I'm not sure that was even your fault. It sounds like you tried to do the right thing by breaking it off with her."

"Even if I try to do the right thing, I wind up fucking things up."

"I'm sure that's not true."

Caine was quiet for a long time. When he spoke again, his voice was pained. "My best friend Liam and I started our band when we were twelve. He was a pretty incredible songwriter. The only problem was, he did his best work wasted."

"I've read that Dylan wrote most of his best work on heroin."

"Yeah. Sex, drugs, and rock and roll. It's not just a tagline to sell T-shirts. The year things really started to take off for our band, so did Liam's drug hobby. At first he drank a few Red Bulls to stay up and play or write songs—eventually the Red Bulls turned into Adderall because it's easier to take a pill, and we were playing gigs near college campuses, and students take that shit like it's M&Ms. But the Adderall keeps you up for twenty-four hours, and you need to crash, so you take another pill to help you come down."

"Are you talking about Liam or about you?"

"I dabbled, but nothing like Liam. At the time, I didn't see it as clearly as I see it now. I guess I thought it was the norm. Me and the other guys didn't even know how bad things were for a while. Then one night, we tried to wake him for a gig, and we couldn't get him up. When the hospital pumped his stomach, there were so many drugs in there—and not just pills—it was a miracle he'd survived. I had no idea the Adderall had turned into coke and meth."

"Oh, God. I'm sorry."

"Liam went to rehab the first time, and we went back to Red Bulls for a while after that. But it never lasted long. He'd build back up to out of control, and we'd drop him off at rehab. We got a recording contract offer during his last stint in rehab. I should've known it was too much for him to handle. Part of our deal was that we had to bring five new songs. That's a lot of pressure on someone who's just getting out of rehab."

I already knew one of his band members died from an overdose. I didn't want him to have to say it.

"I read about your friend when I Googled you after we first met. I'm so sorry."

Caine was quiet for a long time. He shut his eyes, and when they opened, I could see them glistening, even in the dark.

I stroked his cheek. "You can't control someone with addiction."

"No. But I didn't have to pile on the stress. We shouldn't have taken the deal and put that on Liam."

"Was Liam happy about the deal?"

"We all were. We were twenty-one with a record deal from a major label."

"What happened wasn't your fault. Addicts look for reasons to justify what they're doing. If it wasn't that, it would have been something else."

Caine sighed. "I don't have a good track record, Rachel. Even when I try to do the right thing, I fuck it up somehow. I haven't told you about even half the bad choices I've made. About Liam's girlfriend, who was too damn young to be on the road with a band, but I let it happen anyway. About when I was sixteen and met this girl—"

I'd heard enough. Just like he'd done to me earlier, I silenced him by pressing two fingers to his lips. "Shut the fuck up, Caine."

He smiled through his sadness. "You wanted me to talk to you."

I climbed up his body and straddled his hips. I'd been holding the sheet around me and let it fall to my sides. "Thank you for sharing with me."

He gripped my waist and surprised me by lifting me up to my knees. Reaching down, he grabbed his cock and held it up, positioning it at my opening. "I'm not done sharing yet."

Chapter 27

Rachel

Things between Caine and me changed last night. The struggle that had been ever-present in his demeanor toward me seemed to have ended. The dawn of a new day brought a lighter—even happy—version of Caine.

After kicking him out of the shower so parts other than my breasts and between my legs could get cleaned, I took a few minutes to reflect on everything that had transpired. The pulsating stream of water massaged my neck as I closed my eyes.

Caine had opened up to me. He carried around a lot of guilt and weight on his shoulders, much of it seemingly unearned. Yet I hadn't shared much of my past with him. I didn't know if I'd ever be ready to talk about some of it.

After I dragged myself from the shower, I rummaged in Caine's closet to find a T-shirt. His walk-in was bigger than my kitchen. Grabbing an old, worn Brooklyn College shirt, I pulled it on and ran my fingers through my wet hair.

I found Caine sitting at the dining room table with a pile of papers and his laptop open. He was wearing those glasses I loved so much on him and looked up to watch me walk down the hall.

"What?"

"My T-shirt. It looks better on you."

When I reached the table, he immediately slipped a hand underneath it and grabbed my ass.

I wagged my finger at him. "Uh-uh-uh, Professor. Looks like you have work to do."

"My TA should be grading these papers."

"You didn't ask. I would have."

He pulled me down onto his lap and buried his face in my hair. "Why don't you grade them now? I'll finger you while you read through the essay on the art of rhythm."

"You're so crass."

He looked up at me. "What's crass? Fingering you? You like my fingers inside of you. And my tongue. And my cock. I wish I had more parts to put in there. I'd never come out."

I shoved at his chest and laughed. "I'm starving. You need to feed me."

"What? That's what I was trying to do. Warm you up to feed you."

"How about you make us something to eat, and I'll finish grading?"

"Deal. I fucking hate grading papers."

I finished marking the tests while Caine whipped us up some breakfast. Pancakes with a side of sausage.

"This is really good. But it's the same thing you made at my house." I pointed my fork at him. "Do you only know how to cook pancakes?"

"No, wiseass. I know how to cook a lot of different things. I just don't do it often because it's easier to grab something on the way home."

"I'm not that great with meals, but I can make a hell of a cake and pastry."

"Oh yeah?"

"Rose, my aunt who raised us, was a pastry chef. She liked to try to bond with me and my sister by baking together all the time when we first moved in."

Caine seemed contemplative. "Did your aunt and uncle have kids of their own?"

"No. Rose couldn't have kids. They were actually foster parents for a long time. After they adopted my sister and me, they stopped taking in fosters. They had their hands full enough with me and Riley."

"You've mentioned that you had some wild years. I would've liked to see that."

"No, you wouldn't. We put poor Rose through hell. Teenage girls are bad enough without an excuse to raise hell. I was no angel, but my sister was downright awful."

Finishing my breakfast gave me the perfect excuse to get up and try to change the subject. I wasn't a good liar, and it was only a matter of time before Caine would stumble onto a question I wasn't ready to answer. I took our plates to the sink and decided to wash them by hand rather than load the dishwasher.

Caine came up behind me and kissed my shoulder. "Do you have to work tomorrow night?

"No. I work evening tonight and day tomorrow."

"I want to take you somewhere tomorrow night."

"Where?"

"It's a surprise."

I smiled. "Okay."

"Get dressed up."

Finishing the last dish, I turned off the water and turned to face him. "How dressed up?"

"As much as you want to be."

I couldn't remember the last time anything had felt so right. Caine read my goofy smile. "What?"

"This feels...right."

His eyes searched mine. "It does. As much as I fought it, and it's against every rule at work, nothing's felt this right in a long time. Maybe I couldn't get you out of my head because you're supposed to be there."

We spent the next few hours being lazy, snuggled up on the couch watching old *Law & Order* reruns. I hated for the day to end, but eventually I had to ask Caine to drive me home so I could get ready for work. We dressed in his bedroom together.

I made the bed while he changed into jeans and a polo and brushed his teeth. There was a half-empty box of condoms tossed aside on the nightstand.

The master bathroom door was open so I yelled, "Where do you keep these?"

"What?"

"The condoms."

"Nightstand. But you can leave 'em out if you want. We'll be finishing those off soon."

I smiled as I opened the drawer and went to place the box inside, but a small, silver-framed photo caught my eye instead. Nosy, I picked it up to examine it. It was a picture of Caine's old band. He was probably in his early twenties and was arm in arm with another guy about the same age. The rest of the band hovered in the background.

Caine appeared and caught me with it in my hot little hands. "I'm sorry. When I opened the drawer, I saw it. I couldn't help myself. You were so sexy."

The bed dipped as he sat down next to me. "Were?"

I was relieved he didn't seem upset at my snooping. Knocking shoulders with him, I teased, "Well, now you're old and mature, so you're more handsome than sexy."

He took the photo from my hand. "Is that so?"

I watched him look down at it, rubbing his finger across the photo. "Me and Liam and the band."

"You all look so happy. Why do you keep it in the drawer?"

"I don't know. I guess it's not easy to see some days."

I knew the feeling. When I first decorated my apartment, I had days when I passed by the photo of my mother and it made me sad. But eventually I got used to seeing it, and over time, I started to smile at her each morning.

"It gets easier if you leave it out. When you tuck it away, you're burying it, and it never heals."

Caine looked at me and nodded in silence. Then he shut the nightstand drawer and set the small photo up on the end table. "You ready?"

I held back on showing him how giddy it made that he took my advice. The first few times he looked at it would probably be rough, but maybe it was time. Plus, I was hoping I'd be around to help him feel better as he slipped into bed each night.

Grabbing my purse in the living room, I rummaged through to find my cell as Caine slipped on his shoes. There were some loose coins on the bottom next to my phone, which gave me an idea—something I hadn't done in a long time.

"Hang on," I said. "I forgot something in the bedroom."

Walking back to the end table, I took one last look at the old photo of Caine and Liam before closing my eyes and making a little wish. Then I tossed the two copper pennies in my hand on the floor for Caine to find later.

Find a penny, pick it up, and all day long you'll have good luck.

Satisfied, I smiled and turned around to head back to the living room. Not expecting to see Caine filling the doorway, I jumped at finding him there. My hand clenched at my chest. "You scared me."

Caine's eyes flicked to the floor to look at the pennies and then came back to roam my face. "What the hell did you just do?"

Chapter 28

Caine

W*hat the fuck?*
I'd been pacing since I returned from dropping Rachel at her apartment. She'd known something was off, known I was full of shit when I said I had the start of a migraine coming on. I don't even get migraines, yet I was pretty sure the pounding in my head was leading in that direction.

It couldn't be a coincidence.

Could it be a fucking coincidence?

I dragged my hands through my hair. *Think, West, think. What the hell was that little girl's father's last name?*

Then I remembered the file in my desk drawer. Or maybe it was in the cabinet in the office where I kept old band crap. I was certain I'd kept a copy of the police report. God knows why I'd saved it when my parents had paid a fortune to have the incident expunged and make sure my records were sealed.

I ripped my files apart looking for it. By the time I came across the faded yellow page, my office looked like it'd been ransacked.

Victim's name: Benny Nelson

Nelson. I'd thought for sure finding out would make me relieved it wasn't Rachel's last name, but instead it only raised new questions.

The little girl's mother had died the year before. That would've made her around nine or ten when she lost her. Same timeline as Rachel losing her mother.

Fuck.

That feeling. That goddamned feeling I'd had since the day I met her. I knew her from somewhere, but could never put my finger on it. What was it that made me feel that way? I never really saw the little girl close up—only a flash of a ten-year-old face across the span of a church and through lattice work more than fifteen years ago. Nothing was clear.

Fuck.

Rachel had said she was raised by her aunt. She'd never mentioned a stepfather. Then again, if my stepfather was an abusive child molester, it wouldn't exactly be conversation to bring up during a date.

Bypassing the wine, I grabbed the scotch from the liquor cabinet and poured myself a double. It burned as it slid down my throat, but it felt good, like I should be on fire at the moment.

I knocked back another gulp.

Rachel had said she'd grown up a town away from me. *Pleasantville is a small, blue bicycle ride away from St. Killian's.*

Another gulp.

The little girl had an older sister.

Rachel has an older sister.

Teen years where she spiraled out of control—living with that fucker Nelson would definitely make anyone turn to shit trying to forget.

I tossed back the rest of the glass and stared out the window, trying to bring the picture of the little girl to the forefront of my mind. But it was so long ago and so distant.

Finally feeling the liquor seep into my blood, I collapsed on the couch and rested my head on the arm to stare up at the ceiling.

How the fuck was I going to find out? I needed to know.

It wasn't like I could come straight out and ask her. *Say, did you befriend a priest as a child? A man you trusted with all your secrets?*

Yeah. That was me. A stoned sixteen year old who got his kicks listening to a little girl talk about her shitty home life.

By the way, were you molested as a child? Or was that just your sister?

Fuck!

FUUUUCK!

I hurled my empty glass at the window. Luckily, it bounced off of a wood panel and only the glass shattered, not my floor-to-ceiling windows.

I closed my eyes and let my head spin some more.

How do I find out?

How do I find out?

Chapter 29

Rachel

I felt like Cinderella.

Unsure of how to dress, I'd bugged Caine until he told me where we were going. I'd never been to an opera and thought it was sweet of him to want to take me, knowing how much it meant because of my research with Umberto.

I didn't have anything fancy enough to wear, so I'd borrowed from Ava—a simple black dress that crisscrossed in the front and wrapped around my neck. The plunging neckline revealed a lot more than I'd normally show off, and I was glad she'd had the foresight to send me home with double-sided tape, as well as the dress.

Promptly at six, the buzzer sounded, and surprisingly, I was just about ready. While I waited for Caine to ride the elevator up, I went into the bathroom to finish lining my lips. *In for a pound*, I thought as I painted my mouth with a bright red lipstick I also never wore.

I'd left my apartment door cracked open after Caine buzzed, and he knocked before entering.

"Rachel?"

"I'll be out in a second!"

"Take your time."

While that was a normal person's response, I'd expected a comment about my always being late. The last two days, Caine had seemed off his game. He wasn't as sarcastic as usual, and his texts weren't even pervy. It had only been forty-eight hours since he'd dropped me off after our spectacular night together, but I missed the intimacy we'd shared already.

Stealing one last look in the mirror, I liked what I saw and took a deep breath before going out to greet Caine. I was nervous tonight—outside of my comfort zone and all dressed up to go to an opera.

I found my date in his usual spot at my wall of framed photos.

"What do you think?" I did the whole girly-twirly thing—also out of character for me.

The expression on Caine's face when he turned was priceless. His jaw went slack, and he had to clear his throat to speak. "You look gorgeous."

"Thanks. You don't look so bad yourself." He wore a dark, slim-cut, three-piece suit that looked like it could have been made for him. Seeing the way it hugged his broad shoulders and biceps, I realized it probably had been. *Pure class*. It was all in the way he wore the suit, and the effect it had on me was probably similar to what lingerie does for a man. Suddenly I was warm in my sleeveless dress with barely any material up top.

Caine stood in place, his eyes sweeping over my body, and waited for me to walk to him. With my five-inch stilettos, I didn't have to press up on my toes to greet him for a change.

"I like you in a formal suit. It does things to my girly parts."

He smirked. "Oh yeah? We could stay home, and I'll leave it on while *I* do things to your girly parts—with my tongue."

God, forget peanut butter and jelly. There is no better combination than a dirty mouth and sexy suit. Caine gripped the back of my neck and kissed me roughly, not caring that he smeared my lipstick all over the place.

I swooned a little when he whispered, "I love the dress, but I can't wait to take it off of you later."

I felt myself beaming. Who knew I could beam? "I just need to change my purse, and I'll be ready in a minute."

In my bedroom, I fixed my lipstick, applying a fresh layer to my kiss-swollen lips, before grabbing a tiny, black, beaded clutch from the closet and tossing in the essentials.

"Ready?"

"You don't have any pictures on the wall of you when you were little."

That's because there weren't a lot of good times I want to remember. "There aren't very many." I shrugged. "You know, second child and all."

Caine looked at me. "Do you have one? I'd like to see what you looked like when you were little."

"My sister has most of them. But I can probably dig a few up."

He nodded.

Outside, I was surprised to find he hadn't driven. He'd hired a town car to take us, and when we approached, a driver hopped out and opened the back door. I really felt like Cinderella then.

"A car? You went all out. But I'll let you in on a little secret—you were already going to get lucky tonight. You didn't have to impress me."

Caine smiled, but it felt sort of off. I couldn't put my finger on it, but he just didn't seem like himself. Our conversations were normal; any person looking in from the outside would see nothing but a couple on their way to a great night out. Yet, I had a pensive feeling for some reason.

On the way to the Met, we talked about school and work. I chalked my uneasiness up to nerves, or maybe things changing a little now that we weren't fighting our togetherness. Maybe it was just a new feeling of being settled. I wasn't sure.

Inside the theatre, we had a half hour before the show was to start, so we went to the lobby bar and ordered drinks. I ordered my usual diet soda, and Caine ordered a double scotch.

"Is everything okay?"

"Yes. Fine. Why do you ask?"

I shrugged. "No reason."

After he polished off the first scotch, he went back for a second. Just because I generally refrained from drinking didn't mean I frowned upon others partaking. Yet, once again, the two doubles and Caine's quietness while we waited seemed a bit off.

When the lights flickered, the usher showed us to our seats. Looking around the theatre, I told myself again that I probably just felt like a fish out of water. Although I liked the music, the thought of going to an actual opera had always felt pretentious. The place was a designer emporium—I smirked, thinking there wouldn't be any bootleg T-shirts sold outside afterward like the last show I went to.

Caine must have noticed me eyeing the people around us. He leaned in. "If I take off my jacket and lay it across your lap, I can probably finger you and get you to sing along during the opening scene."

The woman taking her seat on the other side of Caine looked his way, so I shot him a warning glare and whispered, "Shhh. Keep your voice down."

He smirked, and when the lights went down at the start of the show, he stood and took off his jacket, giving me a wink. To be safe, I clasped my hand with his when he sat back down.

Music filled the air almost immediately, and it gripped me, catching me off guard. It sucked me in from the first note and didn't spit me out until the very end. It overpowered my senses—the orchestra, amplified voices, the beauty of the theatre and costumes. I'd expected to enjoy the experience, but I hadn't expected to be moved to tears.

I was speechless when it was over. We walked to the waiting town car hand in hand.

Caine squeezed my fingers when we were inside. "So, what did you think?"

"I think it was the most magical thing I've ever experienced."

He rubbed his thumb on the top of my hand. "The first time is definitely something else."

"Thank you for taking me. I'm glad I got to experience that with you."

Caine smiled. "What did you like best?"

"Honestly, I don't know how to explain it. It made me feel something I've never really experienced. Consumed with emotions—like I couldn't feel or see anything else."

His eyes were tender. "I know the feeling."

I'd felt Caine watching me instead of the show at times, but I was too invested to peel my own eyes from the stage.

"As odd as it might sound, I think what I experienced was love in some form. At least the feeling that being in love gives you—that all-consuming and full feeling, you know?"

"I thought you said you'd never been in love."

It was in that moment that it hit me. I was figuring it out because I was falling for Caine. Just like the opera, he'd overwhelmed me since the day I met him. It was an inexplicable connection, although I was afraid to admit my realization out loud.

I shrugged. "I've read about it."

Caine's lip did that little twitch thing I hadn't seen in a while. "You've read about it, huh?"

It felt like he could see through me, so I changed the subject and rounded back to his original question about what I liked best.

"I think my favorite scene was the one where the mother dies. That's kind of morbid, isn't it?"

"What did you like about it?"

"The way her husband sang afterward. There was so much pain and emotion in his voice that I just knew he would never find another love in his life." I covered my heart with my hand, feeling choked up just thinking about that scene. "It reminded me of Umberto and Lydia—the devotion she has for him. At least they had more than fifty years together, but this guy was so young, and the love of his life was gone. It was heartbreaking, but beautiful."

Caine nodded and seemed to ponder my comment as he stared out the window into traffic. When his gaze returned to mine, his face was serious. "Did your mother never remarry after your father? You've never mentioned a stepfather in the picture before you were adopted."

"No." The lie came out before I even gave it a thought. "I had no stepfather." After I said it, I felt badly for not being honest with him.

But that didn't last very long because Caine surprised me by reaching over, hoisting my butt out of the seat next to him, and setting me down on his lap. It wasn't a very ladylike position, considering the elegant dress I was wearing, but I didn't care. His serious mood had been replaced by playfulness. He smiled wide, and it made my belly flutter.

Locking his arms around my back to hold me in place, he said, "You know what we're going to do to celebrate?"

I laughed. "What are we even celebrating?"

"Us. We're going to celebrate us."

The reason didn't matter, only the look on Caine's face.

"That sounds good to me. How are we going to celebrate?"

"Headphone sex."

"I have no idea what that is, but it came out of your mouth and had the word sex in it, so I'm game."

Caine bent his head back in laughter. "That's my girl."

Chapter 30

Rachel

It had definitely been my nerves. After a playful car ride back to my apartment, things took a more serious turn as we entered my bedroom. Caine stopped me at the foot of the bed. Standing behind me, his fingers caressed up and down my bare arms.

His hot breath tickled my neck as he whispered in my ear. "Do you trust me?"

"Yes."

"Close your eyes."

I followed his instructions without hesitation. His hands left my arms, and I felt him moving behind me, but he stayed with his front to my back. A loud *whooshing* sound made me gasp. He'd yanked his tie from around his neck. Then I felt the silk on my cheek.

"I'm going to deprive you of your senses so you can focus on nothing but what I'm doing to you."

I barely heard my own voice, my words stuck in my throat. "Okay."

Caine covered my eyes with his tie, securing it in place like a blindfold. I didn't even bother to try to open my eyes—I was too eager to feel what he wanted me to feel.

"You good?" he whispered.

I nodded.

He slowly unzipped the back of my dress. I wasn't sure if it was the anticipation or if my hearing was actually heightened because I was blindfolded, but the sound of my zipper slowly coming down had my entire body on fire. My nipples swelled, and every nerve ending seemed to come alive—I could feel my own skin.

Caine took his time sliding the dress down my body, using the silky material to caress my curves as he prompted me to step out. Cool air assaulted my skin when he stepped away, leaving me standing alone in nothing but lingerie and stilettos. I heard rustling in the room, but had no idea what he was doing. When his warmth returned behind me, his fingers dug into my hips and pulled me flush against him. He'd removed his shirt, and I could feel his hard chest against my back. Through his pants, the thick length of his cock pushed against my ass. He kissed his way up my neck until he reached my ear.

"You're so beautiful. I can't wait to be inside of you. I want to take you bare—nothing between us tonight. Is that okay?"

My answer was half yes, half moan.

"I'm going to cover your ears now. You good?"

I nodded again. I would have agreed to anything at that point. My body was vibrating with need. Caine slipped something over my ears. He'd taken my noise-reduction headphones from the nightstand table. His voice was muffled when he spoke.

"I've connected you to my playlist. I'll start the music low so you can get used to it and increase the volume slowly."

After a bluesy instrumental began, Caine removed my bra and panties. He then removed the rest of his clothing and stood behind me, his warm cock sandwiched between his abdomen and the top of my ass. He lifted one side of the earphones and the music that had been playing was replaced by his raspy voice.

"Shoes stay on."

He guided me to the bed and spread me out on my back. Once I was settled, he raised the music's volume. Unable to see or hear him, I let out a loud gasp when he began sucking my nipple. My back arched off the bed at the erotic feeling of being touched without warning, of succumbing to his will without question. Instead of feeling captive because I was unable to see or hear, I had the opposite feeling—one of total and complete freedom.

The anticipation of what he might do next was unlike anything I'd ever experienced. Each pinch, lick, stroke, and caress of my body made me that much more desperate for him. I was panting with need, even though I couldn't hear myself.

Caine raised the volume to the music again just as another instrumental started. It was a slow, building piece where the sound and intensity grew, and his actions seemed to mimic that ascent. He took my mouth in a passionate kiss, stealing my breath with the depth of feeling it ignited inside my chest. I was consumed inside and out—the deprivation of everything around me leaving nothing to focus on but him and the way he made me feel.

He broke the kiss on a pant, his body pulling away from mine as I felt him lift up. I couldn't see him, but I was certain he was kneeling over me, taking in my body. I pictured his eyes dilated, nostrils flaring, and desire burning on his beautiful face. Laying spread eagle, blind to everything around me, should have made me feel vulnerable, but instead I felt empowered.

I reached up, knowing he was there even though I couldn't see him, and pulled him gently down to me. Caine's lips brushed over mine as he covered my body with his. Underneath his weight, I opened my legs as wide as I could, inviting him inside. I felt his groan vibrate on my skin as he moved his erection up and down through the wetness between my legs. Then suddenly, the volume in my headphones rose, and Caine pushed inside of me.

The music blared.

The only thing I could see was blackness.

But God, could I feel.

It was the most decadent, erotic, beautiful feeling in the world as Caine eased inside. So many emotions overwhelmed me. My eyes welled up as the music hit its crescendo and Caine buried himself deep—filling me in so many ways.

I'd been on the edge of glory for so long, it didn't take long for the throb inside of me to start. His thrusts were hard, driving in and out with powerful movements that brushed my clit on each downward glide. My world began to splinter as I headed toward climax, everything and anything falling away as my sole focus became the two of us—this moment.

I moaned loudly as it hit me, uttering Caine's name over and over as I rode the wave blindly. Our hips gyrated in unison, somehow moving to the music encasing us. I thought I'd peaked at the top of the roller coaster, but apparently I hadn't. Caine gave one last deep thrust, and I felt the heat from his release spill into me—which set me off riding a whole new wave I hadn't seen on the horizon.

I was utterly spent by the time we stopped rocking back and forth. My body felt spineless, as if I would collapse in a puddle on the floor if I tried to stand. Caine untied the blindfold first and then slipped the headphones from my ears.

He waited for me to speak, but it wasn't easy. Every ounce of energy had been drained from my body.

"That was crazy," I finally managed to croak out.

Caine's lip twitched—which I still loved for some inexplicable reason. He wiped my damp hair from my face. "Yeah."

"I've never..." I didn't know how to explain what I'd just experienced. "It's never...that was."

Caine smiled warmly. "Yeah. Me too."

I laughed. "Is it always like that...with headphones and blindfolded?"

"I have no idea."

My brows drew down. "You've never done that before?"

"Nope."

My jaw dropped. "So how are you so damn good at it, then?"

He chuckled. "I'm not. It's us."

"Us?"

"Together. It just works. I felt it the first night we met. Just didn't want to accept it."

He was right. The connection between us had been there from our first meeting—a spark we could step on and try to extinguish or blow on to fan the flame.

"Do you accept it now?"

He brushed my lips with his and whispered against them. "I never really had a choice, Feisty."

The sound of a cell phone ringing jarred me from a deep sleep.

"Shit." I propped myself up on my elbows and was met with a stream of light directly in my eyes. I squinted my dismay at the open blinds allowing the sun to blare through and reached to my end table for my cell.

Missed call flashed on the screen by the time I grabbed it. I checked the call log, looked at the time, and turned to Caine, lying on his stomach.

"Caine?" I whispered.

His eyes pressed closed more tightly. "Mmm?"

"It's almost ten o'clock. You have class in an hour."

"No, I don't. My TA is teaching today for me."

I smiled. "Your TA was not on the schedule to teach today and has to be at her other job at noon."

He groaned. "My TA sucks."

Grabbing my waist, he pulled me back down to the bed and hovered over me. His erection nudged at my leg.

"You're—"

"Hard."

"Yes, that."

"It's morning, and I just woke up with you naked next to me. My body wants to greet you properly."

"We don't have time. It will take you at least thirty minutes to shower and get to class."

His mouth went to my neck. "I'll be a little late."

My eyes widened. "Late? You? Professor Punctuality can't be late."

Caine's hand slid down my body, his thumb finding my clit and beginning to massage. "I can be late. It's my students and TA who can't."

"That's hypocritical of you," I said, though I'd already lost my fight to his fingers.

He stopped massaging and flashed a knowing smirk. "You're right. I should get going."

I grabbed his wrist. "No way, Professor. Just get the job done quickly."

Fifteen minutes later, Caine had given us both orgasms and was already out of the shower. I was enjoying the sight of him gathering his clothes while wearing nothing but a towel when my phone rang.

"It's my sister again. She called this morning and woke us up."

"Tell her I said thank you."

I smiled and answered. "Hey."

"Hey," she said. "I was beginning to think I might have to send a search party out for you. I haven't heard from you in so long."

"Sorry. I've been busy—between O'Leary's, school, and my new TA assignment—time is flying by this semester."

"How's the ogre working out?"

"Ogre?"

"The new professor you told me about?"

I'd forgotten that the last time I spoke to Riley was my first day as Caine's TA. I looked up and caught his eye as he buttoned his shirt. "Turns out he's not so bad after all."

Caine's brows raised.

"Oh good. I'm glad it's working out," she said. "You didn't forget about dinner tonight, did you?"

I had totally forgotten. "How could I forget our monthly dinner?"

I shook my head, letting Caine know I was lying, and he chuckled as he tucked in his dress shirt.

"I work until seven today. I should be there about seven-thirty."

"Okay."

"Alright. See you later. I need to jump in the shower so I'm not late to work." I was just about to hang up when I made a spur-of-the-moment decision. "Wait. Would it be okay if I brought someone?"

"You're seeing someone and I don't know about it?"

"It's new."

"Of course." I heard the excitement in her voice. "I can wait to meet him."

"I'm not sure if he can make it or not. I'll text you in a bit. Okay?"

"Sure."

Caine finished dressing and grabbed his phone. He'd called an Uber after he got out of the shower.

"Car's almost here," he announced. "I gotta go."

I was still sitting on the bed, naked on top with a sheet draped around my waist. He walked over and rubbed his knuckles against my nipple as he leaned down to kiss me.

"I'll pick you up at work at seven."

"You'll go with me to my sister's?"

"I assumed from your conversation you want me to."

"I do."

"Then I'll see you at seven."

I smiled long after he was gone. He had no idea how much it meant that he'd agreed to come along without any prodding. It felt like we'd broken through to a new place together, and I couldn't wait to walk on the other side.

Chapter 31

Caine

I could get used to that smile greeting me. Rachel waved from the table she was helping when I arrived at O'Leary's a few minutes early. It had been less than twelve hours since I'd been inside her, and yet I felt my body react to seeing her.

Charlie greeted me at the bar. He shook my hand with a firm grip meant to get my attention. "She's floatin' around this place. I take it that's because of whatever the two of you got going on?"

"If you're asking if we're seeing each other, the answer is yes."

"You ain't married, are you?" He narrowed his eyes.

"No, I'm not married."

"You do drugs?"

"No drugs."

"Got a record?"

I was basically being interrogated by a cop—no reason to share something that happened years ago and no one had access to anymore.

"No record."

Charlie spread his pointer and middle finger into a V and pointed to his eyes, then to me. "I got my eyes on you."

Rachel appeared next to me. "Charlie, what are you doing?"

He grabbed a glass from a full crate and started to stack them behind the bar. He'd been in my face, but with Rachel he was kowtowing.

"Just talking with the good professor."

She squinted. "Just talking, huh? Not interrogating?"

Charlie looked me square in the eye. "We were just talking about the Yankees. Third baseman got injured when he was trying to steal home. Should have stayed at third until he got the all clear from his coach. *Right*, Professor?"

Rachel rightly looked suspicious.

"Sure, Charlie," I said.

I wasn't sure if she believed Charlie's shit or chose to ignore it. Either way, I was glad she had someone looking out for her.

"Table three is almost ready to close out," she told Charlie. "I told them to bring their check up to you." She looked at her watch. "Ava's not here yet. You want me to wait? Table five ordered appetizers and hasn't put in their dinner order yet."

"I got it. You two kids take off."

"You sure?"

Charlie thumbed toward the door. "Go on. Get outta here. I don't want people to see your professor friend here and think the place is changing over to yuppies."

I laughed. "'Night, Charlie."

Rachel's sister lived in Queens, and traffic was still heavy from the evening commute home. She was quieter than usual as we inched our way up the parkway.

"Busy at work today?"

"No. It was actually kind of slow."

More quiet as she stared off out the window.

"Something bothering you?"

She shifted in her seat. "There's something I should tell you about my sister."

"Alright."

"She's a drug addict. Well, she's in recovery. But I suppose that still makes her a drug addict, because once an addict, always an addict. It's the same thing as an alcoholic, right? You still call yourself an alcoholic even if you haven't had a drink for five years. Is there actually a time when you stop referring to yourself that way? Like maybe those chips they give out—one might signify that you're sober? Do all of those chips mean different things? I thought they were timeline accomplishments—like one for a month, and another for a year? But maybe—"

She hadn't taken a breath yet. Run-on sentences were one of her tells when she was nervous. I interrupted, "Rachel?"

"What?"

"You're babbling. I don't care if your sister is an addict. I wouldn't even care if you're sister wasn't in recovery. I'm not going to judge her. I'm coming to dinner because you wanted me to come. Do you still want me to join you?"

"Yes."

I reached over and took her hand, bringing it to cover the gear shifter beneath my own. "Okay then."

From my peripheral vision, I saw her shoulders relax a bit. She looked out the window, seeming lost in thought, and then turned to me.

"She lost custody of her son because of her addiction."

"I'm sorry to hear that."

"She only gets to see him twice a week—supervised visitation. Her ex-husband left her a few years ago and took her son with him."

"Her son? It's not her ex-husband's child."

"No. It's a long story. But she had Adam when she was young."

I squeezed her hand beneath mine. "Shit happens, Rach. Addiction is tough." God knows I knew that first hand after Liam.

"I know. I just wanted to tell you that."

"Thank you for sharing with me."

Even though I meant it when I said I had no judgment of her sister—I had definitely visualized her as something different. I'd expected an addict to open the door for us when we arrived—thin and unkempt, in a small apartment, maybe bad teeth. But the woman who greeted us was nothing like that. She was an older version of Rachel.

Healthy and smiling, she welcomed me into her home with a hug.

"It's so nice to meet you. My sister's told me absolutely nothing about you."

Rachel laughed. "Ignore her. She tends to be a wiseass."

"So you two have a lot in common then, along with your looks."

Riley shut the door behind us, grinning from ear to ear. "I like him already."

The apartment's entrance led into the kitchen, so we stood around talking for a while as Riley checked on the dinner she had in the oven. It had been hot as hell in class today, so I'd guzzled a few extra bottles of water while lecturing and needed to relieve myself.

"Excuse me, I need to use the restroom."

Riley was stirring a pot at the stove and pointed down the hall. "Sure. Through the living room, down the hall, first door on the left. I basically live in a railroad car, so you can't miss it."

I noticed a wall full of frames, similar to what Rachel had in her apartment, but didn't stop to look before going to the bathroom. On the way back, I noticed most of the pictures were of the same little blond boy at various stages of growing up. Assuming it was Riley's son, Adam, I didn't want to stop and call attention to it, in case speaking about him was difficult.

I'd almost made it past the picture-lined hall when a small photo caught my eye. It was of two little girls standing in the grass—the younger girl was probably three or four, and the older was maybe eight or nine, but it was definitely Rachel and her sister.

I stopped and zoomed in on the younger girl. The photo was old and grainy, but something about it set off an alarm inside of me. My posture straightened as I stared.

"She always insisted on making her own ponytail. It was always crooked, but she was adamant that she had to do it herself." Riley joined me at the wall of photos and handed me a glass. "It's iced tea."

I took it without moving my eyes. There was something so familiar about the picture. Of course, it would be familiar to me considering Rachel hadn't changed all that much—but it was more than that. My eyes darted all over the wall.

"Do you have other pictures of the two of you?"

Rachel joined us. "You asked to see a picture of me when I was little the other day." She bumped my shoulder playfully. "If Riley is going to show you embarrassing pictures, I better get to see some pictures of you when you were little."

I think I nodded, but I couldn't be sure. My mind was still too focused on Rachel's little face in the picture. After a minute, Riley returned with an album.

"Come on, I'll show you how chunky my sister was when she was a baby. Our mom used to like to take pictures of her naked while she gave her a bath in the sink. Rachel had dimples, but not on her face."

The three of us sat down together on the couch, a sister on either side of me, and Riley began to flip through an old photo album. She pointed to a photo, which I assumed was Riley holding a newborn Rachel. "I hated her when Mom brought her home. She stole all my attention."

Rachel chided, "My mother told her to keep small objects away from me because I could choke, and she used to flick pennies at the bassinet."

"I did not." Riley turned to me and winked. "It was quarters. Those were too big for her to really choke on anyway."

I attempted to seem interested, but something gnawed at me. I knew what it was, but figured it was my imagination running wild. Still, I couldn't seem to let it go. Riley flipped through most of the album—in almost all of the pictures Rachel was very young.

"There aren't too many pictures of us after Rachel was about five or six. That's when our mom got sick."

"Rachel told me. I'm sorry for your loss."

Riley nodded. "Thank you. The two years after she died, before we moved in with the Martins, weren't good times we wanted to capture in photos anyway."

"I didn't realize you hadn't moved in with your aunt and uncle right away after your mother died. Did you live in foster care or something?"

Rachel and Riley looked at each other. There was a silent exchange before Rachel spoke.

"No. We lived with our stepfather after Mom died."

I looked at Rachel. "I thought you said your mother didn't remarry."

Riley looked between the two of us and closed the photo album. "We both like to pretend he never existed." She stood. "I'm going to check my sauce."

After Riley was gone, Rachel took my hand. "I'm sorry. I didn't mean to lie to you. It's just...my sister's right. It's easier to pretend there was no Benny." She spoke softly. "He wasn't a nice guy."

Benny.

Fucking Benny.

The name hit me like a blow to the gut.

I wasn't sure I was going to make it through dinner. I kept sneaking looks at Rachel, and every time I did, I saw the little girl from the confessional. It was goddamn clear as day now, even though I hadn't seen it at all before. Suddenly I couldn't get the one clear look at her I'd stolen across the length of the church all those years ago out of my head. Whenever I looked at her, I was staring right into her sweet little ten-year-old face.

Willing myself to snap out of the fog, I finally noticed Rachel looking at me with concern. Abruptly, I pulled back from the table and stood.

"Excuse me for a moment."

I went back to the bathroom and stared at my reflection in the mirror. Beads of sweat had formed on my forehead and top lip. I'd never had a panic attack, but I was sure this was exactly what one felt like. My heart ricocheted against the wall of my chest, and the simple act of breathing was an effort. I bent over the sink and focused on inhaling and exhaling for a few minutes before splashing water on my face.

I wasn't sure how long I'd been locked in the bathroom, but when I emerged, Rachel waited for me in the hall.

"Are you okay?" Her hand went to my clammy forehead. "You don't look so good."

"Actually, I'm not. I don't feel so well. It started in class today, and I thought it was the heat, but it must be some sort of a virus."

"Oh, I'm sorry. What can I do? Do you want some ginger ale or a cool rag? Maybe you should lie down on the couch for a while."

"I'm okay. But I think I should go."

"Oh. Okay. I understand. Let me just tell Riley, and I'll grab my purse."

"No," I said, probably a little too quickly.

"No?"

"You should stay. I don't want to ruin your evening. Is your sister able to drive you home?"

"I guess so..."

"I'm sorry. I'll see you tomorrow in class, alright?"

"Yes, okay."

While her words said everything was fine, Rachel's face conveyed a whole different story. I wasn't sure she was even buying my sick act, but I needed to get the hell out of here.

After a quick apology and goodbye to Riley, I was out the door. Feeling off-kilter, I questioned whether it was a good idea to get behind the wheel. When I arrived home, I realized it had definitely been a bad idea. I didn't remember driving from Rachel's sister's place to mine.

I poured myself a stiff drink and paced back and forth for a while, remembering the last time I'd seen the little girl from the church—the day I'd followed her home. After everything that happened, my parents had sprung into action to protect me—calling in favors from everyone and anyone, local politicians and police. So much of what went down that day was a blur by now—except one thing. I'd lied to the little girl I now knew as Rachel for months, instead of doing what I could to get her out of that hell as soon as possible.

Chapter 32

Rachel

After ten minutes, the class was getting antsy. I texted Caine, then decided I'd better start the lecture or the students would begin leaving any minute. There was an uneasy feeling in the pit of my stomach. He still hadn't responded to the text I'd sent last night when I got home from my sister's—even though I could see he'd read it.

I lectured for a while and then took a break to play the class a few pieces we would analyze. As the music filled the room, I checked my phone from behind the podium. *Nothing.* Yet the text about class had also been read.

At first, I'd been concerned that Caine had gotten much sicker, maybe had even gone to the hospital or something. But if he was able to read my texts, why wouldn't he be able to respond?

After about an hour of the ninety-minute lecture, I was so distracted, I cut the class early. Caine wouldn't be happy about it, but that wasn't my immediate concern.

Anxious, I dialed his number before the classroom had even emptied. It rang once and went to voicemail.

When a cell is turned off, it goes immediately to voicemail. When someone is unable to answer it, it rings a bunch of times before dropping to voicemail. But when it goes to voicemail after one ring, the recipient is hitting ignore. *What the hell?*

I left a message. "Caine, it's Rachel. I'm worried about you. You haven't responded to my texts and didn't show up for class. Can you please let me know everything is okay so I don't start calling emergency rooms like a crazy person?"

I wanted to drive over to his apartment and check on him, but I had to be at work in an hour, and there wasn't enough time to get there and back. Tuesday was also the only day I worked alone. I opened for Charlie because he did his grocery shopping and went to visit his wife's grave every week like clockwork. No way was I going to interrupt that because my boyfriend wasn't answering my calls.

Is he even my boyfriend? The entire drive to O'Leary's, I found myself debating anything and everything to do with Caine. One little hiccup and my mind was a frenzy of paranoid observations. By the time I parked, I'd come full circle. The man wasn't avoiding me—he simply didn't feel well. Unfortunately, when I checked my phone, that theory was obliterated.

Caine: *Feeling better. Thank you for covering class.*

That's it? No damn explanation? The knot I'd had in my stomach all morning wrenched into anger. I deserved more than that. Tossing my phone into my bag, I unlocked the front door at O'Leary's and sprang into my opening ritual on autopilot. I flicked the lights on, turned the oven on in the back, unloaded the dishwasher, and brought out the first crate of glasses to stock behind the bar before counting out the register. Promptly at twelve, I turned on the open sign. Then I checked my phone again. *Nothing*.

The hours dragged by after that. Ava popped in at four—an hour before her shift started—to visit me, and I was ripe for a verbal explosion. She took a seat at the bar. There was just one other patron at the other end, a retired cop friend of Charlie's who didn't say much and only required a beer an hour.

"So you *are* still alive?" she said. "I figured maybe you'd been fucked to death by the angry professor."

Ava took one look at my face and hers fell. "Oh no. What happened? That asshole screwed you over? Is he married, because I'll seriously go ballistic on his ass."

I sighed. "No, it's nothing like that."

"Then what is it?"

"I wish I knew."

I then proceeded to verbal vomit on my poor friend, telling her all the details of the last few days. Well, not all the details—the incredible sex parts I kept to myself—but I told her everything that might be relevant.

"Do you think he got cold feet because you took him to Riley's? Some men have ridiculous *meet the family* fears—they think that's the last step before you drag them down the aisle."

"I suppose it could be...although I don't think that's it. He never hesitated or showed any concern about going with me, and the first ten minutes or so after we arrived, he was fine."

"What happened between the time you arrived and when he said he wasn't feeling well and bolted?"

"Nothing, really. I've replayed it over and over in my head. We were sitting down in the living room looking at photo albums."

I stared into space as I visualized the three of us—me, Riley, and Caine—sitting on the couch. Photos. Pigtails. Mom dying. *Benny*. It figured something would go wrong at the mere mention of that man. Then it dawned on me. Could Caine possibly be pissed because I'd lied about not having a stepfather? It was so insignificant; I couldn't imagine that was it.

"*Family* photo albums? He bolted because he felt pressure."

"But I didn't pressure him. He had *asked* to see a picture of me when I was little."

"Doesn't matter." She shrugged. "He's a commitment-phobe."

"I really don't think that's it."

"Well, then maybe he was really sick? Maybe he went into your sister's bathroom, got a bad case of the shits, and didn't want to clog the toilet."

I scrunched up my nose. "Do you really need to describe it like that?"

Ava shrugged. "Do you want me to justify him running out so you can pretend he doesn't have commitment issues or not?"

Honestly, all I wanted was to get rid of this unsettled feeling. If Caine did have commitment issues and a visit to my sister gave him cold feet, I could deal with that. All I needed was honesty.

Chapter 33

Caine - Fifteen Years Ago

This was the fourth stop she'd made to pick flowers on the side of the road on her ride home. Her life sounded like a clusterfuck of bad shit, yet she spotted the beauty in the middle of weeds and tall grass.

I stayed at least two blocks back, and she hadn't seemed to notice me at all. Which reminded me, I also needed to have a heart to heart with my little lamb about being aware of her surroundings. Any psychopath could be tailing her.

Well...

It had to be a good two miles before she finally pulled into a driveway. The house was actually pretty nice. I'd envisioned a run-down trailer down at the end of a long dirt road, with sheets hung to conceal the windows and heavy brush camouflaging any sign of life—probably three or four rusted-out, non-functional cars on the lawn. But the driveway she pulled into was paved and led to a small but well-maintained Cape Cod-style house. The grass was mowed, open curtains framed the windows, and neighbors were outside nearby, going about their business. The single car in the driveway was a few years old and had one of those Jesus fish symbols on the back. *Nothing* like I'd expected.

I watched as the little girl disappeared around the side of the house and came back to the front door without her bike a minute later. Without hesitation, she walked inside.

I stayed there looking around for a good half hour after that. For the first time, I questioned whether maybe she was making things up. She could've had a vivid imagination. The seed of doubt was planted, but my gut told me she wasn't telling a tall tale. I took one last look at the ordinary house and turned to head back home. At least I wouldn't have to wait much to find out—so long as she showed with her sister tomorrow.

I waited six hours. At a little after one in the afternoon, I gave in to the fact that she wasn't coming this morning. Before I'd followed her home yesterday, I'd had zero doubt something was going on. But now, after seeing an ordinary-looking house in a normal neighborhood, doubt had crept in. Then again, Ted Bundy looked pretty fucking normal, too. I groaned and stood from the back pew where I'd listened to three masses this morning as I watched the door. I had no idea what I was going to do, but I knew where I was heading.

Four blocks from her house, I realized I needed gas. Since I also needed to figure out a game plan, I made a pit stop at a full-service station with a mini mart and headed inside to pay the attendant. My hand was on the door handle when, from the corner of my eye, I saw something that caught my attention. Parked on the side of the station was a car that looked damn familiar—the same make and model as the one parked in the little girl's driveway yesterday.

Benny is a damn mechanic.

I walked over and took a look at the back of the car. Sure enough, there was the Jesus fish symbol. Looking over at the mini mart, I saw a two-bay garage attached to it. One of the doors was closed, but the other was open about two feet. The lights were also definitely on.

I lingered inside the mini mart, pretending to read the back of a bag of chips while the two customers finished paying. When it was just me and the woman working the register, I took a can of soda and a Snickers bar to the register.

"Is the auto shop still open? My car has some rattling I'd like to get checked out."

She looked up at the clock. "Closed at noon today. But I think Benny's still inside."

My body tensed. "Thanks. Is there an office or something?"

The cashier waved toward a door at the back. "Go right through that door. He's probably in one of the bays."

My breathing became deeper with each step as I headed into the dim garage. There was a screwdriver sitting on the top of a red tool chest. I picked it up and shoved it into the back pocket of my jeans.

"Hello?" The garage held four cars, but there didn't appear to be anyone inside.

A man poked his head out from underneath the hood of one of the cars the next bay over and nearly scared the shit out of me.

"What can I do you for?"

I stared at him. I had no plan.

He pulled a towel from his pocket and started to wipe his hands as he took a step toward me. "We're closed. I need to be getting home to my girls. There's a station about a mile north of here, if you got car problems."

His girls.

"You Benny?"

"I am. Who's asking?"

I needed a stick to poke the bear. A light bulb lit in my head. "I'm a friend of your daughter's."

Suddenly I had his attention. His entire demeanor changed. He stopped wiping his hands and looked me square in the eyes. "My daughter's not allowed to have any boy friends."

"Why is that?"

His face contorted with anger. "Because she's a little slut."

We had been standing on either side of a car, but he started to walk around it toward me.

"You sniffing around my daughter? Let me give you a little advice. You want a nice girl. That one...she's no good. Fifteen years old and nothing but trouble already."

"Keep away from them both."

Benny looked momentarily taken aback. He paused his advance toward me. A slow, evil smile spread across his face. It gave me chills. I was staring into the face of a monster.

"You think you know something? Why don't you go on and spit it out."

"You like little girls. You sneak into the older girl's room at night and threaten her to keep quiet or you'll do the same thing to her little sister. Keep away from them both, or I'll go to the police."

He narrowed his eyes, searching, as he seemed to piece together a puzzle. Seeing the full picture for the first time, a sardonic smile grew on his lips. His tone matched the evil of his face.

"You got something to do with them packing a bag, planning to run away, don't you?"

I said nothing.

He took a step closer. "They won't be running anywhere after last night. Taught them a lesson, just like I'm going to teach you." Benny reached into his overalls pocket and pulled out a small remote. Staring at me, he aimed it at the partially open garage door, and it started to come down. I followed his eyes as they locked on a tray full of tools within his reach. Everything after that seemed to happen in slow motion.

He reached for a wrench.

I pulled the screwdriver from my back pocket.

I was scared shitless, until he spoke again.

"Get your own damn pussy."

Chapter 34

Caine

"What are you looking at?"

Murphy rested his head on my lap, his big brown eyes staring up at me. I scratched his favorite spot behind his ears, and he let out a big sigh.

"Jesus. Your breath stinks, buddy." At least I thought it was Murphy's. It was possible it was actually my own.

I shut my laptop and took off my glasses to rub my eyes. How the fuck was I going to tell her? I'd been cooped up in my apartment for two days, hadn't showered, barely ate, and felt completely defeated. Rachel must've taken the hint that I was blowing her off since she hadn't texted me since yesterday.

I realized just how crazy about her I was when I debated never telling her for the hundredth time. It wouldn't be such a difficult decision if there weren't so much to lose. And I'd definitely lose her. How could she ever trust me after she found out we'd known each other fifteen years ago? That I'd lied to her for months? That I'd taken something she held so sacred—a priest she trusted—and manipulated her through a screen each and every week.

If I told her, I was going to lose her. Hell, I wouldn't trust anyone who pulled that kind of shit.

But if I didn't tell her, everything we had and everything to come would be based on even more lies.

I'd been selfishly trying to justify never telling her. Telling myself I'd be hurting her twice by coming clean. I knew she cared about me. I'd be reopening old wounds I doubted she wanted to revisit. Why not let sleeping dogs lie?

There was one thing I couldn't get past—I didn't want to be another man who let her down. She deserved better than that. *Fuck*. She deserved someone better than *me*. I tugged at my hair as I raked my hands through.

Tell her the truth and lose her—while hurting her in the process.

Lie to her face and try to move on with that lie always between us.

Even though I'd wasted two days debating the issue, deep down I knew there was no real fucking choice. I couldn't keep lying to her.

The only consolation was that once she hated me, it would be easier for her to move on. At least it would be easier for one of us. And my prolonging things was only being selfish.

I reached for my phone just as it illuminated. We hadn't had contact in more than twenty-four hours, so the timing of her text was impeccable.

Rachel: How about some chicken soup? I could stop over after work tonight.

I stared at my phone for a while, hesitating. It was one thing to live on death row, but another to have your execution date set. Before I could grow a pair of balls to answer, a second text came in.

Rachel: I get off work at eight.

I didn't want her driving at night while she was angry or upset. It was time I grew some balls.

Caine: I'll come to your place about nine.

After a shower, I decided to take Murphy for a long walk to clear my head and kill some time. We'd made it a block and a half when a thought crossed my mind.

"What do you say to an afternoon road trip?"

Murphy wagged his tail, so I took that as a yes. If I stayed cooped up in my apartment anymore, I was going to lose it. I needed to get out and clear my head. Might as well make the day a good one for someone...

An hour later, we were walking into the main building at Regency Village. I'd called ahead to make sure it was okay to stop by, and the nurse had said she'd let Lydia and Umberto know I was coming. Lydia was waiting in the reception area. Her eyes lit up when she saw me and Murphy.

She bent to pet him. "He looks just like our Max."

"This is Murphy. I figured Umberto might like a visit."

"You have no idea. This is going to make his day—probably his year. No matter where his head is, he never forgets that damn dog." Lydia looked around. "Is Rachel with you?"

"No, just me. I was in the area so I thought we'd stop by," I lied.

"That's so sweet of you, Professor West."

"Call me Caine, please."

"Caine it is." She smiled and nodded as she stood from petting Murphy. "Umberto is taking a nap right now. He should be up soon. Would it be alright if we took a walk? It might seem odd, but I'd love to hold the leash and walk around the property. My husband and I used to take a walk with Max every night after dinner, right before we had our tea and cookies."

"Of course." I offered Lydia the leash and my arm. She took both, and we headed outside for a stroll under the blue skies.

"So tell me, Caine. Are you married?"

"No, not married."

"Handsome young man like you with such a sweet dog, women must be falling at your feet."

I'd never been the type of person to talk about a woman I was seeing—not even in college when the other guys couldn't keep their mouths shut. But what the hell.

"There's a lady in my life, but I did something stupid and screwed it up."

"Oh? I'm sorry to hear that. Do you want to talk about it? I have more than fifty years of marriage experience. Maybe I can help you fix things."

"It's not something that can be fixed so easily."

Lydia was quiet for a long time. "Do you love this lady?"

I'd been avoiding figuring out the answer to that question. But lying to Lydia was harder than lying to myself for some reason. I nodded.

"I think I might. I have no idea when it happened, though."

She smiled. "That's how it happens. You just turn around one day and it hits you right in the face as if it's been there all along and you were too blind to see it. That's the thing about true love—we never see the beginning or the end."

Great. No end in sight. Just what I need to hear before Rachel dumps my ass.

Lydia must've noticed my dejected face. She squeezed my arm. "Don't worry, sweetheart. It's all going to work out. When you're in love, mistakes can be fixed."

"I'm not sure some mistakes are fixable."

"Have you told her about whatever it is that you've done wrong?"

I shook my head.

"We all make mistakes. Life doesn't come with instructions. Someone who loves you will forgive you for them. But when you hide them or lie about them, they're no longer mistakes—they're decisions."

"To be honest, I've been avoiding her for a few days, knowing that when I come clean, she's going to get hurt."

"Well, unfortunately, the truth does hurt sometimes. Another woman makes my husband happy now after more than fifty years of marriage. It's not always easy. But in the long run, it's better to hurt someone with the truth than make them happy with lies. Because she can make the decision to move on with the truth. Lies keep you stuck in place."

Lydia wasn't kidding that she'd learned a thing or two in her fifty-plus years of marriage. The window of doubt about telling Rachel the truth finally slammed shut. I reached over and squeezed Lydia's hand. "Umberto's a very lucky man."

The look on Umberto's face when he saw Murphy might have been one of the best things I'd ever witnessed in my life—although I mentally kicked myself in the ass that I hadn't come with Rachel. She would have loved to see this. I would have loved to watch the smile on her face.

Umberto's other lady was nowhere in sight today. With Lydia crouched down at his side, Umberto smiled and laughed as he scratched Murphy's head. My unfaithful four-legged friend lapped up all the new attention. I stood back and took a moment to watch the three of them. Then I gave them some privacy. At least one decision I made was a good one today.

I spent the hour driving home from visiting with Umberto and Lydia thinking about tonight. Then I dropped off Murphy, took a shower, and practiced what I was going to say—how I was going to explain what I'd done without sounding like a total asshole.

I'd even convinced myself I could pull it off, until I arrived at her building and couldn't think of one way to even begin such a conversation. It was as if I'd just found out who she was all over again. Everything I'd thought about, the words I'd carefully considered, seemed to escape me as I stood outside my car and looked up at her window.

It was an unusually warm fall night with a nice breeze, so her third-floor window was open. Her bedroom light was on, her shade pulled almost all the way down, and I couldn't bring myself to do anything but stand in place and stare. My heart almost stopped when her silhouette appeared. She was in profile, looking away from where I was standing. At first she didn't move, just stared off into space, but then I saw one hand reach for her wrist, and she started to play with her watch.

Yeah, I'm nervous, too, Feisty. I'm sorry I've made you feel this way the last few days.

I needed to get this shit over with for both our sakes. Taking a deep breath, I finally headed toward her building. The elevator was slow to arrive and even slower to crawl to the third floor. By the time I stepped off, I had perspiration beading on my forehead. Walking to her door was excruciatingly difficult.

I knocked and waited with my hands in my pockets, staring down at my shoes. Under my breath, I said a little prayer—the irony of that not escaping me.

Rachel opened the door, and I immediately felt a kick to my gut. She looked more beautiful than ever in a green sundress with thin straps that showed off her beautiful, long neck. Her wild, dark hair was down and pushed to one side, and I had the strongest urge to lean in and devour that neck. Unlike her normal, understated makeup, tonight her face was all done up. A bright red, glossy lipstick coated her plump lips, and her lashes were thick and dark, which matched the dark liner that made her almond-shaped eyes look even larger. I was sad that I might not get to brush my lips against hers one last time.

I raised my gaze to meet hers, and my heart beat out of control. *I've fallen in love with her.* In that moment, I wanted nothing more than to tell her. But I didn't want the first time I said those words to be muddied by the conversation we were about to have. I only hoped I'd get to say them one day.

"Hello, Rachel."

Chapter 35

Rachel

"Hi."

Caine was staring at me funny—as if he wasn't really seeing me, even though he looked straight at my face.

"Caine?

He blinked a few times. "Sorry. You look beautiful."

"Thank you." I stepped aside for him to enter, noting that he hadn't leaned in for a kiss. I tried to brush it off, but it elevated my already jittery feeling to full-blown panic.

Caine came inside, and things became even more awkward—worse than a bad blind date. I was standing in a room where this man had recently cooked breakfast for me, yet he felt like a complete stranger.

"How are you feeling?" I attempted to make some conversation.

"Better. Thank you. I'm sorry for the way I rushed out of your sister's apartment and left her to make sure you got home."

"It's fine. I understand. You weren't feeling well."

Caine nodded and dug his hands into his pockets. After another minute of awkward silence, he cleared his throat.

"Listen, Rachel, we need to talk."

"Okay. Why don't we sit down? Can I get you something to drink?"

"No, thanks. I'm good."

He followed me into the living room. I sat on one end of the couch, which left plenty of open space for him to join me. But he chose to sit on the adjacent chair.

Caine looked at his feet, then dragged a hand through his hair. Though he could totally pull off the disheveled look, I got the feeling he'd been doing that a lot the last few days, and it had nothing to do with styling. He blew out a loud breath before starting to speak.

"I can't start a relationship with lies."

Oh, God. My little lie about Benny had been niggling in the back of my mind ever since I'd talked to Ava about what was going on with Caine. I felt sick. But I refused to let that horrible man take anything else from me.

"I'm sorry about lying. It's just…it's not easy for me to talk about."

Caine attempted to speak, but I cut him off, going into my usual nervous ramble.

"I said I didn't have a stepfather because I wish I hadn't had one. I try to pretend he never existed. He wasn't a nice guy. He was abusive…to me and my sister once my mother died."

Caine's jaw flexed. "He abused *you*?"

I nodded and looked down. "It wasn't the same for me and my sister. He..." Even after fifteen years, I could barely say the words. "...he sexually abused my sister. But I was too young."

"So he didn't touch you?"

I shook my head. "Not the same way he touched my sister."

A look of relief crossed Caine's face. "Thank God."

"But as long as we're being honest, I told you another small lie. The scar on my back isn't from falling out of a tree when I was a kid. It's from my stepfather. The night before the police removed us, he came home earlier than we'd expected. Riley was packing because we were planning on finally going to get help the next morning. Benny ransacked my room and found the bag I'd packed. He lost his mind and started kicking us with his steel-tip boots. That's what left the scar on my back."

I'd been too stubborn for a lot of years to allow myself to cry about everything that happened. But the memories from that night were still vivid when I talked about them. I could see my sister sneaking into my room after Benny had passed out to do wound care on me. My tears felt cool, running down my warm face.

"My sister taped it closed, but it probably needed a dozen stitches."

Caine came to kneel at my feet. I leaned my head into him, burying my face in his shoulder to hide my emotions.

"I'm so sorry, Rach. I'm so sorry. I didn't know."

Once the faucet was open, I couldn't stop the water from coming. Caine holding me made me feel safe for the first time in a long time—safe to cry. And so I did. I cried and I cried, allowing myself to let it out. I didn't know where it was all coming from, but the cry turned into an ugly sob—one that had me gasping for breath. Caine sat and held me quietly, stroking my hair and saying he was sorry over and over. When I finally calmed down, I sat up to find him with tears welling in his own eyes.

"I'm sorry for falling apart like that. I've never told anyone about that night, except the social worker who took us the next day. I've never even said my sister was sexually abused out loud." I looked Caine in the eyes. "That's why I lied to you and said my mother never remarried. It's easier to pretend she never did and those years never happened."

Caine looked so sad. His voice was full of hesitation. "You went to a social worker the next day, after he did that to you?"

"Actually, she came to us. Benny got into a fight at the garage the next day, so the police came to find us with a social worker."

"A fight?"

"Yeah. He had a lot of rage. I wish it had happened sooner for my sister's sake. We were both so afraid to tell anyone. But the social worker knew something wasn't right when she showed up. Benny was put in the hospital, and we were taken to stay with my aunt. Eventually, my sister told the social worker what was going on, and Benny was arrested while he was still in the hospital. A month later, he died of a heart attack while in custody." I shrugged. "And life just moved on. Our aunt adopted us, and we never looked back."

"I'm so sorry, Rachel."

I half laughed-half sniffled. "Stop saying that. It's not your fault. I just wanted to explain why I lied because I know you were upset about it. And now I'd like to go back to pretending Benny never existed. Can we do that?"

Caine looked like he was going to argue. His mouth opened to speak, then closed, then opened again. But eventually he nodded.

After a trip to the bathroom to wash the streaked makeup from my face, I felt like a weight had lifted off my shoulders. Unfortunately, I couldn't say the same about Caine. While unloading and a good cry had lightened my mood, it seemed I'd passed that heaviness to him. We decided to turn on the TV and relax by watching a movie, but each time I glanced over at him, he seemed lost in thought.

When the movie ended, I thought things might return to normal in the bedroom. Although when I mentioned being tired and ready to go to bed, Caine surprised me by saying he needed to sleep at his own place because he had an early meeting.

That unsettled feeling I'd had was back as I walked him to the door. "Are we okay, Caine?" I hated to ask, hated to sound needy, but I'd already had two sleepless nights and knew I would be up again if he left without us talking.

Caine cupped my cheeks. "You're the most amazing

woman I've ever met. Never forget that, Rachel." He brushed his lips with mine and said goodnight.

I leaned my head against the closed door after he was gone. While the sentiment was sweet, especially given everything we'd talked about, why did it feel like Caine was saying goodbye?

Chapter 36

Caine

I didn't have the heart to tell her after she'd broken down—at least that's what I told myself. I was keeping it from her for her own good, not because I was a selfish prick with no balls.

But after a week of being half in and half out, I realized I was doing the same thing to her that I'd done when she was a kid—stringing her along, week by week, and not taking any action because I was unsure of myself.

Only back then I was a confused teenage boy, and now I was supposed to be a man. I sure as hell wasn't acting like much of one. I'd avoided Rachel almost every night this week, except in class when I had no choice but to face her. She knew something was off.

"What's going on with you?" my sister asked as she took my plate. She'd had another doctor's appointment this afternoon, so I'd been babysitting. Evelyn must've been pretty desperate to use me again, considering I almost killed one of her kids last time.

"Nothing much."

She went into the kitchen and put my plate in the sink before returning for her interrogation. "Bullshit. I can tell when something's wrong."

"How?"

My sister leveled me with a stare. "For starters, you're still here. Normally when I ask you to babysit, you dart out the door the minute I get back, as if having a family is contagious or something."

I guess she had a point. I tried to play it off as nothing. "I was hungry, that's all." I shrugged.

She scrutinized me. "Where's the woman you had here with you last time? The girls talked about her for a week. Rachel, wasn't it?"

"How would I know?"

"Don't give me that crap. Your face changed as soon as I said her name."

"You're imagining things."

"Really?" She leaned in. "Rachel." Her voice grew louder. "Rachel. Rachel. Rachel."

"I think you should add a shrink to that list of doctors you're visiting." I stood and began to clear the rest of the table to put some space between the bulldog and me.

My nieces had already disappeared with a box of elbow macaroni and Elmer's glue, and they were unusually quiet as they stuck food to construction paper in the living room.

Where were the little motor-mouths when you needed them to interrupt a conversation?

My sister and I cleaned up from dinner, and surprisingly, she was quiet. I should have realized she was busy reloading.

Pushing the dishwasher closed, she turned and leaned against it, cornering me in the kitchen as I put away the last of the plates.

"What did you do?"

"What are you talking about?"

"Either she dumped you, or you did something wrong. I can tell. You're moping around. And since you generally get fired up when someone screws you over, I'm going to go out on a limb and guess that *you* screwed something up."

Damn. She's good. I sighed. "I got myself into a mess."

"You want to talk about it?"

"Not really."

"Okay. So how do you get yourself out of this mess?"

"Without hurting her, I can't."

"Did you cheat on her?"

"It's nothing like that. "

Evelyn contemplated me for a minute. "Listen, little brother, you carry around a lot of baggage for things you think are your fault that aren't. You take responsibility. Are you sure you actually did something that bad?"

My sister was always biased when it came to me. When I didn't respond, she shook her head and continued. "You're a good man. Whatever's going on, I know you'll make the right choice. I can't imagine you ever caring about someone and intentionally hurting them."

My sister was right about one thing. I never intended to hurt Rachel. Or Liam, for that matter. But I'd made a lot of bad choices over the years, and other people suffered the consequences. I'd missed doing the right thing for Liam—didn't see that the pressure was too much, that the band and the label contract were more than he could handle until it was too late. With Rachel, I should have told someone what I suspected the day she walked into that confessional. But instead I lied to an innocent girl, pretending to be a priest for months. She had scars left by my mistakes. I'd done enough damage to her.

I hated that her eyes brightened when I asked her to go for a cup of coffee after class the next day.

"So, according to *Cosmo*, I like you," she announced.

We'd ordered two coffees and sat at a quiet table in the back of the coffee shop. Rachel was attempting to act like nothing was wrong, but I heard the shake in her voice and noted the way she twisted her watch back and forth.

"More quizzes?"

"Yep. Question nine was iffy," she teased. "It asked if I'd still be physically attracted to you if you gained sixty pounds, went bald, and suddenly became unemployed. My pen was hovering over a certain answer, but then I remembered you like to blindfold me anyway." She smiled and *fuck, it hurt.*

When I didn't respond, Rachel thought I was offended. "I'm teasing, you know," she said.

I nodded and cleared my throat. It felt like my balls were stuck in there as I attempted to get out the words I needed to say.

"Listen, Rachel...I can't do this anymore."

Her smile wilted. She knew what I was saying, yet still found a way to cling to hope.

"What? Hang out on campus? No one thinks it's odd. I see TAs and professors together all the time."

"I didn't mean spend time on campus. I meant spend time at all. We can't see each other anymore."

"Why? I don't understand?"

I'd decided after talking to my sister last night that there was no use in telling her anything about the church, about us fifteen years ago. Why hurt her by dredging up more shit when I didn't have to?

"You're my student. What happened between us shouldn't have ever started."

Sadness transformed into anger on her face. "That's bullshit. You don't care about that. And besides, the semester is halfway over."

"I'm sorry." I looked down because it was too hard to lie to her beautiful face. "It should have never happened."

"*Screw you.*"

"I'll stay on as your thesis advisor. This is my fault and shouldn't affect you in any way."

"It shouldn't affect me?"

"Rachel..."

She stood. "You know what, Caine? For a long time I felt unworthy of love, *ashamed* of things that happened in my life, *regretting* my choices. It wasn't until the last few weeks that I started to realize I'm *not* my past. I don't ever want to be someone's regret. So go fuck yourself."

On instinct, I grabbed her arm as she brushed past me. Tears filled her eyes, and I knew she wanted to leave before I saw them, didn't want me to see her upset. God, I wanted to rewind and erase everything I'd just said. But instead, I released her arm and let her go. It was the best thing I could do for her, even if it didn't feel that way in the moment.

I couldn't turn around and watch her walk out. Squeezing my eyes shut, I listened to the sound of her footsteps become more and more distant until I couldn't hear her at all anymore.

Rachel was right about one thing—she was my regret. Just not in the way she thought. I'd always regret letting her go.

Chapter 37

Rachel

O ut of habit, I began to walk to the seat I'd occupied since the beginning of the semester. But then I stopped. *Screw this.* There was no reason to subject myself to a front-and-center view of the mighty professor. I'd do my job, attend the classes I was required to sit in on, teach the extra-help sessions, grade papers—all of it. But I didn't have to sit where he'd told me he preferred I sit. Not anymore.

Looking around the room, I smirked, seeing an open seat next to Mr. Ludwig. Let him have a close-up view of my body so he can sketch—someone might as well appreciate it.

It was almost seventy-five degrees today, but my seatmate still had his wool beanie on.

"Hey." He smiled at me. "Professor Stick Up His Ass let you off lockdown? I thought I was going to have to move up to the front just to get to ask you to go for coffee after class one day."

"Did you need help with something? You haven't come to any of my extra-help sessions."

Beanie boy smiled. He was cute, in a college frat boy, dimpled kind of way. "Nope. Don't need extra help. Just need coffee with you."

I felt a presence behind me. Seeing the flirt's eyes lift from my breasts to over my shoulder and his cheeky expression disappear, I knew who it was.

I kept ignoring him, hoping he would take the hint. *No such luck.*

"Rachel." Caine cleared his throat. "Can I see you after class, please?"

I closed my eyes. I wanted to respond with '*Go screw yourself*', but I wouldn't give him the satisfaction of that much emotion. Nor was I going to let myself turn into one of the rumors I'd heard about Professor West before I even met him.

Plastering on my best imitation smile, I turned to face him, offering a fantastic view of my pearly whites. "Of course, Professor."

I was adamant about showing him I was fine. But what I saw when I looked up erased my fake smile. Caine looked awful. His bright eyes were bloodshot, his naturally warm-colored skin looked cold, and his appearance was disheveled—not the intentionally stylish kind. No, Caine looked like he'd either been on a bender that ended a few hours ago, or he was sick as a dog and dragged his unhealthy ass out of bed for the first time in days to show up to class.

Even though I was pissed at him, I hoped it was the latter.

Caine nodded and his eyes moved to the student next to me. I caught the slight tick in his jaw as he glared at Mr. Ludwig a few heartbeats longer than normal. My emotions were clearly all over the place, because it pissed me off that he felt he had the right to give anyone a hard time for flirting with me. I owed him nothing.

For the next ninety minutes, I avoided looking at Caine, preferring to pretend to take notes while my mind wandered. When class was finally over, I waited in my seat until the last of the students were piling out and then walked down to the front of the room. I stood ten feet away from Caine, feeling terribly awkward. He was packing up his bag.

"I thought it might be best if we talked in my office."

"I'm fine here."

Caine looked up at me. "I'd like privacy."

"I'd like a lot of things, but I don't seem to get them all, now do I?"

He nodded. "Fine. Can we at least sit?" He held out his hand to direct me to the front row. Begrudgingly, I went.

I was acting like an insolent teenager, but I refused to look at him. He waited, assuming I would eventually stop playing with my phone and give him my full attention. But he assumed wrong. After a few minutes, he took the hint and began to speak anyway.

"I got an email from the dean about your request to change your thesis advisor."

"And?"

"That's not necessary. You're almost done, and if you don't want to spend time with me, we can handle most of it over email."

I finally looked up at him. "I don't want your opinions on my work. And I don't want to rehearse my thesis defense with you. I don't want to defend anything to you."

Caine reached out to touch my arm. "Rachel."

I pulled back. "Don't touch me."

He held both hands up. "I'm sorry. I didn't mean to upset you."

I scoffed. "It's a little late for that, isn't it?"

He took a deep breath and blew out a loud stream of air. "Let me start over. We're able to be professional to each other during class, so why create all the extra work for yourself by requesting a new thesis advisor? Most professors will want to put their own touches on your work, and you'll wind up with rewrites for months."

"I guess you prefer to put your *touch* on my work in a different way."

From his tone, I could tell Caine was losing his patience. Which is exactly what I wanted. I wanted to piss him off...wanted to get a rise out of him in some way. Our ending had been too anticlimactic. It made me feel like I'd never been worth his energy. And that just sucked.

"I'm trying to be professional, Rachel."

My spine straightened. "So am I, Professor. If it was my choice, I wouldn't be your TA *or* have you as my thesis advisor. I could request a new thesis advisor without raising suspicion since we hadn't worked together that long and you weren't my original advisor. But I couldn't come up with a reason to be removed as your TA without raising suspicion. I thought telling them we were *fucking* before and *now we're not* might not be the most professional way to handle things."

Caine raked his fingers through his hair. "I'm sorry for hurting you, Rachel. I don't know how to fix things and make us go back to friends."

"We were never friends, Caine. And as far as fixing things, it takes two to make any relationship work. We can't fix anything, because only one of us knows what was broken." My voice softened. "I still don't understand what was broken."

The crack in my voice on the last few words brought Caine's eyes to mine. I wanted to stare him down, shoot angry daggers at him, but when I looked deep into his eyes, all I saw was hurt.

In a moment of weakness, I allowed my heart to show. "What happened, Caine? Why did you cut me off? We were fine one day and then the next..."

Instead of looking away like he'd been doing lately, Caine allowed me in for the briefest of moments. Our gaze locked, and I saw inside of him—the man I'd met was still in there, down deep. I'd started to think I'd imagined who he was since it had all disappeared so quickly.

"You're an amazing woman, Rachel. You deserve better."

One minute I was vulnerable and soft, and the next I was impervious and hard. I stood abruptly, losing my equilibrium and almost losing my footing before I steadied myself. "You don't get to tell me what I deserve. I get to choose what I want."

Caine stood and grabbed my elbow as I went to turn. The loud clank of the heavy classroom door opening echoed through the empty lecture hall. Voices followed behind it as students began to filter in for the next class. I waited, curious to see how important keeping me in place would be to him.

It hurt all over again when he just let go.

"Think about it, Rachel. Don't cause yourself extra work just because you're mad at me."

Even though the students were at the top of the hall, I leaned in to make sure no one could hear. I might have also done it for effect.

"Go fuck yourself, Professor," I whispered in his ear.

"Talk to me." Charlie leaned his elbows on the bar. He was done for the day, but still hanging around. I'd suspected he was waiting until the last afternoon stragglers called it a day.

The dryer cycle of our dishwasher had stopped working a year ago. Charlie had no intention of fixing it. Oddly, that worked for me—especially today, since I found the motion of wiping down glasses soothing. I pulled a dripping soda glass from the crate I was working on and shoved the dishtowel inside.

"What would you like to talk about? Current events? Music?"

"Don't give me that, missy. You know what I'm asking."

I smiled at Charlie, completely aware of what he was asking. "I'm not sure I do."

"You've been moping around here for a week. What's going on? Boy trouble?"

Charlie was tough on the outside, but had an ooey-gooey soft center. It was one of my favorite things about him.

"Everything's fine, Charlie. Just a busy week is all."

He shook his head. "You're full of shit. Twenty-eight years on the job. I know when someone's full of shit."

I was about to deny it when I thought of something. "How can you tell when someone's full of shit? I mean, what are the telltale signs?"

"There's body language that can give you an idea on most people, if you pay attention."

"Like what?"

"Well, there are the obvious ones—the person won't look you in the eyes, they get fidgety, they touch their mouth or face. Although most good liars know those signs and work to control them. There're smaller things that are better indicators. For starters, their shoulders sometimes rise a bit. It's because their breathing gets a bit shallow when they lie, and that's the body's natural reaction to the change in breaths. Some also stand rigid still. When people are talking, they have a natural sway to their body. But when they lie, they lose that natural comfort. Aside from that, there are hints in speech—like saying the same words or phrases repetitively. "I didn't. I didn't."

"Interesting."

"Who's lying to you?"

I exaggerated raising my shoulders and repeated myself. "No one. No one."

"Wiseass."

Charlie cared about me, and I knew he wouldn't pry too deep into things like Ava would, so I was honest with him. "The guy I was seeing broke things off. I get the feeling he's not being truthful about why." I sighed. "Maybe I'm just looking for a reason that doesn't exist because of my own ego. I don't know."

"We talking about that professor?"

"Yeah."

"You want to know whether his heart's still in it or not? You're thinking there's some crap in his head that doesn't reconcile with what's inside his chest?"

I nodded. "I guess so."

"Well, there's only one way to find out if a man who's running the other direction really loves you."

"What's that?"

Charlie looked me in the eyes. "Move on without him. A man comes to his senses really quick when he thinks you're not waiting around for him anymore."

Chapter 38

Caine

I was full of shit.

Only this time, I was lying to myself, too. The department chair had emailed to ask that I do a write up of my observations on Rachel's thesis project to pass around to the other professors to help solicit a new advisor. I'd been dragging my feet to give her a chance to reconsider, and now I was using it as a reason to see her—pretending I needed to turn it in fast when I had no intention of doing any such thing.

It was the mid-semester break, and six days of not seeing Rachel was about all I could take. If anyone got a hold of what I'd resorted to, they'd think I'd lost my mind—and they might be right, but I didn't give a fuck after six days.

This month's *Rolling Stone* magazine had one of those quizzes Rachel was obsessed with. I'd noticed it while thumbing through two weeks ago and put it aside so she could take it. Missing her this morning, I might have taken it myself.

What Your Music Says About Your Love Life asked a series of questions based on which songs you related to most. When I tallied up my score, the prediction it assigned to me about my future was, of course, completely inaccurate. Curious, I read the other predictions anyway. One hit home, only I hadn't scored between a 52 and 68. That particular answer couldn't have been any more perfect for Rachel to read today if I had made the shit up myself. It read:

You've already met your destiny! Although you may not know it. You're an old soul who connects with people on a cosmic level. Trust can be an issue with you, and you often avoid relationships because you follow your head instead of your intuition, sometimes blindly. In love, sometimes you need to throw caution to the wind and jump in with both feet. You've known your soulmate for a long time, but only recently have realized it was meant to be. Stop fighting it and feed your soul.

The quiz was a series of fifteen questions. I retook it, only this time I answered as Rachel would. Drinking a scotch on the rocks, I rattled the ice around in the glass as I tallied up her answers. Her score would be somewhere between 40 and 43. *You've yet to meet your destiny!*

"Yeah. Not happening," I grumbled.

Sucking back the rest of the scotch, I figured she needed a boost of eighteen to twenty points in order to be safely ensconced where she was supposed to be. I picked the four questions where I was most certain of her answers and manually changed the point rating to increase it by five each.

"Much better. "

Jesus Christ, I've been thoroughly pussified.

I tossed the magazine on the table and scrubbed my hands over my face. What the fuck was I doing? I'd resorted to editing love quizzes and taking them as Rachel. I needed to *not* have a second drink, sober up, shower, put some clean clothes on, and go down to O'Leary's before I resorted to calling and hanging up on her just to hear her voice.

Growing some balls, that's exactly what I finally did.

I'd decided not to text her before showing up so she didn't have the opportunity to tell me to email over the unimportant stuff I was pretending was important for her to take a look at. I drove to O'Leary's at almost the end of her shift. The thought of seeing her soon had me in a better mood than I'd been in for two weeks. I whistled along with the music on the car ride over.

Ava was behind the bar when I walked in. I remembered Rachel had said her friend's bartending abilities were limited to covering quick breaks and trips to the bathroom, so I figured she must be in the restroom or doing something in back.

I took a seat at the bar to wait, opting for the emptier side, opposite where Ava stood with her back to me while she talked to a patron. Still in my good mood, I tapped my fingers on the bar to the sound of Jack Johnson's "Better Together" playing overhead.

Unfortunately, my good mood came to a screeching halt when I glanced around the restaurant. Rachel was at a table, only she wasn't delivering food. My hands clenched into fists as I watched her sitting in a booth off in the corner with some guy. Their hands were intertwined in the middle of the table as they sat in what appeared to be deep conversation. I stared until the guy moved his head and I could get a clear look at his face. *Davis.*

What the fuck?

My first instinct was to walk over and find out what the hell was going on. I even stood and took a few steps. But then I saw something that made me freeze in place. Rachel bent her head back, laughing. Instantly I went from angry to an odd mix of feeling crushed and guilty. She was smiling again instead of looking like she was sad. Wasn't that what I'd wanted all along?

Conflicted, I watched from a distance until I was unable to take it any more. Then I turned around and quietly walked back out of the bar. I was angry, though I knew I had absolutely no right to be. And my anger was mixed heavily with regret.

It was my fault she was holding hands with another man. I'd walked away because I didn't deserve to have her, yet no one else was worthy of her either. There was no logic to my thoughts. Somehow, though, I was aware that no one would understand the decisions I'd made. So, I kept to myself, even though I needed to work out what I was going through out loud.

The entire break, I'd been cooped up in my apartment. My only daily activity, other than hitting the gym, was listening to music. If I didn't keep myself out for at least a few hours now, there was a good chance Rachel would be getting a mix tape. I was that pussified.

Left with nothing to do with myself, I decided to go for a drive. I'd let the road and my little car take me where they would. I didn't have to be at work until Monday. Getting out of the city for a night or two might be just what I needed. Pulling a U-turn, I headed for the bridge instead of the parkway that took me back to my apartment. I honestly had no particular destination in mind. So, I just drove. For hours. And when I arrived, I realized I was exactly where I needed to be.

The stairs had been replaced. Worn red brick was now white marble. Some of the bushes were new, and the little fence that surrounded the statue of the Virgin Mary hadn't been there before. But otherwise, St. Killian's looked exactly like the last time I'd walked through its doors fifteen years ago. I still remembered that visit. I'd snuck out of the house—having been punished after the shit that went down with Benny the week before. I knew she was gone. My parents had told me that much since I'd refused to even talk about anything that'd happened until I heard she was safe. But I didn't care. I needed to be here that Saturday in case somehow she came back to talk to me. I wanted to explain why I'd done what I'd done.

That afternoon, I sat in that dark booth for six straight hours. Of course she never did show up—she was long gone. I realized I'd have to live with the guilt of betraying her trust and hope she moved on.

The irony didn't escape me that I was here once again after seeing her *move on* today.

Inside, the church was empty. I had no idea why I'd come or what I was going to do when I got here. My eyes went right to the confessional, which was still there, but I wasn't about to go sit inside. Instead, I took a seat in the back pew and just looked around. It was peaceful tonight. The smell of musty incense warmed my senses. Closing my eyes, I took a few deep, cleansing breaths, spread my arms along the top of the pew, and bowed my head.

I stayed that way for an indeterminate amount of time, until the sounds of footsteps close by caused me to lift my head. An older priest came toward me. I hadn't even heard him until he was only a few pews away.

"Ha-ware-ya, son?"

It took me a minute to realize he had an Irish brogue and had just asked *how are you?*

I smiled. "I'm good. I hope it's okay to be in here."

"No locks on these doors. We're very lucky. Very few churches can say that anymore. Great community here. You can come whenever you want."

"Thank you."

"Is there something you'd like to talk about?"

"I don't think so."

"You sure? I'm known as a pretty good listener."

"No offense, Father, but it's a woman—not sure that's your area of expertise."

The priest smiled warmly and took a seat in the row in front of me. Turning to the side, he lifted a knee onto the seat and slung one arm over the back of the pew to face me.

"I might be married to the Lord, but I got a mother and four sisters." He held up four fingers. "*Four* sisters. None of the bunch ever shut the hell up, so I know a lot about women."

I chuckled. "I don't think I've ever heard a priest say hell unless he was referring to eternal damnation."

He smiled. "It's the new millennium, son. I have to keep up with the times. Even watch some of those *Real Housewives* shows when I go over to my sister Mary's place. She's addicted to that stuff.'"

"That sounds like a penance."

"Yeah, well, the Lord works in mysterious ways."

"*That* I can wholeheartedly agree with."

"So what brings you out this fine evening? Don't think I've seen you around at any of the masses. Are you new to the area?"

"No, actually I grew up here. St. Killian's was my church when I was a kid."

"Ah." He nodded. "You back in town visiting family, then?"

"No. Dad passed away years ago. Mom doesn't live here anymore. I just...I was..." No use lying to a priest. "Thought I'd go for a drive to clear my head, and somehow I found myself here."

"Sometimes the path is created for us, and we can only follow."

"I suppose…"

"So tell me about your girl. What's her name?"

"Rachel."

He nodded. "From the book of Genesis."

"If you say so."

"What's been going on with Rachel that has you lost?"

"It's a long story, Father."

"I've got nothing but time."

"You won't like it very much. I haven't honored the church too well. Or priests for that matter."

His smile was inviting and nonjudgmental, even after I'd warned him off. "We all make mistakes, son. Sometimes getting it off your chest helps."

There was nothing to lose, except his respect. I already had none for myself. Maybe a real confession was a long time coming.

So, I took a deep breath. "Alright. Don't say I didn't warn you."

***

The priest took off his glasses and rubbed his eyes. "Well, that was a doozy indeed, son."

"Tell me about it."

"Let's start at the beginning. What you did all those years ago…while it might've begun for the wrong reasons—you skipping out on working, hiding in the confessional—you came back even after you didn't have to be here anymore."

"Yeah."

"Tell me, why did you keep coming back each week?"

"I knew something was off. The little girl...Rachel, I mean. She was scared. She seemed like she really needed someone to talk to about whatever was going on."

"So you wanted to help her?"

"Yeah." That was the truth. I had wanted to help. "But I didn't go about it the right way. I should have told someone on day one, involved the police when I had my suspicions. Instead I played detective and got her hurt."

The priest contemplated for a moment. "Why didn't you go to an adult? There must have been a reason."

"She was scared, skittish almost. I wasn't sure what I suspected was right. I was afraid I'd scare her off and she'd trust no one after that."

"Perhaps if you'd run off and informed the police after the first time you spoke to her, Rachel and her sister would've been too scared to admit the truth and denied anything was going on."

I shook my head. "Maybe they would have told the truth and been taken out of that hell sooner."

"Sometimes in life, pain is unavoidable, son. We do the best we can. It seems to me that you brought the situation to an end. Had you *not* come back that next week, it could have gone on for years. Many teenage boys wouldn't have given up their Saturday afternoons to befriend a young girl."

I raked my fingers through my hair. "I don't know."

"Do you believe in God, son?"

It had been a long time since I walked into church, but that didn't change my faith. As miserable as I was, and as screwed up as my connection to the church was, I still believed in a higher power.

"I do."

"That's good. You need to heed the destiny He has chosen for you. And the only way to honor that is to accept it and embrace it with truth."

"I'm not sure I understand."

"There is no such thing as coincidence. Coincidence appears to be a remarkable concurrence of events that have no plausible connection. But there is always a connection. God is always the connection."

I was skeptical. "So you think God put us both in that confessional at the same time?"

"I do." He was steadfast in his answer. "And even more importantly, I believe God brought you back together again for a reason."

"And what's that reason?"

"That." He pointed a finger at me. "Is for you to figure out. It appears He's giving you a second chance. What you do with it is up to you."

I shook my head. Maybe he was right. Maybe we were back together for me to come clean with Rachel, or maybe this second chance was about something more. But doing the right thing by her was fifteen years in the making.

"Thanks, Father."

He reached over and extended a hand to me. "I'll give you some space so you can do what you came here to do—think."

We shook. "Thank you."

He stepped out of the pew, took a few steps toward the altar, and then turned back to me. "Four Hail Marys, two Our Fathers, and an act of faith." Seeing the look on my face, he explained. "Your penance. I don't believe in just saying prayers to atone for your sins. Sometimes I give an act of virtue of some sort as part of your contrition—an act of charity, an act of hope... I'm going easy on the prayers for you, but I want the act of faith to be significant."

I sat alone in the back of the church for almost another hour, thinking. Eventually I decided it was time to go. But as I headed out, I couldn't resist taking a look, returning to the scene of the crime.

I smiled when the door to the old confessional creaked open just like it used to. The inside looked almost exactly the same, maybe a little more time-worn. Taking a seat in that chair where everything had started, I took a look around. The decor hadn't changed much either. Only a simple gold cross hung on the wall. I stared at it for a while, then my head fell into my hands and my eyes closed.

So many questions swirled around. *Could there be some truth in that Rachel and her sister might have denied anything going on if I'd told someone right away? Could she forgive what I'd done and all the lies then and now? Even if she could, had Rachel already moved on? Is it better that she did?* Seeing her earlier with Davis—the happy look on her face as she laughed—hurt like hell. I wanted to be the one to make her smile. Maybe that was my act of faith, part of my penance of sacrifice.

I didn't know what the hell I was supposed to do. It was possible I was more confused now than when I'd wandered in. *I know I've been a crap parishioner, but a sign might be nice.*

Feeling defeated, I opened my eyes and looked down at the worn carpet. A shiny penny stared at me, heads facing up. I laughed and reached down to pick it up. Even after all these years, I could still hear her little voice.

"Find a penny, pick it up, and all day long you'll have good luck."

God, she was still with me. Even after all these years and everything we'd been through. How could I let her go?

And then it hit me.

I could let her go physically. But she'd be taking my heart with her. I needed to at least give her the truth and let her decide what to do with it.

Just like I'd done before when I sat in this seat, I flipped the copper penny over and over between my thumb and pointer. Closing it into my palm after a minute, I looked up at the cross.

"Thanks. I'm gonna need it."

Chapter 39

Rachel

If he really cared, he would have done something about it.

That was tough to accept. Even though Caine had given me no reason to hang on to hope, I had been. But tonight I felt like whatever I'd been clinging to had finally snapped.

"It's killing me to see you like this," Ava said.

We'd just locked up O'Leary's at the end of the night. Since it had been slow, I'd done everything I needed to before we closed, except total out the register, which I was currently doing. I stopped counting and looked up at my friend.

"I'll be fine. It was just a rough night."

She took a seat at the bar. "Maybe you shouldn't have told Davis you weren't interested. He's a nice guy. Might help you to get over the fuckwad."

I smiled. Ava had been Team Caine right up until the moment I told her he'd broken things off. Now she had a wide assortment of names for him, none of which were Caine.

"I just don't understand why he showed up here tonight."

"Caine? I don't know. But he didn't look happy. He stared at the two of you sitting in that booth over there and didn't even hear me call his name. I thought for sure he was going to storm over and throw a punch."

Although that would have been upsetting, at least it would have shown me he cared. No man sees a woman he has feelings for and walks out. *Especially* the moment Caine had apparently walked in on. Finding out he'd stopped by O'Leary's and left when he saw me holding hands with Davis felt like it was finally the end. I'd been imagining seeing something still there in his eyes. But Charlie had been right—if you want to know whether a man's heart is still in it, show him you've moved on. I'd been seeing what I wanted to see instead of the truth.

"Well, he didn't. And that says more to me than anything."

"Men suck."

I finished counting out the register and put the money in the leather bag we used to store it in overnight in the safe.

"That about summarizes things."

On the drive home, I gave myself a pep talk. I was over Caine West—I hadn't really fallen in love with him. It was just lust. My nine-month dry spell had me confusing the two. I needed to get out more, maybe date people my own age. This was for the best. Goodbye, Caine West. Tomorrow comes with or without you, so I don't need you to continue.

I prescribed my own musical therapy on the way home. Listening to Rachel Platten's "Fight Song" had me feeling that I was not only going to be fine, but was actually better off without Caine. *I'm pumped to be dumped*, I thought to myself, laughing.

I parked my car in the overpriced lot near my apartment and sighed audibly. Convincing my head was a heck of a lot easier than convincing my heart. And with those two at odds, my emotions were all over the place. I went from pumped to plummeted in the span of turning off the car and walking five blocks home alone.

Lost in thought, I wasn't paying attention to my surroundings. My footsteps were sluggish, and an unexpected panic hit me as I turned the corner to my building. I looked over my shoulder, across the street, up and down the block—all the while feeling a strong wave of anxiety. That feeling grew as I walked faster toward home. It wasn't until I opened the outer door to my apartment building that the reason for my anxiety made itself known.

I jumped and screamed as I found someone standing in the vestibule. On instinct, I pulled back and punched as hard as I could, squeezing my eyes shut.

"Shit!" the intruder yelled.

Only...that voice. It wasn't an intruder at all.

"Caine! What the hell? You scared the shit out of me. Again!"

His hand went to his face where I'd just decked him. "I can see that. You're packing a pretty nice punch, Feisty."

"I'm sorry. Are you okay?" My heart was beating out of my chest.

"Yeah, I'll be fine. Don't worry about it. I didn't mean to scare you. I was ringing the bell. I figured you'd be home by now since O'Leary's closed at midnight."

"Are you sure you're okay?"

He moved his hand, and I could see his cheek already starting to turn red and swell.

Caine nodded. "I deserved it anyway."

Once the rush of adrenaline began to wear off, I realized my hand hurt, a lot. Opening and closing it, I wondered if I might have broken something.

"You hurt my hand."

Caine pulled his head back. "*I* hurt your hand? You punched me."

"Yeah, but it's your fault for scaring the crap out of me. Again. What is it with you waiting in here anyway?"

"Let me see your hand."

I held it out. It wasn't cut or anything, but the knuckles on the middle and pointer fingers had started to swell.

Caine took my hand in his and gently ran his thumb over my knuckles. A bolt of electricity shot through me that had nothing to do with the injury. I pulled my hand back quickly.

"That hurt?"

I lied. "Yeah."

"We should put some ice on it."

Hearing him say *we*, reminded me *he* shouldn't even be here in the first place.

"What are you doing here?"

Caine looked down, then up at me. His beauty kicked my pulse up again. He looked tired and stressed, and had a lump growing on his face where I'd punched him, yet he was still absolutely gorgeous. The kind of handsome that never grows old because each time you're amazed at the effect it has on you.

His voice was tender. "I need to talk to you. Please."

"It's late."

"It can't wait."

When I hesitated before opening the door, he took that as a sign I might not be comfortable inviting him up.

"We could go get a cup of coffee or just take a walk, if you want."

I dug into my purse for my keys. "No, it's fine. I want to change out of my work clothes anyway."

The elevator ride was awkward. The doors were silver and reflected Caine looking at me. I kept my eyes trained up, watching each floor illuminate as if the car was dependent on me for movement. The damn thing moved at a snail's pace.

Inside my apartment, I went to the kitchen, dug a bag of frozen peas from the freezer, and handed them to Caine. "Your cheek is swelling."

"It's fine. Use that for your hand."

I set the bag down on the kitchen counter and practically ran to my bedroom to change, needing to gather my thoughts. "I'll be out in a few minutes."

Twenty minutes ago, I'd been angry-singing "Fight Song" in the car, wishing the man a good riddance, and now I was getting my hopes up because he'd showed up at my door. I was pathetic. What was he doing here? Had he been drinking? He'd better not think he was showing up for a booty call. *Sex with Caine.* I cursed my libido for even considering it.

I changed into a pair of yoga pants and a tank top, brushed my hair, and washed up. I might have even spritzed on some perfume. (Don't judge.) As I was about to walk back to the living room, I realized I wasn't in the right frame of mind yet. Grabbing my iPhone, I opened my playlist and scrolled until I found something to change my mood back to pissed off. I stopped at Three Days Grace's "I Hate Everything About You."

That'll do.

Lying back on my bed, I shut my eyes, popped in my earbuds, and reset myself. After, I felt stronger and ready to face Caine.

He was in his usual spot, looking at the photos on the wall when I finally emerged.

"Can I get you something to drink?" I walked past him and headed to the kitchen for a bottle of water, though I really could have used something stronger.

"No, thanks."

Twisting off the cap, I took a long drink while his eyes followed my every move. "So what do you need to talk about?"

"Could we sit?"

Caine waited for me to take a seat. I was closer to the couch but intentionally sat in the chair across from it so we wouldn't wind up sitting too close. Tonight our roles were reversed. But I needed space to think straight when he was near.

After he sat, he clasped his hands together, rested his elbows on his knees, and dropped his head, staring down at his feet. I'd never seen Caine look so nervous. He was generally the epitome of composure. The longer the silence stretched between us, the more anxious I became.

After what was probably only two or three minutes, yet seemed like an eternity, Caine blew out a ragged breath. When he finally raised his head to look at me, his eyes were glassy and filled with pain. I wanted to reach out so badly, but I had to protect myself. Whatever was hurting him would soon be hurting me.

"I don't know where to start," his voice was hoarse.

There's only one answer when a person looks as troubled as Caine did. "How about at the beginning?"

He nodded. "That's where I should have started weeks ago." He searched my eyes. "I know you don't owe me anything, but can you promise me something?"

"What?"

"Hear me out until I finish."

"Okay..."

Caine just kept shaking his head. "Do you remember the first night we met?"

"In the bar? Yes."

"I said you looked familiar to me. You thought I was feeding you a line. At the time, I couldn't place it, but after finding out you went to Brooklyn College, I chalked it up to having seen you around."

I furrowed my brows. "Are you saying we met before?"

Caine nodded. His face was so solemn. "It was a long time ago."

"Where did we meet?"

"In church."

What the heck was he talking about? My head tilted to the side. "Church?"

Caine dragged his fingers through his hair and stared at me. The look on his face was breaking my heart.

"Do you remember going to St. Killian's to talk to a priest every Saturday?"

My eyes widened, and my body went still. "How do you know about that?"

He searched my eyes. "It wasn't a priest. It was me."

I think I was in shock. I didn't understand what I was feeling. I wasn't upset or angry—I just felt sort of...numb, like I was lost in a heavy fog and couldn't figure out which way to go. My palms were clammy and legs heavy, even though I was sitting. A wave of lightheadedness mixed with nausea washed over me, and I held on to the sides of the chair.

"Rachel?"

I heard Caine say my name, but I wasn't really listening.

"Rachel? Maybe you should lie down."

That was probably what I should've done, considering how I felt, but I needed answers.

"When did you figure out it was me?"

Caine smiled sadly and reached into his pocket. When he pulled his hand out, he opened his fist to show me a dozen or so pennies in his palm.

"I kept them all. I have no idea why. But I did. All these years."

Confused, I took one from his hand. "These are..."

He nodded. "The ones you used to toss into the confessional so I'd have good luck."

"You kept them?"

"Honestly, I knew I was doing something wrong even then, but after I realized you believed in good luck despite all the shit swirling around you, I couldn't have walked away if I'd wanted to. I don't know why I kept them, but when I saw you toss pennies on the floor of my bedroom a few weeks ago, it just clicked."

"Why didn't you tell me then, if you realized that day?"

"I wasn't sure. I guess a part of me didn't want to believe it was you, that *you'*d lived with that fucking monster. I needed to be positive. Tossing pennies could have just been an odd coincidence. So the next time the opportunity presented itself, I asked you if your mother had ever remarried."

My face dropped. "And I said no."

Caine nodded. "Then at your sister's—"

"She mentioned Benny."

He nodded again. "That's not all. There's more, Rachel."

What else could he possibly be hiding? "More?"

"You know the fight Benny got into at the shop?"

"Yeah?"

"It wasn't a customer. It was me. That Saturday after I'd told you to meet me the next morning, I followed you home, just in case you didn't show up. Then when you didn't show up at the church on Sunday, I was coming to check on you. A few blocks from your house, I stopped to get gas, and I saw the same car parked at the station that had been parked in your driveway the day before. I stopped at the place he worked, completely by coincidence."

"And what happened?"

"I told him to keep away from you and your sister. He said some horrible stuff, and then he came at me with a wrench."

"He hurt you?"

"Couple of cuts and bruises, but I was fine."

My head was spinning. "I don't feel so good."

"I'm so sorry, Rachel. For everything. For lying to you all those years ago. For not going to the police and getting help sooner. For getting you hurt. If I hadn't told you to come meet me, that animal wouldn't have caught you packing, and he..." The pain in Caine's voice was agonizing. "He wouldn't have hurt you. I'm so sorry."

As much as it upset me to see Caine distraught, I needed to be alone. I needed some time to think. It was too much to take in at once.

Talking to that priest had been a lifetime ago. I couldn't remember all the things I'd told him, but back then, I was lost. He was the only person who made me feel safe. Finding out none of it was real made me feel... confused, angry, *violated.*

But worst of all, I was ashamed. I'd always regretted hiding what was going on for so long, and I felt responsible for not stopping what my sister went through sooner.

"I need to lie down." I felt Caine looking at me, but I couldn't bear to meet his eyes. "You should go."

He was quiet for a moment while I continued to look away. Then I heard him stand. His voice was a whisper.

"I'm sorry, Rachel. I'm so sorry."

Chapter 40

Rachel

I'd wanted to come back for so many years. But that part of my life was a locked box, and I'd been afraid to open it for fear of finding things inside I couldn't stuff back in. Yet over the last four days, since Caine had revealed so much, the call to come back here had gotten so strong I couldn't ignore it any more.

There was no service going on, but in the last ten minutes people had started to wander in and sit in the pews near the confessional. Perhaps, they were waiting for a session to start. I sat on the other side of the church, lost in my thoughts for the better part of an hour. My attention kept drifting over to the people going in and out of the confessional door—the sinners. A woman with a young child walked in and sat down. The little girl was probably about ten years old, not much older than I was when I'd started to come on Saturdays.

After an older gentleman exited the confessional, the woman leaned over and said something to the little girl before going inside for her turn. It reminded me of when I used to come with my mom before she got sick. I closed my eyes and saw Mom and me sitting in those pews twenty years ago.

"You know how when you have a stomachache or a fever and you go to the doctor?" she said as we waited for her turn to go into the weird room.

"Yeah."

"Well, this is where you come when something is bothering you inside here." Mom patted her chest.

"When my chest hurts? Like when Riley had pa-noma?"

Mom laughed. "Pneumonia and no. Not your chest. What's inside of you that makes you feel a certain way."

I crinkled up my nose. "What's inside of me?"

"Your soul. It's the thing you can't name. It's the truth of what makes you you."

I laughed. "I don't understand."

Mom smiled. "You don't have to right now. Just remember this is a place you can come to talk to God about anything."

"What if He's busy?"

She leaned over and kissed the top of my head. "Then one of His angels will be listening."

I hadn't even realized I was crying until a tear landed on my folded hands. Opening my eyes, I looked over to where the little girl was sitting, and the pews were all empty. She was gone, and so was her mother. They'd gone without my even noticing. The open confessional door caught my attention. Looking around, I realized I was the only person left in the church. My chest had a crushing sensation inside from the old memories of my mom.

"Well, this is where you come when something is bothering you inside here."

"What's inside of me?"

"It's the truth of what makes you you."

Before I could debate it, I'd stood and headed over to the confessional.

It was surreal to step inside after all these years. I might be twenty-five now, but it was a ten-year-old girl who took a seat. Nothing had changed. The room looked the same as it had the last time I'd stepped inside. I could hear breathing on the other side of the confessional—the priest was waiting. And this time I'd seen him walk in. I knew it was actually a priest.

Eventually, after I debated walking out over and over, I took a deep breath and slid open the wooden window that covered the lattice screen.

"Bless me, Father, for I have sinned. It's been fifteen years since my last confession."

Except for a few *go on* and *tell me more* comments, the priest had been relatively quiet. After a rocky start where I wasn't sure how to begin or what to say, I miraculously babbled on for the better part of half an hour. It was the most I'd ever spoken to anyone about my mother, my sister, my guilt, or the years of struggle over being ashamed for what I'd allowed to happen.

"What brought you here today? It sounds like you've been doing a lot of *tinking* of late." *Thinking*—I thought I'd heard a brogue.

Even though I'd come here with confusion over Caine, we really hadn't spoken about him much. What was bothering me, I'd realized, had little to do with him and more to do with me.

"It's a really long story."

"I've got nothing but time, my dear."

I guess priests have heard it all, because after I finished my crazy story, he didn't sound even the slightest bit shocked.

"Is there anything else you'd like to confess today?"

"Well, it's been a really long time, so I'm sure I have a ton. I use bad language pretty frequently."

The priest was quiet for a moment. "For your penance, I want you to say one Hail Mary and one Our Father and complete two acts of forgiveness."

"Okay."

I stood and looked at the lattice. The priest was facing the door, and I could only make out a vague profile.

"Thank you for listening, Father."

I had one hand on the door when he stopped me. "Rachel?"

"Yes?"

"That first act of forgiveness should be easy. You haven't done anything wrong. You need to forgive yourself."

After I said my prayers, I returned to my car. It wasn't until I was halfway home that something dawned on me. I hadn't told him my name, yet the priest had called me Rachel.

On the way back, I did a lot of thinking. I decided to stop in at O'Leary's and ask for a few days off. My head wasn't in a good place, and I really needed to work on my thesis anyway. It was late afternoon, and the bar was quiet, with just few ex-cop regulars hanging around with Charlie.

"Hey, Charlie. You have a minute?"

"Sure, sweetheart. You're a heck of a lot more pleasant to look at than these two old guys." He thumbed his finger at his buddies with a smile.

I took a seat at the other end of the bar, and Charlie filled a glass with Diet Coke before coming to talk to me.

"Would it be okay if I took a few days off? I can ask Ava to cover me."

"Everything okay?"

"I just need to get caught up on some schoolwork."

"Sure. Of course. And don't worry about getting Ava to cover you. I'll cover your shifts."

"Thanks, Charlie. I really appreciate it."

"Oh, by the way." He walked to the register and lifted the money tray, removing an envelope from underneath.

"Glad you and that professor broke up. I ran him. He's got a record."

"You ran him?"

He tossed the envelope on the counter. "Yeah. Told you I was going to check out the guys sniffing around you girls from now on. Guy's got a record for assault. It's old, and it was sealed because he was a juvie. But not too many criminals change their stripes."

Rather than attempt to explain anything, I just said thank you. It was a fitting end to the day I'd had. When a few new patrons came in, Charlie went to make some wings, and I decided to open the envelope.

It was surreal to read a police report that involved Caine and Benny. The top half was all informational—name, date, location, time of incident. At the bottom of the page was a section labeled Narrative of Incident, and a paragraph had been written in an officer's chicken-scratch handwriting:

On 8-3-02 at 15:35 hours, suspect committed an act of assault on an unrelated thirty-nine-year-old man. There were no witnesses to the attack, but when I arrived on the scene, the suspect was standing over the victim, who was unconscious. I observed cuts and blood on the suspect's knuckles, consistent with the victim's assault. Ambulance number 4631 was dispatched and arrived on the scene at 15:48 hours. The victim regained consciousness during the time the paramedics were treating him. The suspect admitted he had assaulted the victim but refused to give a statement other than requesting that police and social services be sent to 3361 Robbins Lane within the town of Pleasantville. Units were dispatched to the address to investigate. The suspect was searched and cuffed and placed into the back of the squad car while the scene was secured. He remained there until 16:50 when he was transported to the 33rd precinct for processing of charges on second-degree assault.

While I'd already known everything I read, somehow seeing it all on paper hit me. Caine had put my sister and me before himself, making sure we got the attention we needed before even considering what might happen to him. He'd done the same thing again a few weeks ago—or, at least he thought he had—choosing to sacrifice his own happiness for mine when he'd broken things off to avoid dredging up the past.

I closed my eyes. The memory of my mom that had come back today as I sat in the church once again flooded my thoughts. She'd told me to come to the church if I ever needed to talk, and God would listen.

"What if He's busy?"

She leaned over and kissed the top of my head. "Then one of His angels will be listening."

Suddenly everything was clear. It wasn't Caine I needed to forgive. He'd never done anything but try to protect me. I needed to forgive myself in order to accept him into my heart. I could run the other way, but it was too late, he already had my heart.

Charlie must have noticed me in deep thought and mistook that for being upset.

"You okay?" He pointed to the ripped envelope on the bar and the papers I'd been reading.

"I am now. Thanks, Charlie."

Chapter 41

Caine

Rachel's text was the last thing I expected. I read back through the ambiguous exchange from an hour ago.

Rachel: *Could we talk tomorrow after class?*
Caine: *Of course. Is everything okay?*
Rachel: *Yes. Everything is fine.*
Caine: *Do you want to discuss something related to school or your thesis?*
Rachel: *No.*

I knew she generally ran off to work on Tuesdays after class.

Caine: *Don't you have to work after class?*
Rachel: *No. I took a week off.*

There was no damn way I was going to get any sleep tonight. I was too anxious. Of course, my mind started to screw with me, imagining all sorts of shit—like why she'd taken a week off. I pictured her sitting on a plane, heading to some exotic destination with that Davis tool. Even though a chunk of time had passed since our last text, I picked up the phone in an attempt to find out something that might help me relax.

Caine: *Are you going somewhere?*

She typed back a few minutes later.

Rachel: *No. Not going anywhere.*

Further attempts to relax after that were just as futile. Eventually I grabbed my keys and decided tomorrow was way too long to wait to hear what Rachel had to say. I'd given her the space she'd asked for, but if she was finally ready to talk, I had a lot I needed to say, too.

After I got to her place, I realized it was pretty late. Not wanting to scare her by buzzing the door at almost eleven, I decided to text first.

Caine: *Are you awake?*

The dots started to jump around. That answered that question.

Rachel: *Yes.*

Caine: *Think we can do a little earlier than after class tomorrow?*

Rachel: *Sure. What time?*

Caine: *Right now.*

Rachel: *I think it's better if we speak in person.*

Caine: *Me too. I'm downstairs. Can I come up?*

My phone rang a minute later.

"Are you joking?"

I pressed her bell in response. "That's me."

After she buzzed me in, I waited in front of the elevator. The damn thing was too slow. Now that I was here and she'd let me in, I was desperate to see her. My heart beat unnaturally fast in my chest as I waited. Impatient, I looked around for a door leading to a stairwell. Once I found it, I flung it open to take the stairs two at a time.

Rachel's door opened just as I arrived on her floor. "You're really here."

I couldn't tell whether she was happy or upset that I'd come without warning—her face was mostly just shock.

"I am."

She stood in the doorway in a thin, cotton T-shirt and shorts. Her hair was pulled back into a ponytail, and her face was wiped clean of makeup. I'd seen her looking beautiful all dressed up for an opera, but she was never more beautiful than in this moment.

"Can I come in?"

She stepped aside. "Sure. Of course."

On the drive over, I'd decided that before she said whatever was on her mind—whether that be telling me off, telling me she was seeing someone else, telling me to fuck off, or even on the long shot that she'd be telling me she was willing to give me another chance—I was going to tell her how I felt about her. I was done keeping secrets from this woman.

"Can I get you something to drink?"

My mouth was parched from nerves and the race up the stairs. "Some water would be great. Thanks."

While Rachel got me some water, I looked around the room, finding the wall of photos that always caught my attention. My eyes fixated on the photo of Rachel and her roommates. *Davis*, to be specific. I needed to know. So, when she brought me the water, I asked point blank without any preamble.

"Are you seeing Davis again?"

"No."

"I saw you with him last week at O'Leary's."

"I know."

"You saw me?"

"No. Ava saw you. Why didn't you stay to talk to me if you came all the way there?"

I hung my head. "I was trying to do the right thing."

"The right thing? What does that mean?"

"Let you be with someone better for you than me. Walk away."

She seemed to contemplate that for a moment. "Why are you here now then?"

I sighed. "Because I'm a selfish asshole."

"I don't understand."

I waited until she was looking in my eyes and decided to say what I should have said weeks ago. "I lied to you. I kept things from you. I got you hurt. I'm the reason you have a scar on your back. You have zero reasons to want to trust me or give me another chance, but I have to try."

I took a deep breath. "I have to try because I love you, Rachel. I'm so fucking desperately in love with you."

She looked like she might cry. Dread knotted in the pit of my stomach.

"I don't blame you for anything that happened, Caine. That's not why I couldn't see you for a while. I couldn't see you because I couldn't *look* at you. I'm so ashamed of everything that happened."

"Ashamed? What are you talking about? You have nothing to be ashamed of."

Rachel looked down. "I let things go on for a long time and didn't tell anyone. I should have gone to the police. Or told a teacher. If I had been less afraid, maybe my sister wouldn't have gotten things so badly. Maybe she wouldn't have spent half her life in and out of rehab. I was the only one who could have done something about what was going on, and I didn't."

I placed my hand under Rachel's chin and lifted, forcing her to look at me. My heart broke when I saw tears streaming down her face.

"You did nothing wrong. You have *nothing* to be ashamed of. *Nothing*."

"I should have—"

"You should have been a ten-year-old girl who went out and rode her bike without a care in the world. That's what you should have been doing. The only person who did anything wrong to your sister was *Benny*. You were ten and scared and didn't even fully understand everything that was happening. And even then, you *did* try to tell someone. You told me. I was older. I should've known better and gotten help."

"You *did* help. If it weren't for you, I don't know how long it would have gone on."

"I should have stopped it sooner."

She shook her head. "The other day I was thinking about what made me go into that church to begin with, and I remembered a conversation I had with my mom. She told me to go there if something was ever bothering me inside. She said it was a place I could go to talk to God about anything. I was probably only about five when she told me that, so I took her advice very literally. I asked her what would happen if God was busy. And you know what she said?"

"What?"

"She told me if He was busy, one of His angels would listen."

I stared at her, mesmerized by how strong and smart she'd been even back then. "Your mom sounds like a really special person, very spiritual."

"She was. And she was also right, Caine. Don't you see that? God was busy, so He sent me an angel. My own guardian angel. God sent me you."

It didn't matter that I looked like a pussy, I started to cry.

Rachel placed her hand over my heart. "It's time we both let go of the past."

"I'm so sorry for everything, Rachel."

"There's nothing for you to be sorry for."

Leaning in, I cupped her beautiful face in my hands and kissed her with everything in me. Her cheeks were flushed when it broke.

"I almost forgot," she said.

"What?"

Rachel took a step back and lifted her T-shirt off of her body. She wasn't wearing a bra, and I couldn't hide the expression on my face.

"Hold that thought, Professor. I want to show you something else."

She turned around and looked at me over her shoulder. On the bottom left side of her lower back was a big bandage.

"What happened?"

"Take the tape off. But do it gently because I'm still a little sore."

As I began to peel back the tape, I realized the area she had covered was her scar from Benny fifteen years ago.

"Did something happen to your scar?"

She smiled. "It's not a scar. It's just a cut that healed. The real scars are the ones you can't see—those are the hardest to heal."

Lifting the dressing, I had no words, seeing what she had done. I could no longer see the long scar that had marred her beautiful skin. It was covered by a tattoo of an angel.

"That's you," she said. "I'd buried so much so I wouldn't have to deal with old emotions. Everything coming out now wasn't easy, but I finally feel like I'm on the other side of those memories. They'll always be there, but I can see them in the rearview mirror now instead of in front of me."

I was so choked up, my voice croaked when I spoke. "It's beautiful. Just like you."

"I can keep the bandage off now. The guy at the tattoo parlor told me to leave it on for up to eight hours. I just got it done today."

Rachel turned back around to face me. Her tits were so damn full and perky, I couldn't help but be distracted by them.

"Caine?"

"Huh?" My eyes lifted back to meet hers.

She looked amused. "There's just one problem."

"What's that?"

"I can't lie on my back."

"That's not a problem, Feisty. I can think of a lot of ways to be inside you without you being on your back."

I leaned down and scooped her into my arms. Cradling her, I walked to the bedroom.

"Tell me, do you want to ride me, be on all fours, bend over the footboard, or spoon fuck? Or maybe you'd just rather sit on my face?"

I set Rachel down on the edge of the bed, removed her shorts and panties, and began to shed my own clothes. When I got down to my boxer briefs, I hooked my fingers in the sides and looked at her as I pulled them down. My cock was painfully hard.

"What's your pleasure, sweetheart? Which one are you in the mood for?"

Rachel licked her lips. "I have to pick just one?"

I stepped out of my boxers and stroked myself a few times. "No, babe, you're picking the first position. We're going to do them all. Tomorrow you're going to be so sore, it will hurt when you sit down in class. And I'm going to watch you sit and know exactly why you're squirming in your seat. Then I'm going to have a hard-on for the entire class. Pick one so we can start making you sore."

"Ride you. I want to ride you."

Her face was so sexy with that impish smile. I climbed up on the bed, settling my back against the headboard, and lifted her onto my thighs. I wanted to watch her face while she took my cock into her body.

"Are you wet?" I slipped my fingers between her legs and found her completely soaked.

She nodded.

Gripping my cock, I held it near the base. "Take it. Nice and slow. I want to watch it disappear inside your pussy."

Rachel lifted onto her knees, placing her hands on my shoulders for balance, and hovered over the glistening crown of my cock. I had the strongest urge to thrust up and bury myself deep inside her, but I didn't. She wanted to ride me, and I wanted to give her anything she wanted.

"Christ," I groaned as she began to lower herself onto my cock. She was so tight and hot. I was captivated by the sight of her pussy sucking me inside. It had only been a few weeks since we were last together, but I was starving for her like it had been years.

She lifted up and down a few times, easing me farther and farther in until she was seated with me fully inside, her ass pressed against my balls. When she started to gyrate her hips, I pressed my thumb to her clit and rubbed small circles, while I grabbed hold of her ponytail with the other.

"Ride me, Feisty. Ride me *hard.*"

She moaned, so I yanked a little harder. With her head back, her magnificent tits were right at my eye level. I watched them bouncing up and down, taking my eyes off only long enough to lean forward and suck a nipple into my mouth—one and then the other. Rachel's speed increased—bobbing up and down, lifting halfway off my cock and taking me back in with a rhythm that was so fucking perfect. Just fucking perfect.

Whimpering, she began to lose steam as her orgasm took hold. I grabbed her hips and took over where she'd left off, thrusting up into her from underneath while she met me with whatever she had left. The tight squeeze of her pussy and her moaning my name over and over as she came undone had me thrusting harder and harder until my name was barely a whisper from her lips. I swallowed every last one of those moans in a kiss. Then I buried myself as deep as I possibly could and came long and hard inside of her.

"I love you, Rachel Martin," I mumbled against her lips.

"I love you, too, Caine West."

We stayed like that for a long time, her sitting on my lap, me caressing her face.

I just couldn't get over the way things had turned out. I was awestruck by her beauty, inside and out—and by the way fate had brought us back together again.

"What? You're looking at me funny," she said.

"It's just so crazy how many years this has been in the making, how we found our way back to each other."

Rachel smiled and tilted her head. "You know you're the reason we met again, right?"

"I think Professor Clarence dying had something to do with it."

"Maybe. But if it weren't for you, I might not have even discovered the power of music for therapy. All those years ago, you gave me your headphones and told me to listen to music—to concentrate on the words whenever I was upset. I listened, and it really helped. That's how I really got into music."

I thought back. "I did give you headphones, didn't I?"

"You did. You know I wrote you a letter the morning everything happened. Well, not you, but fake-priest you."

"Oh yeah? Did you get to bring it to the church?"

"No. I don't even know what happened to it. Got thrown out when we went to live with my aunt and uncle, I guess."

"What did it say?"

"I don't remember exactly. But I know I thanked you for talking to me every week."

"I went back on Saturdays for a month just in case you came back. It felt like something was missing each time I went and you weren't there."

"There was. A little piece of your heart." She smiled. "I kept it and brought it back to you."

"No, you didn't, Rachel. You've always had my heart, and I don't ever want it back."

Epilogue

Rachel

"If you're going to ban sex, you need to start wearing a bra around the house," Caine grumbled as he leaned down and planted a chaste kiss on my lips. He also slipped his hand under my shirt and pinched my nipple. *Hard.*

"Oww."

"You love it, and you know it."

My fiancé was grumpy, but he was also right. I secretly loved that he was growing more irritable by the day since I'd cut him off almost two weeks ago.

My eyes softened as I looked up at him. "What time will you be back?"

"Probably not until six. I need to go over all the grading my shit-for-brains TA has done before turning the final grades in."

Caine was extremely unhappy with the TA he'd been assigned this year. I smiled.

"Once you've had the best, everyone else seems inferior."

"You were a good TA. But I might've been influenced because of your great T and A. Come to think of it, since you're not even giving me T and A now, *you* should at least give me the TA and do my grading."

"No can do, Professor. I have a full day ahead of me. I need to finish packing the last of my things here this morning. Your sister and I are taking the girls to pick up their dresses and then out to lunch. After that, I have to go see Father McDonald to give him our readings and music choices. So you're going to need to take care of things yourself."

He pouted. "I've been taking care of myself for two weeks."

I stood from the chair where I'd been sipping my morning coffee and pushed up on my tippy toes as I wrapped my arms around Caine's neck.

"It's just two more days. Think how much more exciting it will be when we finally go to bed Saturday night after the reception is over. And the next time you make love to me, I'll be Mrs. Caine West."

His eyes softened. "I do like the sound of that. Although I only agreed to wait until after the wedding. I never said anything about after the reception."

"What did you think? We're going to have sex in the car on the drive from the church to the restaurant?"

"I was thinking we could do it in the confessional, right after the priest says you're stuck with me for the rest of your life."

"That's twisted on so many levels, even for you."

Caine laughed. "I gotta run or I'm going to be late starting the exam. So give me that mouth and kiss me properly to get me through another day of celibacy."

In one motion, he reached a hand around my back and squeezed my ass as he lifted me. My legs wrapped around his waist. His mouth melded to mine, the kiss hard and passionate. I moaned into his mouth as he backed me up to the wall and pinned me against it, using his hips so his hands could roam my body.

Yes, my soon-to-be husband definitely knew how to kiss me properly.

After he begrudgingly left my apartment without getting laid, I looked around at the sparse furnishings I had left to pack. Since we'd decided I was moving into Caine's place, we'd been taking stuff there over the last month. Pretty much the only things left to box up were my wall of framed pictures, my books, and some personal things in the bathroom. I took on the books first and then moved to the wall.

I'd added some new pictures to my display over the last year: Caine and me at my graduation from grad school. I was facing the camera, smiling proudly about getting my degree, and Caine was looking at me with the same proud smile. Me and the crew from O'Leary's on my last night working there. Charlie had his arm draped around my shoulder. He'd been a hard sell on accepting that Caine wasn't a violent criminal. Ultimately, one night after Caine and I were back together, I'd told Charlie my entire story.

After so many years of keeping everything pent up, it was odd to share it openly—but the more I talked about it, the farther back in the rearview mirror those ugly days went.

I missed working at O'Leary's, but I loved my new job as a musical therapist. I worked as an independent contractor for a school district, doing one-on-one therapy with autistic children. It was a job that felt more like a reward than a grind. Caine and I had dinner with Charlie every week at O'Leary's. He might not be my employer anymore, but he was the closest thing I'd had to a father figure since my uncle passed away. In fact, Charlie would be giving me away in two days. I suspected Caine would be getting a good eye-squint warning at the altar from him.

Even though my research was done and my thesis published, we still kept in touch with Lydia and Umberto. The first Sunday of every month, Caine and I brought Murphy to visit. I wasn't sure who got more from our visits—us or them.

I packed two boxes of framed photos, feeling sentimental as I folded the bubble wrap over each memory. The last one I packed was the photo of my mother on the swing in our yard. I brushed my fingers over her beautiful face through the glass. *Thanks, Mom.* Without her advice to seek the church, I might never have met Caine.

The small slide-locks that kept the back of the frame on and the picture in place must have moved when I took the photo from the wall. As I reached for the bubble wrap, the cardboard back of the frame opened, and something fluttered to the ground. It was a folded-up piece of paper.

Thinking it was probably a receipt or the sample picture that had come inside the frame, I picked it up and unfolded it.

I froze when I saw the handwriting on it.

Because it was my own.

It was less developed and messier than it was now, but it was mine. And I knew exactly what it was—the letter I'd written to the fake priest sixteen years ago. Until that moment, I hadn't remembered putting it behind Mom's picture. I steadied myself and took a deep breath before reading what I'd written.

Dear Father,

I'm sorry I didn't get to meet you when I was supposed to. My stepfather found out we were going to run away and got really mad. He said if he ever caught the person who was going to help us, he'd hurt them. So I can't come talk to you on Saturdays anymore, because I don't want him to hurt you. But I wanted to say thank you. Thank you for the headphones and for telling me how to listen to music to make everything better. Thank you for listening to me even when I was too afraid to talk. But most of all, thank you for being my angel when God was too busy. I hope I get to see you again someday.

-Rachel

I stared down at the page. And I read the letter a second time. Then a third. Mom had sent me my angel. I had no doubt about that.

Two days later, I walked down the aisle to marry the love of my life. My new little nieces, Lizzy and Alley, were flower girls. They walked ahead of me, dropping rose petals. When they reached the altar, Alley looked back with a giant smile, and I nodded my head, indicating it was time to drop the other things I'd slipped into her basket. She looked up at her uncle, then tossed two pennies at his feet. They both landed face up.

Charlie walked me down the aisle to a folksy remake of an old Gene Clark song, "Full Circle." There were tears in Caine's eyes as I came to stand next to him at the altar. He took my hand as the song finished playing, and together we smiled and turned to look back at our confessional. Just as the lyrics said, we'd come full circle. We'd traveled different paths to get back to where we'd started, but finally we were finished. Now it was the first day of the rest of our lives, and I couldn't wait to start.

THE END

Acknowledgements

As always, I owe enormous gratitude to my amazing readers. Thank you for allowing my world to become a part of your world. I'm honored that so many of you have been with me for multiple books and can only hope we have many more years together.

To Penelope – The journey wouldn't be the same without you traveling it right next to me. Thank you for putting up with all my craziness, especially while I wrote this one!

To Julie – Thank you for your unwavering friendship.

To Luna – Your support and friendship are a gift. I pen the story, but you bring it to life with your imagination. Thank you for all that you do, and I can't wait for October!

To Sommer – As always, you covered my words with beauty.

To my agent and friend, Kimberly Brower – I'm proud to call you both. I can't wait to see what the second half of 2017 brings!

To Elaine and Jessica – Thank you for all of your hard work in bringing this story to its full potential.

To Dani at Inkslinger – Thank you for organizing everything for *Beautiful Mistake!*

To all of the generous bloggers – Thank you so much for all of your support. I am blessed to have such wonderful partners to spread the love of books. Your enthusiasm is contagious and makes every release more exciting than the last. Thank you for taking the time to read my work, write reviews, make videos, create teasers, and help launch so many books! Thank you! Thank you! Thank you!

Much love
Vi

Other Books by Vi Keeland

Standalone novels
EgoManiac

Bossman

The Baller

Mister Moneybags (Co-written with Penelope Ward)

Playboy Pilot (Co-written with Penelope Ward)

Stuck-Up Suit (Co-written with Penelope Ward)

Cocky Bastard (Co-written with Penelope Ward)

Left Behind (A Young Adult Novel)

First Thing I See

Life on Stage series (2 standalone books)
Beat

Throb

MMA Fighter series (3 standalone books)
Worth the Fight

Worth the Chance

Worth Forgiving

The Cole Series (2 book serial)
Belong to You

Made for You

CPSIA information can be obtained
at www.ICGtesting.com
Printed in the USA
BVOW09s1925300717
490637BV00001B/1/P

To Larry and Lancelot

❧ Contents

❧ Acknowledgments

The spirit and message of this book came from a community of persons unique in their isolation but united in their dedication—the caregivers. In one-on-one interviews or in support group sessions, they shared their stories with little idea that what they do in caring for another adult human being takes special courage, perseverance, and skill. I thank them and hope that this book begins to give them the recognition they deserve.

A number of individuals took time to contribute to the content of specialized sections of the book. These persons include Harry Krout, Joyce Barry, Margaret Jass, Augie Bergemann, Henry Juncker, Manny and Lu Gallert, Valerie Stefanich, Cathy Rickheim, Kay Brown, Mary Pelnar, Lisa Atherton, Gail Seim, James Sasser, Barbara Capstrand, Margie Smerlinski, Peg Wagner, Edith Giese, Carol Stankiewicz, Paulette Auclaire, Barbara Keyes, Greg Spzak, and Lee Ullman.

Every day the staff, clients, and caregiving families of St. Timothy's Senior Day Care Center added to the project.

Finally, I thank Elaine Goldberg, my editor, whose personal and professional expertise contributed immeasurably to the content of this manuscript.

ꭗ Foreword

Jo Horne's *Caregiving: Helping An Aging Loved One* is a very timely book. While family members have always assisted aged relatives, caregiving has received widespread public attention only in recent years. It has emerged as an important issue for several reasons. One critical factor is that the population has been aging, and there are more people in need of assistance. Because of the improvements in modern medicine and public health, more people are now living to old age. At the turn of the century, only 39 percent of persons could be expected to live to old age (sixty-five), while today over 70 percent can expect to grow old. The increase in the number of people living past eighty is especially dramatic. This aging of the population creates the need for more caregiving because chronic ailments that can limit, in varying degrees, a person's ability to function independently become more common with advancing age. Researcher Elaine M. Brody has even suggested that caring for a relative is becoming so common that it should be regarded as a "normative" life event, that is, as expected a milestone as getting married, working, or retirement.

At the same time, however, other changes in the population have resulted in fewer people being available to take on caregiving responsibilities. Today's elders had smaller families than in the past, so caregiving tasks can potentially be assumed by fewer people. This trend will become even more pronounced for subsequent generations. Women, of course, have historically been caregivers, but as more women seek work outside the home, there may not be anyone within the family to assist if caregiving has to be full-time. One other factor that limits the availability of caregivers is that as more people live to old age, the caregivers are themselves likely to be older, too, whether they are the spouses or even the children of the persons needing assistance. Children who are caregivers might themselves be in their fifties, sixties, or even seventies and not be physically able to take on some caregiving tasks.

Putting all these changes together, the result is that more people are in need of care, but fewer people are available to give it—though families usually are involved, often making heroic efforts to assist an impaired elder. This dilemma of increased need and decreased resources is at the heart of the problem many caregivers face. In this situation, caregivers need to make the maximum use of resources that are available to them and to plan carefully for the care of their relatives so that it does not deplete them emotionally, physically, or financially.

Jo Horne provides useful guidelines for responding to the emotional and practical demands of caregiving. One important aspect of caregiving is its emotional burden. Taking on caregiving responsibilities often creates conflicts with other obligations to work or family. Caregivers also experience the emotional pain of seeing a parent or spouse incapacitated. The tasks of caregiving can themselves be physically and emotionally exhausting. As a result, caregivers experience the whole range of human emotions: guilt, anger, frustration, exhaustion, anxiety, fear, sadness, love, and the satisfaction of having done a good job. As Jo Horne points out, these strong emotional reactions are a normal part of being a caregiver. Caregivers sometimes think that they are the only ones experiencing these strong emotions, but when they find out that others are having the same feelings, such as when they have a chance to discuss their experiences in a support group, they often have a sense of relief. Somehow, learning that difficult feelings are a normal part of caregiving seems to help people cope with them better.

Going beyond the emotional reactions, caregivers can take some pragmatic steps to lessen the day-to-day strain. The area in which *Caregiving* excels is in helping families identify the type of assistance that could help them deal with their relatives' problems and the stress they are under. Jo Horne carefully shows the steps involved in deciding when to get help, tells how to find what types of assistance are available in one's own community, and advises on how to choose what is best in a particular situation. Getting occasional help with or relief from caregiving chores is critical, both for full-time and part-time caregivers. By getting assistance when the demands of care are too great, families are able to conserve their energies for the tasks that no one else can do, and that makes them better caregivers in the time they devote to their relatives.

Perhaps the overriding theme in *Caregiving* is that families can take positive steps to deal with the stresses with which they are confronted. They can learn how to understand and cope with their relatives' problems more effectively and to find ways of getting help when they need it. It is not always easy to find help, and sometimes no good alternatives may exist. But it can be surprising how far practical planning will go in alleviating the emotional and physical strains on caregivers. Toward that end, *Caregiving* will be a valuable resource for anyone who is a caregiver.

STEVEN H. ZARIT, Ph.D.

Associate Professor of Gerontology and Psychology
Director, Andrus Older Adult Center of the Andrus
 Gerontology Center
University of Southern California

✵ Introduction

When people think of life in the "olden days," it is assumed that families took care of their own. Often three generations lived under the same roof. Such conditions have been romanticized in books and films as the time when many families were like the Waltons of television fame—loving and unified against all odds. Many people feel that today's family is splintered and disinterested. The facts are quite different.

Americans *are* taking care of their parents and spouses and relatives whether or not those family members are disabled. The four-generation family is common in today's society, and one generation providing care for another on some level is the rule rather than the exception. The generations do not always live under the same roof, but even in the good old days that may not necessarily have been an act of love but rather one of economic necessity. Today the members of all generations prefer to maintain as much independence as possible for as long as they can. Moving in with another generation is usually done out of necessity, not because the person is loved more or less.

For years caregivers—spouses, adult children, sons-in-law and daughters-in-law, sisters, brothers, friends—have taken on the job of caring for their aging relatives with little support and no compensation. *Newsweek* reporters in a cover story about Alzheimer's disease summed up

1

the plight of all caregivers: "They drive themselves to physical and emotional exhaustion while rendering continuous care. . . . And amid all this, they may see their life savings consumed in the crushing task of caring." The article goes on to say that Alzheimer's as a disease has been overlooked by legislators in their attempt to plan for a national health policy. In that same way, caregivers have been overlooked.

The care being provided today is more often for chronic (sustained) illnesses than for acute (temporary) emergencies. Caregivers are being asked to learn new skills and to juggle several life roles within a single twenty-four-hour day. While most caregivers are women, many males are assuming the care for disabled spouses and/or parents. Whether the caregiver is male or female, increasingly there is the chance that he or she will in one lifetime assume the caregiving role for more than one person.

To become a capable caregiver for someone who is aging means to understand the history of that person and his or her impairments and disabilities. It means getting a clear diagnosis of the ailments from a qualified physician, or other source, and then researching carefully how to give care for each incapacity. It means considering the decision to become the person's primary caregiver with all the care and introspection one might give to making a decision about accepting a major career change or having a child. It means reorganizing one's life to allow another person to share in that daily routine. It may mean dealing with one's own aversion to illness as well as the behavior that may result from a person's chronic illness. It means finding the time and having the fortitude to stand up for one's own right to a life beyond caregiving.

Caregiving has been written for you if

— you are considering the idea of becoming a primary caregiver for another adult.

— you have been caregiving for a time and need some fresh encouragement and ideas for coping.

— you are one of the thousands of caregivers throughout the country living in a rural area or small community where support systems and community service organizations are limited.

— you are part of a family network supporting in some way a caregiver and a care recipient.

Caregiving is a handbook, a reference tool. You can read straight through the entire book when you have time. In the meanwhile you can turn to those sections that directly apply to your current caregiving situation. There are written exercises for you to do that will help you identify both your own needs and those of the care recipient. And throughout the book resources that can make the job of caregiving easier for the novice or for the experienced caregiver are listed and discussed.

Aging—the Facts

Older people have the same needs as everyone else. Most of the aging population in this country comes from a work-oriented society. To work is to be successful. To work is to carry one's own weight. To work is to be American. When such people become physically and/or mentally impaired and unable to work, they may begin to feel useless, lazy, and slovenly. Just like all other humans, regardless of age, older people need social contact, love, understanding, self-esteem, and recognition.

As persons age, they experience a number of losses— more losses than gains. Children leave home to pursue their own interests and to establish their own families. Jobs are taken over by younger people. Homes are sometimes sold in favor of more practical living arrangements. Friends die or move away. A spouse may die. In addition to these losses, an older person may also experience a number of bodily changes.

- Hair color may change to gray or white.
- The skin may wrinkle and become drier.

- Teeth may be lost and replaced by dentures.
- Eyesight and hearing may be diminished or impaired.
- Movement and communication may become more difficult.
- Bones become more brittle and may break more easily.
- There may be decreased circulation of the blood and less resistance to temperature changes.

If you are considering becoming a caregiver for another person who is older, you need to consider these changes that have occurred as part of the aging process, as well as the physical and mental incapacities reported to you by the person's doctor. For the older person, coping with additional changes at this time in his or her life may be especially difficult. Yet most older persons cope quite well because these changes occur over time, allowing for preparation and adaptation. Caregivers can make the difference in a person's ability to accept a major change or to reject it.

Choosing a Caregiver

Whatever circumstance or disability has led to the consideration of one member of the family giving care to another, it is important that you and the other members of the family understand that caregiving is a *family* matter. Before the selection of the primary caregiver is made, the family needs to come together to make some very tough decisions that will affect every life—the care recipient's, the chosen caregiver's, and the lives of the other members of the family. Consider the range of feelings and emotions that are bound to be present at such a gathering.

The Care Recipient

Regardless of the extent of his or her incapacity, the care recipient is still human, with needs and dreams and angers and fears. He or she may be facing anywhere from a very limited to an almost total loss of independence, privacy, and freedom. This person needs to have the opportunity to express his or her feelings (if possible) about what is going to happen. The care recipient, regardless of his or her disabilities, is still a unique personality, and that individuality needs to be recognized and respected by the potential caregivers.

The Caregiver Candidate

The potential caregiver will possibly be called upon to make enormous personal and financial sacrifices for the care recipient, depending on the extent of the care needed. Such sacrifices may include giving up a career, moving the person into the caregiver's home, or cutting back considerably on an active and enjoyable social life. If the care recipient is a parent, the caregiver may find himself or herself in the dual role of parent and child to the same person. If the care recipient is an in-law, the caregiver may resent the intrusion of the spouse's parent. After a time the caregiver may have to deal with a range of feelings that can include guilt, resentment, and anger.

Some caregivers may mistakenly plan to take over the person's life totally, thinking it is an act of kindness to do so. But the most successful caregiver will be the one who works to help the care recipient maintain as much independence and control over his or her life as possible.

Other Family Members, Friends, and Neighbors

Other persons who may be indirectly or secondarily involved in the caregiving process may come forward at this time with lots of advice and statements that include the words *should* and *should not*. There may be numerous stories of others they know or once heard about in the same position. There will be friends and family who loudly proclaim their willingness to help in any way they can and others who will want to sweep the whole distasteful mess under the rug (or into the appropriate institution). These people should have their say, but it is the chosen primary caregiver and the care recipient who should have the final word.

Issues to Be Resolved

Once a decision has been reached about who is to assume the role of primary caregiver, there are other issues to be resolved. Where will the person live? What help from other people or from agencies in the community is the caregiver going to need? Who is going to pay for this? How can the person's ability to make sound judgments regarding his or her legal and financial affairs be determined? Who is going to see that a complete diagnosis of the person's problems is made? How is the caregiver going to get the training he or she needs to deal with those diagnosed incapacities? How much help is the care recipient going to need with just the basic routines of everyday living? How is the caregiver going to deal with those unpleasant feelings that are bound to arise out of the days and weeks and months of hard work? How is the caregiver going to find some time off—some time to take a break? How is the caregiver going to know when enough is enough and the time has come to stop being a primary caregiver?

Rewards of Caregiving

Caregiving is hard work, but it does not have to be unrewarding, sorrowful, or depressing. One caregiver whose father was in the advanced stages of Alzheimer's disease told me, "Someone needs to teach the public that *senility* doesn't mean 'gone' and that *caregiver* does not mean 'sentenced' or 'dead.'" In every caregiving situation there can be moments of incredible warmth and comfort and pleasure. Older people may have to deal with a number of losses, but they do not lose their sense of humor. They do not lose their individual personality traits. They remain people—with faults and feelings, ideas and opinions. The rewards of caregiving lie in keeping those unique qualities alive and functioning.

For some of you there will be no choice either because you are the only available candidate or because the role is cast upon you by others. Sometimes before you have even had a chance to define what you are doing as caregiving, you will already be deeply involved in the job. You may have to find alternative sources of support other than family and friends because you and the care recipient may have no other family close enough to offer support, and you may have gradually isolated yourselves from the rest of the community.

Whether or not you make a conscious choice to become someone's caregiver in even a limited way, it will help if you have a kind of Olympic spirit about the whole project—to decide at the outset that if you are going to take on the job, you are going to be the best caregiver you can be for that person and that when you are finished, you will have no regrets about how you did it. Some caregivers approach the job with dread, anger, and revulsion. They live day to day growing more depressed by their lot in life. The most successful caregivers are those who accept the role with the attitude that it is not the end of either their lives or the care recipients', who fight every day to maintain quality in their own lives and in the lives of those for whom they are caring, and who hold firmly to their sense of humor through days of pain and emotional punishment.

Until you have experienced the role, it is hard to comprehend the task ahead of you. After you get into the job, it may be very hard for other family members and friends to understand the complexities you face every day. Make no mistake. If you are considering becoming a primary caregiver, the job is hard, sometimes thankless, and certainly exhausting. But you can do it if you choose to do so for the right reasons. In taking on the job, you can be richly rewarded in terms of learning and developing a range of new skills as well as by establishing relationships with the care recipient and others that will continue to inspire and stimulate you long after your role as caregiver has ended.

Part One

❧

Should You Become a Caregiver?

People shrink from the idea: The day may come when independence for their parents will end, when their apartment must be closed up and a frail, elderly mother or father taken to a nursing home. . . . Everyone would like to postpone that day as long as possible. But how can grown children provide for parents who are ailing, who can no longer manage?
—Ellie King and Deborah Harkins

1 ✌ Life Sentence or Life Style?

It was Christmas, 1982. In the midst of hurrying and worrying and overspending I sighed aloud and wondered whatever happened to that fabled "spirit" of the season. Somewhere in the attic of my mind, I recalled an old Sunday school lesson equating that spirit to love. But the television commercials assured me that I could buy the spirit at the local shopping mall.

The last thing I needed to add to the growing list of things to be done before the Big Day was an interview with two eighty-year-olds. I had started to do research for a book about people caring for their older family members, and Fred W. had agreed to talk with me about his experiences in caring for Lillian. I had no idea that the hour I was about to spend with the couple was going to be the best of gifts to myself.

FRED AND LILLIAN

Their neighborhood was one of change—empty storefronts next to some vacant lots. For the most part the houses seemed to have seen better days, though they were neat and well kept. I rang the bell of the upstairs flat and waited. Fred answered the bell and led me up the well-lighted and carpeted stairway. The living room was immaculate and filled with good furniture. There were some antiques and some bare spaces where antiques had stood and been sold—not so much

11

for the money, Fred told me, as for the fact that they could no longer be cared for.

Lillian sat quietly near a large window. She was dressed in navy blue, which accented her soft white hair. She smiled shyly as I sat in the rocker across from her. Fred positioned himself on a sofa, choosing the end closest to Lillian. I noticed as we talked how his hand would sometimes reach over and rest on the arm of her chair, an unconscious gesture of tenderness I found more moving than actual handholding.

Fred and I talked of many things. Lillian listened and spoke only when directly addressed, yet Fred never treated her as if she were not there. He would include her always with a smile or a touch or a question that required her gentle nod or smile.

I asked how long they had been married, and Fred told me they were two years away from their sixty-fifth anniversary. "That," he informed me, "will be some celebration. Isn't that right, Mommy?" He calls her Mommy. They have no children. It is a nickname born out of some private joke or teasing many years ago.

Our conversation moved to more immediate, less pleasant concerns—health, finances, the future. Fred told of how he and Lillian had established their own health fund, having been denied insurance in the past. He told me how, at eighty-five, he still works part-time in his trade as a plumber. On those days Lillian attends an adult day-care center in the community. Fred mentioned that his eyesight is not what it once was and that he is not sure how long he will be able to work. The idea of not working depresses him.

He still drives, and he and Lillian do their own shopping and housework. They attend their neighborhood church when they can.

Fred's day begins at five, when he gets himself dressed and groomed and then showers, dresses, and grooms Lillian. The daily morning routine for caring for her medical equipment—a catheter made necessary by a paralyzed bladder, and a colostomy bag—takes a couple of hours. Fred is so thorough and particular about these procedures that Lillian's doctor once asked him to demonstrate his techniques for the office nursing staff.

Fred's greatest worry is that he will become incapacitated. In anticipation of this event, he has taken all precautions to assure that Lillian will be lovingly and properly cared for. He and Lillian have toured nursing homes and interviewed staff members and chosen the one Fred thinks will take the best care of his Lillian. Their home is hooked to a telephone security system; if Fred does not call in every morning by a certain time, the system calls a neighbor or the paramedics and police. Whenever he and Lillian travel, together or separately, each carries a small notebook with detailed instructions about medical care for Lillian's multiple problems.

Fred had words of high praise for their neighbor, a young mother in her thirties who works part-time at the neighborhood pharmacy. Every day she calls or visits Fred and Lillian. The two neighbors have worked out a light code for the evening. When Fred fails to light a lamp in their kitchen window, his neighbor seeks immediate help. She has a key to their house and all the emergency information. A few months before my visit they had had a chance to test their system when Fred fainted one evening and had to be taken to the hospital for several days. Because of Fred's careful planning, Lillian had only one thing to fret about—not her medical care or personal care but when Fred would be home.

I asked Fred and Lillian if they had one holiday or special gift that stood out in their minds. Fred thought for a long time and finally, with a shrug, mentioned a ruby and diamond brooch he had given Lillian once. It was the only piece of really fine jewelry they had ever been able to afford. He glanced at Lillian. Their pale blue eyes met, and she gave him a girlish smile. In that moment I knew how truly unimportant that brooch had turned out to be when held next to the decades they had shared together.

It was time to leave. I had work to do. Fred wanted to get Lillian ready for lunch out and a visit with an old friend. Fred gave me a strong handshake—the hand-shake of a man used to hard work and responsibility. I turned to Lillian. I had noticed that sometimes her realities were confused, her memories dim, but one thing she was very clear about—the love and devotion of her Fred.

As Fred and I walked down the stairs, he repeated his praise of their neighbor. "I don't know how she does it, all that patience and care. She is such a giver. I don't think I could ever do what she does."

I was dumbfounded and turned to protest. But I did not say anything. Not about the rising at five every morning. Or about the cooking and cleaning and laundry and medical care. And not about the constant worry and responsibility. No, I did not say anything. Fred would not see things that way.

There is an old saying about how love is not love until you give it away. When I left Fred and Lillian, I knew that love and the spirit of giving had a lot to do with each other.

In many ways this book started with Fred and Lillian and that morning I spent in their front room. Fred was the first caregiver I had met. Because of his devotion and zeal to excel as a caregiver, he was a hard act to follow for the dozens of other caregivers I was to meet over the next two years, as I did research for this book. I talked to husbands caring for wives and wives caring for husbands. I met daughters and daughters-in-law caring for mothers and/or fathers. I met sisters who cared for brothers and sisters who cared for sisters. I met sons—some widowed or divorced—caring alone for their aging parents.

The range of medical problems was broad—multiple sclerosis, Parkinson's disease, Alzheimer's disease, stroke, arthritis, diabetes, heart disease, depression, and drug dependency. Some of the people I met were short-term caregivers—caring for a loved one who was recovering from an acute illness or accident such as a broken hip. Others were caregiving by long distance, like the son in Texas who flew to and from Wisconsin weekly to attend to his eighty-year-old mother. Some were the primary caregiver for a few hours each day, bringing in meals, checking up on the person, and then going home. Most were the full-time, twenty-four-hour-a-day variety. Their willingness to share their stories and methods of coping is the backbone of the coming chapters.

ALICE AND ED

Alice stands about five-one and weighs around a hundred pounds. She is sixty-nine years old, but her untinted hair is the color of copper. She loves long walks, good music, and plants. Ed is over six feet, more than two hundred pounds, and seventy-four. He is confined to a wheelchair for the rest of his life. He can barely speak. He has Parkinson's disease. They have been married for nearly fifty years. Their son and daughter are both married and live in other cities.

Alice remembers how it started. "About ten years ago he started to make excuses for staying home whenever we were to do anything. 'You go, Alice,' he would say. It wasn't like him at all. He was a man who loved activity and people. He never missed a home football game and daily walked five or six miles with me."

She thought that perhaps his early retirement depressed him. She thought it might be a recurrence of an earlier problem with a bladder infection. But the doctors could find nothing. And then one day Ed could not straighten his neck. His chin hung low on his massive chest. At night he asked for two pillows to support his frozen neck.

They sought therapy for the stiffened muscles. The therapist advised using hot packs and only one pillow at night. "It will relax on its own," he told them, and Ed's neck did. Without the extra pillow Ed's neck slowly straightened as he lay in bed. They were relieved, but within days they were told that a diagnosis of Parkinson's disease had been made. There was medication, but a side effect could be urine retention. Ed had an old bladder disorder that made him especially prone to infection. Medication to treat his parkinsonism was going to be risky.

Over the next few years Ed's condition continued to deteriorate, and the job of caring for him became full-time and more. When a friend suggested that Alice find some help, she called the local chapter of the Visiting Nurse Association. Ed was still ambulatory, but Alice could see that the problem would only escalate. The VNA sent a nurse to the home, and that same nurse assisted Alice throughout Ed's illness.

The first thing the nurse did was to show Alice how to do range-of-motion exercises with Ed (see pages 131-132). Then she suggested that Ed be seen by a neurologist. He had tried the medication in spite of his chronic bladder problem but was having some serious side effects.

"I didn't like the neurologist," Alice said. "He wasn't interested in my questions. He just wanted to tell me what he thought. He prescribed a new medication for Ed. Well, I was always one to read up on things, so I read about this medicine. It was for severe arthritis and other things Ed didn't have at all, and the description also gave some pretty scary side effects. I gave Ed the medicine for a few weeks, but he got so dopey from it and the bladder problem didn't go away. Finally he was back in the hospital, off the medication but scheduled to have a catheter installed."

That was five years ago. Once Ed left the hospital, Alice's day began and ended with the routine of emptying the catheter bags and caring for the equipment that allowed Ed to relieve himself. The process takes time (anywhere from twenty minutes on up) to do on a mobile person. As Ed's mobility lessened, the time necessary for the daily routine care increased dramatically. No longer was there time for Alice to take her daily walk. Rarely could she get out for a concert or church meeting. Her day began and ended with Ed. In between she cooked and cleaned and paid the bills and fought with doctors for the best care she could get for her husband. She was often exhausted, frustrated, and lonely.

Ed was confused and bewildered by his illness, yet he rarely complained except to comment from time to time about his inability to do some seemingly simple task. He and Alice could still walk around the block, but it was a slow and tedious process. At home Ed had started to fall more often.

The nurse suggested that Alice get a Hoyer lift (see page 153), since she was alone much of the time and insisted on moving Ed from his wheelchair and bed to his favorite chair in the living room, where he could listen to his treasured classical records. That was not all Alice insisted on for Ed. Every day she dressed him completely, and she gave him a bath. She insisted on the same standards for herself. No robe and slippers for her, no hair uncombed. "It was a matter of respect and dignity," she told me.

After a visit Alice's children insisted that she hire an aide to come to the house twice a week. Alice gratefully accepted this help. When the aide came at eight two mornings a week, Alice escaped for a couple of hours to resume her beloved walks while the aide bathed, groomed, and dressed Ed and gave him his breakfast. There was another bonus to having the aide come. Twice a week Alice had another person to talk with and another person to help in the constant monitoring of Ed's condition, especially when his powers of communication failed.

Alice got other help. A couple from their church came once a month. The man stayed with Ed while the woman took Alice with her to the women's guild meetings at the church. Neighbors were sometimes helpful when Alice needed to have a chance to get away to the bank or for a dental or doctor's appointment of her own. Occasionally she was able to ask neighbors to pick up milk or some other grocery item, and on the weekend a niece would stay with Ed while Alice did the weekly shopping. "Groceries," she told me. "I didn't have time for other shopping."

But she could never count on these favors from others, and she spent the majority of her time alone with Ed. "We were always close, sharing the same interests. When he could no longer communicate with me, I would talk to him. I'd tell him everything about the church, the neighbors. We'd watch the news. I'd read him the paper. We'd listen to the music we both loved." Sometimes they were able to call a medical transport van and go to the doctor's or to some other appointment or meeting.

Through the years Alice developed some procedures for giving care to someone twice her size who was almost totally incapacitated. First, she organized the room where Ed slept. Everything she would need for their morning and evening routines was within reach either in the drawer of a nearby chest, under the bed, or on the nightstand. She started the day with the range-of-motion exercises and found that, because of his love of music, Ed seemed more responsive to the routine when she made up songs to accompany the motions. She used the same trick to get him to walk when he still could—chanting a rhythm to prod his response.

After the exercises Alice emptied the catheter bag and bathed Ed. She discovered that an empty plastic honey container had the exact-sized nozzle needed to place the vinegar and water solution in the catheter bag. Also, the honey bottle was easier to squeeze and held more of the liquid than the syringe normally used for the procedure. That completed, Ed and Alice went into their morning ballet of rolling him to and fro while she dressed him. Using the Hoyer lift, she moved him to his wheelchair and got him to the kitchen table for breakfast. By then it was ten or ten-thirty. Alice used the rest of the morning to clean, do laundry, and catch up on the financial and legal matters that needed her attention.

After lunch Alice would take Ed back to bed to

rest, getting him back up in the late afternoon to watch the news or listen to music. Then dinner, some television or music, an evening snack, and the night routine of getting Ed ready for bed. To be certain Ed was getting the proper amount of fluids, Alice would get him ready for bed and then give him two glasses of water from a special cup with a spout that made it easy for him to drink lying down. She had discovered the cup at her local pharmacy. Her day ended alone as she returned to the living room to read the paper, have her own evening snack, and just unwind before going to bed.

"And then," she said, "I'd get up and do it all over again." She said it with a gentle laugh and no resentment, but she assured me that there had been many days when she had dreaded facing the exhausting routine and the loneliness and isolation that permeated her life.

About a year ago Alice learned of a care co-op—a volunteer group of people who would come into the home and care for a disabled person when there was a sole caregiver for that person, thus affording the caregiver a few hours or even a whole day of respite. Alice called and started having a volunteer come to the house. Then she was able to spend one day a week for herself. After years of caring for Ed, she now had the time to see a movie or get her hair done or window-shop. She began to wonder why she had never allowed herself a day off before.

And then it was over. Ed ate dinner one night, sat in his chair, and then was put in his bed. But this night Alice heard him moaning softly as she sat with her paper and snack. She called their doctor, who told her to get Ed to the hospital. After a long night of tests, Ed seemed to be resting comfortably. Alice sat with him through the morning. Just before leaving, she leaned close and sang one of their favorite songs to him. Then, at the staff's insistence, she went home to rest. An hour later she got the call to return. By the time she got there, Ed was gone.

"Afterward, at first I would remember him the way he was at the end, and then I would start thinking about him when he was himself and we'd always do things together. It was sort of a confusion—almost like two people, like I had lost him twice."

Since Ed's death Alice has filled her days with answering the letters and cards of their many friends and relatives. She has had a multitude of details to handle in the settling of the estate and has been grateful for these distractions. A few months after Ed's death as she was beginning to have large blocks of time once devoted to Ed and now without purpose, she received a letter from a group asking if she would be available to testify before a state commission appointed to review the rights of the disabled.

In her usual determined way Alice set about finding out all she could about the state and federal policies on those matters that would be discussed by the commission. She called her state legislator and congressperson. She spoke with local health experts and providers of home care services. She testified to that commission and went on to become more actively involved in efforts to get greater benefits on both local and national levels for care recipients and caregivers. Alice found these activities therapeutic as she adjusted to life after full-time caregiving.

BETTY, GEORGE, AND BEA

Betty and George have four children ages fourteen to twenty who live at home. Down the block lives George's seventy-eight-year-old mother, Bea. Bea has Alzheimer's disease. A year ago she was working as a volunteer in the community and enjoying spending time with her children and grandchildren. To Betty and George she seemed fine. They did notice some slight disorientation and forgetfulness but chalked up those experiences to the simple "normal" changes of the aging process.

Before her husband's death, Bea and her husband

had managed a very successful business in another state. After his death she had moved to the town where George lived to watch her grandchildren grow up. She always appeared in control; she was loving, giving, and kind. A quiet, introverted person, Bea seldom allowed anything to upset her and often hid her feelings. Perhaps that is why it was several months before George and Betty realized something was different.

They saw her several times a week, taking her to dinner or shopping or to some school function in which one of the grandchildren took part. On these occasions she was sociable and seemingly fine. Then one Sunday when they were all at her home for dinner, she served an apple pie for dessert. While George raved about his mother's prowess at baking apple pies and marveled that after all these years she had attempted one, Bea smiled and cut the pie. Eagerly they all dug in. Betty and George tried to hide their discomfort when with the first bite they realized Bea has used salt instead of sugar, but the children were not so diplomatic. "Yuk!" exclaimed their youngest and spit his bite out onto the plate. "That's the worst stuff I ever tasted." There was silence around the table, and all eyes focused on Bea.

Cornered, she burst out, "It isn't my pie. That woman across the street came and took my pie and left this. She hates me—always has men in her house, and she knows I call the police on her, which is only right . . ." By this time she was raging around the room.

"Mom," George said softly as he tried to reach out to her.

"Get away from me," Bea shrieked. "Who are you people? I don't know you. Get out of my house before I call the police."

The incident was isolated. Nothing so dramatic had ever happened before. Nothing close to it happened again. George and Betty got Bea to the doctor the next day. After several days of tests, the tentative diagnosis came back—Alzheimer's. The doctor told George and Betty that Bea could probably continue to live alone with some support. He suggested that Betty visit frequently and that Bea be included in as much of George and Betty's family life as possible.

At first Bea seemed to do fine. She continued to prepare most of her own meals, clean her own home, and maintain most of her contacts with friends and neighbors. She seemed fine, and Betty and George began to hope that perhaps the diagnosis had been wrong. Then when she visited, Betty began to notice seemingly unimportant details—things that by themselves would have been forgotten, even laughed about. But these insignificant incidents grew too numerous to laugh about.

The first thing Betty noticed was that Bea's home seemed to be in constant disarray—nothing drastic, just as if someone had been looking for something. Then Betty would find certain items misplaced in inappropriate areas. Bea's sweater turned up in the freezer one day, the house keys were found in the laundry chute, and Bea's eyeglasses were finally found, after a long search, in the bottom of a flowerpot.

One day, while helping Bea do the laundry, Betty noticed strange stains on the underarms of Bea's blouse. She sniffed and touched and discovered that Bea had used toothpaste under her arms instead of deodorant. Betty also became aware that some of Bea's actions had changed—she paced all day and often called George and Betty in the middle of the night for no apparent reason. Betty began to spend more and more time at the home of her mother-in-law. When Betty was not actually there, she was worrying about Bea and what she might be doing.

At night Bea would watch for George's car to pull into her son's driveway. Barely before he had had time to get inside the house, the phone would ring. Bea would be calling to talk with her beloved son. On weekends George would take both Betty and Bea to the shopping mall. "Arm in arm the two of them would walk through the mall, window-shopping and laughing," Betty said. "I felt like a third wheel. My kids say Dad's just trying to give me some relief since I'm with her all week, but I get green-eyed all the same. There is no time for me. Between running back and forth to her house and taking care of George and the kids, there just is nothing left over for me. Once I asked one of the kids to stay home in case Bea would call so George and I could go to a movie, and George said, 'Can't we take Mother?' Doesn't he see that I need him too?"

Sometimes when Betty would visit her, Bea would ask to be taken home. Betty thought she was asking to move in with them—a move she wanted to postpone for as long as possible. But gradually she came to understand that what Bea meant was the home where she had lived as a child. Sometimes she would ask where her parents were and when they were coming to get her. When her mother-in-law's erratic behavior began to cause problems of sleeplessness and nervousness in Betty's own health, the doctor suggested that George and Betty join the local support group for Alzheimer's families.

Once in a great while Bea would come to Betty and tell her how confused she felt. "Why can't I remember? You just told me that, didn't you?" There were other moments when she seemed especially lucid and aware of her illness and Betty's and George's care. "I call that the teasing part of the disease," Betty said, "those moments when I am sure she's all right and the whole diagnosis was some terrible mistake. And then something totally new will happen like last week when she wandered out of her house in the middle of the night and the police called us. I was so embarrassed. I can see it coming—the day when she won't be able to live alone. Then what?"

Betty has a part-time job that allows the family to afford some of the extras they enjoy such as weekends in the country and movies and dinner out now and then. Betty is beginning to realize from the support group that caring for someone who has Alzheimer's can be more than a full-time job for more than one person. Betty does not want that job, though she understands that she will be the logical candidate when the time comes. Because Bea is from another city, her only close contacts where she now lives are her son's family and one or two neighbors. Betty could hardly expect the neighbors to care for Bea. Betty is beginning to understand that she should start planning now for her role as a full-time caregiver—planning that will protect Betty's right to a life of her own.

Already she is beginning to familiarize herself with community services that will help her in her caregiving role. When she insisted that the family get away for a long weekend without Bea, the leader of the support group suggested she call nursing homes in the area until she found one willing to have Bea stay with them for a few days. Betty helped Bea pack and move into her room at the home. Betty posted labels around the room—on the bathroom door, on the closet door, next to the call bell. She installed a night-light and taped to the door a large calendar that would allow Bea to check off the days until their return. She placed photographs of George and the grandchildren on the dresser and hung Bea's favorite robe in the closet. Then she sat down with the nursing home staff and gave them detailed information about dealing with Bea.

She could see that Bea was unhappy with this move, but Betty told her mother-in-law gently but firmly that she and George needed time away for a few days, that they would be back as her calendar indicated, and that Bea would be well taken care of by the nursing home staff. She did not allow George to accompany her to the nursing home and assured him that his mother was fine when they left on their trip. She knew that if George had seen his mother's sad face, he would have capitulated and insisted that she come along with them.

When Betty returned, she found Bea relieved to see her. During the week that followed, she learned that Bea had some pleasant associations with her weekend at the nursing home. Betty knew that she had done the right thing. She had needed the break from the constant monitoring of her mother-in-law's activities and from the knowledge that the day would come when

Bea would have to live with Betty and George. George had seen that it was possible to have a family life that did not always include Bea and still be a good son.

"How are you ever going to be able to manage?" Betty's friends ask her when they discuss the possibility of Bea's coming to live in Betty's house.

"Bea gives a lot back in spite of her illness," Betty tells them. "Because of caring for Bea and learning about her problems, I am changing. I look at life differently. I'm more organized, and even though I'm doing more and I'm often exhausted, I am feeling better about myself and my ability to cope with almost anything."

"But what about you? What about your life—your rights now that the kids are almost grown and you and George are about to have some time for yourselves?" her friends persist.

"Let's face it," Betty says. "I don't want to do this. It's not what I would have chosen for these years, but as I tell the kids, life isn't always fair. Bea was always there for us—she and George's father and my folks denied themselves plenty so that we could have a better life than they did. It's scary, and sometimes I really resent the whole idea that I might have to sacrifice my life in order to care for her, but there simply is no one else."

These are three of hundreds of thousands of stories of one human being's caring for another. Some, like Fred, do it almost totally alone with little help from family or friends. Fred is lucky to have one neighbor who is willing to take an active role in Lillian's care. In caring for Ed, Alice often found that her neighbors could not be counted upon to be there when she needed them, though they professed a willingness to help. Her children lived out of town and so could not share in the care of their father and support of their mother. Betty is one of thousands of women today who are caught between raising their own children and caring for their parents and in-laws. She will have to make major sacrifices in her own life to care for her mother-in-law.

Need for Caregivers

In an article entitled "The Oldest Old," Alan J. Otten of the *Wall Street Journal* writes, "Men and women 85 and over constitute the fastest-growing age group in the U.S. It is these 'oldest old' . . . who pose the major problems for the coming decades. It is they who will strain their families with demands for personal care and financial support."

According to Mr. Otten's research, families of four generations are already commonplace in American society, thanks to modern science and its strides toward treatment for once major killers such as stroke, cancer, and heart disease. One day a cure, or at least a remission treatment, for Alzheimer's disease may be found, adding even more years to life expectancy. The number of persons who will be called upon to give care to another will continue to increase as life expectancy expands.

Female family members who once dropped out of the labor force to care for their children are now dropping out to care for an aging parent or spouse. And others who intended to rejoin the labor force after rearing their children may never have that opportunity because they are needed as caregivers. The lower birthrate will show up in years to come with fewer citizens of working and tax-paying age to share the burden of the costs of caregiving for the aged. These three factors will increase the financial strain many families in the United States are already beginning to experience in their later years. Still, despite stereotypes to the contrary, Americans are rising to the need. Statistics show that most frail older persons live outside of an institution and that the primary caregiver and financial supporter is a family member.

But what happens when the primary caregiver becomes ill or disabled as in the case of a seventy-five-year-old woman who is caring for her ninety-six-year-old mother or the seventy-year-old man caring for his wife? For years the caregiving process has been intergenerational—the children or grandchildren have assumed the role of primary caregiver. Still, as this society ages, people are going to have to seek innovative programs and ideas for giving care and give equal attention to finding support and respite for the caregiver.

Writing Your Own Story

If you are considering becoming a primary caregiver for another person, you are about to write your own unique story. Some of you will find that there are others who are not only willing to help but who will be there for you and the person you are caring for in concrete, supportive ways. Others will find that within your communities there are agencies whose services can make your job as a primary caregiver easier in the absence of supportive friends, neighbors, and family members. And some of you—hopefully, a minority—will find that you are doing it alone with little or no outside support and often with unwanted interference from other family members who, while unwilling to take on the role of primary caregiver, are not unwilling to offer constant advice on how you can do the job better.

Sometimes your days will seem to be filled with exhaustion, frustration, and stress. Sometimes there will be moments when the whole situation seems ridiculously funny. And sometimes there will be moments of tears— moments when you remember the person in better days when his or her health was intact, moments when you cry for joy with the person as the smallest step toward improvement or remission is made.

You will share one part of your caregiving story with every other man and woman who has walked the same road. *You will be a different person for the experience.* You will get to know yourself and your capabilities and tolerance very well, and you will begin to look at your own life and the lives of others in a very different and unique way.

2 ❧ Getting to Know the Person Who Needs Care

The role of the caregiver is not necessarily to give *total* care. Frequently the person will need only minimal support. Sometimes the caregiving role will be one of coordinating services from the community that will allow the person to remain independent. At other times the person will be living with you or relying heavily on you and various community support services. However extensive your role may be, your first step, ideally even before you decide to take on the role of primary caregiver, is to find out as much as you can about the person who will need care. This, unfortunately, is a luxury few primary caregivers will have. More often a crisis will precipitate the need for care, or the caregiver will be selected on the basis of being the only one available or the logical person to do the job. However, if there is time before the actual caregiving begins to consider the person needing care as well as the extent of the care needed, by all means take the opportunity and make the most of it.

What Is Normal in the Aging Process?

Some changes in mental and physical capacity are common to aging persons. In general, as people age, they can expect a variety of diminished capacities—some that may occur all of a sudden, some that may occur in a limited way, and others that they may anticipate but that may never occur at all. For example, aging persons may expect their eyesight and hearing to diminish. For many, sight and hearing do weaken, but for some, these senses remain complete for all their lives. Likewise the circulatory, respiratory, and digestive systems may slow down, and bones and muscles may weaken (including those muscles that control bladder function). Mental health may be affected by the numerous losses and changes with which an aging person must cope; the person may become depressed or show signs of poor judgment, impaired memory, or confusion. Any or all of these capacities may be diminished, but it is a mistake to assume that changes in the performance of vital organs and systems of the body will be automatic. Such changes may never happen. Those that do may occur over a period of years, even decades. When vital organs and systems do begin to operate at a diminished capacity, there will be symptoms.

Hearing Changes

The most affected area will be sounds in the high-frequency range. Frequently an aging person will have trouble hearing conversations, especially if there is any sort of background noise. Strides are being made in the science of correcting hearing loss or improving hearing capacity that has been diminished. Encourage the person to check with his or her doctor. For further information about hearing loss, see pages 173-174 and page 175.

Sight Changes

Even slight visual impairments can be helped by making sure there is a regular examination of the person's vision. The caregiver can seek the advice of professionals about the possibility of correcting the person's visual impairment through surgery or medications and can make minor changes in the home and in his or her care for the person that can also aid the person's visual security. For more detailed information, see pages 173-175.

Changes in the Other Senses

As people age, the senses of touch, taste, and smell may also diminish, giving rise to some safety concerns.

For example, an older person may not be as sensitive to the smell of smoke or may be very sensitive to heat from a heating pad or even the sun. In the normal process of aging, a person's reaction time may become slower. Such slowing *may* mean that an older person will have some forgetfulness, will be less creative than he or she once was, and will take longer to find a solution to a problem.

The Circulatory, Respiratory, and Digestive Systems

Aging people may need more rest simply because less blood and oxygen may be getting into the bloodstream. It is very important to have blood pressure checked at least every six months and for the person to be examined by a doctor after any incidence of ankle swelling, shortness of breath, or chest pain. The digestive system may become more sensitive to the aging person's emotional state. Being depressed or upset may affect digestion.

Changes with Muscles and Bones

Because of illness or simply a reduced activity level, there may be some loss of bone mass and muscle tone in the aging process. The best way to control the rate of such loss is through regular exercise and diet. Inactivity can lead to faster deterioration and even more pain. Because of loss of muscle tone, older persons may experience a need to urinate more frequently, or constipation may be a problem. (See the discussion of incontinence on pages 121-123.) Loss of bone mass can lead to a serious condition known as osteoporosis (see pages 195-196).

Emotional Changes

Loneliness is one of the most frequent emotions experienced by aging persons, though there can be a range of emotional changes such as anger, unrealistic fears, and depression. Such loneliness can be caused by a multitude of problems including physical limitations, loss of friends and family, lost opportunities for socialization, and isolation within the home. Loneliness that gets no relief can turn into depression if the older person becomes withdrawn, apathetic, and negative.

Who Is the Care Recipient?

What is the personal history of the individual? What is the history of your relationship according to you? according to the person? What disabilities (mental and/or physical) does or will this individual have? What is the prognosis for the person? What are the possibilities for treatment or remission?

Of course, it is overwhelming. Deal with one question at a time. Write things down. You are going to have a lot to decide in a very short period of time and while under a great deal of stress. Do not try to rely on your memory. Keep a notebook or file and put things down about the person and yourself. List questions you want to ask the doctor or social worker (see page 172) and questions you need to ask yourself and the person (see pages 49-50 and 37). Be as thorough as possible.

Dan was an executive responsible for supervising many employees. He was an intelligent, loving, active man who, at the age of fifty-four, was diagnosed as having Alzheimer's disease. His wife is his primary caregiver. His two teenage children are his secondary caregivers. Dan is no longer able to work. His speech is nearly gone, and he rarely recognizes his friends.

Joan, fifty-eight, has multiple sclerosis. Until a month ago she could ambulate with a walker. Now she uses a wheelchair and is becoming incontinent. Her husband is her primary caregiver. Almost daily Joan loses another skill. Almost daily she and her husband shut the door on another part of their lives.

Sara is seventy-two and in the hospital again. Since her husband's death following a long illness nearly a year and a half ago, Sara's life has been out of control. She feels useless after being relieved of her full-time job as caregiver for her husband. Her children seem to run their own lives without needing anything from her. When she is not in the hospital, she lives alone in a small apartment. She has become reclusive and depressed. Her daughter is on call as her primary caregiver.

John, sixty-seven, is recovering from a stroke. While his mental capacities seem intact, his motor and speech skills have been damaged. John is scheduled for release from the hospital in two days. His wife is dead. His only child, a son, lives several hundred miles away and will become his long-distance primary caregiver.

These are four brief descriptions of a care recipient and his or her incapacity. Each identifies the primary caregiver. Try writing a similar description of your relative for your notebook or file.

Can you write ten things about the person (not bringing in anything about yourself) and allow only three of them to deal with the illness? For example, John's son might start by writing the following:

1. Dad is quiet and shy with a great sense of humor.
2. Dad is a very good grandfather.
3. Dad has always done his own cooking.
4. Dad's parents immigrated to the United States when he was four years old.
5. Dad is very frugal—stingy.

From these brief statements one can begin to see a human being rather than a medical problem.

Write ten statements about your relative for your notebook or file.

Here is another exercise that will help in further identifying the individual. Ask members of the family to come up with their own list of statements about the person. If possible, get the person to tell you about himself or herself. Use these questions as leaders for such an interview: When you were younger, what was your favorite thing to do? If you could be anything in the world, what would you be? Tell me what it was like for you when . . . (choose a time such as when the person was a teenager or during the Depression or during World War I or World War II). Listen carefully to the answers and observe the person as he or she responds.

You do not have to "do" anything with this information. Just store it all away in your file or notebook. What a person chooses to relate will be colored by the situation now. For example, a father might tell his son that the Depression was a terrible time "but at least I could work." Then he could work; now he cannot. It is a clue to help you understand the feelings the person is experiencing at the moment.

What Is the Care Recipient's History?

Think about the individual in terms of what has shaped his or her life. Did your father immigrate to this country? Under what circumstances? Was it to escape poverty? to avoid persecution? Did he come alone? with his parents? How did he deal with and how was he affected by the major historical events of his life—war, depression, unemployment? How was his work affected? How was his economic status affected?

Now think about the person's private life. What do you know of your mother's parents? childhood? siblings? What was school like for her? How much education does she have? What about her marriage? How was she at being a parent in your eyes? in her eyes? What were her dreams and disappointments? How does she normally react to change? to illness? to children? to emergencies?

There is a great deal to think about and probably not a lot of time to think. You can hardly expect to get to know this person in depth if you have barely known him or her for twenty or forty or sixty years. Here are a couple of exercises that may help.

In a notebook write ten statements about your relative's past before you knew that person. Base your statements on what the person has told you about that past and on what you know about the person's past from others.

Are there any areas of conflict such as money or religion you can see already that may cause a problem in your relationship? For example, if the person's way of life is to think everything through three times before acting and you are prone to action first and thought later, that is a potential problem. Do you see any other situations where the two of you may be in conflict? List them. Put that list in your notebook or file along with your profile of your relationship with this individual.

What Is the History of Your Relationship?

Write the answers to these questions in your notebook or file.

1. How long have you known the person?
2. How often have you been together over the past five years?
3. If you were a child when you first knew the person, how has your relationship changed now that you are an adult?
4. If you could change just one thing about the person, what would it be?
5. What do you think the relative would change about you?
6. Do you look forward to the times you are together? Who dominates those times? Are both of you comfortable with that?
7. Have there been any major conflicts in the history of your relationship according to you? according to the relative? For example, did the person object to your choice of lifestyle? If there have been major conflicts, how have you resolved them? Were both of you happy with that solution?
8. Do the two of you respect and trust each other?

Your past relationship with the person can offer many clues for your future relationship. Generally speaking, you can expect that both of you will deal with the frustrations of this change in your lifestyles in the same way you have dealt with such matters in the past. This, however, is not carved in granite. Dan's wife found that her gentle, intelligent, loving husband turned into an angry, critical, and agitated man who lashed out both verbally and physically at her and their children.

When the individual's lifestyle is first beginning to change, you may see more dramatic changes in behavior than later. A lot may be happening to him or her, and often the person feels out of control. Even the most docile person may reach a point of saying, "No more." And the person you thought could cope with anything may suddenly surprise you.

Sara, who was known to her children as an independent, take-charge lady, became a clinging and frightened shell of that person when faced with the dramatic changes in her lifestyle following her husband's death. John is perfectly agreeable and polite to the social worker, the doctor, and any other outsider, but to his son he is resentful, paranoid, and bitter.

Is your relative meeting his or her crisis in the manner you might have expected? How does the way in which he or she has chosen to deal with the situation make you feel and why?

Is Medical Help Needed?

If you have not yet gotten a medical diagnosis of your relative's condition, prepare for your visit to the doctor by answering the following questions.

1. What has prompted your concern? What symptoms have you observed? What behavioral changes have you noticed?
2. Can you obtain complete copies of recent medical visits, tests, prescriptions, and evaluations?

3. Have you paid attention to what the person is saying about himself or herself, not just about physical complaints but about what is happening in his or her mind? Have there been expressions of worthlessness? thoughts about suicide? concern over memory loss?

4. Has there been any recent major loss or a series of minor losses for the person? Has the person recently retired, and, if so, how did he or she feel about that? Make sure you are looking at the person's feelings and not your own. Many people look forward to the day when they can stop work and do all the things they have dreamed of. Your loved one may have found that retirement is not the television holiday it is often projected to be.

5. Do you have confidence in your relative's doctor? Does your relative? Do you feel that the doctor will accept any information you bring and then act on it?

6. Does the person's doctor understand the aging process? Will he or she give the older person complete, competent care, or will the doctor chalk up changes to "aging" and not pay attention to conditions that might be cured or reversed?

7. Finally, are you prepared to ask the doctor the tough questions that are eating away at your imagination? Will she walk again? Can this be cured? Will he get better? Ask. If you are to be the primary caregiver for this person, you must have some idea of what you are facing before you can get ready to deal with it. See page 172 for specific questions to ask the doctor.

There are any number of impairments that may afflict an older person. Sometimes there will be more than one incapacity. Sometimes impairment will be both physical and mental. Do not try to make your own diagnosis. Some symptoms are common to many illnesses, and sometimes there is a cure or treatment and sometimes there is not. Plan to seek professional advice from the physician or social worker as soon as possible in the caregiving process so that you and your relative can know from the beginning what you can expect.

How Does the Care Recipient Feel About the New Relationship?

If the person needing care, whether the needed care is limited or total, is able, consider finding time to discuss the changes the relationship of caregiver and care recipient will make in both your lives. Asking the person some of the following questions may give you valuable insights into that person's feelings and ideas about the new relationship.

1. How do you feel about what is about to happen (for example, moving in with the caregiver or having the caregiver take an active role in the person's daily life)?
2. If you could choose anyone to be your caregiver for the next several months or years, would that person be me? Please be honest. Why or why not?
3. How do you feel about moving in with me and giving up your own home?
4. What are the emotions you are feeling when you think about the changes that are about to take place in your life? Anger? Fear?
5. Do you think we are making the right decisions about your needs now?
6. What do you expect your life to be like now? Will your friendships and social life be affected? Will you have to make sacrifices or changes that you do not want to make?

Not all of these questions will be relevant to every caregiver and care recipient. They are simply here to give you an idea of some of the topics that may need to be discussed. There are some questions that are applicable only to the caregiving situation where the person is about to move in with the caregiver. Keep in mind, however, that no matter how limited the needed care or support may be, it is important that you as the caregiver candidate try and understand the person's feelings about those changes that are about to take place in his or her life.

At this point it may be less important for you to have

detailed medical information than it is for you to try and solicit the feelings of the care recipient. The physician may underestimate or overdramatize the need for care, and you and the person may find out that there is more or less to the job only when you are well into it. Therefore, for now, concentrate less on gathering information about the illness and potential treatments and cures and more on diagnosing whether or not this other person and you can coexist in the same house or in separate homes as a person in need of care and support and the person who is expected to provide that care and support.

3 ❧ Making the Decision

Not every primary caregiver will be called upon to live with the care recipient or have that person move into his or her home. Sometimes the role of the primary caregiver will be limited to occasional long-distance phone calls or visits to see whether the care recipient is managing. In some cases the caregiver may be needed to drop in to help with one or more specific tasks such as shopping, balancing the checkbook, or monitoring medications. But how does someone *become* the primary caregiver for another person? Frequently the call for help comes suddenly, perhaps following a hospitalization. Decisions must be made within a number of days or even hours, and these are decisions that may alter the course of at least two and perhaps many more lives for years to come.

When a spouse becomes incapacitated, the partner may assume that there is no choice but to become the primary caregiver. Never mind that the couple has just seen their last child through college. Never mind that the two of them have finally earned the time to be together, to enjoy their golden years. For many the long-planned-for golden years turn into decades of grayness spent in one partner's caring day and night for the other. For others the opportunity to give comfort to a loved one in his or her last years is its own reward.

Occasionally an adult child (usually a daughter) will become the primary caregiver. There may be other brothers and sisters in the family, but because of the mobility of the United States population in recent decades, adult children may be scattered across the country at the time it becomes apparent that Mom or Dad can no longer live totally independently. In other cases all the children live nearby. Still, each sibling may have an excellent reason for not taking responsibility for the parent—finances, children of his or her own, inadequate time or space, an unwilling husband or wife. The list is endless. Usually there is one adult child who seems the natural candidate to assume the role of caregiver. Is it because this person is more nurturing? because he or she has training in caring for frail, aging people? More likely the choice will be made on the basis of such factors as geography, available space, and/or who will be the least inconvenienced. If there are no daughters (and in some cases where there are), a daughter-in-law often becomes the elected caregiver.

In almost every case where one person becomes dependent in even a limited way and someone else becomes a caregiver, everyone involved is called upon to face situations for which they have little or no training, information, or frame of reference. Most people are ill prepared to face the reality of their own mortality as mirrored in the faces of their parents or spouse. If failing health includes a dimmed mind or confusion, fears and aversion to the task may quadruple: "Will this happen to me?" "I couldn't remember where I left my glasses today. Yesterday I could not recall a name. *Is* this happening to me?" Some people are unable to deal with that.

In some families there are members who prefer not to deal with the future, especially if that future involves possible unpleasantness. Family members may say that they are prepared to "do whatever is necessary *when the time comes*," and others may believe that to prepare for such eventualities as nursing care or incapacity is to create a self-fulfilling prophecy for the individual. In their way of thinking, if Dad sees his children preparing for the possibility that he may someday become incapacitated, he will believe that such a possibility must be true and will indeed become incapacitated.

Other potential caregivers have the idea that any necessary services will be there when a catastrophe strikes and allow little or no time to arrange for these services. They believe that Mom will not be released from the hospital unless there is an adequate support system in the community ready to receive her.

Whether the family has months, weeks, or merely hours to make a decision, it is important for everyone to keep uppermost in mind the fact that what they decide may affect many lives for an undetermined period of time and that the chances are good that decisions made today will still be in effect several months or even years from now. Any situation that has an effect on the caregiver and the person who needs care must be considered. Does the caregiver have a family of his or her own? Does he or she work? Does he or she have retirement plans that will be severely limited by taking on the caregiver role? What about those others who are unable or unwilling to be the primary caregiver—what kind of role do they plan to play?

Before one can honestly debate the idea of whether or not to become a primary caregiver for a spouse or parent (or anyone else), it is essential that the individual gather as much information as possible. The potential caregiver should have an honest, no-holds-barred conversation with the person who needs care (if possible) and with anyone else who will be a part of the process either directly or indirectly. This includes the person's doctor, the hospital social worker, and any members of the family who may act as secondary caregivers.

Caregiver Candidates

The potential caregiver needs to examine his or her past and present relationship with the person who needs care. Research has shown that both the caregiver and the person can be expected to react to stress and crises in the same way they always have even if the care recipient is mentally impaired. If stress has caused the person to rant and rave and throw things in the past, it would be unrealistic to expect that the person would be able to handle a crisis in a calm, rational manner.

Consider the marriage where the husband has been the chief breadwinner, check writer, decision maker. If that man has a brain-damaging stroke or becomes afflicted with Alzheimer's disease, his wife will probably find herself taking on his roles in addition to her own plus the new and unfamiliar role of caregiver. Still, her husband's personality traits honed on his years of multiple responsibilities during their marriage will not suddenly disappear. He probably will not become a docile, accommodating follower. On the contrary, frightened by his awareness that something terrible is happening to his mind, he may fight back by becoming demanding and aggressive. He may manifest his personality through constant worry and pacing. He may repeatedly try to return to a job he no longer holds in an effort to regain some control over his life.

A daughter who has waged a lifelong battle with her mother to run her own home and raise her children in her own way may find her whole world turned upside down if Mom moves in. Mom, displaced from her own household where she was in charge, may try to stay in the background, but if it has been her nature to take charge, to do things her own way, she may soon almost unconsciously start to try to gain a foothold in her daughter's home. "I just want to help," she may say and be quite sincere, but in fact she is at a loss to deal with the feelings of anger, sadness, and loss she feels at having to be taken in by her daughter.

If the daughter has a family of her own, she may find herself torn in two or three different directions. Her children will have major adjustments to make if they are still living at home, and their initial joy at having a favorite grandparent come to live with them may soon fade if that grandparent becomes critical of their behavior, friends, or music. Daughter's husband will also have an adjustment to make—the adjustment of having to share his family with someone else. He may bury resentments about money, privacy, or space and manifest them in other ways such as impatience with the children or spending more time at work.

When the primary caregiver is a daughter-in-law,

there are other possible conflicts to consider. If the care recipient is her mother-in-law, the caregiver may experience the old rivalry that can sometimes exist when two women have cared for and loved the same man over a period of time. The way in which the daughter-in-law and her mother-in-law or father-in-law have coped with their relationship through the years of good health could affect how things will go in situations of adversity such as when the daughter-in-law is called upon to give limited or full-time care to her husband's parent. She may resent having to care for this person who is part of her family only through marriage. She may feel angry at the need to postpone dreams and aspirations she and her husband and children have looked forward to. Often in-laws do not see very much of one another through the years of the marriage, or they have not established workable patterns for communicating their feelings with one another— especially if those feelings are in any way unpleasant such as anger, jealousy, or resentment.

Such conflicts (between daughters and parents or daughters-in-law and husbands' parents) may not be solved but can certainly be anticipated if there are open and frank discussions at the beginning. Adult children who expect to bring parents into their homes to live must forget the television ideal of Grandma as some modern cheery fairy godmother. A woman who has worked outside the home all her adult life may not suddenly become a baker of chocolate chip cookies and a teller of stories to her grandchildren. A grandfather used to running the affairs of a large corporation or used to hiring others to make repairs around his own home may not suddenly become a man who is content to spend hours puttering around the basement workshop or out in the garden.

The dependent parent will feel displaced, lonely, and in the way regardless of how welcome you make him or her. The person may be up at all hours of the night, become progressively more frail, and act out fears and angers in ways that are embarrassing for the caregiver. An adult child who is about to become a caregiver needs to total the anticipated costs—physical, psychological, and financial. In their book, *When Your Parents Grow Old,* Jane Otten and Florence Shelley offer some very good advice: Never ask a parent if he or she would like to live with you unless you are fully prepared for the answer to be yes.

Outside Pressures

Pressures to "do the right thing" are very strong in the United States. Adult children are told that they owe their parents reparations for their years of sacrifice and self-denial in rearing them. And they do respond. As of 1981 approximately 20 percent of America's aging population lives with their children, and fully one-third of older Americans can and do depend on relatives to help when they become ill. However, it is unrealistic and self-defeating to expect adult children to "repay" parents with care similar to that which they received in childhood—aging parents are not similar to children.

Another social pressure is the one on institutionalization. According to society, this is to be the absolute last resort—to be used only after all else has been tried and abandoned. The message that placing one's loved one in a nursing home or other institutional setting implies that the caregiver must have failed is one of America's most unjust myths. There comes a time in any situation when, far from failure, the act of placing a loved one in a long-term nursing facility for either skilled or custodial care may be the greatest act of love left to the caregiver and other family members. However, the idea that America's older population is being warehoused in institutions is a gross misrepresentation. Research shows that throughout the country adult children and older spouses are taking care of their own, often under incredible conditions of hardship, red tape, and self-denial.

In addition to guilt trips imposed by society, there are land mines within the indirect relationships that surround the caregiving situation. A caregiving husband may find that his adult children, while unwilling to assume responsibility for their ailing mother themselves, will be critical and skeptical of his methods of meeting the challenge. An adult child who has assumed the role of caregiver for a parent or in-law may find himself or herself constantly under the microscope by one or more siblings. Even the two people most involved in this new relationship, the caregiver and the care recipient, carry their own sets of emotional baggage into the relationship. The person who needs care may be repressing feelings of guilt at having burdened the caregiver and may fear speaking out because he or she thinks that may result in institutionalization. The caregiver (especially if the prime motive for assuming the role was a sense of duty or obligation) may be suppressing resentment at the apparent freedom of the others in the family and at the stress caused by the situation and, therefore, by the person needing care.

When the Person Needing Care
Is a Spouse

A caregiving spouse may be drawn immediately into the role with little thought or planning based on the idea that there is no other choice. The for-better-or-for-worse syndrome leaves little room for choice. Societal pressures are strong. Suppression and denial of feelings such as anger, fear, bitterness, and depression could become second nature for the caregiving spouse who believes such feelings are wrong.

Another problem of one spouse caring for another may be the simple fact of age. When one aging adult cares for another, there may be the dual stress of the care recipient's health and the caregiver's health. (This can also happen in the parent/child relationship, especially if the parent is over eighty and the child is in his or her sixties.) Spousal caregivers may find themselves experiencing the reactions of a widow or widower. Indeed many of those interviewed for this book expressed just such feelings, calling the act of caregiving, especially for an Alzheimer's victim, "a never ending funeral." In such situations long-standing patterns of intimate response, such as touching and holding each other, as well as private humor between loved ones may simply no longer exist, leaving the caregiver with an almost overwhelming sense of abandonment.

The caregiving spouse as well as the caregiving adult child faces this new role at a time when his or her own life may be going through a number of changes—retirement, physical impairments, financial shifts, reduction in social position, inability to move about, and even housing. These are all normal later-life changes.

One myth is that "senility" is a normal later-life change. Nothing could be further from the truth. *Senile* is a term frequently used by society to cover a range of mental illnesses or disabilities. The word literally means "old" and refers only to the fact that a person is older or aging. What most people mean when they use the word *senility* is in fact "senile dementia," a condition associated with a collection of symptoms including forgetfulness and confusion often wrongly identified as senility (see chapter 11). In addition to senile dementia, there are other forms of dementia that can result in mental deterioration or mental impairment.

When mental impairment, such as sometimes occurs following a stroke or such as that experienced by someone who has Alzheimer's disease, is a part of the caregiving package, the process may be complicated. A spouse may relinquish cherished roles of friend and lover to become an almost impersonal nursemaid in some cases. Long-standing problems in the marriage that have been postponed over the years may be exacerbated by the paranoia often exhibited by mentally impaired persons. Friends may drop away, and family may be overwhelmed by a once articulate, vibrant, loved one who is now unable to put together a complete sentence.

The caregiving spouse may be totally ignorant of available benefits and services that will ease the caregiving task load, and, if both the caregiver and the care recipient are older, may be tied to the house because of an inability to drive or a fear of getting out.

When the Person Needing Care
Is a Parent or In-law

In the situation in which the caregiver is an adult child and the care recipient is a parent or in-law, there is an added burden. In a parent-child relationship it is rare when the two people have attained equality as one adult to another. The parent-child relationship may remain intact regardless of the ages of the two people involved. This inequality can make caregiving even more difficult.

The caregiving adult child must also consider factors such as his or her own spouse and children, a career that may be interrupted or forfeited for the caregiving responsibility, and a personal life that is separate from the personal life of the care recipient. In most cases in which an adult child becomes a caregiver for a parent or in-law, both parties have been living separate lives for many years.

When an adult child becomes the primary caregiver, he or she may have a picture of the parent who needs care as an individual who has few needs and who is basically independent. In fact, the parent may have many fears, anxieties, and depressions, all of which may come suddenly to the fore when that person is placed into this new role of being dependent in even a limited way on someone.

Frequently adult children who are caregivers are surprised to find that these parents who have always seemed strong and self-sufficient can be very tentative and/or demanding. The picture the adult child may retain is the portrait of that parent at a younger age when the parent was more or less in charge of not only his or her own life but the child's as well. When the parent suddenly starts to ask the adult child for advice and guidance, the child may be put off by what seems to be a sudden reversal in roles.

Family Interaction

In the process of deciding whether or not to become a caregiver, an adult child may have to deal with siblings whose interest in the situation ranges from none to suffocating. Caregiving spouses may find that they are having to negotiate power struggles between their grown children at a time when their total focus needs to be on what is best for the person who needs care. Ego may play against ego. Sibling rivalries and familial power plays will surface. To be sure, choosing a caregiver is a family affair, and certainly everyone directly or indirectly involved needs the opportunity to have his or her say—even if there are tears, angry outbursts, and much gnashing of teeth.

However, once the assignment has been made, it is time for those indirectly involved to step back and allow the primary caregiver to get on with the job. Other family members need to be supportive in any way they can but also need to accept the caregiver's lead and take their cues from him or her. Advice and ideas can be shared, but always this sharing should take place in an atmosphere of support rather than one of criticism.

Making the Choice

How does one finally reach the decision to accept the role of primary caregiver for another adult? Start by asking yourself the questions that follow. If possible, allow yourself plenty of time and privacy to form your answers. Write the answers down and answer each question with all the honesty and soul-searching you can muster. This is the time to admit to yourself once and for all that you find your father-in-law's voice loud and abrasive and decide whether, if he is going to live with you, (1) there is any possible way you can change him or (2) you honestly believe you could overlook it and get used to it every day for the next several years. This is the time to consider honestly whether it is possible to work, continue your role in rearing your family, *and* drive back and forth to your mother's house twice a day to give limited care.

By putting your answers in writing, you actually are forcing yourself to voice your complete thoughts on each question. Do not form your answers with the thought that you have no choice but to become the primary caregiver. That may very well be the bottom line, but for the purposes of this self-examination, assume that should you reach the conclusion you definitely are not caregiver material, there will be other options.

1. What is the relation of this person to you?
2. What physical and/or mental disabilities does this person have at this time, as far as you know?
3. How do you feel about the person's disabilities as you understand them? Are any of them repulsive to you? If so, do you think you might learn to accept them?
4. Has the person's physician given you any idea of how quickly the person's health may decline?
5. Have you thought about the fact that the person's condition is likely to deteriorate? Have you thought about how much time it is likely to take to care for this person now and in the future when the condition worsens?
6. How long do you expect the caregiving to last? (Be specific.) What do you anticipate will happen to end it? (Be realistic.)
7. Where will the person live? Will anyone be required to move? From one town to another? Within the town? From one room to another?
8. Whether the person will live with you or in his or her own home, what do you anticipate will be the inconveniences of the living arrangement?
9. Will the person you may be caring for have to make changes in his or her life that will mean moving away from familiar friends and places? Is the person likely to feel lonely or isolated?
10. What are the financial arrangements for caring for this person?
11. Will the person have special needs regarding such things as diet and clothing?
12. What is the person like? How well does he or she cope with stress? with change?
13. Whom do you think the person wants to have act as

his or her caregiver? If that person is not you, why is it not possible for that other person to become the primary caregiver?

14. Have you and the person resolved any major differences you may have had with each other in the past? If so, how did you resolve them—by arguing, by giving in, or by not talking about them? How will you resolve problems in the future especially if the two of you are to live together?

15. How do you feel about this person? Can you name three traits this person has that you like? that annoy you? Which three traits were easier to come up with?

16. How good are you at placing yourself in another person's shoes—at understanding another person's feelings?

17. How well do you cope with stress and change? Do you have a good sense of humor? How is your patience? your flexibility?

18. What are your current responsibilities? Which of these cannot be changed? Which of these will have to be sacrificed?

19. Is your life enough in order to allow you to take on the responsibilities of caring for another adult?

20. Will caring for the person require a good deal of physical strength? Do you have that strength? (For example, if the person uses a wheelchair, will you have to lift the person into and out of the wheelchair?)

21. Why are you doing this—considering becoming someone's caregiver? (Try to write down every reason you have for taking on this responsibility.)

22. What are good reasons you have for *not* taking on this responsibility?

Involving Others

Before you make the final decision to become another adult's primary caregiver on any level, limited or total, meet with those other members of the family or household who will be involved in any way in the caregiving process. Your spouse, children, siblings, and anyone else who will be a part of the relationship need to take part in this meeting. If you are single, living alone, and with no family, it would be wise to arrange a similar meeting with a trained counselor—your clergyperson, the hospital social worker, or a family counselor—and perhaps a few close friends. At this stage you may not know yet the full extent of the caregiving role. You may not have all the answers as to what specific types of help will be needed. At a later time you can meet again with these same secondary caregivers to assign specific caregiving tasks (see pages 102-104). For now you simply want to make sure everyone understands what becoming a primary (and secondary) caregiver will mean.

A word here about the necessity of seeing that your own children, if they are in the home, have the opportunity to express their thoughts and reservations about caregiving if the care recipient will be living in their home. As a parent, spouse, and child who may be about to bring all three roles under one roof, you are part of a burgeoning new segment of the United States population—the so-called Sandwich Generation, or Women and Men in the Middle. Your children need to have a clear understanding that this new role of caregiving that you may assume will definitely cut into the time you will have for them just as a change in careers or a new baby would. Even if the person will not be living with you, the children need to be aware that your routine is about to change and that in the future there may be even more changes and requests for sacrifices from everyone. Children are very perceptive, and you may be amazed at the insights they will offer through their questions and ideas.

At this meeting of all who will play a part in the care of the individual, it is probably a good idea not to have the person who needs care present. On the other hand the presence of a trained counselor may be a very good idea. If you are to conduct the meeting, you might consider the following points for discussion.

1. If you assume the role of primary caregiver, is everyone satisfied with that solution?

2. Does everyone agree that once the full range of caregiving tasks is known, there will be another meeting to divide those responsibilities fairly?

3. If the care recipient is to live in the caregiver's home, is there enough room for everyone? Are there enough bathrooms and bedrooms? Will there be enough privacy? If not, what compromises and changes need to be made?

4. In what ways do you each believe the care recipient will have to adjust to the new arrangement? In what ways will the primary caregiver and his or her family have to adjust?

5. Will everyone try to get along with everyone else if the person is to live in the same house? Can any differences be resolved before the move is made?

6. What are the financial and legal ramifications of the situation as it stands today? Who will pay for what? What extra burdens will caregiving place on the primary caregiver's budget?

7. What are the feelings of each person who attends the meeting and who is about to become a secondary caregiver about the new arrangement?

8. Does everyone at the meeting understand that if the caregiving role is accepted, that responsibility is likely to expand as time goes by?

9. What information does the primary caregiver need to gather before a division of duties can be outlined? Are any of the secondary caregivers willing to help collect that information?

Keep in mind that for many caregivers there will never be a meeting with potential secondary caregivers from the family because there will be no one else. On the other hand, for some—especially spouses and adult children—the role is accepted not because there is no choice but because caregiving is seen as a natural extension of the relationship to the care recipient as child or spouse. For others the decision will boil down to whether one person alone is willing to assume care for another adult. If, after examining your feelings about taking on the responsibility and your feelings about the care recipient, you can think of nothing rewarding or fulfilling about the job, you and the person will be entering a no-win situation. Before you make that final decision to accept the responsibility, seek some counseling if you feel obliged to take on the role but fail to see the potential rewards of caring for another person.

Pluses in Caregiving

One positive in taking on the role of caregiver is that accepting the responsibilities in the first place takes a person with extraordinary qualities. Also, you are about to receive a terrific education—about your own talents and strengths, about the person's disabilities, and about aging in America. For some the skills attained through caregiving could translate into a new career or position in the community in later years. In addition to those pluses, your bonds with the care recipient will be strengthened in significant ways. You may begin to relate to your mother as a friend and "sister." You may find a deeper love and commitment with your spouse.

What to Expect

Make no mistake. Becoming a caregiver means embarking on a voyage over largely uncharted waters. For centuries the job has been done with little guidance, recognition, or support. There will be incredible demands made on every facet of your life. Some of the things you enjoy most will have to be sacrificed. Family members and friends and neighbors may constantly criticize the way in which you are doing the job. At times you may feel that you are having to fight major battles to get any care at all for the person who is impaired or disabled. Services will be complicated or nonexistent. There will be inconceivable strains on your time, your physical and emotional resources, and your budget.

However, if you learn to make the services that are available in your community work for you and the care recipient, you can do a very good job of giving care without wearing yourself out, having to sacrifice your own life, or bankrupting yourself or the care recipient. Assuming you have decided to take on the role of caregiver, the following chapters will tell you how to make those choices that will make life easier for both you and the care recipient. Start a notebook or card file to record the information you will gather as you go through the rest of this book. It may prove a crucial reference for you in the years to come.

Part Two

❧

Getting Started

As our population grows older, we are faced with the responsibilities of aging parents who, somewhere in the process, can no longer be self-sufficient. Not only can the aging process be painful emotionally for our beloved elderly but also for us. In addition, growing very old can be financially exhausting with many persons outliving their resources, leaving their families to provide financial support often at a time when they themselves are either struggling to get the last of their children through college or are dependent on retirement income. The difficulties are awesome.

—Ruth Seegrist

4 Ꮼ Living Arrangements

Now that you have been elected the primary caregiver (whether by choice or default), the time has come to go into action. This is the time to consider not only housing but such things as how you will maintain as normal and complete a life as possible for yourself, the person you are caring for, and the others you love. If it appears that a new location is necessary for the care recipient, you will need to explore all the living alternatives available in your community before you both choose the one that seems best at this time. And you will need to keep in mind that somewhere down the road one of the other alternatives may be needed.

Whatever choice you make for living arrangements, keep in mind that the present "home" for the person may be the last outpost of his or her existence as an independent person. To move the person from that place means to take away a part of the self. Do not plan *for*—plan *with*—unless mental incompetence leaves you no choice. Even when your relative is confused, making him or her a part of the planning process can help alleviate some of the stress of relocation and the accompanying major lifestyle change.

In a *Newsweek* article entitled "Growing Old, Feeling Young," the writer gives this advice for understanding the feelings of older citizens when they are faced with change in their later years: "The frustration many of [our elderly] feel comes partly from the sense of being depersonalized—of being regarded as units of need instead of as sentient yearning human beings."

Using the following checklist, determine what type of arrangement would be best for your relative. Each alternative is explored in detail following the list.

   — Person can continue to live alone.
   — Person can continue to live alone with the following types of support: _____
_____ .
   — Person needs a structured setting such as an apartment or unit in a building that caters to aging persons or a retirement village with organized activities and help with shopping, chores, transportation, and emergency health care.
   — Person can live with you or another family member.
   — Person needs skilled nursing care twenty-four hours a day and should be in a nursing home.

Care Recipient Continues to Live Alone

In many cases your relative can continue to function quite well alone, and one might think that even though that person is aging and becoming more frail, there would be no need for a caregiver. But a caregiver can play an important *limited* role now that may delay escalation into a more active role at some future date. This assessment of the person's ability to function independently is more important than a medical diagnosis for determining whether a person can stay at home.

To determine whether the person can continue to manage alone, ask this: Can the person prepare meals? keep up a house or apartment? financially afford the upkeep of a home? get out for shopping and socialization? handle emergency situations by calling for help or going to a neighbor? If so, the person probably can continue living alone without help, and your role as caregiver may be limited to visits and phone calls. The person will still be self-sufficient, and what will be needed from you will be gentle concern and discreet monitoring.

You will want to pay attention to such things as what your relative is eating and how often, whether he or she is getting any exercise or opportunities for social activities, and whether, when you visit, the home seems to be in good order and a safe, secure place.

While this may be the easiest of caregiving roles, it, like all the others, has its pitfalls. If the relative is your parent or in-law, you may find yourself from time to time thrust into a role-reversal situation that makes both of you uncomfortable. The person may accuse you of "mother-henning" or nagging. In wrestling with your own fears about growing old, you may become understandably angry when your parent or in-law refuses to do everything possible to maintain his or her health. It is hard to understand why a person will refuse to see a doctor. But sometimes older persons with disturbing symptoms are told again and again, "That's just something you have to expect when you get old." Often they are told that by their own doctors. It hardly seems worth the trouble of making another appointment to hear the same thing. The number of physicians who are trained in the treatment of the special needs of aging patients is limited. Frequently aging persons who live in small towns and rural areas are seeing doctors who have had no special training in the field of geriatrics. Whenever possible, an aging person should seek the services of a physician who specializes in treating the older patient.

Regardless of who the person is, he or she will struggle to maintain control and may fear that admitting a need for help will lead to a drastic curtailing of his or her independence. Many older persons become secretive and refuse to discuss their health problems for fear they will be placed in a nursing home or at least removed from their own beloved home. Caregivers at all stages who are faced with this problem can help the situation by (1) putting themselves in the place of the person, (2) thinking how they might react faced with the same decision, and (3) discussing these fears with the older person.

The best thing you can do as a caregiver for a person

who is continuing to manage alone is to be supportive and prepare for the day when living alone is no longer possible. Finally, whether the person continues to live alone with or without help, it is part of your job as caregiver to assess the home to see if any changes might be needed for the safety and comfort of your loved one. Use the checklist on pages 133-135 as a guide. Once you are satisfied that the person can live alone with a reasonable degree of safety, back off and do not hover. Part of living an autonomous and independent life at any age is being allowed the freedom to make choices and to take risks.

Care Recipient Continues to Live Alone with Help

Some older persons may want to continue living alone past the time when they are capable of total independence. Help may be needed in one or more of the following areas: meal preparation, housekeeping, lawn maintenance, shopping, laundry, basic hygiene, and taking medications.

Getting your relative to accept basic household help (as opposed to home nursing care) may be a major undertaking, especially if the person is a woman who has prided herself on her home and cooking for decades. If more than household services are required, you will need to investigate the types of home health care services available in your community. (Home health care is discussed in detail on pages 76-81.)

Exploring the Resources

How do you go about getting a person who is fighting hard to remain in control of his or her life to accept help, especially if that help is to come from an outsider? Allowing someone from an agency to enter the home and take over responsibilities may be seen as the first step down the path toward total dependence. That makes accepting the help a mixed bag of both relief to have help and fear of what that aid can mean in the long run. You can start organizing yourself to help your relative get the help he or she needs by listing the areas where help is needed in your notebook. An example is given below.

HOUSEHOLD HELP	PERSONAL AND MEDICAL HELP
Help with meal preparation.	*Help with bathing.*
Help with home maintenance.	*Help with medications.*

Next, explore the resources in your community. This is discussed in detail in chapter 5. Who or what agency can provide the types of help your relative needs? How do these agencies operate? What do they charge? One of the pitfalls for the caregiver in this situation is to hear what outside help costs and then immediately say, "You're kidding! I'll do it myself." Be very careful what you volunteer to take on. Consider these points before you decide that you are willing to do the work yourself.

- What will happen if you are sick?
- What happens if you want to go away?
- Are you really prepared to make every meal or do the laundry or do the shopping for both your own household and your relative's for the next year? the next five years?

In the beginning, when you want so much to do everything possible for this person you love and/or feel a responsibility for, it is so easy to say, "I'll do that." But think of this as a long-term commitment before you volunteer. You can easily take on more after you see how things are going, but if you try to do everything in the beginning, you may be overwhelmed by the magnitude of the job and feel trapped and resentful rather than loving. And once you have taken on the task, you may meet even more resistance from your relative when you try to hand that part of the caregiving role over to an outside agency.

List in your notebook or file each of the problem areas you outlined above and every possible solution you can think of for that problem. Do not rule out anything at this stage. This is the time to consider *all* the alternatives—even those that are not especially attractive to you. (If you are unfamiliar with community resources, see chapter 5.) Here is one example.

PROBLEM	RESOURCE	SERVICE	COST
Evening meal.	1. Meals on Wheels.	Delivers hot lunch and cold supper.	Minimal.
	2. Eat with me.	I shop for and prepare meal.	Depends on menu.
	3. Senior nutrition site.	Hot lunch.	Minimal or free.

Continue listing in your notebook the areas in which your relative needs help and the resources available for providing that help.

In addition to the services mentioned earlier, have you found any of the following services available in your community: errand services, home repairs (at times run through a local or county agency at minimal or no cost to the person), telephone reassurance services, Life Line paging systems, transportation services, legal assistance, and counseling for emotional and mental impairments?

In smaller communities services may be available at the county or regional level if not in the community itself. Whether or not your relative can make use of such services now, it is a good idea to do research and know what is available for the future. (See pages 148-149.)

Do not overlook the untapped resource of the local teenage population in your community. These young people often can be relied upon to run errands, provide simple maintenance services such as lawn cutting or snow shoveling, or perform routine tasks for the care recipient such as helping the person with meals or going with the person for a walk. There are advantages for everyone in such an arrangement. The teenager assumes some responsibility and earns spending money. The care recipient meets a new friend from another generation. And you, the caregiver, have one less responsibility to fit into your already busy schedule.

Convincing the Care Recipient to Accept Help

Once you have explored what resources are available, you have done only half the job. You still have to convince the relative to accept this help. Before you do anything, try this exercise: Make a list of those things in your own life that you do without the help of others, especially those things you take special pride in such as your career, your work in the community, your role as a parent, and your fame as a gourmet cook. Now imagine that one by one those skills are taken away—you can no longer work or get out into the community, your children are grown and no longer seem to need your nurturing, your arthritis makes slicing vegetables and other cooking routines impossible.

How would you replace each loss? What would you tell yourself to get you through? Spend some time at this before you try to convince your relative to accept outside help. When you fully understand that the person who needs help is aware that these services and outsiders are well-meaning and certainly a blessing but at the same time cannot shake his or her own sense of loss and failure, you are ready to try to talk the problem out and get some resolution. Here are some pointers that may help.

Do try to involve the relative in the selection process and the decision.

Do present the need for help in a positive light, avoiding such statements as, "You can't do that anymore."

Do consider a change in routine if it will provide the

best solution. For example, if your relative can get a balanced hot meal at noon at a senior site, try to convince him or her to let that be the major meal of the day regardless of the fact that for forty years the evening meal has been the hot meal.

Do keep an open mind and be flexible. Not everything will work. On the other hand something might.

Do not make blanket statements such as, "I'll never put you in a nursing home," or "Mom would never agree to have someone clean her house."

In a few cases the necessary help may be temporary. A recently widowed woman may be afraid to stay alone at night. A person recovering from a mild stroke or heart attack may fear that such a thing can happen again, especially in the first few weeks following the incident. The person may be afraid to bathe for fear of blacking out or falling. In such cases professional help even on a temporary basis may be unnecessary. A neighbor or college student may be interested in taking care of the person for an hour or so or staying over for the night. In any case—whether the help is temporary or permanent, professional or not—there is an added bonus. The person who comes in to help will function as a social contact, someone to talk to and look forward to seeing at a specific time.

Getting Medical Help

If the help that is needed is as much medical as it is practical, look for home health care services available in your community. In such cases your hospital social worker or local visiting nurse association can give you leads and valuable advice. If the person is currently hospitalized with a traumatic illness that will seriously change the way he or she will be able to function at home (for example, stroke, broken hip, heart attack), a meeting with the hospital health team is essential.

The health team is made up of the hospital social worker, the floor nurse, the physical therapist (and any other special therapist who has been involved in the care), and the doctor as well as representatives of any home care agencies the doctor has recommended for continuing care after the patient's release. This meeting should give the family and the person a clear idea of what and how much improvement to expect, what and how much help will be needed, and where to go for that help. If you are to be the primary caregiver, take notes in your notebook, get the phone numbers and names of agencies and contact persons, and ask about any eligibility requirements those agencies may have regarding health status or finances.

Care Recipient Moves to a Structured Setting

Retirement villages, board-and-care or group homes, shared housing, co-ops, and low-income apartment complexes are being developed as alternative living arrangements for the growing older population. In many cases an older person who needs help does not have a family support system living close enough to cope with the problems. Families are widely scattered in the United States, and the number of long-distance caregivers is on the rise.

In such structured housing the person usually has a room or small apartment of his or her own and shares common areas and features such as dining rooms, activity rooms, and laundry facilities with other residents. There may also be such services as transportation for shopping and medical appointments, a clinic for routine health checkups, counseling, and planned social activities. There are sometimes levels of care that allow the person to move to ever increasing structured care as the need arises.

While there will still be the trauma of giving up a home and familiar environment, there is the self-esteem of making the move to a setting that allows choice, encourages some independence, and, most of all, does not put the person in the position of living with family and feeling like an intruder. For those who have become increasingly depressed and reclusive while living alone, such settings can provide the added advantage of opportunities for creative expression and social contact.

On the debit side many of these new concepts in alternative living have no government backing—that means no funding—and residents must pay the full cost of the services. For some families the costs of such programs can be out of reach, and the low-income housing that is available in many communities has long waiting lists. It is hoped that the demand for alternative living arrangements will prompt the government and private insurance companies to find ways to compensate alternatives to nursing home care and hospitalization.

Role of the Caregiver

If your relative chooses one of these alternative living plans, it is your job as caregiver to stay informed. If you are a long-distance caregiver, stay in touch. Call and write often and visit whenever you can, even for a day or two. During the months of the adjustment period, send your relative lots of newsy letters, items from your local paper that might be of interest, and photographs. Another very good idea is to give your relative a cassette recorder and blank tapes and send him or her taped messages from your family. Have the grandchildren do the same, and encourage the person to tape messages back to you.

If you live nearby, make a definite commitment to spend certain times with your loved one. For example, one grandfather had lunch every Sunday with his grandchildren without their parents. Plan a definite shopping trip. Do not make idle comments on the phone such as, "We'll have lunch soon, Mom." Instead say, "Let's go out to lunch on Saturday."

Invite your relative to your house for dinner, and, as social contacts are developed at the new residence, include a guest in the invitation. Occasionally drop by unannounced, perhaps with an extra casserole for the freezer or a special treat from the bakery. This will give you a chance to see your loved one at a time when he or she has no opportunity to be "on" for you. Be careful that such unannounced visits do not appear to be for the purpose of intruding or investigating.

Whenever possible, involve your relative in some family project. I had never had much contact with my mother's only sister until I planned a special surprise for my parents' fiftieth wedding anniversary and needed some family history. The result of that initial contact has been a warm correspondence that has grown through the years until today each of us looks forward to the next letter.

Care Recipient Moves in with Adult Child or Other Family Member

Many older persons have their own homes and continue to live independently well into later life. Of the rest, possibly as many as one-half live with their children, who are themselves moving toward retirement years. As the World War II baby boom ages, the need for caregivers will grow in direct proportion to the rapid growth of the over-sixty-five population.

What are the positives and negatives of living with a parent or in-law? Is it something everybody wants? Have all the possibilities for alternative care been explored? Is everyone prepared to make changes and adjustments to accommodate the new living pattern?

On the positive side there is a sense of continuity, especially for the extended family such as grandchildren, when parents move in with their children. If the caregiver is widowed or single, companionship for both the caregiver and the parent may be a major plus. Increased peace of mind is another benefit as is the advantage of combined incomes and expenses plus shared work loads. Of course, sometimes the person is incapacitated in ways that negate some of these advantages.

One large negative the caregiver may experience is that of becoming a child again, this time in his or her own home. In cases where the caregiver is caring for a sibling, childhood rivalries and power positions may make the caregiving process difficult. The kitchen usually is the battlefield for women, while men tend to clash over changing mores in society.

It may be possible to prevent or overcome such problems if careful ground rules between the caregiver and the person needing care are established early in the caregiving relationship (see chapter 7).

Another problem may be caused by the simple increase in the number of people who are expected to share the same space and interrelate with one another. Values may conflict. The extra person's presence may increase the amount of work you have to do while at the same time rob you of privacy. At a time when you were about to be free of the responsibilities of child rearing and career building, you may find yourself faced with a new role that requires even more responsibility and carries with it even more tension and stress.

Even in the best of relationships, there will be some ambivalence about living together under one roof. There may be old family power struggles that have lain dormant for years and will now resurface under the pressure of shared living. If you have a spouse and children, the number of feelings and personalities to be considered may be quadrupled.

Getting Ready

When the care recipient is coming to live with you, your first task is to set up for that move, handling as many of the details as possible before the actual moving day. Depending on what has precipitated the move, you may have anywhere from several hours to several weeks to plan. Regardless of how much time you have, start with the health team meeting discussed on pages 64-65 and include any family member who will be directly affected by the decision to have the person move in with you.

Once you know what the needs of your relative will be, spend some time assessing your home's ability to meet those needs. Start by making your home accident-proof, such as providing grab bars in the bathroom and handrails on stairways. (See the safety checklist on pages 133-135 for a detailed list of suggested safety measures.) Then consider the following questions.

1. Will the person have his or her own room?
2. How is the room decorated and furnished now? Is that suitable? What is the possibility you might redecorate using the person's own furniture and allowing him or her to help in the selection of colors and accessories?
3. If the person must share the room, is there enough space for both roommates to have privacy and a place for personal property? Sharing a room is not a good idea and should be avoided if at all possible.
4. What about the rest of the house—will the person feel welcome or like an intruder? Could you add Dad's favorite chair to your living or family room? Could you use Mom's dishes? Does the person have a special collection or painting you might make part of this new home? Have you thought about the person's hobbies and made room for those?
5. If the person is mentally incapacitated, have you made the house as familiar as possible and provided security for one who might be prone to wander?

Anticipated Changes in Daily Routine

Once you have looked over the house and decided what physical changes are needed, spend some time thinking about the changes that are about to happen in your daily personal routine:

1. How much time will you and your relative spend together? Both you and the person who needs care will need time for your normal life free from guilt and resentment.
2. What will the person pay for, what will you pay for, and what will other members of the extended family pay for?
3. If you work, how will your relative spend the day?
4. What responsibilities, if any, will the person have for maintaining the household?
5. If there are children who will be living in the house, what power of discipline will the person have over them?

6. Have you and your spouse discussed how you will maintain your marriage with the addition of another adult to the household?

Moving Day

Prepare the person's room and the rest of the house as much as possible before the actual moving day, and then be prepared to make some additional adjustments or accommodations. When your relative arrives, strive to have the environment one of comfort and welcome and as free of turmoil and stress as you can make it. One emotion prevalent among older people who are moving in with their adult children is the idea that they are intruding and not really wanted. If they have to witness a lot of changes being made to accommodate them, it will make them feel they are a burden, and they will be even more anxious and withdrawn.

Do not expect compliments and reactions of delight from your relative when he or she sees all you have done. The person may be grateful and even touched but unable to show those emotions as he or she struggles with feelings of loss and guilt at having put you to so much trouble. If the care recipient is a sibling, you and that person may have to work your way through some old rivalries and jealousies. Especially if you and your sibling have had limited contact during your adult years, you may find that it will take some time to relate to each other as adults rather than on the basis of your childhood personalities.

Regardless of the relationship, both you and the care recipient are embarking on a new lifestyle. Do not try to pretend this is something that happens to either of you every day. Life is going to be different for both of you, and there is a time when those feelings of uncertainty and anxiety should be shared.

Care Recipient Moves into a Skilled Nursing Home

Sometimes the mental and/or physical incapacities are such that there really is no alternative to nursing home placement. At other times the family support system is nonexistent or so slight or the family members live at such distances that there may be no other choice. Another instance when a nursing home may be the best solution is in the case of someone who lives in a small town or rural area where community service agencies or alternative housing projects are nonexistent or limited. A complete discussion of nursing home placement can be found in chapter 16.

"I'm ready to give him to God," one caregiver said, "but not to a nursing home."

Nursing homes have gotten the same bad press mental institutions got several years ago. In fact, the nursing home industry has come a long way, and more homes now provide an environment that is as noninstitutional and warm as possible. Caregivers should not assume that a nursing home is a "last resort." It may be one of several alternatives, and in some cases it may be the best alternative (see chapter 16).

If a nursing home is the answer for your relative, there are still choices to be made. You will want to visit a variety of homes—private, for-profit homes as well as those sponsored by religious groups, and other nonprofit agencies. If possible, take the person you are caring for with you on some of these visits. Even if the person is mentally incapacitated, you can get a feel for how he or she will respond to the setting and be received by the staff. See whether you can stay for a meal or observe an activity session. Ask for a copy of last month's activity calendar and menu. If the person is too ill to come with you, ask if a member of the nursing home staff will call on the patient at home or in the hospital.

In selecting a home, follow the checklist given on pages 287-289. Keep in mind that you can change your mind if, after your loved one has been in residence for several weeks with ample time to adjust, the arrangement does not seem to be working out. Although moving is traumatic for everyone, do not be afraid of upsetting your relative further by yet another move. It is better to make the extra move than to tolerate a bad situation.

Stress of Relocation

In her article "Relocation Stress and the Elderly" in the *American Journal of Occupational Therapy*, Betty Risteen Hasselkus defines relocation as a "complex sequence of experiences and events beginning with the situational changes that precipitate a *decision* to move and ending with the months of adjustment that *follow* a move."

Men may be more vulnerable to the stress of relocation than women. If mental impairment is part of the problem, men and women are both particularly vulnerable because impaired memory does not allow them to prepare for a move, and they have been relying on familiar surroundings to disguise their failing memories. If the person's state of mind prior to the move has been one of depression or despair, his or her ability to cope will also be severely affected. Also, nonambulatory persons are more affected than those who are ambulatory.

But for any older person relocation is not simply a matter of moving to a new home. There is a vast social and psychological adjustment to be made. In many cases the person is being asked to give up things that have been a part of a lifetime of experiences—a home, furniture, mementos. The person is asked to accept all at once a new setting including different meals, different shopping, different transportation, and different social contacts—not to mention an entirely new daily routine that may mean adjusting to one or more other people after years of living alone or with someone else.

Try to recall those experiences in your life when you felt uprooted and lost. Perhaps it was when you had to attend a new school, move to a different city because of your job, or start a new social life after a death or divorce. How did you feel? How long did it take for you to feel comfortable?

Give your relative as much voice as possible in the move. Both of you will be under a lot of stress for the first several months. Expect that, and if you feel unable to cope alone, get some professional help. Continue to remind each other that this is different and that you know it is often hard but can be survived and might even evolve into a pleasant lifestyle.

For more information.   Your physician and hospital social worker can be invaluable in giving you information about services and facilities that are available in your area. You can also contact your local or regional Office on Aging, a county health department social worker, a local home care agency social worker, or a local nursing home social worker. For more information about housing options throughout the country, contact the following:

Administration on Aging, U.S. Department of Health and Human Services, 400 6th Street, SW, Washington, DC 20201   1-202-245-0724

American Association of Homes for the Aged (AAHA), 1050 17th Street, NW, Washington, DC 20036   1-202-296-5960

American Association of Retired Persons (AARP), 1909 K Street, NW, Washington, DC 20049   1-202-872-4700

American Nursing Home Association, 1025 Connecticut Avenue, NW, Washington, DC 20036   1-202-296-5636

National Caucus of the Black Aged (NCBA), 1424 K Street, NW, Washington, DC 20005   1-202-637-8400

5 ⚓ Getting Help from Others

Regardless of what living arrangements you and the person you are caring for make, both of you may need help from sources outside the home. Not every person will need every source of help, but the best caregiver may be the one who prepares for the possibility that help may be needed from a variety of sources at some point in the process.

In her article "'Women in the Middle' and Family Help to Older People" in *The Gerontologist*, Elaine M. Brody, director of the Department of Human Services for the Philadelphia Geriatric Center, has given a very good description of what it is that caregivers, even those playing a limited caregiving role, do. "They shop and run errands; give personal care; do household maintenance tasks; mobilize, coordinate and monitor services from other sources; and fill in when an arranged care program breaks down."

As the primary caregiver for another person, the task of finding resources to meet the needs of your relative will often fall to you. Be prepared by exploring those resources now.

Help from the Hospital

If the person who needs care will be coming home after hospitalization, a major source of help could be your learning by watching as hospital employees do their jobs.

Take notes for your file and ask questions. Be in the room when nurses and aides give basic care. Will the care recipient have to be bathed in bed? Will he or she need help getting in or out of bed? getting in or out of the bathroom? How is that done without injury to the person? to the caregiver? Ask whether the staff can let you try lifting and moving the disabled person with them there to assist and teach.

Learn what to say to reassure the patient while you are helping with painful therapy procedures or trying to get the person to eat or take medications. Learn how to give medications and treatments and how to clear the throat if choking occurs. Ask for tips for dealing with a stubborn or confused patient. Ask your library for Lois Barclay Murphy's *The Home Hospital* if your relative will be in bed for some time following release from the hospital.

Neighbors, Relatives, and Friends

The ideal family member or friend, of course, is the one who sees the need and finds some way to help without being asked or told. However, people are often well-meaning but unable to judge what they might do to help you or your relative. If you see that the offer of help is not just a mere social grace but rather a sincere desire to be of service, you may have to make concrete suggestions to the person offering help: "Could you sit with Mother for an hour while I run to the store?" "Could your son shovel the snow for us? I'll be glad to pay him." "Would you call me at work if you think there is a problem at my parent's house?"

Occasionally a caregiver is hurt and frustrated when his or her own friends and neighbors or those of the person drift away. Depending on the extent of your caregiving role, you may find it necessary to seek new opportunities for making friends for both the person who needs care and yourself.

When it comes to diseases that affect the mind, people still live in the Dark Ages in many ways. To many, mental illness is frightening, and many laypersons know little about such diseases as Alzheimer's and other forms of dementia unless they have experienced such illness within their own families. They may know even less about the complexities of caring for such a person.

If someone offers a helping hand and you think it is a sincere offer, keep in mind that it may take some gentle encouragement from you to see that sincere offer through to reality. Think of things others might be able to do to help you in small but important ways and list them.

Examples: 1. Neighbor will call Mom at noon to remind her to take medication.
2. Uncle Jack will drive Mom to doctor when I have to work.
3. Barb wants Mom to call her in an emergency when Mom cannot reach me.

Home Health Care and Community Services

Aside from family, friends, and neighbors, the caregiver may need to depend on services outside the home. One of the fastest growing industries in the United States is the home health care service market. Consumers can now purchase a variety of services and products for both medical and wellness needs in the home. In addition to outpatient services provided by clinics and hospitals, there are visiting nurses, public health agencies, private health agencies, fitness clubs, and major corporations all getting into the business of home health care. Products to make life easier for the caregiver and the person needing care are available for rent or sale from hospitals, clinics, pharmacies, independent retailers, and even mail-order houses.

Your Yellow Pages can help you find the available resources in your community. But shop carefully. As in any business, there are excellent products and services, and there are those that are of questionable quality. Apply the same techniques you would use in shopping for any high-cost item or service. Shop around, compare costs, and get references. Even though some services will be available through public agencies, you should still compare the cost and quality of those services to those being provided by private, for-profit organizations. Not all services will be available in every community. Find out what your community offers at the public level as well as in the private sector. Record each service that is currently available in your community in your card file or your loose-leaf notebook. Whether or not you plan to make use of a service now, research it for the future—when you may need it, and in a hurry. Below is an outline of the information needed for each type of service. You may have more than one entry for each category.

1. Home nursing services may offer a variety of services including registered nurses who will call on the person needing care at home; physical, occupational, and/or speech therapists who can give the person therapy at home; nutrition counselors who will advise on diet; and social workers who will assist the person and the caregiver in planning a care program. The home nursing service may also have home health aides who can come to the home to assist the caregiver with such tasks as bathing the care recipient or administering certain treatments such as the range-of-motion exercises.

Not every home nursing service will offer every one of these services, and some may offer other services that are listed below. The home nursing service should be the first agency you call along with the Area Agency on Aging.

Offered by _____

Contact _____ Phone _____

2. Geriatric hospitals and clinics specialize in the care and treatment of illnesses that particularly affect older persons.

Offered by _____

Contact _____ Phone _____

3. Emergency services such as ambulances and paramedics respond immediately to calls for help.

Offered by _____

Contact _____ Phone _____

4. Mental health care centers offer counseling for both the care recipient and the caregiver. Some may offer materials and/or programs on coping skills. Others may offer therapy for those who suffer from mental illnesses such as depression.

Offered by _____

Contact _____ Phone _____

5. Medical equipment and supplies are needed for certain treatments or disabilities. There are retail outlets for such supplies as well as pharmacies that offer such products and clinics or hospitals that may have certain products for rent.

Offered by _____

Contact _____ Phone _____

6. Medications delivery service is offered by many pharmacies. If the care recipient is unable to go to the pharmacy and has no one to go for him or her, this can be an important consideration in choosing a pharmacy.

Offered by _____

Contact _____ Phone _____

7. Telephone reassurance systems and/or paging systems are two services that may benefit the care recipient who is living alone. The telephone reassurance system is often offered by local police departments. The care recipient makes arrangements to call a certain number at a specific time or times each day. If the service does not receive the call, someone will call the person. If there is no answer, a family member or neighbor will be called to check on the person. If no one is available, the service will dispatch an agent or emergency team to check on the person.

The paging system consists of an instrument the person wears or carries that is connected electronically to a central dispatcher. If the care recipient falls or feels he or she needs help, the device will signal the central dispatcher, who will call the person. If the person does not answer the telephone, the dispatcher will send emergency help immediately.

Offered by _____

Contact _____ Phone _____

8. Meals delivered to the home or offered at specified nutrition sites are often county or other government programs supported by public funds and offered to the participants at a very minimal cost.

Offered by _____

Contact _____ Phone _____

9. Homemaker services offer help with the mechanics of maintaining a home such as meal preparation, laundry, and cleaning.

Offered by _____

Contact _____ Phone _____

10. Home maintenance services offer help with maintaining the structural soundness, security, and appearance of the home such as repair services, yard work, and similar chores.

Offered by _____

Contact _____ Phone _____

11. Home security services will survey the home and recommend security measures. Some may also be engaged to patrol the home.

Offered by _____

Contact _____ Phone _____

12. Transportation services again are frequently community services that are supported by public funds. Such services often include vans or buses for the disabled and can be called upon to transport care recipients to and from doctors' appointments, therapy sessions, and/or day-care programs.

Offered by _____

Contact _____ Phone _____

13. Legal services that specialize in counseling older persons are becoming more common. Some programs are offered through the Area Agency on Aging; others are privately run.

Offered by _____

Contact _____ Phone _____

14. Adult day-care centers offer a variety of services including meals and activities for care recipients and respite for caregivers. (See pages 265-268.)

Offered by _____

Contact _____ Phone _____

15. Other agencies to contact for help include these:

Area Agency on Aging
Contact _____ Phone _____

United Way or United Fund
Contact _____ Phone _____

Medicare (a federal health program) See pages 90-91.
Contact _____ Phone _____

Medicaid (a state and federal health program) See pages 91-92.
Contact _____ Phone _____

Social Security Office
Contact _____ Phone _____

Veterans Administration
Contact _____ Phone _____

16. Other resources are available in your community, such as care co-ops, board-and-care group homes, and volunteer programs through local churches, synagogues, or schools.

One last word about services in your community: Remember, many first-time caregivers romanticize what they believe will be out there to help them in their enormous task. Americans believe that the government will provide at *some* level of help or assistance. Never having dealt with Medicaid or Medicare or state or county support services, these caregivers often live in a mythical kingdom where they assume they will have ample services available at every stage of the caregiving process. The truth is that while there are many good agencies out there, too often the community is apathetic, services are token, doctors are patronizing, paperwork is endless, the care recipient's own anger manifests itself in demands the caregiver cannot fulfill, and the caregiver is angry and exhausted and drowning in guilt.

Professional Services

Getting help from the professional community should be fairly standard throughout the country. Within the medical community there are certain services you should learn to expect. The best advice is to learn to deal with all professionals in a forthright, courteous, and businesslike manner. Keep in mind that while they sympathize with signs of stress and diminished coping ability, they have little time for rambling stories about what your relative did last night or how hard your life is. What you want from them is help, and the quickest way to get it is to present yourself in a calm, no-nonsense, pleasant manner. Professionals or not, human beings are more likely to go out of their way for the person who, in the face of an incredible task, maintains his or her composure and sense of humor.

Who are these professionals, and how should you expect them to serve you?

The Social Worker

You should be received by this professional with an attitude of listening and comfort. It is the social worker's job to help you wade through all the bureaucratic red tape, make a plan for caring for your relative, and give you some of the practical and emotional support necessary to carry out that plan. The social worker has the right to expect from you total honesty about your feelings, your finances (and the finances of the care recipient), the living conditions you are prepared to provide for that person, and your needs in terms of help from outside agencies in order to provide the best possible care for the person. The social worker is not a mind reader, and you will need to understand that finding solutions to your particular needs will take time.

The Doctor

You and/or your relative may already have an established relationship with your relative's physician and may have fallen into some bad habits that will waste both your time and the doctor's. For example, it is not uncommon for an older person to give his or her caregiver a litany of symptoms and problems at home and not mention one of them to the doctor. Some older persons do not wish to take up too much of the doctor's time and may downplay the very symptoms that have alarmed you in the first place.

As soon as you become the person's primary caregiver, make an appointment with his or her doctor for an office consultation without the care recipient. Explain that you are interested in discussing the person's condition with the doctor as well as your role as caregiver. Go prepared to get the maximum amount of information in the minimum amount of time. That means thinking about the interview before you go and writing down the questions you want to ask. See page 172 for some suggested questions.

Whether the doctor is an established contact or someone your relative has just started to see, you need to evaluate the doctor based on the following questions.

1. Does the doctor allow enough time for visits?
2. Is the doctor accessible during emergencies?
3. Is the doctor sensitive to the fears and needs of older persons?
4. Does the doctor make light of the person's symptoms and problems?
5. Does the doctor understand the aging process?
6. Does the doctor have experience in or interest in geriatric medicine? (If not, look for a different doctor, one familiar with geriatric medicine, who is more knowledgeable about the problems of the aging. References can be obtained from hospitals.)
7. Does the doctor know his or her own limitations?
8. Is the doctor willing to work with you in providing care for this person?

In her book, *Caring—A Daughter's Story*, Diane Rubin says, "The line between courtesy and groveling is very fine. I cross it every time I act as medical representative for my folks. I will do most anything to make things comfortable, including shuffle."

It should never be necessary to grovel or shuffle. However, the physician does have some rights. He or she has the right to expect that you will ask clear, concise questions and that you will not expect him or her to be doctor, psychiatrist, *and* confessor. If you find that after presenting yourself in a businesslike manner—organized and efficient—your doctor still treats you like little Mary Smith with a patronizing pat on the head, change doctors.

Brokers for Long-Distance Caregivers

If you live out of town and your relative is hospitalized, you should rely heavily on the social worker to coordinate plans and keep you informed. Many long-distance caregivers use up their own energies as well as their funds by making numerous trips back and forth trying to care for their family members. Some trips may be unavoidable, but there should be people on the relative's end working for you, making excessive travel and expense unnecessary.

In some cities health care professionals are organizing businesses that coordinate care for persons whose primary caregivers live out of town. These people think of themselves as brokers for services for these older people and their absent families. Such firms offer counseling for family members about services available to the older person. Once choices have been made, the brokers follow through to make sure that the selected service is being provided and that the person is receiving sound support. Caregiving relatives who live in town can also make use of the service and receive the added benefits of ongoing counseling in group sessions with other caregivers.

Unfortunately, at this writing such brokers for services are rare and concentrated primarily in the large metropolitan areas of the country. Ask your relative's doctor, clergyperson, or hospital social worker if such a service exists in your relative's community. You can also check that community's Yellow Pages under "Social Workers."

Networking

Sometimes in the midst of all you have to do, there simply may be no one else to take that extra step and build that necessary support system so vital to your ability to give quality care over the long haul. In the business world it is known as networking. In business it is the old idea of "It's not what you do; it's who you know." Applied to caregiving, networking can be an important way of finding services and respite. Someone you know may know someone who can help. Follow these four steps to establish your networking system.

1. Make a list of everyone you know who might be able to help you. Include everyone who has offered help, pro-

fessionals in the field, and people who might know someone who could help. Make a card for each one to include in your file.

2. Start talking to these people. Tell them you are looking for information and ask them specific questions. Remember, people want to help not only because of you and your relative but also because it makes them feel good about themselves. If you are talking to professionals, plan your questions in advance. Write down what you want to know. Ask for pointers on how to handle the particular problem, where to go for additional help, what to expect, and what steps to follow in giving proper care.

3. Take the time to follow up, especially with people in the professional community. Send a thank-you note. Mention some piece of advice you have already acted on. End with a request to keep you in mind for more information that may become available in the future. Make sure friends and neighbors know how much their time and efforts are appreciated. Keep several small inexpensive gifts in the house at all times—fancy soaps, special teas or coffees, notepaper or calendars. Then when someone does something to help, write a short note and drop off the gift with the note the following day.

4. Do not accept no for an answer. If one agency or service tells you that your relative is ineligible or that the service has been discontinued, do not hang up until you ask, "Can you suggest someone else who may be able to help me?" Be appreciative, but set a goal of coming away from every phone call with either a successful solution or the name of someone else to call.

Networking is like a chain reaction. One suggestion leads to someone who has information that leads to an agency that can help. Keep at it, and keep adding information to your file or notebook. Get names and numbers and file them under the appropriate headings. Record everything even though you may not plan to make use of the name or service at the time. At some future date that one piece of information may be just what you need to help your relative.

Emergency Help

Are you prepared for emergencies—not only emergencies that happen to the person you are caring for but emergencies that could happen to you? What plans have you made if you get sick? What if you have to be hospitalized? Plan now for such contingencies, and let everyone know of these emergency procedures. Put together in your file the steps to your emergency plan along with details such as phone numbers, names, addresses, and other information the substitute caregiver may need.

A good bit of advice for handling emergency situations is to be sure that the gas tank is always full. Perhaps it would also be a good idea to keep a small overnight bag packed if either your relative or you is prone to the sudden attacks of some illnesses. Enlist the aid of neighbors and relatives who might be willing to be on call for a short time while you attend to a minor emergency. But even if your neighbor agrees to be on call, plan on a backup caregiver just in case the neighbor is unavailable.

Whatever outside help you choose, planning ahead is your best bet for successful caregiving. Know what is available *before* you need help, and when you do need that help, do not be too proud to call for it.

6 ✧ Financial and Legal Matters

What does it cost to care? What financial and legal recourse does the caregiver have? What are the caregiver's rights, and what are those of the care recipient? What is the difference between Medicare and Medicaid? What about estate planning—wills, guardianships, trusts? If you do not have an attorney and/or financial advisor or cannot afford either of them, to whom do you turn for advice?

Defining Costs

In the United States only 5 percent of people over sixty-five live in institutions. While the love and concern caregivers lavish on their relatives are priceless assets, the financial costs of caring for older persons are substantial.

If you are a caregiver for an older person, what are the costs? Consider the lost wages of the care recipient if that person was currently employed as well as the lost wages of those family members who provide supervision and care. Include in that figure any lost benefits such as pensions, insurance, and other employee bonuses that result from early retirement if those persons have stopped working or reduced their working hours. Are there costs because of changes in housing (having to move to another home or apartment), or does the present home have to be remodeled in any way to accommodate the relative and his or her impairments? Are there additional transportation costs because the person can no longer drive or uses a wheelchair and needs special transportation?

And what about the myriad of medical costs? How many medications will the person need? Will you need to hire special aides or nurses? What about sickroom supplies—wheelchairs, special beds, or other special equipment? Is the person on a special diet because of his or her illness? Will there be a need for ongoing physical or speech therapy? Will there be ongoing doctors' bills?

One area of costs for caregivers with live-in relatives that is often overlooked is respite care. Adult day-care centers in some states are supported by public funds; in others they are not. If you want to go away for a vacation or long weekend, what will it cost to have someone stay with the person or to place the person temporarily in a nursing home? Can you afford to hire an aide or nurse once a week to give yourself a break from the full-time job of caregiving? Have you budgeted for counseling for yourself and/or the care recipient if the grueling details and emotional strains of the job begin to get you down?

List in your notebook or file the approximate costs for each item.

ITEM	COST PER MONTH
Lost wages	
Lost benefits	
Housing changes or remodeling	
Transportation expenses	
Medical costs (Some of these may be covered. See pages 90–93.)	
Medications	
Special help (aides, nurses)	
Sickroom supplies (wheelchair, hospital bed)	
Special diet	
Physical therapy	
Speech therapy	
Occupational therapy	
Doctors' bills	

ITEM	COST PER MONTH
Respite costs	
Day care	
Vacation care	
Once-a-week relief at home	
Counseling for both the care recipient and the caregiver	

Keep in mind that costs may escalate with the economy and will no doubt increase if the person's condition worsens.

Governmental Programs

Probably your list is staggering. Perhaps you are fortunate that the care recipient still has some major medical insurance that will cover some of the expenses. Perhaps you can rely only on what the state and Medicare and Medicaid are willing to cover. The governmental giants in the health industry can be pretty confusing. Here are some basic facts.

Social Security Administration

Within the Department of Health and Human Services in the federal government is a division known as the Social Security Administration. It is the responsibility of this administration to administer three major income and health maintenance budgets:

1. Retirement and Survivors Insurance (RSI)—monthly checks paid to retirees and their eligible family members or eligible surviving family members.
2. Disability Insurance (DI)—insurance to protect primary wage earners and their dependents from loss of income following disability. (That disability must be to the extent that the person must be expected to be unable to work for at least one full year or that the disability must be expected to result in death.)

3. The Supplemental Security Income (SSI) Plan—a program that administers funds to low-income citizens of all ages who meet certain eligibility requirements. (See pages 92-93 for a more complete discussion.)

Health Care Financing Administration

The Health Care Financing Administration (HCFA) handles health insurance, more commonly known as Medicare, Part A, and Supplemental Medical Insurance (SMI), more commonly known as Part B of the Medicare program.

Each program has its own set of rules for eligibility including age limits and financial restrictions. You will need to contact your local Social Security office to find out what benefits the care recipient or you are eligible to receive. You need to note that Medicaid is not listed above. Medicaid is a *state*-administered program but is funded jointly by the state and federal governments and is subject to federal standards.

Medicare. This is a broadly based federal health *insurance* for people aged sixty-five and over as well as for many disabled people. The program is divided into two parts: *Part A* is basic hospital insurance, and *Part B* is voluntary medical insurance. Under Part A, Medicare will cover reasonable and necessary treatment for an illness or injury as determined by a review committee. Part A covers hospital care, skilled nursing or rehabilitative care, and some home health care. You are covered under Part A if you are receiving benefit checks from Social Security or railroad retirement, are aged sixty-five and still working, have been entitled to Social Security disability checks for two years, or have end-stage renal disease. If you are sixty-five or older but are not eligible for Social Security or railroad retirement benefits, you may have to pay for Part A coverage. Finally, federal workers may now qualify for Medicare depending on the length of their employment with the government and the starting date of that employment.

Part B helps pay for those items not covered under Part A, such as physicians' and surgeons' services, some home health care services, some outpatient hospital services, and/or other items such as tests and special sickroom equipment. You are eligible to enroll in this voluntary Part B program if you are eligible for Part A benefits or are sixty-five or older. You pay a small monthly premium ($15.50 as of 1985), and you can join the program at any time after you meet the requirements, but you must pay a higher premium if you join late.

Your relative's Medicare card will state whether he or she has elected to pay the extra premium that will enroll that person in Medicare Part B (medical insurance) and cover certain medical expenses over and above the hospital costs and nursing provided under Part A. You need to understand that Part B will pay for what Medicare has determined to be "reasonable" charges in those areas it covers at a rate of 80 percent.

Sometimes the person's doctor will bill the person above the "reasonable rate" established by Medicare; those additional charges must be paid by the patient. Some doctors are willing to accept the fees Medicare has determined to be fair for specific services. Such doctors are said to be willing to "accept assignment," meaning they will accept the going rate with no additional charges. Medicare pays 80 percent of the assigned rate, and the patient is responsible for the rest. For a list of those doctors in your area who "accept assignment," call your local Social Security office, Blue Cross office, or Area Agency on Aging and request the Physician/Supplier Assignment Rate Listing (PARL).

As of this writing, the following services are not covered under either Part A or Part B: custodial care (when care for the person requires no special skills or training), routine medical examinations, dental care and dentures, eyeglasses and routine eye examinations, hearing aids, orthopedic shoes, medications, and acupuncture. Medicare will cover only skilled care in a nursing home for a short period of time after a hospital stay.

Medicaid
This is a federal and state health assistance program that pays medical bills for low-income people who cannot

afford the costs of medical care. (In California the program is called MediCAL, and in Arizona there is a program called Access.) Anyone who has no other or limited assets may apply, especially people who have dependent children and low incomes; who have high medical costs, such as long-term care in a nursing home, in relation to their income; or who are blind, aged, or disabled with little or no income. You can apply at the local welfare office. In some states, if you are eligible for SSI, you are automatically eligible for Medicaid and do not have to file a separate application.

What Medicaid covers will vary from one state to another, but basically these items are included: inpatient hospital services, outpatient hospital services, outpatient laboratory and X-ray services, skilled nursing facility services, home health services for those entitled to skilled nursing facility services, physicians' services, and family planning services. The amount and duration of coverage will vary. In addition Medicaid may cover special services to children and in some states will also cover costs for prescription drugs, dental services, eyeglasses, private-duty nursing, pacemakers, intermediate care services, physical therapy, emergency-room services, visits to podiatrists and chiropractors, counseling for emotional problems, and ambulance services. *You should call your local public health office or social service office to find out what services are covered in your state. Do not assume that the state covers all the items listed above.*

In some cases a person would be covered by both Medicare and Medicaid. Start by finding out what benefits under these two programs the care recipient (and you if you are over sixty-five) is entitled to receive. A person may become eligible for Medicaid if he or she is able to transfer or disburse personal assets at least two years before institutionalization. But this takes careful planning.

Supplemental Security Income (SSI)

This federal program is for those persons sixty-five or older who are disabled or blind, receive less than a specified income, and have minimal assets. Social Security will count both unearned (for example, interest and pensions) and earned income (that is, wages). The person's resources for the purposes of this program will include real estate (with the exception of that person's home), stocks, bonds, savings and checking accounts (including joint accounts), and some personal and household property (depending on its value and use). Countable resources (after certain exclusions are made) cannot exceed $1,600 for an individual and $2,400 for a couple. These figures will go up every year from 1986 to 1989.

To be eligible for an SSI payment, the person's income cannot exceed a certain amount. In 1985 the maximum federal payment rates are $325 for an individual and $488 per month for a couple. In some states, a person would also be eligible for a state supplement to these rates. In the case of a couple where only one person is in need of SSI benefits, a part of the other person's income may also be counted unless the couple has been separated or living apart for at least six months or the other person's income is very small. In addition, if the person lives with someone else and does not pay his or her fair share of the household expenses, Social Security will reduce the SSI benefit by one-third of the federal benefit rate. Consult an attorney if the situation applies to your relative's case.

Certain exclusions from total income are allowed including tax refunds on real property, food stamps, housing assistance from federal programs, and funds set aside for burial expenses up to $1,500 for each person and spouse. There are several deductions that apply if the person is blind, disabled, or has children living at home. To determine whether your care recipient or you are eligible for SSI benefits, call your local Social Security office.

Making the System Work for You

Some middle-class Americans who have always taken care of themselves without government support may view such programs as charity. However, the programs are there for everyone, and those who use them most successfully are those who plan ahead for the possibility that such assistance may be needed. In some states the caregiver may need to be concerned about establishing residency, disbursing joint bank accounts, and recording expense vouchers for services rendered during caregiving in order to be eligible for benefits from Medicaid.

If the person wants to transfer assets in order to become eligible for Medicaid and to protect that estate for heirs, the key is to plan ahead while the potential care recipient is still healthy and to get sound legal advice. If the state Medicaid agency determines that assets were disbursed solely to make the person eligible for Medicaid, benefits can be denied and the person determined to be ineligible for two years or more.

The issue is very complicated, and again what is allowed will vary from one state to another. The best course is to get an attorney and make sure he or she knows the applicable state as well as federal Medicaid laws. Caregivers can also get advice or references from the following:

National Senior Citizens Law Center
1424 16th Street, NW, Suite 300
Washington, DC 20036

American Bar Association
750 North Lake Shore Drive
Chicago, IL 60611

AARP Legal Counsel for the Elderly
1909 K Street, NW
Washington, DC 20049

Preventing the Impoverishment of Spouses

When a person has moved into a nursing home and has exhausted his or her available resources in paying for care, that person can apply for Medicaid to cover the cost of his or her continuing care. However, by the time this happens, that person's spouse, who has remained in the community, may be living in poverty. How is this possible? Such circumstances can occur because current Medicaid regulations in some states do not allow the spouse living in the community (most often the wife) to keep enough of the nursing home spouse's income to allow her to meet expenses. The spouse remaining in the community is generally required to live at a level comparable to the SSI monthly income level.

According to a March 1985 bulletin of the Institute on Law and Rights of Older Adults at the Brookdale Center on Aging, Hunter College, New York, the community spouse may seek an order of support through the family court from the income of the nursing home spouse in that state. The amount awarded by the court is then considered exempt in determining the Medicaid budget for the nursing home resident.

If you are in danger of becoming impoverished because of the need to have Medicaid support for your spouse in a nursing home, seek immediate legal aid and counsel. If all your funds are being used for the nursing home resident spouse, you may be placing yourself in a position of being institutionalized simply because you can no longer afford to live in the community.

Legal Capacity

In the event a care recipient becomes incapacitated to the extent that he or she cannot manage personal affairs, what recourse does the caregiver have? The standard remedies—those taken by many families *after* the person has become incompetent—include guardianship and conservatorship. (Traditionally, a guardian is a person appointed by the court to handle the personal affairs of the person, and a conservator is a person appointed to handle the financial affairs of the person, or the person's estate. In some states there is no longer a differentiation in terms.) In either case the appointee may be whomever the court chooses. If the person is living *solely* on Supplemental Security Income (see pages 92-93), Social Security, or veterans' benefits, a representative payee may be appointed. Basically these appointed representatives are custodians of the person's financial estate appointed *after* incapacity or incompetency has been declared by the court. Definitions vary from state to state. The person appointed may or may not be the caregiver or some other member of the person's family. The procedures for having a person declared incompetent will be controlled by state law. Consult your attorney for the requirements in your state.

If the care recipient and the caregiver are organized and plan ahead for the unlikely possibility of incompetency or incapacity, they may elect to create, if your state authorizes one, a durable power of attorney (designating a person of the care recipient's choice to manage his or her affairs in the event of incapacity) or a living trust that will allow assets to be disbursed before the death of the person (see pages 97-98).

What is competency? A competent person in the eyes of most states is one who understands the nature of the action he or she is taking, who understands and can account for his or her own assets and personal property, and who recognizes and understands his or her relationships to others. An incompetent person is one who in the eyes of the court is incapable of managing either himself or herself and his or her own property. These are the extremes. A person may be losing certain facets of his or her ability to manage while retaining others; for example, a man may still be able to manage his bank account but be unable to drive.

Incompetency

The first step then is to determine capacity. In an incompetency hearing a person may come into court, and the court will review the petition and then appoint another person (not a family member) to investigate evidence of incapacity. If the reviewer finds the person to be incapacitated and unable to manage his or her affairs, the court may then appoint another person (perhaps a family member) to act for the person in limited or unlimited ways. It can be an expensive and time-consuming procedure, and in some states it stigmatizes the person with the public declaration of "incompetency." Also once the decision has been made, it is very difficult to have it reversed. However, in cases where there has been no prior planning and the care recipient is perhaps a danger to himself, herself, or others, such legal intervention may be necessary even though the person may be an unwilling participant.

Some state laws provide that if a person is not totally incapacitated, he or she retains the legal capacity to make certain decisions. Such laws provide for limited guardianships and limited conservatorships. In addition, the appointment of either a guardian or a conservator does not necessarily mean that the person has lost the legal capacity to make a will or a health care decision. You should consult an attorney to determine what rights are taken away when a guardian or conservator is appointed under your state's laws.

Legal Safeguards

In the case in which the person and his or her family have planned for the possibility of incapacity, there are several options available. In some states a person who is disabled may nominate his or her own conservator, and the arrangement can be of limited duration. In states that allow a living will (a document that states what the person would like in the event of his or her inability to function, such as turning off life-support systems), a person can plan for possible incompetency. But be careful. State laws on living wills vary greatly. In some states living wills are not legally valid but may be helpful to a court in determining the individual's wishes.

Power of Attorney

If you can persuade your relative to plan ahead, it is possible in most states to establish a power of attorney or the broader-based *durable* power of attorney. The difference is that the simple power of attorney ends when the person becomes incompetent, and the durable power of attorney continues. Also the durable power of attorney can be established now to go into effect after the person becomes incapacitated or incompetent. In most states the durable power of attorney has only financial powers, but in some states medical and health care decisions can be determined by the durable power of attorney.

Your greatest stumbling block may be to get the prospective care recipient to agree to consider some arrangement for handling his or her financial affairs in the event of incompetency. First of all, people are reluctant to give such broad powers to another person, even a son or daughter or spouse. Older people are especially sensitive to any loss of control over their own destinies at a time when already so much is changing for them. You best can handle these problems by making a thoughtful selection of the person who will handle the financial end of the caregiving process, by including the care recipient in all plans for the eventual need for such a representative, and by structuring the arrangements so that it becomes effective only when it is needed.

Living Trust

If the person is still unreceptive, the caregiver might consider proposing a living trust arrangement. Under this plan the person signs a document (called a trust agreement) that names one or more persons (not necessarily family members) as trustees. The trust agreement contains specific instructions about the management and distribution of the person's assets. The person then transfers his or her assets to the trustees, and the trustees are bound by the guidelines contained in the agreement.

Getting Help with Financial and Estate Planning

Whatever form of financial and estate planning you and your relative choose, start by getting the best advice you can afford. It is available in every community, often at no charge. Talk to your local banker, legal aid society, bar association, or Area Agency on Aging. Have your questions ready, and take notes. Get the names and addresses of additional sources of help, and follow through. Get as much information as possible before making a final decision. To get yourself and the care recipient started, include these forms in your notebook or file.

Financial Planning

Area Office on Aging _____

Contact _____ Phone _____

State Bar Association _____

Contact _____ Phone _____

Bank _____

Contact _____ Phone _____

Local Social Security Office _____

Contact _____ Phone _____

Care recipient is eligible for: Medicare ___ Medicaid ___

Veterans Administration Benefits _____

Railroad Retirement _____ SSI _____

In this state the following services are covered by Medicaid: _____
_____ .

In this state the following services are *not* covered by Medicaid: _____
_____ .

Care recipient does (not) have major medical insurance. ___
If he or she does, the following items are covered: _____
_____ .

VA and other benefits will cover _____
_____ .

Of the expenses listed on pages 88–89, the following are covered by either Medicare, Medicaid, or some other support: _____
_____ .

Of the expenses listed on pages 88–89, those that are not

covered by either Medicare, Medicaid, or some other support will be covered by
the person's own assets _____ the caregiver's
assets _____ a secondary caregiver's assets _____.

Estate Planning

Care recipient is competent _____ or
incompetent _____.

Care recipient lacks capacity in these areas: _____
_____ .

In the person's home state the following estate planning
options are available.
guardianship _____ conservatorship _____
durable power of attorney _____ living trust _____
living will _____ other _____
_____ .

After discussing the options with counsel and the care
recipient (if possible), the two best options at this time
appear to be _____ and _____
_____ .

After discussing each option with the person and within a
meeting of all the primary and secondary caregivers, the
best choice appears to be _____ .

List in your notebook or file what the care recipient and
the caregiver must do to put that plan into action.

It is never easy to plan for such finalities as wills and
distribution of estates. Perhaps you have not planned for
yours either. In that case it might be an easier adjustment
for the care recipient if both of you plan for your own
estates at the same time. If you are making a will and
planning for your own possible incapacity, perhaps it will
not seem so ominous and threatening for your relative to
allow you to help with the planning of his or her affairs.

The key is to make sure that these financial and legal
matters are handled as early in the caregiving process as
possible. All over the country there are stories of people
who waited until a few weeks or months before entering a
nursing home to make arrangements for their estates

only to find that legally their assets and in some states personal property would be used until nearly depleted to pay for their care.

For more information.   For further help consult the following reference.

Medicaid/Medicare, Which Is Which? U.S. Department of Health and Human Services, #HCFA-02129

Your local Social Security office should have the following free materials.

A Brief Explanation of Medicare, #10043
Home Health Care Under Medicare, #10042
How Medicare Helps During a Hospital Stay, #10039
Medicare Coverage in a Skilled Nursing Facility, #10041
Your Medicare Handbook, #10050
A Woman's Guide to Social Security, #10127
If You Become Disabled, #10029
Supplemental Security Income for the Aged, Blind, and Disabled, #11000
Your Social Security, #10035

For information about funerals and living wills, write to the following:

Concern for Dying
250 West 57th Street
New York, NY 10107

Continental Association of Funeral and Memorial Societies
1146 19th Street, NW
Washington, DC 20036

Books that may help include these:

What to Do with What You've Got by Peter Weaver and Annette Buchanan.

The Essential Guide to Wills, Estates, Trusts and Death Taxes by Alex J. Soled.

It's Your Choice: The Practical Guide to Planning a Funeral by Thomas C. Nelson.

The Social Security Book by Jack E. Gaumnitz.

7 ✤ Setting the Ground Rules

As the primary caregiver, how will you set ground rules for yourself and the person you are caring for and for those who will be secondary caregivers so that the process of caregiving can run as smoothly as possible? How will you clearly define what each person's role will be? How will you get the person to express his or her feelings and needs? How will you protect your rights to a life of your own?

For Secondary Caregivers

Begin setting the ground rules by calling a meeting early in the caregiving process of everyone who will be helping you, the primary caregiver. At this meeting it is probably a good idea not to have the person you are caring for present.

Present these secondary caregivers with the list of needs you have prepared in studying your relative's impairments—medical needs, social needs, financial needs, and emotional needs. Add to this list your own inventory of what you will need from these people in the way of support and respite.

Make it clear that this is the time to be frank, to say whatever needs to be said, to air whatever complaints there may be, and, finally, to draft a written agreement that clearly outlines responsibilities and the plan for care. Yes, *written*. "But this is my family," you say. Exactly. And family members have a tendency to play even more political games than total strangers. The agreement can be quite simple. For a live-in caregiving situation, the agreement may be something like this:

Name of person who needs care: _____

Name of primary caregiver: _____

Names of secondary caregivers: _____

    (Then list each caregiver's name and the responsibilities that person has agreed to assume in the caregiving process.) A sample is shown below.

Mary, the primary caregiver, will take Mom into her home to live, providing shelter, food, laundry, and personal and health care. She will pay with her own funds one-fourth of the expenses for those items not covered by Mom's own assets or any benefits to which Mom is entitled.

Bob, secondary caregiver in town, will handle Mom's bills and arrange for benefits such as Medicare and insurance payments, will schedule and provide transportation for all visits to the doctor, and will take over total care of Mom one week per quarter to allow Mary respite. Bob will share in Mom's expenses at Mary's house by paying one-fourth of everything not covered by Mom's own funds.

Joan, secondary caregiver out of town, will visit Mom at least three times per year and at that time will take on total care for Mom with Mary's limited help. Joan will contribute one-half of the monthly expenses of care not covered by Mom's own funds.

    Have each person write down what he or she is willing to contribute, and compare that list with the list of needs you have already shown the group. If the person is to manage independently for a time, it is still a good idea to hold such a meeting to discuss those what-happens-if questions that are sure to be on everyone's mind. Keep in mind that this is no place for role-playing. If you have always been the peacemaker, the one who goes along with whatever the others want, and now you are about to become the primary caregiver, make certain that you are firm in stating exactly what you and the care recipient will need and expect to get from the others.

For the Person Receiving Your Care

Setting ground rules with your relative will depend on the mental and ambulatory capacities of that person. If the person is capable of making decisions and maintaining some independence, by all means sit down and outline a plan for both of you. However, except in the very early stages, a person who has Alzheimer's disease or is otherwise brain-impaired may not be capable of such a conversation. Some of the questions you should bring up have already been covered: How much time will you spend together? How will each of you take time for yourself without offending the other?

Looking at things from the view of the care recipient (especially if he or she is coming to live in your home), try to think how you feel when you visit friends. You are not always sure what is expected, are you? You are always on the alert for any sign that you might be intruding or overstaying your welcome. No matter how well you know these people, things are different there. Your relative will experience similar thoughts and may be receiving messages you never intended.

For example, if the person sees a television set in his or her room, the message received may be that he or she is to retire to that room after dinner and leave you and the rest of the family alone. You may have added the television with the idea that Dad might want some privacy from you. These things have to be said. How much time do you want the person to spend with the rest of the family? Is he or she free to go throughout the house at any time? Are there times you want to be alone with your spouse or without the person? What about meals? Do you want or expect your relative to help prepare them? serve them? clean up after them? What about other household chores? You might consider a written contract between you and the person receiving care similar to the one you have made with the secondary caregivers.

As the two of you adjust to your new routine, situations you may never have considered will occur. For example, your father-in-law may disapprove of the hours you allow your teenaged children to keep. If you are caring for your mother and she still lives in her own home, she may wrongly assume that you and your family will spend every weekend with her or at least include her in your planned activities. Unless such matters are discussed honestly and at the time they first come up, they can mushroom into major disagreements. If your parent is coming to live with you, try to get off on as equal a footing as possible. Do not play child to your parent or in-law. At the same time resist the temptation to turn him or her into your child. If the person you are caring for is your spouse, try to maintain the relationship on as normal a level of equality as possible.

Whether the person you are caring for is living with you, is living alone with your support, or is living in another community, it is important that at the beginning of your relationship as caregiver–care recipient, each of you understands exactly what is expected of the other. It is also important that, as the relationship changes and the need for care increases, open lines of communication be maintained.

For You, the Caregiver

And what about setting some ground rules for yourself? Your major ground rule has already been stated: Do not keep saying, "I'll do it. I can manage that."

Before your relative becomes an integral part of your life, you must make some decisions that will protect your right to a life of your own. If you find yourself giving up every activity you have ever enjoyed—work, bridge games, singing in the choir—you are giving up too much. You will be of little use to either the care recipient or yourself if you sacrifice your entire life for that person.

Especially if your relative is mentally incapacitated, you need to find concrete ways of having time for yourself alone and for yourself with others without the relative. This type of respite is the last thing many caregivers seem to allow themselves. That is a mistake. A regular routine that allows you some rest and relaxation or respite every day should be as much a part of your schedule as giving out medications to the care recipient (see chapter 14).

Start by drawing a twenty-four-hour Pie of Life for your routine as it is now without your relative. Draw a circle and divide it into sections that approximately correspond to the amount of time you spend doing things during the day. For example, if you work, one-third of the pie would be labeled "Work." How much sleep do you need? Take another section for that. If you need eight full hours (most of us do not), that is another third of the pie. Now you have one-third left to divide between all those other things you must accomplish during each day: meal preparation, laundry, exercise, recreation, caring for other family members, and so on.

Sample.

**24-Hour Pie of Life
Before Caregiving**

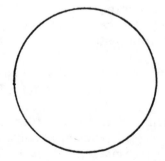

Draw your pie.

Next, draw a pie that includes the care recipient as part of your daily routine. What things will have to be sacrificed? Where does the person fit in? You can assume that care for another person will take probably twice the time you think it will whether or not the person is mentally incapacitated.

Sample.

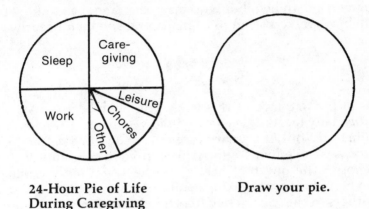

24-Hour Pie of Life During Caregiving

Draw your pie.

Once you have completed this exercise, you can begin to see the need for protecting your life from the possibility of giving up everything in order to care for another person.

Possibly you will be able to include the person in some of those activities you enjoy and not have to sacrifice your own pleasures. Perhaps you can enroll your relative in a day-care or senior center program and still maintain your career. These are things you need to consider and that you will explore in depth in Parts Three and Four of this book.

You should also recognize that there is every possibility that, once you become a primary caregiver, you will be going through some emotional states that are unfamiliar to you. Support groups are filled with beginning caregivers so filled with anger and the horror of this situation taking over their lives that they were for a time unable to accept any help at all. Every suggestion for relief was met with a negative answer. "It won't work." "There is no one else." There is always someone else—maybe not in the family but perhaps in the circle of friends, the church or synagogue, or the community. When you find an idea that seems to work, make that service or technique a regular part of your routine. Expect other persons to live up to their part of the caregiving agreement. And do not take so much on yourself that you leave no room for others who may want to help but who may be at a loss as to how to help when you seem to be managing so magnificently.

In Part Two of this book, you have been exploring the many facets of becoming involved in another person's life as his or her primary caregiver. You have researched the available living alternatives in your community and chosen the one that best suits the situation; you have explored ways of seeking additional caregiving help from others in the family, neighborhood, and community; you have examined the financial and legal ramifications of the job of caring for another person; and you have established some ground rules for the job with the care recipient, yourself, and others. Before going on to Parts Three and Four, review your progress by answering the following questions.

1. Have you explored all the possible living alternatives in the person's community, and are you satisfied that the one you have chosen is the best alternative?
2. Have you studied the person's home (or your own if the person is to live with you) for safety and security?
3. If the person is moving in with you, are both of you clear about expectations in terms of privacy, responsibilities, and finances?
4. Have you met with those friends and neighbors who have expressed an interest in helping and told them in specific ways how they might help?
5. Have you explored community service agencies whether or not you think your relative or you will need any of their services, and do you know what they provide and at what charge?

6. Have you made an emergency plan in the event that you are unavailable to continue caregiving for a period of time?

7. If you are to be a long-distance caregiver, are you comfortable with the arrangements that have been made for caring for your relative? Are you satisfied with the personnel, and do you have a single contact who can take charge if necessary?

8. Have you a clear understanding of what caregiving will cost? Are you sure about how those costs will be met? Have you determined your relative's eligibility for Medicare and Medicaid?

9. Have you gotten sound legal advice about the person's status in the event of incapacity? Is there a will? Is there a clear designation of who will act for the person in the event of mental incapacity?

10. Have you set the ground rules for your new living arrangements or your new role as caregiver with everyone who will be directly or indirectly involved?

11. Are you satisfied that the secondary caregivers understand their roles and will live up to their specific commitments?

12. Have you discussed the daily routine with the person you will be caring for? Have you solicited his or her questions and comments about what is expected?

13. Have you set some ground rules for yourself to protect your privacy and right to a life independent of your role as a primary caregiver?

Part Three

❦

Meeting the Care Recipient's Needs

About 8 to 10% of [noninstitutionalized older people] are as functionally impaired as those in institutions. . . . Overall estimates of the proportion who need supportive services hover about the one-third mark, or about 8 million people.

—Elaine M. Brody

8 ✌ Getting Down to Basics

Sometimes the role of the caregiver is to give simple basic care to an older loved one. Such basic care may include help with such daily routines as hygiene (bathing, dressing, and grooming), medications, diet, exercise, ensuring safety, recreation, and socialization. In many cases there is no catastrophic illness either physical or mental. In most cases the care recipients are people who have for years run their own homes and lives. Just because they may need occasional support and basic care from time to time does not mean they have stopped being individuals who like to be respected for their own value and to be treated as adults rather than as children.

Most older persons prefer living in their own homes to living with their children. They have developed a way of life that suits them, and they should be encouraged to maintain as much of their routine as possible. When you as caregiver are called upon to help in some basic and limited way, it is important that you not try to impose your way of life and routine on the older person. Allow that individual the dignity of personal values and standards whether or not you agree with them.

In the case where an adult child is caregiver to an aging parent even in a limited way, it is important to keep in mind that relationships between children and parents are complicated. Many adult child caregivers feel guilty when their parents need help because they have not always had the best of relationships, and the child may even dread being needed. Such guilt and fears can lead to a real martyr complex if the caregiver is not careful. It is imperative that both parties establish from the outset what help is needed, how much the adult child is willing to give, and where the boundaries lie (see chapter 7).

Sometimes the older person needs more than just minor help with basic care routines. Sometimes the person is bedridden or uses a wheelchair or is mentally incapacitated in ways that make routine care such as dressing and grooming a problem. Caring for such persons is more of a full-time job. Still, the requirements of such basic daily routines as hygiene, nutrition, and activities are the same. Some ideas for administering basic care and planning for socialization and safety regardless of the extent of the person's impairments are outlined in this chapter.

Hygiene

Whether the needed care is total or limited, the primary caregiver may need to assist the person with some of the tasks of daily hygiene. The help needed may be as simple as an occasional reminder or as detailed as bathing and dressing the care recipient.

Bathing

It probably is not necessary for the person to bathe every day. Occasionally a sponge bath will be enough. Some care recipients, though unable to manage alone, may resent any invasion of their privacy, especially in the bathroom. At such times you may want to get everything ready for the task to be performed and then leave the person alone, making sure the door does not close completely by placing a towel over the top. You can wait nearby, alert to any sound of distress while at the same time preserving the person's privacy.

When preparing to bathe the person, follow this procedure.

1. Gather everything you will need: soap, washcloth, towels, oil or lotion, shampoo, robe or clean clothing,

slippers, and shower stool or chair. Use the same brands of products your relative has used in the past if at all possible.

2. Be sure the bathroom is warm and free from drafts and that the water temperature is comfortable and safe.

3. Help the person undress and get into the tub or shower if necessary. (If possible, protect the relative's privacy by allowing the person to do this alone.)

4. As the person bathes, check for any signs of skin irritations or sores, especially if the person spends most of his or her time in bed or sitting.

5. Help the person out of the tub or shower and apply lotion or oil to dry skin areas as you dry the individual thoroughly.

If the person prefers a bath to a shower, a detachable shower hose will make the job easier. As long as the person is in the tub or shower, you can attend to several grooming needs at once such as shampooing (use baby shampoo—it will not irritate sensitive skin or eyes), shaving, and nail care (if the person is sitting down).

One of the hazards of bathing and showering is in regulating the water temperature. The caregiver may have to preset the water temperature by running the bath or starting the shower for the person. If the person is taking baths or showers with no help, the water heater thermostat can be set at a lower setting to avoid the possibility of the water being too hot. If the person is confused, the caregiver might consider setting the water controls and then blocking or covering them so that the person cannot change them.

Falling in the tub or shower is another problem for aging people, especially when trying to climb into and out of the tub or shower. If the person is especially weak or unsteady, consider renting or buying a shower stool from your sickroom supply house. Be sure that the feet of the stool have rubber tips so the stool cannot slide. For any older person trying to bathe or shower alone, there should be grab bars on the sides of the tub or walls of the shower stall. In place of a stool, you can use an aluminum lawn chair. Be sure it is a sturdy one that does not fold up *too* easily. Just be sure to place it on a rubber mat to prevent sliding.

If the person is mentally impaired, many caregivers use bar soap rather than liquid. The liquid sometimes looks like something to eat or drink to a confused person. In some cases bar soap might also resemble food, so you will have to try both and see which works the best for your relative.

Some older persons are incapacitated to such an extent that getting them into a tub or shower is impossible. For such persons you will have to rely on sponge baths for bathing. To administer a sponge bath while the person is in bed, use the following technique.

1. Time the sponge bath for a part of the day when you are least likely to be interrupted by ringing phones or other outside demands.

2. Take everything you will need to the bed. Cover the mattress and bedding with a protective sheet before the person gets into bed (if the person is completely bedridden, place a sheet or protective covering under the individual by gently rolling the person from one side to the other while you work the covering under him or her).

3. Put water of the correct temperature in a small basin. If the water supply is not conveniently nearby, fill a larger container with extra water slightly warmer than you will be using on the patient and bring along an empty container to dump used water into as you bathe the person.

4. Keep the person warm by uncovering only one part of the body at a time. Wash, rinse, dry, and apply lotion to each part of the body before proceeding to the next part. (A bath mitt is sometimes easier for a sponge bath than a washcloth. Bath mitts are available at pharmacies, linen departments of stores and mail-order houses, and bath shops.)

5. Change the bath water frequently.

If you are caring for someone who is bedfast, seek help from a home health care agency. The help from the agency does not need to be permanent, but you will need to learn some very special care techniques in order to forestall complications that can arise from being confined to bed for long periods of time such as decubitus ulcers (bedsores), muscle wasting or contractures, kidney complications, and/or bowel dysfunction.

Whether your relative bathes in a tub, takes a shower, or needs a sponge bath, protect the person's dignity and right to privacy in every way that you can. Encourage the person to do as much as he or she can alone.

Oral Hygiene

Dentures are fragile and expensive. Handle them with extreme care. Remove them carefully and brush them under running water with a toothbrush and toothpaste. If you wish, use one of the many soaking solutions available on the market.

While the dentures are out, have the person (if possible) brush any of his or her own teeth. If the care recipient is bedridden, hold a small basin under his or her chin so the person can spit into it. Be sure the person brushes his or her tongue and rinses thoroughly with mouthwash or salt water.

Pay special attention to mouth care if the individual frequently breathes through his or her mouth and the lips are dry and cracked. Moisten the lips with some petroleum jelly or cold cream—never use glycerine—to keep them from becoming infected.

If the person is completely helpless, wipe the tongue and gums and the inside of the mouth gently with a soft gauze cloth moistened with a hydrogen peroxide solution or plain water.

Dressing

Older persons, regardless of their health problems, are still interested in looking their best. Taking pride in one's appearance is a sign that a person has held on to his or her self-esteem. Such people are more likely to feel good about themselves and the world around them. If your relative no longer cares about appearances, you should be concerned about that person's mental attitude.

When selecting clothing for the person, you should be aware that as people age, their bodies change, and what once fit may no longer be suitable. Many caregivers find that separates work better than suits or dresses. Such tailoring details as raglan sleeves, soft gathers, and undefined waistlines may be more convenient than more fitted styles. Another thing to consider is that many older people are affected by stiffening of the joints and arthritis. For this reason selecting clothing that is easy to put on and take off is important. Stretch fabrics and garments that open in front will help. Fasteners should be easy to see and operate.

Because of body changes that are normal to the aging process, such as changing hair color and skin tone, you may be surprised to find that colors that once were quite flattering for the person are no longer attractive. If the person can still go shopping, that can be a very good activity. It gets the person out of the house, allows the opportunity to make selections and express opinions, and makes the individual aware of his or her self-worth.

Sometimes selecting the clothing to be worn for the day can be a major problem for a person, especially if he or she is mentally impaired. The colors and patterns of many outfits hanging together in one closet may be too confusing. Some people mask their confusion by refusing to get dressed, hiding behind the excuse that it is too much trouble and there is no point. You can alleviate this problem by choosing two complete outfits and offering that simple choice to the person rather than facing him or her with an entire closetful of clothes.

Most successful caregivers are very organized. Hanging clothing for yourself and the person you are caring for by outfit, complete with shoes and accessories, can save a lot of time for both of you. Another tip that may help speed the process of dressing is to lay out clothing in the order in which it is to be put on. Do not give up. Get dressed yourself and have the care recipient get dressed every day regardless of the schedule. Do not fall into a habit of saying, "What for? We aren't going to see anybody." Yes, you are. You are going to see each other.

If your relative uses a wheelchair or has been partially paralyzed by a stroke, you may need to give special considerations in choosing clothing for that person. Clothing items with back closings may be easier for you to manage without having to lift the person out of the wheelchair. When the person who uses a wheelchair is going out, you may find it easier to use a cape rather than a coat, or a shawl instead of a sweater. These garments are also easier for someone who is paralyzed on one side to wear, since there is no wrestling with sleeves and buttons. Another convenient garment for those who have lost the use of one hand is mittens instead of gloves; mittens are easier to put on and take off. When you are dressing a person who is partially paralyzed and/or in a wheelchair, put the weakest arm in the sleeve of the shirt first, pull the shirt across the back, and then put the strongest arm in its sleeve. Undress the person in reverse order.

There are companies that specialize in clothing for the disabled. Sears, Roebuck and Company and the J. C. Penney Company have health care catalogs that include clothing as well as health care supplies. You can also order catalogs and clothing from the following places.

Comfortably Yours, 52 West Hunter Avenue, Maywood, NJ 07607

Amputee Shoe and Glove Exchange, 1635 Warwickshire Drive, Houston, TX 77077

Fashion-Able, Rocky Hill, NJ 08553

Geri Fashions, 301 East Illinois Street, Newberg, OR 97132

National Odd Shoe Exchange, 3100 Neilson Way, Santa Monica, CA 90401

New Look Patient Apparel, 505 Pearl Street, Buffalo, NY 14202

Wheelchair Fashions, PO Box 99, South Windham, ME 04082

The following sources are not in the clothing business but may be able to offer advice.

American Gerontological Society, 10 Columbus Circle, New York, NY 10019

American Physical Therapy Association, 1156 15th Street, NW, Washington, DC 20005

Arthritis Foundation, 3400 Peachtree Road, NE, Atlanta, GA 30326

Also, Adeline Hoffman has written a book entitled *Clothing for the Handicapped, the Aged, and Other People with Special Needs.*

Grooming

Good grooming is important in the caregiving process because of what it does for self-esteem—both the caregiver's and the care recipient's. Aside from bathing or showering, oral hygiene, and dressing well, there are other grooming rituals that need to be observed every day such as hair and nail care. For as long as possible the person should be encouraged to continue these routines unassisted. Sometimes the caregiver can help by laying out the necessary paraphernalia and then leaving the person to complete the task.

Men who are caregivers may be stymied by the ritual of applying makeup for their impaired wives or mothers. However, with a little practice, simple routines are easily mastered. Keep in mind that many of the best makeup people in Hollywood are men. One idea is to go to a shopping mall or department store and seek some instruction from a cosmetics specialty store or department. The woman's hairdresser or a neighbor or relative may be able to advise you. Do not just give up on applying makeup for your wife or mother. Such a seemingly small thing can be of major importance to the person's mental attitude.

Women who care for men may have to shave their relative if it is not possible for the person to continue to perform that task on his own. Shaving is relatively simple, but if you need help, have a male relative or friend or the person's barber give you some pointers.

Hair care is another very important part of the grooming routine. Keep styles short and simple to manage. If it is not possible to get the person to a barber or beautician, see if there are any hairdressers who will make house calls. If money is a problem but you and the care recipient can get out, try making an occasional appointment with a local beauty school or barber college. Costs are much lower, and the students are directed and supervised by professionals. Better yet, learn to cut the person's hair yourself.

Other time-savers and step-savers are the dry shampoos on the market. These allow some of the set to stay intact while removing surface dirt and oils. An attractive wig might also be helpful occasionally when unexpected company arrives. When brushing or combing hair of any length, work in small sections from the ends to the scalp, especially if the hair is matted or tangled.

Nail care for both men and women is important, especially if one hand and/or foot is paralyzed. Sometimes the paralyzed hand stays bent into a fist most of the time, allowing nails to grow unnoticed. Keep nails short, and if polish is used, make it clear or a light shade. Pay attention to foot care as well as hand care. If the person sits in a wheelchair or is confined to bed, the caregiver may not pay attention to the continuing growth of nails because there is so much the caregiver has to manage. Check the paralyzed hand and/or foot regularly and maintain care of those body parts as well as of the functioning hand and foot. Regular examinations by a podiatrist are also recommended.

Incontinence, a Special Hygiene Problem

Sometimes an older person who appears to be perfectly healthy in every way suffers from the loss of urinary or bowel control. Urinary incontinence is especially common in older women but can also be a problem for men. The figures according to the National Institute on Aging are that one in ten persons over sixty-five years of age has a problem with urinary incontinence. Many withdraw from normal social routines and try to hide the problem from their families.

As a caregiver, you should know that in many cases incontinence can be treated and controlled. In some cases it can be cured. If you know or suspect that your relative has a problem, seek medical attention for that person at once. Some common types of urinary incontinence include the following:

- stress incontinence brought on by exercise, laughter, coughing, or other actions that stress the bladder
- urge incontinence, the sudden onset of a strong urge to urinate that may be associated with such conditions as bladder infection, stroke, Parkinson's disease, multiple sclerosis, and senile dementia
- overflow incontinence, which occurs when the bladder is swollen or distended and which may affect men generally and both men and women with diabetes

Sometimes incontinence is caused by such situations as being afraid to go to the bathroom at night or when in a strange place. It can also be brought on by an emotional reaction if the person is upset, as in the case of being moved from his or her home to an unfamiliar location. Another psychological cause of incontinence may be anger, and at other times the condition is the result of use of medications such as diuretics.

If the person is confused, incontinence may be a result of that confusion. Sometimes the individual may simply forget where the bathroom is or what to do once he or she is in there. Pictures and labels may provide just enough cues to aid the confused person. Put the care recipient on a regular schedule and stick to it if the person is having trouble making it to the bathroom on time.

You can help the person suffering from any form of incontinence by doing the following:

- evaluating the person's need for assistance and offering that aid in whatever *discreet* way you can
- leaving the toilet lid open at all times and installing grab bars and a call bell near the commode

- taking along extra clothing for the person when he or she is going out. This avoids embarrassment if an accident occurs in a place outside the home.
- familiarizing yourself with products that aid an incontinent person, such as disposable pads and underpants
- installing a portable toilet near the person's bed if night incontinence is a problem
- keeping the diet rich in fiber and keeping track of bowel movements
- stocking the bathroom with disposable pads, premoistened towels, and other aids that will help the individual change and clean himself or herself
- restricting liquids after 7:00 P.M.

Accidents will happen, and sometimes the odor and stain of such an accident is the most embarrassing for the person and the most frustrating for you. To clean fabric stained with urine, soak the fabric in a solution of boiling water and Lysol. To clean fabric stained with feces, soak the fabric in cold water and then wash with Tone soap (toothpaste also works to reduce the odor) and hot water. Use a brush to scrub out the stain.

One of the most important things you as a caregiver can do for the incontinent person is to be sensitive. Incontinence is not something the person does on purpose. Your attitude is clear to your relative. Be sure it is a positive one.

Medications

Used correctly, prescribed and over-the-counter drugs can improve health. How do you make certain that your relative is getting proper medication? How do you know what to expect from a prescribed drug? Do you know what will happen if that medicine is taken in combination with other prescribed drugs or over-the-counter formulas? The two major sources of sound advice and information about the drugs you and your relative take are your physician and your pharmacist.

The Physician

The doctor is not a mind reader. He or she can only know what the problems with the care recipient are if you or that person communicates those problems. Likewise, he or she needs to know some of the habits of the individual that can have an effect on the performance of some medications. For example, does the person drink or smoke? Another vital piece of information you need to share with the physician is whether the person is seeing other doctors and taking medications prescribed by them.

From time to time, you need to review with the doctor what medications are being taken and for how long they have been taken. Patients can build up a tolerance over a period of time, and the medicine may no longer be effective. Doctors with experience in geriatric medicine are more aware that older persons react differently to drugs than do younger persons. Such physicians may prescribe dosages that are more or less than they would prescribe for younger patients. Is your relative's doctor aware of this? If you do not think a medicine is doing what it should, or if you see any new or unusual symptoms, you need to contact the doctor. However, you should not expect the doctor to prescribe medication for every little symptom.

The Pharmacist

A pharmacist is an expert in both prescription and nonprescription medications. He or she can be your best friend when it comes to getting advice on medications. Get to know the pharmacist and take your prescriptions to the same pharmacy to be filled so that you build a relationship with one professional staff and have someone to call in an emergency. Many pharmacies offer home delivery services, and many pharmacists will inform the patient and the physician if they see a threatening combination of medications on a patient's record.

You need to ask both the doctor and the pharmacist for information on any side effects medications may have. You also need to seek the pharmacist's advice on any over-the-counter medications the person you are caring for plans to use in combination with prescribed drugs. Besides the medications prescribed by physicians, most people have several over-the-counter medications on hand at all times. It may interest you to know that there are over 300,000 different nonprescription formulas available for your purchase—an endless list of cold remedies, cough medications, laxatives, painkillers, and so on.

The pharmacist can also help by providing safety or easy-to-open caps on bottles, giving you an accurate measuring device for dispensing medicines, telling you whether old medicines are still good or need to be thrown out, and advising you on the availability of generic brands that may save you money.

The Medicines

What information do you need about any medicine you or your relative will take? Make a chart or keep a notebook and fill in the following information for every medicine, prescribed or not.

- Name of medication
- Purpose of medication
- Dosage
- Times medication is to be taken
- How medication is taken
- Possible side effects

Be sure that you ask the pharmacist how the medication is to be taken (with water or milk, before eating or after, and so on), how the medication will react with other medications already being taken, and how the medication should be stored.

Some patients inadvertently take the effectiveness out of prescribed medications. Drugs are prescribed to be taken in a certain way at a certain time for a certain purpose. If the medicine is to be swallowed whole or melted under the tongue, there is a reason for that, and taking it any other way reduces or even cancels the effectiveness of the drug. Prescriptions also have instructions about when they are to be taken. If those instructions are vague (three times a day), get specifics from your doctor or pharmacist. Ask what to do and what not to do if one time is accidentally missed.

Ask the doctor before discontinuing any prescribed medicine. Some patients decide on their own to stop taking a medication because they feel better. Other patients decide they can save money by making a prescription last longer by taking it less often than prescribed or by cutting pills in half. And one of the biggest problems of improper use of medications is sharing medicine with someone else. This is a very dangerous habit and *under no circumstances* should medicines for one person be used by someone else.

Old drugs can lose or change strengths, and holding on to a medicine can be dangerous. Speak to your doctor before resuming any medication that has been stored for any time. Storing drugs properly is important. Heat, light, and humidity can cause drugs to change strength. Be sure to ask the pharmacist if any medication needs refrigeration or special storage conditions.

Finally, keep all medications in their original labeled containers. Sometimes, especially when traveling, people will take medications and mix them together in one pillbox. Many pills look alike, so pills should never be mixed together.

Administering the Medications
Many caregivers find that being sure that prescribed medications are taken is one of the most difficult parts of their job. The care recipient sometimes fights taking the medicine or has trouble swallowing it. If the person is still living alone, he or she may simply forget to take the medicine. If any of these situations apply, try these suggestions.

• If the medicine is liquid, have the person suck an ice cube before taking the medicine. The ice cube will numb the taste buds.

• If the person is bedridden, administer liquid medicine in a cup rather than with a spoon. There are special cups available for those who are bedridden.

• Set a kitchen timer or alarm clock to remind the caregiver or the care recipient that it is time to take medications.

• If the person lives alone, try calling or having others call to be sure meals are being eaten and medications are being taken on schedule.

• If the person remembers to take medications on time but has trouble sorting out multiple medications, there are containers available at pharmacies or medical supply houses that have individual lidded cups for days of the week or even for several-times-per-day doses. Medications can be sorted out a week at a time in these devices by a caregiver who visits.

Some people with Alzheimer's disease have been found to have unusual reactions to medicines that work fine for others. Be aware and watch for side effects.

For more information.   Ask your librarian for these books.

Consumer Drug Digest by the American Society of Hospital Pharmacists.

The Essential Guide to Prescription Drugs by James W. Long, M.D.

Joe Graedon's The New People's Pharmacy by Joe Graedon.

The Pill Book by Harold M. Silverman and Gilbert I. Simon.

Diet and Nutrition

The mom who once admonished you to finish your vegetables because "people are starving in China" may now be starving herself either by not eating at all or by eating fat-loaded convenience foods. The dad who taught you the value of a dollar may have a problem dealing with the seemingly simple task of shopping for food. Why do older people seem to lose interest in food? One culprit might be their diminishing senses. For many, the sense of taste diminishes with age. Some researchers think this may be due to a lack of zinc. Appetite is stimulated by the sight of attractively prepared food as well as by the smell of food in the process of preparation. Poor eyesight may change the way foods look. Poor eyesight can also make shopping tedious and frustrating. And perhaps the worst culprit for appetite loss is loneliness. Too many older people are expected to eat alone day after day and still maintain an interest in the ritual of mealtime.

Other factors can affect the appetite such as medications, digestive problems, and special diets that limit food choices. And do not forget that many members of the older population have to deal with dentures and other mouth problems that restrict food choices. Arthritis may make the manipulation of utensils difficult, if not impossible. And finally, finances can play a role—when money is tight, unfortunately many older people will sacrifice a balanced diet in favor of meals that are cheap and filling.

What are the special nutritional needs of the aging? For most there is a need for less calories, due to reduced activity and exercise. Women need to be especially aware of their calcium intake. Over 80 percent of older women in the United States have some amount of calcium loss from their bones, and many suffer from the condition known as osteoporosis (see pages 195–196). Products rich in vitamin D such as milk, yogurt, and cheese need to be included in the diet at least twice a day. Another nutritional need for older people is iron. Enriched whole grains and green leafy vegetables will help meet this need. Research has shown that fiber is a necessary aid to the ability to digest foods. Eating foods that are rich in fiber and drinking plenty of water help considerably in preventing constipation.

If the older person needs fewer calories but still needs to take in such foods as dairy products, red meats, and whole grains, how can weight be controlled? Sugars and other fats will have to be watched strictly. For snacks, offer fruits, nuts, and cheese or peanut butter on crackers instead of pies, cakes, and cookies. Be careful about serving too many snacks that are high in salt. For dessert offer a baked apple with raisins or serve yogurt with unsweetened fruit.

Helping the Person Eat

With a person who suffers from Alzheimer's disease or is confused, playing with food or utensils at mealtime may actually be a device for masking an inability to choose. The simplest solution is to limit choices. Cut up the meat before serving and eliminate the need for a knife. Offer the person either a spoon or fork but not both. Serve one food at a time if necessary. Prepare the coffee with cream and sugar away from the table and serve it. Simplify foods—serve soup in a cup or mug, offer finger foods such as fish sticks, french fries, drumsticks, and finger gelatin. Use the chain holders that allow one to carry eyeglasses on a chain around the neck to hold a napkin in place bib style or sew ties onto a dish towel and use it as a bib-style napkin. Such precautions should only be taken when the person is having problems with the usual food utensils. Try not to anticipate problems. These aids can be dehumanizing if they are introduced too early in the caregiving process.

Be aware that the person may forget to eat food placed right in front of him or her. Gentle reminders even as simple as touching the fork lightly may be enough to stir action. Also pay particular attention to consumption of liquids. Confused persons may be unable to express thirst, so serve liquids at frequent and regular intervals throughout the day. Finally, many confused persons will try to eat objects that to them resemble food—dog food, flowers, printed napkins, soap, plants. If this is a problem for your relative, remove those items from the home; if that is not possible, keep them out of sight.

Checking Up on Your Relative

Follow these suggestions if your relative is not living with you and you suspect that he or she is not eating properly.

• Find a time or excuse when you visit to look in the refrigerator. Notice what foods are still there from last time and the freshness of all the foods that are there.

• Ask what the person ate for the most recent meal.

Do not judge; just show some interest.

• Drop by with a meal to share that is divided into three serving-sized portions—one for the person to have that night, one for you to eat with him or her, and one for the freezer.

• Find ways for the person to avoid eating alone. You might check into senior nutrition programs and/or invite the person to share a meal with you occasionally.

• Offer to take the person shopping for food or, if shopping is a problem, investigate the possibility of a store that will deliver or a home shopping service.

• If the person uses a wheelchair or is disabled, write for *Mealtime Manual for People with Disabilities and the Aging*, Institute of Rehabilitative Medicine, NYU Medical Center, Box 38, Ranks, PA 17572 ($3.25) and *The Wheelchair in the Kitchen*, Kitchen, Paralyzed Vets of America, Inc., 7315 Wisconsin Avenue, NW, Washington, DC 20014 ($2.50).

Exercise

Many older people mistakenly feel that when they start to age and their frailties become more pronounced, they must "take things easy." They fear moving. Movement may be painful, and because of that pain the individual may move as little as possible. This is a mistake. Exercise is a vital part of everyone's lifestyle—young, middle-aged, or old.

Perhaps you have just started an exercise program after a long period of a more sedentary life. Remember the aches and pains after the first few days of that new exertion? It will not be any different for an older person. And there will be positive benefits after a short time just as there were for you. Of course, any person who has been without exercise for any length of time should check with a physician before beginning any program.

What are the benefits of exercise for an older person? For starters, regular exercise will increase maximum oxygen consumption (that means conditioning will be better), and it will lower the heart rate (that means the body's other organs will not have to work as hard.) On top of that, regular exercise can decrease blood pressure, burn off body fat, and improve strength and mobility. Perhaps one of the biggest positives is that regular exercise—because it makes a person feel better—has the power to stimulate feelings of self-worth and create a sense of well-being.

Regardless of the physical impairments of the individual, he or she can benefit from a regular daily routine of exercise. Set a certain time of day and stick to it. If you have trouble disciplining the person to a regular exercise routine, investigate the possibility of joining an organized class or program through the local senior center or YMCA or YMHA.

Walking is one of the best and least boring exercises. It is also one of the least expensive. It is not quite free, for a walker will need a good pair of walking shoes with solid support and cushioning. In the last decade heart patients have discovered the positive benefits of walking briskly for at least half an hour each day. In many communities shopping malls open their doors at six or seven in the morning to accommodate these walkers. It is a great way to exercise because the weather is always the same, there is something to look at, and there are other walkers on the premises.

Not everyone can walk though. Some cannot even stand. There are good programs of graduated exercises available for such people—exercises that give every part of the body a workout without standing. Such programs are available on video cassettes or on tape cassettes, and most are done to music. Perhaps your local library or Area Agency on Aging can recommend such a program. Each program is usually about twenty minutes long and involves such simple props as a chair and perhaps a towel. Most programs should be used for a few minutes at first and the time gradually increased until the entire twenty minutes can be used.

For the bedridden there is also a program of exercises called the range-of-motion exercises. In this case you, the caregiver, assist the person in exercising by gently moving each part of the body in sequence. It is imperative that helpless people be exercised in this manner. Even totally helpless people can benefit from these routines. For proper training in these programs, call your local home health care service, which can supply you with an illustrated brochure about the range-of-motion program or will send someone to show you how to do the exercises with your relative.

Whatever you and your relative choose as an exercise routine for your relative, keep in mind that exercise will benefit people of any age. Remember, anyone who is thinking of starting a regular program of exercise should see his or her doctor first. Once you have the doctor's permission, follow these suggestions for establishing an exercise routine in cooperation with your relative.

- Begin with some simple warm-up stretches. This will minimize the risk of injury. And when the formal exercise period is ended, do not forget a cool-down period. There needs to be a gradual transition from strenuous exercise back to the normal resting state. For example, after a brisk walk go one more time around the shopping mall at a normal or leisurely pace or repeat the warm-up stretches more slowly.

- Train yourself and, if possible, the care recipient to take his or her pulse so that throughout the exercise period you can monitor heart rate. Your doctor can advise you on what is a proper heart rate range during exercise for someone of the person's age and condition.

- Choose your exercise activity to suit the needs of the person. Walking is easy and familiar if that is possible. If not, check with the local library or senior center for an exercise program that can be done at home or for a class the person can join. If nothing is available, you can order the following:

Adult Physical Fitness, U.S. Government Printing Office, Washington, DC 20402 (#040-000-00026—70¢)

Join the Active People Over 60, Maryland State Office on Aging, 861 Park Avenue, Baltimore, MD 21201

The Fitness Challenge in the Later Years, U.S. Administration on Aging, U.S. Government Printing Office, Washington, DC 20402 (#017-062-00009—75¢)

Fitness for Life: Exercises for People Over 50 by Theodore Berland.

• If the person experiences any pain or discomfort, discontinue the exercises until you can check with his or her physician. But keep in mind that some muscle soreness will happen and is a sign the program is working.

• How often should the individual exercise? At least three times a week is a good pattern in the beginning. Later you can add days, but avoid exercising every single day, especially if the program is strenuous. You may want to have the person alternate the types of exercises he or she is doing—walking one day and doing aerobic exercises (those that build heart and lung performance) the next. This prevents boredom and allows different muscles to be worked each time.

Safety

Accidents in the home are one of the most common causes of injury and death in the United States. The problem can be exaggerated for those over sixty-five, as they become less agile and more prone to falls and other accidents. Follow these suggestions to help secure the home and daily routine from the opportunity for needless accidents.

• Make sure there is adequate lighting both inside and outside the dwelling.

• Make sure electrical cords, all small appliances, and lamps are in good working order. They should all bear the Underwriters Laboratories label. The UL seal guarantees that the electrical cords and wiring are safe when properly used.

• Do not use extension cords unless they are absolutely necessary, and then tape them into place to prevent the person's tripping over them.

• Make certain every room and hallway is well lighted. Install night-lights in the bathroom and bedroom and the hallway between the two. Place a flashlight or lamp within easy reach of the person's bed.

- Replace worn carpets and rugs and tack them into place. Avoid scatter rugs if possible, or at least make sure they have nonskid backings.
- Make certain uncarpeted floors are not slippery.
- Install nonskid strips on uncarpeted stairs. Be sure stairways are well lighted with switches at both the top and bottom of the stairs. Install handrails on all stairways.
- Make sure inside and outside stairs are in good repair. Add handrails and ramps where necessary.
- In the kitchen be sure appliances are in good working order and that the stove is well away from any curtains or materials that might catch fire. If the person is confused, mark the stove controls and hot-water faucets in red.
- Be especially aware of heat-producing or power appliances that may burn or injure the care recipient who is confused or whose eyesight is faulty.
- Install nonskid strips in the bathtub and shower. Install grab bars in the bathtub and shower and next to the toilet. Set the hot-water heater at 110 degrees or lower to prevent accidental burning.
- Post emergency numbers in large print next to every telephone.
- Store medications in their own labeled containers in a cool, dark place.
- Store any poisonous substances in properly labeled containers and away from foods or medications.
- Install smoke detectors in the kitchen and stairways. Place fire extinguishers nearby, and make certain the person can use an extinguisher if possible. If the person lives in an apartment complex, be sure he or she knows the exit route in case of fire. Also check to see whether the building has a sprinkler system.
- Have the furnace and exhaust systems checked regularly, and replace filters on a regular schedule.
- Be sure all storm windows and doors and all screens are in good repair, and place proper locks on all doors and windows.

• If possible, discuss with the person what to do if someone breaks into the home. Make the person aware of any con games or service contract scams that may operate in the area. (*Keeping Out of Crime's Way: The Practical Guide for People Over Fifty* by J. E. Persico with George Sunderland deals in depth with con games and scams.)

• Get to know the neighbors if you do not already know them. Make sure they are aware of the person who is in need of care and living alone or living with you.

• Finally, repair those items that need attention and install those extras that will ensure safety for the relative.

If the relative is still living alone, observe the individual's movements and be sure he or she is steady and balanced. If not, suggest the use of a four-pronged cane or walker. Call and visit often. Make sure the neighbors are aware of anything out of the ordinary and have emergency numbers (including yours) to call if they suspect a problem.

You might also consider contracting for a telephone reassurance system, especially if the care recipient is living alone or with an elderly spouse. These systems are widely available through hospitals, telephone centers, and police departments. Call your local police department, phone center, or hospital for information.

Recreation

There are several reasons older people stop doing those things they once enjoyed. Some reasons, such as depression, are treatable. Others, like Alzheimer's disease, may not be as of this writing. One thing is certain—losing interest in life is not part of growing old. Most older people maintain a zest for living and a curiosity to try new and interesting things.

If your relative is apathetic and there seems to be no physical cause, pay close attention to what he or she says and does and report these observations to the doctor. Everyone has bad days, and that is normal, but prolonged disinterest in life is not. If the doctor tells you it is, get another doctor.

Do not overlook the obvious problems such as failing eyesight or hearing or pain in joints and fingers. Check the individual's diet. A diet too rich in fats and sugars can result in apathy and sharp mood swings. Be sure that medications are being properly taken and that there are no side effects from mixing medications. Also, be sure the person has meaningful activities to fill his or her days—nothing is more depressing at any age than busywork, with no meaning or purpose.

In planning a recreational or activity program with your relative, start with what interested him or her in the past. Are those activities still a part of the individual's life? If not, why not? Is there a health reason? Can it be treated? If health is not the reason, determine whether there has been sufficient opportunity to pursue the hobby or pleasure or if there is still any purpose to the activity in the eyes of the individual.

Hobbies

You might be able to rekindle interest by asking the person to use his or her skills to create something for a special occasion such as a school bazaar or to sell at a local consignment shop. Another way to rekindle interest is to show an interest in learning the skill yourself, placing the individual in the role of teacher and advisor. Be sure that you are sensitive to any physical disabilities that may make pursuing the hobby impossible or, at the least, uncomfortable for the individual.

Confused or mentally impaired persons may give up hobbies because of their realization that they can no longer remember the steps necessary to perform the skill. Such people may cover their embarrassment at the realization that their minds no longer work in this area by refusing to perform any activity. You may find through trial and error that the person is still capable of some simple skills, but keep in mind that you may have to give instructions each time the individual performs the task involved.

Television

If the person must remain at home, one of the most likely sources of entertainment is the television set. While you do not want the television set to become a substitute for life itself, a favorite TV program can be an enjoyable evening's pastime for both of you. Make a production of it—fix some popcorn or a snack, or order in pizza or Chinese food. Pour some wine or soda. Take a real break, put your feet up, and enjoy the show.

Reading

Do not overlook your local library as a source of entertainment supplies. Besides the usual books and magazines, many libraries now offer films, tapes, and records. If you have a record player or tape machine, you could have a sing-along. If you have one of the new video cassette recorders, you can borrow films and programs to show on your television. Some libraries even offer a home delivery program for those who cannot leave the house. There are books on tape for the person who has problems seeing or reading; also, books in large print are available through most libraries.

Traveling

In some cases your relative may be able to travel either alone or with you. You should, of course, clear any travel plans with the physician first if there has been a medical problem. There are a number of things you can do to make the trip more comfortable for the older person.

Call the airlines and book a seat in advance. Request wheelchair assistance, if necessary, and any special diet. Most airlines will assist older passengers in boarding ahead of other passengers, whether or not the person is in a wheelchair or using a walker. If the individual uses a walker, be sure the one being used is collapsible for a plane ride so it can be folded and stored while in flight.

Book all hotels in advance, and request any special needs; then confirm the requests in writing. For example, you may wish to request a room on the lowest floor in the unlikely event of a fire or other emergency. Perhaps you will want to request twin beds or a wheelchair-accessible bathroom. Think of the needs before you arrive, and give the hotel time to anticipate them.

When you and your relative pack for an airline trip, limit the amount of carryon luggage and the number of coats you will have to manage, but do carry a small case that contains all medications and other items you will need in case your luggage goes astray. If you will be traveling as part of a group, make the tour manager aware of any special needs as far in advance of departure as possible, and if the person's disabilities will slow down the tour group, do not go on the tour.

Once you arrive, do not try to do too much, especially if life for the person has been fairly sedentary for some time. Keep in mind that you are each individuals and not joined at the hip—if the care recipient needs an afternoon nap but you are raring to go, plan to do some things on your own. Your relative might appreciate knowing he or she is not holding you back because of physical frailties, and you can share your experience over dinner.

Finally, limit the length of your stay, and try to keep meals and schedules as close to the normal routine as possible. Be flexible and aware of the person's reactions to tours and activities. Plan, as much as possible, in advance for any emergency or need and be appreciative of any special service rendered.

Special Activities

Any primary caregiver may find himself or herself one day at a loss to know what recreational activities to propose to the care recipient. Depending on the extent of the relative's disabilities, there are many possibilities for keeping the individual alert and involved in a full and satisfying life.

• Even bedridden or paralyzed persons can try painting. A number of very talented artists paint by holding the paintbrushes in their teeth because they are totally paralyzed from the neck down.

• Card games can be played by almost anyone, including the confused. You may have to revive some childhood games such as Memory, Go Fish, and War. (Get cards with large face numbers if needed.)

• Making photograph albums is a good activity for the bedridden and those who use a wheelchair as well as for the confused.

• See if any charity or nonprofit or political organization needs help with stuffing envelopes or making calls. If the person you are caring for is able, the two of you might volunteer to canvass your neighborhood for funds for a worthy cause.

• Cooking, gardening (indoors and outdoors), and music are activities many older persons can enjoy in spite of their impairments.

• Consider getting the person a pet.

• Help the person find a pen pal in another part of the city or state.

Socialization

Opportunities for the person to socialize with others may be limited, depending on the nature and severity of the person's impairments. After the first shock of the news of the person's illness, friends may fade away for any of a number of reasons: inability to cope, uncertainty about what to do, problems within their own lives. The caregiver may actively have to seek social contacts for the care recipient and for himself or herself. Some caregivers resent having to add this responsibility to their already filled lives, but caregivers who refuse to pursue social contacts for their relatives may find that they and the care recipients are soon isolated and very lonely. One caregiver said, "I'll be damned if I'll invite people to dinner who have known my sister for forty years just to get them to say hello to her." That person is both right and wrong. No, it should not be necessary to entertain old friends in order to have them keep up the association they have had with the individual for years. But the reality of the world is that it may indeed be necessary to take those extra steps to ensure that old friends do not fade away. As the primary caregiver, you should also be on the lookout for opportunities for forming new friendships both for yourself and for the person who needs care and support.

New Friendships

Because both your lives have changed, you might find yourself exposed to new situations that can be a source of new friendships. For example, if your relative attends an adult day-care center or senior center or eats one meal at a senior nutrition site, encourage him or her to talk with the others who attend these programs. If you have joined a support group, nourish those contacts you make there. These are people who thoroughly understand what your life is like as a caregiver, and although they have their own persons to care for, they can be a source of encouragement and sympathy when what you really need is to talk with someone who understands.

Visitors

You may have to set some guidelines, depending on the condition and wishes of the person being cared for, when visitors come to call. A visitor will need to know what to expect. For example, is the visitor coming to see both of you or to give you a short break while he or she visits with the relative and you attend to some personal task? If the visitor is to be left alone with the person, have you made sure he or she understands the person's condition and limitations? For example, does the visitor have any knowledge of Alzheimer's disease and how the person may react? Or if the disabled person is prone to choking and coughing spells or other attacks that may alarm the visitor, does the visitor know what to do and where to reach you? If you leave the visitor alone with your relative, return to the room every so often to reassure the visitor of your presence should he or she need you. Do not take advantage of the visitor's time and goodwill.

You have to be prepared for the fact that something you have grown used to may be repulsive to a visitor. For example, if the person you are caring for has lost some motor control, the resultant condition may frighten a visitor. A mentally incapacitated person's pacing or incoherent conversation may alarm the unsuspecting visitor. If possible, talk with the visitor in advance and tell him or her what to expect and what not to expect. Encourage visitors to keep in mind that although outward appearances may have changed, this is still the same individual they have always known with many of the same unique personality traits. This is true of people with Alzheimer's disease, who, although their own speech and thought patterns may be gibberish, may be very aware of what is being said to and about them by others.

In a *Woman's Day* article entitled "The Best Medicine Can Be You!" author Maggie Strong (whose husband has multiple sclerosis) offers the following suggestions for visitors.

1. Do not keep asking the person how he or she is. If the person is in pain or losing a mind or dying, there really is no adequate answer to that question.
2. Allow the disabled person the dignity of asking for your help before offering to assist the person to move about in a wheelchair or rise from a chair.
3. Be aware that people who are disabled or impaired may be introverted and shy. The visitor needs to take the initiative in pursuing the friendship.
4. If you see that it is a bad day for the person, keep the visit short.
5. Do not tell the person about other people you know who have symptoms similar to those of the person. One caregiver tells of someone who told her husband when he was describing his illness, "Oh, that's just middle age. I've got that too!"
6. If possible, take the person on an outing with you. Do anything you can to make the person feel less dependent.
7. With the person acting as supervisor (if possible), do a few odd jobs around the house or see whether you can do some special shopping for the person, such as buying a birthday present for that person to give to the caregiver as a surprise.

8. Ask about the caregiver. Show that you understand that the situation has affected two lives.
9. Ask the caregiver about his or her feelings. It may be an incredible relief for that person to be able to admit that he or she is frightened, angry, or depressed.
10. Do not give medical advice. But do pass on any information you may have about services that could help the care recipient and/or the caregiver.

Show this list of tips to your relative's visitors as well as to family members who may come to call. You will be answering questions those people may be unable or afraid to express.

Finally, be sure that the visitor is aware of how much the visit has meant to both you and the person you are caring for. Reassure the visitor that, even though the person may not have been particularly responsive, a visit is never pointless. No one can say for sure what a visit may mean to a person who cannot respond, but research has shown that there is an effect. If the visitor feels that there is no point in his or her time with the disabled person, remind the visitor that there was someone else who benefited enormously from the time spent—you, the caregiver.

Holiday Celebrations

Satisfying both your needs and the care recipient's can be difficult, especially when you feel trapped between the needs of the person and those of the rest of the family. Holidays can be a double-edged sword. On the one hand, a frail older person should not be expected to handle the many preparations and details of a large family gathering. On the other hand, the person is understandably reluctant to relinquish his or her position as the head of the family.

You might meet with other siblings and in-laws and plan ways to divide the work load. Perhaps one person could drop by the week before the big day and help Mom clean and set up the house. Someone else could make plans to help with the baking several weeks in advance.

The big holiday meal could be a combined effort, with Mom making her special recipe and everyone else bringing their own special contributions. Or the family could plan to spend the major part of the day at home with the older person but eat the meal out and make that treat part of the gift giving. It is difficult to buy gifts for older people, and a chance to dress up and get out may be something Mom and/or Dad would really enjoy.

Reminiscing

Talking about the past and one's personal experiences is a way of being a part of a group or the family unit for all people. Giving respect and importance to those stories is one good way to build self-esteem for the person for whom you are caring. Telling the stories allows the older person to put his or her life in order and to see personal achievements. This can be a very crucial part of the therapeutic process for those who suffer from memory loss and/or depression.

Many family members lose patience when an older person again and again starts to tell the same story. In this situation, rather than cutting the person off abruptly with "We've heard that story a thousand times already," try another tactic. Gently say something like, "I remember when you told us that, Dad. That must have been a very special moment for you." Then add, "I'd like to hear you talk about . . ." and choose some part of the person's life with which you are not familiar. Encourage not only the telling of the family history but also the recording of it through tapes, charts, and photograph albums.

Pay close attention to those stories the person tells again and again. There may be a reason they are special. They may give a clue to some agitation or special joy the relative is feeling. Some older persons will devote much of their conversation to the past. Rather than become annoyed by this fascination with what has already happened, you might use this as an opportunity to put together a family history for younger generations. For assistance in getting started on genealogical research, write to the National Archives, Room 1111, 711 14th

Street, NW, Washington, DC 20408.

You can also ask your librarian for how-to books on tracing your family history. One such book that is thorough and easy to follow is *How to Trace Your Family Tree* by the American Genealogical Research Institute staff. Your librarian will be able to suggest other titles.

Participation in Family Matters

Not every minute of every day has to be planned. The person you are caring for will enjoy just being included in the normal routine of the family or household. Many caregivers seek to "protect" their relative from the normal anxieties and agitations of daily life. Often caregivers will go to great lengths to hide bills and keep problems within the family unit a secret, thinking the news will be too upsetting for the older person. On the contrary, often the person's imagination, allowed to run rampant when he or she is left out of such normal family relationships, does far more damage than reality would. In some cases, given the opportunity to be concerned about someone else's needs and problems, the person may improve markedly.

Encourage the individual to talk, and, whenever possible, seek his or her advice and sympathy for a problem or concern. By encouraging someone's interest, you are stimulating a mind, and you are allowing that person to remove the focus from self to someone or something else. Often older people are accused of being boring. You will rarely meet a boring older person. Do not misunderstand. You may meet a number of aging persons whose total focus *seems* to be on their own aches and pains, but the minute you offer them the opportunity to express an opinion about something outside of themselves, they may become more animated, have strong opinions, and be interested and interesting.

Communication of Feelings

A person needs to be encouraged to talk about feelings that lie beneath any surface statement. If an older person says, "I'm not sure I really want to go to the senior center," you might respond by saying, "Are you worried that you won't know anyone there and will feel shy?" At the same time, you need to share your own thoughts and feelings. Do not say, "You've got to start eating," if what you really mean is, "It really has me worried that you are losing weight and don't seem to have an appetite." Your expression of your concerns may just trigger some positive response in your relative. Encourage other family members to treat the person in the same open and honest way whenever possible. Here are some other examples.

Do not say,	*if what you mean is,*
"We all forget sometimes."	"I'm concerned about the extent and frequency of your short-term memory loss."
"Maybe all you need is rest."	"You are sleeping all the time. Have you seen your doctor?"
"Aren't you tired of just sitting and watching TV all day?"	"I'd like to talk with you about the possibility of your getting out more and about doing more things here at home."
"I think I'm going crazy."	"I have too many responsibilities right now, and I'm not doing a good job of any of them. I need some help."

In the caregiving situation it is essential that the two of you learn to talk to each other about your own needs and feelings. Feelings left covered often lead to guilt that leads to resentment that leads to anger that leads back to guilt. Suppose you need an evening of your own just to unwind, but you know Mom is expecting you to spend the evening with her. She has no major problem; she is simply lonely and wants somebody around. Do you feel like a bad child because you want to take time for yourself? Do you deny your need and spend the evening with her but resent the time spent? Do you refuse and then feel angry all evening? Learning to say what you feel and to take care of your own needs is a vital part of the caregiving system. Sometimes you have to say, "I can't do that. I'm sorry."

Religious Affiliation

One visitor that you may be able to depend upon for regular visits and help is your relative's (or your) clergy-person. Many older people find great comfort in their religion as they become more frail. Those beliefs should be respected and, if necessary, tolerated, even encouraged. If you do not share the person's beliefs, have a frank discussion with him or her and explain that while your beliefs are not the same as the individual's, you understand that the pursuit of those beliefs is important to him or her and that you respect that.

If the person is homebound, consider ways that he or she can continue to pursue those beliefs. Perhaps this will include such activities as listening to services on the radio or television; asking the local pastor, priest, or rabbi to call; requesting home visits from local church or synagogue members; and obtaining devotional or other religious reading materials. If the person has always offered thanks before meals and that is not your family's practice, perhaps you could ask your family to respect the person's right to private grace by remaining quiet while the person prays.

The church or synagogue's role in the caregiving process will be as individual as you or your relative. Take your cues from the individual. Is religion important? Is there a long-standing relationship with one priest, pastor, or rabbi, and will the relative be able to continue that relationship? If not, is there a church or synagogue in the new neighborhood that can meet the need?

Talk to the appropriate clergyperson and make him or her aware of your relative's needs and condition. Find out what the clergyperson is willing to do for your relative, and find out if there is anything the homebound individual can do for the church or synagogue to help support that feeling of belonging. Such tasks as repairing hymnals, stapling newsletters, or folding programs might be possible. Your actions will show the person you are caring for and the religious community that your relative's interests and beliefs are important to you because of what they mean to him or her. And you might just inspire some positive caregiving action from some unexpected sources.

Trying New Things

In this chapter you have gotten a lot of ideas about meeting the basic daily living needs of the person who needs care and support. Occasionally, as you read through these suggestions, you may have raised an eyebrow in skepticism. But remember this: No idea is dumb or crazy if it works, and the only way you are going to find out what works is to try everything at least once.

"Order in Chinese food? Are you out of your mind! My father would never stand for that—he's strictly a meat and potatoes man." Maybe. On the other hand, he might just enjoy the idea, and you will have an evening off from cooking.

Or, "My wife would *never* go to a senior site for a meal. That's charity. We don't accept charity." Really? Who worked all his or her life to pay the taxes that have made such charity possible? Take your wife and go. You are not accepting anything except what you already paid for years ago in hard work and taxes. Look at the positives. It is a chance to get dressed up. It is a time to be with other people—old friends and new acquaintances. And if you have a balanced, nutritious meal at the site, you can ease up on dinner and make soup and sandwiches or a salad.

Finally, be very sure that the reasons you have for not trying something are truly objections from the care recipient and not your own inhibitions, prejudices, or fears. If it does not work, what have you lost? If it does, look what you have gained!

Basic Care Aids from the Community

In most communities, regardless of size, there are a number of organizations and agencies with resources for helping the caregiver deal with the myriad of details involved in giving care to another adult. In chapter 5 you researched a number of specific possibilities. Particular needs and community resources for help with those needs are listed below. Check your phone book for addresses and telephone numbers.

Consumer Problems
Better Business Bureau, State Commissioner of Insurance, City Health Department, District Attorney's Office, State Department of Consumer Protection

Counseling
Department of Social Services, family service agencies, local churches and synagogues, Veterans Administration, Salvation Army, YMCA or YWCA, hospital social worker, community mental health centers

Financial Aid
Social Security Administration, Internal Revenue Service, Veterans Administration, State Medical Assistance Program, local bank

Food
County Office on Aging, public school board, public health nurse, hospital social worker

Health Services and Information
Local chapter of the organization that is concerned with your care recipient's illness (American Cancer Society, Alzheimer's and Related Disorders Association, and so on), City Health Department, public health nurse, visiting nurse association, local university medical college (they often have clinic services to serve the older person), mental health association, Veterans Administration

Homemaker Services

County Health Office (Title 20 services), local church or synagogue, local home health care agencies, County Office on Aging

Housing

County Office on Aging, Social Services Department of the County, American Red Cross, Salvation Army, local housing authority.

Legal Counseling

Legal Aid Society, university law school, Lawyers' or Bar Association, District Attorney's Office, local bank, local library

Medicare and Health Insurance

Social Security Administration, County Department of Social Services

Nursing Homes

County Department of Social Services, County Office on Aging, State Department of Health and Social Services, hospital social worker

Transportation

American Red Cross, Area Agency on Aging, any senior citizens service organization, State Department of Health and Social Services

For more information. Many pamphlets and books and other free or inexpensive materials are available to make the job of caregiving easier. If possible, contact the local chapter of the national organization for the particular disease or affliction your relative has. The chapter will be happy to mail you free materials and inform you of support groups and other programs to aid afflicted individuals and their caregivers. To get started, you might consider writing to the following national organizations that publish materials on aging and the diseases of the later years. Be specific in your requests.

American Health Care Association
1200 15th Street, NW
Washington, DC 20005

American Occupational Therapy Foundation
6000 Executive Boulevard
Rockville, MD 20852

U.S. Department of Health and Human Services
Public Health Service
5600 Fishers Lane
Rockville, MD 20857

National Institutes of Health
9000 Rockville Pike
Bethesda, MD 20205

National Institute on Aging
8630 Fenton Street, Suite 508
Silver Spring, MD 20910

National Council on the Aging
600 Maryland Avenue, SW
Washington, DC 20024

American Association of Retired Persons (AARP)
1909 K Street, NW
Washington, DC 20049

American Association of Homes for the Aging
1050 17th Street, NW
Washington, DC 20036

9 ✺ Basic Nursing Techniques and Emergency First Aid

If you are the caregiver for a person who is physically incapacitated, you will need to be prepared to perform certain nursing tasks that relate to that illness. You will also need some special skills that will allow you to deal with emergencies that may arise as a result of the illness. Finally, you will be called upon by your relative to help that person find ways to cope with the daily routine of living with a physical disability. Keep in mind that not all disabilities are visible. Pain, for example, is not visible. If the person outwardly functions well for his or her age, there may still be an unseen problem that that individual is coping with every day—trouble with swallowing or shortness of breath, for instance. A visual or hearing impairment, as discussed on pages 173-175, may make communication difficult for the person, causing a withdrawal from others that can eventually lead to isolation and depression.

Beyond the basic nursing skills and skills necessary to handle emergencies, the caregiver needs to develop some resources for dealing with the daily routine of caring for a person who is physically incapacitated. Fortunately there are a number of patient aids, organizations, and publications available to assist the caregiver for the physically impaired.

Nursing Tasks

Do you know how to take both an oral and a rectal temperature? Can you take a blood pressure reading? a pulse? Do you know how to give an enema? drain a

catheter? Do you know the proper techniques for handling a person who is bedridden or who uses a wheelchair? If the person develops a bedsore, do you know what
to do?

Some skills are better taught in person than through
a book. Call on your home health care agency, hospital
staff, or local American Red Cross to teach you the
following:

- the different ways to take a temperature
- how to take a blood pressure reading
- how to find and count another person's pulse
- how to administer an enema
- how to care for a catheter or colostomy bag

The American Red Cross offers two services that
may be of help in learning basic nursing skills. First, many
local chapters offer a home nursing course. Classes are
held at a community location, and the eight sessions last
for two and a half hours each. Second, the Red Cross
also has published a textbook for the course entitled *Family Health and Home Nursing*. You can order this text at a cost
of $3.95 from your local Red Cross chapter.

Another book that is available for caregivers who
need help with home nursing skills is *The Illustrated Manual
of Nursing Techniques* by Dorothy Erickson Reese, available
through the American Health Care Association, 1200
15th Street, NW, Washington, DC 20005.

Handling the Individual

If the person uses a wheelchair, is bedfast, or needs
assistance in moving, you need to learn the proper
methods for handling the person to avoid injury. If the
person is receiving some type of physical therapy or the
services of a home health care agency, have those professionals demonstrate the proper techniques for lifting and
moving the person without injury to him or her or to
yourself. When you lift, bend your knees and lift with
your legs, not your back. Spread your feet and lift
smoothly and as close to the body as possible (distance
leverages weight).

Can you do the job alone? If not, and there is no one else to help, perhaps a mechanical device, such as a Hoyer lift, will help. The Hoyer lift is basically a tripod that you roll next to the person's bed or chair. Attached to the tripod is a canvas sling or seat. You place that sling under the person, and when the person is securely in place, you swing the arm of the lift (or the wheels in some models) to move the person from one place to the other. When the person is settled, you remove the canvas sling. You must be sure that you have enough room to make the move and that furniture pieces are stable. Also, as in any procedure that involves the person's cooperation, you would need to explain exactly what you are about to do so that the person can relax and assist you. Your home health care agency professional can help you get a demonstration of any piece of special equipment or any special procedure.

Caring for Persons Who Are in Wheelchairs or Who Are Bedridden

Some of the physical impairments described in this chapter may mean that the person is confined to a wheel-chair or to bed. Such persons have special needs. You may find that some changes in the household or in the person's environment are necessary. There may be a need for special clothing, special diets, and special supplies. You will have to be especially aware of the person's immobility when planning for such matters as safety and security.

People who use wheelchairs and those who are bed-fast are often wrongly treated as if not only their bodies but also their minds are affected. It will be your job as caregiver to see that visitors and other social contacts continue to treat the person with respect and dignity. You will have to help the person plan activities that are inter-esting and challenging.

Keep in mind that the more you and the individual can focus on what the affected person *can* do, the happier the person is likely to be. In most cases the mind continues to work. Stimulate that mind. Show the person that even though he or she may be unable to be mobile physically, his or her thoughts, feelings, and opinions are very important to you.

Special needs for those who use a wheelchair. Any person who suffers from an illness that affects the central nervous system will have special needs to maintain some independence in his or her daily routine. Eventually such people may need to use a wheelchair, making mobility even more difficult. If your relative uses a wheelchair, you need to survey the home to make sure that the environment is suitable for wheelchair living. Are there clear paths for the wheelchair to move around the rooms and home? Are there obstacles that make movement difficult such as thick shag carpeting or high thresholds or narrow doorways? Can the person reach those items he or she needs most often—clothing, bathroom supplies, kitchen utensils? Are counters, sinks, stoves, and clothing rods at a height the person can manage? If the person will continue to cook, are dishes and pots and pans lightweight and easy to balance? Would duplicates of certain items in two different places make life easier for the individual?

If structural changes would be too expensive, try to be creative. Perhaps contents of cabinets could simply be rearranged. Perhaps a different style wheelchair—one that is smaller—would be easier. Ask for ideas, and keep as your focus the premise that a person with a condition that requires a wheelchair deserves the opportunity to maintain independence for as long as possible.

Types of wheelchairs. Other than the standard wheelchair, which can be fitted with a number of special accessories to meet the particular needs of an individual, there are a variety of chairs available for special situations, including these:

• the amputee chair, designed for persons with missing legs or arms
• the reclining chair, designed for persons who need special support for the head and trunk area
• the hemiplegic chair, designed for persons who are paralyzed on one side
• the oversized chair, designed for oversized persons
• the narrow chair, designed to adapt to small spaces and narrow doorways and hallways

• the motorized chair, designed to offer greater mobility for the person capable of handling a heavier chair that requires some dexterity to maneuver

Your doctor, home health care agency professional, or physical therapist will help you and the person needing a wheelchair select the proper chair.

Special needs of the bedfast person. With some illnesses the person may eventually become completely confined to bed or may spend a major portion of time in bed. If this is the case, the bedroom should be set up as headquarters for care. Those items you and the care recipient will need most often should be within easy reach even if that means emptying dressers and closets of items usually kept there and replacing those items with towels, pads, dressings, and other equipment. To keep the room looking homelike, look around for unlikely storage areas, for example, under the bed or on added shelves in the closet.

Be sure the room is equipped with a telephone and a list of emergency phone numbers, a night-light and a flashlight, a call system for the person to call you when you are somewhere else in the house, and anything else that will save you steps and make life more pleasant and independent for the person. Some caregivers have sung the praises of such items as a remote control for the television or a bedside caddy to hold such small items as eyeglasses, notepaper, and tissues. (You can make a simple caddy by taking an eighteen-by-thirty-six-inch rectangle of sturdy fabric and sewing patch pockets to one half, leaving the other half plain to slip between the mattress and springs.) Be aware of the person's possible hypersensitivity to noise, light, or odors. Stay alert to the possibility that problems with circulation may develop when a person stays in bed all or most of the time. Finally, have a visiting nurse or a home health care aide teach you how to make an occupied bed and how to feed someone in bed.

Bedsores, or pressure sores. Bedsores (decubitus ulcers) are caused by pressure or irritation. It is important that you and the care recipient be alert to the earliest signs of such sores because they can develop rapidly and are very difficult to treat. Prevention will be far more successful than treating a sore that has already developed. The following suggestions should prove helpful.

1. Prevent the sores by keeping the bed and any chair cushions smooth and free of wrinkles, moving the person frequently, and making sure the person has a proper diet and enough fluids each day.
2. Special devices that help reduce pressure are available, such as water mattresses, special beds, and egg crate cushions for wheelchairs. Seek the advice of your home health care professional concerning what you can do to prevent bedsores and any complications from them.
3. Develop a regular schedule for checking the skin, and stick to it.
4. Watch for signs that a sore may be forming: redness, heat, blue-colored spots, or cracks in the skin. If there are red areas, smooth on lotion frequently if the doctor approves.
5. If a sore develops, call the doctor or visiting nurse at once. Do not try to treat sores without a doctor's advice. Do not use home remedies or follow someone else's suggestions. Bedsores are serious injuries and must be treated only under the advice of trained professionals.

Coping with the Daily Routine of a Physical Disability

The following patient aids, organizations, and publications may be helpful in making your job as primary caregiver for someone who is physically ill and disabled easier.

Patient Aids

> Aids for the Blind and Visually Impaired
> American Foundation for the Blind
> 15 West 16th Street
> New York, NY 10011

Emergency Call Systems
Call your local Office on Aging or
Life Line Emergency Response Systems,
1-800-451-0525

Large-Print Books
Thorndike Books
PO Box 157
Thorndike, ME 04986
(Some popular magazines such as the *Reader's Digest* are
also available in large-print editions.)

Talking Books (tape cassettes or records)
The Library of Congress
Blind and Physically Handicapped Division
1291 Taylor Street, NW
Washington, DC 20011
(First call your local library.)

Aids for the Hearing Impaired
National Association of the Deaf
814 Thayer Avenue
Silver Spring, MD 20910

Check your local sickroom supply store or pharmacy
for these items for the physically impaired.

Air cleaners
Bath lifts
Bathtub seats
Bathtub security
    rails
Bed boards
Bedding
Bed pads
Bedpans
Bed protectors
Bed rails
Bed trays
Bed-wetting alarms
Blood pressure
    monitors
Braces
Canes
Catheters

Cervical collars
Chairs, power lift
Commodes
Crutches
Cushions,
    wheelchair
Diapers, adult
Dining aids
Drainage bags
Dressing aids
Emergency call
    systems
Exercise equipment
Footbaths
Gloves, disposable
Gowns
Guardrails
Heating pads

Hospital beds and
    accessories
Incontinent briefs
Incontinent care
    aids
Oxygen units
Patient lifts
Shower chairs
Thermometers
Urinals
Vaporizers
Walkers
Wheelchairs and
    accessories

National Organizations

> American Coalition of Citizens with Disabilities
> 1200 15th Street, NW, Suite 201
> Washington, DC 20005

> American Veterans of World War II, Korea and Vietnam
> (AMVETS)
> 4647 Forbes Boulevard
> Lanham, MD 20706

> Disabled American Veterans
> 3725 Alexandria Park
> Cold Springs, KY 41076

> National Association for the Visually Handicapped
> 305 East 24th Street, 17-C
> New York, NY 10010

> National Association of Hearing and Speech Action
> 10801 Rockville Park
> Rockville, MD 20852
> 1-800-638-TALK

> National Association for the Deaf
> 814 Thayer Avenue
> Silver Spring, MD 20910

> National Association for the Physically Handicapped
> 7107 Eastman Drive
> Falls Church, VA 22043

> National Easter Seal Society
> 2023 West Ogden Avenue
> Chicago, IL 60612

> National Federation for the Blind
> 1800 Johnson Street
> Baltimore, MD 21230

> National Multiple Sclerosis Society
> 205 East 42nd Street
> New York, NY 10017

Other national organizations are listed in the descriptions of specific illnesses or disabilities (see pages 176-203). To find out whether the national organization has a toll-free telephone listing, call 1-800-555-1212. Before trying to contact a national headquarters, check first to see whether there is a local chapter in your community or area. Often the local chapter will have any publication or aid you may need and will send materials to you or invite you to come to the office.

Publications

The following government agencies offer publications of interest to the disabled.

> Bureau of Education for the Handicapped
> U.S. Department of Education
> 400 Maryland Avenue, SW
> Washington, DC 20202

> Independent Living for the Handicapped
> Department of Housing and Urban Development
> 451 17th Street, SW, Room 9106
> Washington, DC 20210

> U.S. Department of Education
> Clearinghouse on the Handicapped
> 400 Maryland Avenue, SW
> Washington, DC 20202

These private agencies also offer materials.

> Rehabilitation International U.S.A.
> 1123 Broadway, Suite 704
> New York, NY 10010

> SATH (Society for the Advancement of the Handicapped)
> 26 Court Street
> Brooklyn, NY 11242

> American Coalition of Citizens with Disabilities
> 1200 15th Street, NW, Suite 201
> Washington, DC 20005

> The Disability Rights Center
> 1346 Connecticut Avenue, NW, Suite 1124
> Washington, DC 20036

> American Civil Liberties Union
> 132 West 43rd Street
> New York, NY 10036

The following books may be of use if you are caring for a physically disabled person.

The Gadget Book: Ingenious Devices for Easier Living, edited by Dennis R. La Buda.

The Home Hospital by Lois Barclay Murphy.

Independent Living for the Handicapped and the Elderly by Elizabeth Eckhart May.

Emergencies

Unexpected and sometimes life-threatening situations can arise with the healthiest of persons. Someone who is mentally or physically disabled or ill with a chronic disease may be even more susceptible to crises. The caregiver needs to be prepared to deal with situations that may arise that require immediate medical attention such as the following:

Bleeding	Heart Attacks
Burns	Hypothermia
Choking	Overdoses
Coma	Poisonings
Convulsions	Shock (Traumatic)
Dislocations	Sprains
Fainting	Strokes
Fractures	

As you can see, there is quite a disparity in the severity of those situations in the list. However, if you are alone with the person when an emergency occurs, you need to know what to do for any crisis whether that crisis is a sprained ankle or an overdose of medication. If the emergency is one that could be life-threatening, first be sure the victim is breathing, and then phone for help. When you place the call, be prepared to give the following information.

- phone number from which you are calling
- address and any special instructions that will help the ambulance driver locate the address
- description of the person's condition
- your name

Do not be the one to hang up; let the person who is speaking to you end the call. He or she may have questions to ask or special instructions about what you should do until help arrives. Unlock the door and turn on the outside lights whether it is dark or not; it makes it easier for the ambulance driver to locate the house. If you can, get another family member or a neighbor to stand outside and direct the arriving emergency team to the person.

Sometimes there is no need or time for calling an ambulance. The caregiver can manage some emergencies alone with proper training. Do not worry about panicking. Panic usually occurs when you are improperly prepared to handle an emergency. If you plan for the eventuality and know the basic techniques to use, you will be able to handle a multitude of problems. *Some emergency techniques are best learned in a class: CPR (cardiopulmonary resuscitation), mouth-to-mouth resuscitation, and the Heimlich maneuver for aiding a person who is choking. These techniques are lifesavers only if they are properly performed.* You should be able to handle the following emergencies on your own or until help arrives.

Bleeding

There are three methods for stopping severe bleeding: direct pressure on the wound, elevation, and pressure on the supplying artery. To apply direct pressure if the bleeding is from a wound, cover the wound with a sterile gauze pad or soft, clean cloth and press the palm of your hand over the entire area of the wound until you can secure the pad in place with a bandage. Continue to apply pressure for twenty or thirty minutes. If there is no sign of a fracture, an open wound that is bleeding severely and is located on the head, neck, arm, or leg should be elevated above the level of the person's heart. The direct pressure should be continued. If these two techniques do not stop the bleeding, apply pressure to the main artery supplying blood to the wound. Have a health care professional show you the location of these arteries, and do not use this technique unless the other two fail. Call for help as soon as the bleeding is controlled enough for you to make the call.

Nosebleeds are a special case because they can result not only from injury but also from diseases such as high blood pressure, and they may come on quite suddenly without any obvious cause. Keep the person quiet, in a sitting position. Have him or her lean forward, and apply direct pressure to the nostril with a cold compress. If bleeding continues, insert a small pad of clean gauze into the nostril and apply pressure externally with the thumb and index finger. Be sure to remove the gauze when the bleeding is under control. If bleeding cannot be controlled, get medical attention at once.

In the event that you suspect internal bleeding, seek medical attention immediately. Some of the symptoms to look for are pain and tenderness; swelling or discoloration of the soft tissues (those areas that are not muscular) of the body; cold, pale skin; rapid but weak pulse; rapid breathing; restlessness; excessive thirst; and vomiting or coughing up blood or passing blood in the urine or stool. If you suspect internal bleeding, loosen the person's clothing, have the person lie flat with legs elevated, and keep the person warm. Do not give the person any food or drink. Call a doctor.

Burns

Burns are measured in degrees, a first-degree burn being the simplest and a third-degree burn being the most dangerous and complex. First-degree burns are caused by sunburn, scalding, or contact with hot objects. The skin will turn red and be painful. To relieve the pain, apply very cold water, *not* ointments or fats. If the burn is deep with blisters, seek medical attention.

Second-degree burns are caused by a deep sunburn, contact with hot liquids, or such volatile substances as gasoline, kerosene, and other products that may "flash" suddenly when near fire. The skin will probably blister. Apply very cold water (or ice), or submerge the burned part of the body in cold water, or apply a *wet* dressing with a plastic covering. Do *not* try to break the blisters. Seek medical attention.

A third-degree burn can be caused by fire, severe

scalding, or electricity. The skin will appear white and charred, and an ambulance should be called at once. If there is burned clothing, do not attempt to remove it. Cover the burned areas with a sterile dressing or freshly laundered sheet. If the hands are burned, raise them above the heart. Feet and legs that are burned should also be elevated.

A special case is the chemical burn that may occur when the victim has swallowed or spilled some chemical household cleaner such as bleach or drain opener. Usually the product will have instructions for handling accidental chemical burns printed on the label. If there are no instructions on the product itself, wash any external burn with plain water and call an ambulance.

Many cities have emergency numbers for burn centers and poison control centers, and often the operator at the center can give you over the phone proper procedures that will help until emergency personnel can arrive. Post these numbers with other emergency numbers near every phone.

Choking

Many older persons who are disabled either physically or mentally are candidates for choking. Sometimes they must eat from a reclining position, or they eat too fast, or they are unable to chew or swallow properly. If your relative is having trouble with choking, you should call your local Red Cross office or hospital and ask where you can receive free training on the Heimlich maneuver for dislodging food when a person is choking.

When you go for training, tell the instructor what the condition of your relative is so that the instructor can recommend the best method for dealing with a choking emergency. Someone who is bedfast, for example, will have to be handled somewhat differently from someone who can stand or sit erect.

If the person eats too fast, serve soft, easy-to-swallow foods, and stay away from meats and food products that require careful chewing. Serve plenty of liquids. Serve a variety of foods that are cooked in sauces and liquids and therefore easier to swallow. And be sure the person is not storing food in his or her jaws while eating, making large unmanageable lumps that will be hard to swallow.

Coma

A coma is far more serious than simple fainting. There is no response to stimuli, and it is impossible to rouse the person. A person who suffers from diabetes may be a candidate for coma. If you suspect coma, proceed as follows:

1. Make sure the victim's heartbeat and breathing continue. If you are unsure, administer resuscitation.
2. Summon medical help as soon as possible.
3. If you know why the coma has occurred, tell the emergency operator that information and ask for instructions on what to do until the ambulance arrives.
4. Loosen any restrictive clothing.
5. Do not move the person unless absolutely necessary.

Convulsions

During a convulsion the person will become unconscious suddenly; the muscles of the body will go rigid for several seconds; there will be a jerking motion accompanied by bluish color in the face and lips and drooling; and, finally, all movements will subside, and the person will be drowsy and disoriented. The sight of someone having a convulsion can be frightening. Do not panic. The most dangerous time is the period of rigidity, during which the person may stop breathing or bite his or her tongue. If your relative experiences a convulsion, keep the following in mind:

1. Do not try to hold the person down. Your job is to help the person avoid injuring himself or herself while the seizure runs its course.
2. Push any furniture or objects out of the way.
3. To keep the person from biting his or her tongue, place a wadded handkerchief or a rolled towel—even a newspaper or magazine, but nothing hard—between

the person's teeth. Be careful not to get your fingers between the teeth.
4. Keep the person lying down, preferably on the floor.
5. Loosen the clothing, and keep the breathing passage open.
6. After the seizure, check the person's breathing.
7. When the person comes out of the seizure, do not try to ask questions or disturb him or her. Turn the person on his or her side or stomach to prevent vomit from entering the lungs.
8. Stay with the person, and after you are certain breathing is steady, get medical help.
9. Convulsions followed by coma in an older person could signal a cerebral vascular accident, or stroke.

Dislocations

A dislocation involves the displacement of bone or cartilage at a joint after extreme and sudden stress on that joint. Usually the person will experience a great deal of pain and swelling. You should not try to correct a dislocated joint yourself, but rather get the person to a hospital emergency room if possible or call the paramedics.

Fainting

Fainting occurs when, temporarily, there is an insufficient supply of blood to the brain. It is a temporary unconscious state. Before fainting, the victim may be extremely pale, feel cold and clammy, be dizzy or nauseated, and experience blurred vision and/or numbness in the hands and feet. The best thing you can do for a person who has fainted, once you are sure breathing is continuing, is to leave the person alone and wait. Recovery of consciousness usually occurs within minutes or even seconds of assuming a reclining position.

If the person announces a feeling of faintness, have him or her lie down flat and breathe deeply and slowly. If possible, elevate the legs; do not elevate the head.

Fractures

Any time you suspect a fracture or even the possibility of a fracture, get medical help at once. If you can, get the person to an emergency room as soon as possible. If not, keep the person immobilized, and apply ice to the injured area until help arrives.

Heart Attacks

The onset of a heart attack will most frequently be accompanied by a squeezing pain in the center of the chest. Often the pain will radiate down the arms or into the jaw and neck area. The person may also experience profuse sweating, nausea, shortness of breath, and a feeling of fullness or pressure on the chest. If any of these symptoms are present, have the person sit or lie down at once, and if there is a prescription for nitroglycerin tablets, administer the tablets as prescribed. If the pain does not subside after three tablets and ten minutes, call for an ambulance. If there are no tablets, call an ambulance after two minutes. You should not attempt to drive the person to the hospital yourself. Learn CPR just in case. In the event you are alone and CPR is needed, you will not be able to leave the victim to call for help. Instead you should administer CPR and shout for help if you have any hope of attracting attention from a neighbor or passerby. For a discussion of heart disease, see pages 186-188.

Hypothermia

What is hypothermia, and who is at risk? The condition is one in which the body temperature drops below ninety-seven degrees Fahrenheit. A drop below ninety-five degrees can be fatal if not detected and treated in time. Older persons or other persons who have a chronic health problem are susceptible to hypothermia. If room temperatures fall below sixty degrees Fahrenheit, there may be a risk of hypothermia.

The symptoms include bloated face or pale skin color, trembling without shivering, irregular or slowed heart rate, slurred speech, shallow or slowed breathing, low blood pressure, and/or drowsiness. If you think someone may be suffering from hypothermia, assume that the condition is a medical emergency and immediately call for medical help.

If someone you care for lives alone and is a hypothermia candidate, encourage that person to drink warm liquids in the colder weather; dress warmly and keep the heat at a reasonable level; eat food rich in calories such as red meat, bread, rice, and peanut butter; wear socks all the time; and call you once a day. If the person is over seventy-five years of age, the thermostat should never be lower than sixty-eight degrees.

Overdoses

Be aware that anything from alcohol to nonprescription drugs can be abused. Sometimes problems arise because substances that are harmless used alone can be dangerous when taken in combination with another chemical substance such as a nonprescription medication or alcohol. Any chemical substances improperly used can cause an overdose—alcohol, depressants (barbiturates), narcotics, stimulants (amphetamines), or tranquilizers. If any of these drugs has been prescribed, ask the doctor about the symptoms and treatment in the event of an overdose. And check with the person's pharmacist to be sure that the combination of drugs being taken is not potentially dangerous.

Poisonings

While children are the most common victims of accidental poisonings, older adults may be poisoned because of poor eyesight and mistaking one chemical for another. If you have reason to believe the care recipient has taken something poisonous, call your local poison control center at once and ask for instructions. Do *not* automatically induce vomiting, especially if you do not know for sure what the poison is. When you call, be ready to give the following information.

- the age of the victim
- the type and amount of poison swallowed (if possible)
- the first aid given so far
- whether or not the person has vomited

To prevent poisoning accidents, be sure all medications and potentially dangerous substances are kept in containers with easy-to-read labels and are stored in logical places and not mixed one with another. For example, do not keep a bottle of mouthwash and a bottle of drain cleaner together under the bathroom sink.

Shock

This is the name given to a condition in which a person's vital signs—pulse rate, respiratory rate, body temperature, and blood pressure—are profoundly lowered. If a person has been severely injured, be prepared to treat that person for traumatic shock if necessary. The symptoms are clammy skin with sweating on the hands and face, a weak and rapid pulse, and/or vomiting or complaining of thirst. The first step is to call for medical assistance. Then follow these directions.

1. Check the breathing and, if necessary, administer resuscitation.
2. Control any major bleeding.
3. If the person is unconscious, place the person on his or her side to keep the airway from becoming blocked by vomit or blood.
4. Keep the person lying down and lightly covered.
5. Elevate the feet unless there is injury to the head or the person is having trouble breathing.
6. Do not administer food or fluids.

Sprains

In the first twenty minutes apply ice or cold compresses and elevate the sprained joint. After twenty minutes replace the cold compresses with an elastic bandage to provide support for the injured joint. Do not wrap the bandage too tightly or it may restrict the blood supply. If there is any doubt as to whether the injury is a sprain or fracture, treat it as a fracture (see pages 165–166).

Strokes

When a blood vessel in the brain ruptures or a clot forms that interrupts circulation, the incident is called a cerebrovascular accident, or stroke. The symptoms of a stroke can be very different depending on what part of the brain is affected. One or more of the following may occur:

- intense headache
- altered speech patterns
- suddenly impaired vision
- weakness, paralysis, or numbness—usually on only one side of the body
- drooping on one side of the face
- difficulty in breathing or swallowing
- loss of bladder and/or bowel control
- a difference in size between the pupils of the eyes

If you suspect a stroke, be sure the victim is breathing and positioned on his or her side so that secretions can drain. Do not administer fluids, and call for help at once, even if after a short time the person seems to have fully recovered and appears to be functioning normally. For a more detailed discussion of strokes, see pages 198–203.

Medical Intervention

Once you are in the process of caring for a person with identified impairments, how do you judge whether a change in the person's physical or emotional behavior calls for a medical intervention? There are some changes you may observe in the person's daily personal habits or functions that should be cause for some concern—not necessarily cause for alarm—and that should be brought to the attention of the care recipient's doctor. These are changes in the following:

- mental alertness
- memory capacity
- language patterns or capacity
- mobility
- moods or attitudes toward life or other people
- vision or hearing

Anything unusual about the following needs to be reported to the doctor as soon as possible:

- walking patterns (shuffling, stumbling, limping)
- facial, hand, or foot movements
- breathing patterns
- discharges or bleeding
- rashes or skin discoloration
- perspiration, chills, or hot flashes
- swelling, lumps, or tenderness
- coloration of the urine or feces
- weight loss or gain
- odors from body, breath, or discharge from sores

10 ✥ Understanding Physical Incapacities

At every age people are prone to certain diseases. First there are the "normal" childhood diseases (mumps, measles, chicken pox, and the rest), and sometimes the not-so-normal ones (childhood cancer, cerebral palsy, and others). In the adult years people worry about the big three—heart disease, cancer, and stroke—and work their way through numerous viruses and, sometimes, new allergies. But the list of diseases people can anticipate gets longer as a person gets older. There is arthritis, diabetes, various lung diseases, and neurological diseases such as Parkinson's and multiple sclerosis. For women, there is osteoporosis. For men it is prostate problems. For both men and women there is the increased risk of stroke or heart attack and the chronic condition of hypertension (high blood pressure).

Certainly, many people live out their lives without contracting any of these illnesses, but when someone does become ill with a physically debilitating health problem and that person is older, it is likely that he or she will need help beyond the doctor and the hospital. The affected person may be completely dependent or need care in a very limited way. It is important to place the emphasis of care on what the person can still manage to do without help. If you become the caregiver for someone who is physically incapacitated, how do you know what help is needed, and how do you get the additional support both you and the affected person will need?

Start with the Person's Doctor

When the person has been given a diagnosis, you need to meet with the physician(s), the hospital social worker, and any other personnel who have been or may be involved in the treatment of the illness. Get straight answers to the following questions and add them to your notebook or card file.

1. In lay terms, what are all the impairments—mental and physical—the person has?
2. What tests have been run and why? What were the results? (Request a copy of every medical record and keep it.)
3. Has every health professional involved pursued every medical possibility for making the person well or better? (The primary physician is best able to answer this question.)
4. If there is more than one medical problem, have all the physicians involved consulted with one another, and do they all agree with the current diagnosis and prognosis?
5. What is the prognosis?
6. What is the prescribed treatment for each ailment?
7. Does the pharmacist have any questions or reservations about any of the medications prescribed for the individual?
8. Given the current status, what is the projected life span of the affected person? What is the projected need for care?
9. Can this person manage alone? Does the medical community foresee the possibility of the person managing independently again?
10. Will the caregiving relationship be interim or ongoing?
11. What specific equipment will be needed?
12. How much does the affected person know? How much will he or she be told?
13. Based on the ailments, what can you expect the emotional health of the person to be?

Eyesight and Hearing

As people age, they may experience failing sensory perception, primarily impaired eyesight and/or hearing. There are, of course, a number of medical advances being made every day to assist those afflicted with these problems. Cataracts, a clouding of the lens of the eye, once were the fear of many older persons and now in 95 percent of the cases can be successfully treated with surgery. Glaucoma, an increase in the fluid pressure inside the eyeball, can also be cured or controlled if diagnosed and treated early enough.

One visual problem that is unique to aging persons is senile macular degeneration. Simply put, this is the gradual deterioration of the fine vision that allows persons to see details clearly. The onset may seem sudden though the condition may have existed for some time. If a flat object seems to the person curved or distorted at the edges, if the person has difficulty seeing at night, if the person complains that colors are faded, and especially if the person complains that he or she cannot see an object straight on but must look at it from the side, see a doctor immediately. There is a very short period during the course of the disease when some help can be achieved through the use of a laser treatment, so early diagnosis is very important.

Hearing impairments may be caused by nerve damage in the inner ear, a blockage in the outer or middle ear, or a combination of the two. Many impairments respond well to recent advances in hearing-aid technology. Two contributing factors to hearing loss are pride and neglect. Many hearing impairments can be cured if treated in the early stages. If the person complains of such things as ringing in the ears, pressure in the ear, or increasing hearing difficulty, make an appointment with an otologist, or ear specialist.

Some people who have a sight or hearing problem are content to "make do" with eyeglasses or to encourage friends and relatives to talk into their "good" ear. As a caregiver who may be dealing with other incapacities as well as hearing or sight impairment, it is important for you to know how to care for and communicate with your relative to save both of you unnecessary frustration and loss of patience. Talk to the person's specialist or physician for tips on care and treatment at home.

Communicating with the Visually Impaired

The most important service you can provide for the person who has trouble seeing is a stable environment, one he or she can depend on to be the same today and tomorrow. Do not move furniture without warning the person. Walk and sit next to the person and touch frequently. Touching is vital in communication with anyone whose ability to communicate has been impaired through sight loss, hearing loss, or mental incapacity. Why? It shows you care. It gets the attention of the impaired person. It reduces feelings of isolation, and it builds trust.

With a person who is visually impaired, always identify yourself and what you are doing before making a motion or request. Activities that are unexplained can cause undue anxiety for the person who cannot see clearly what is happening. Keep in mind that the person's problem is in seeing, not in hearing. Speak in a normal voice.

Try to stimulate the other senses—smelling, touching, hearing, and tasting. When you are about to move the person, make simple statements: "We're going to walk straight for several feet and then turn right." "Here you are in front of the table—can you feel it?" Place the person's hand on the table while you place the chair behind. Gently touch the person's legs with the chair, and keep your hand on his or her waist or shoulder as the person is seated.

When a sight-impaired person eats, be sure to identify the food, and, if sight is very bad, identify the location of the food on the plate and table. "Your meat is at six o'clock, vegetables at three. Your coffee is just to the right of your plate." Many sight-impaired people find a spoon easier to manage than a fork.

The Center for the Partially Sighted (901 Santa

Monica Boulevard, Santa Monica, CA 90401) has a one-page handout on household tips for the visually impaired.

Communicating with the Hearing Impaired

When you speak, face the person at his or her level and speak in a normal voice. You may want to slow your speech a bit, but you should avoid any exaggerated mouth movements. Keep your hands and anything else away from your face, and do not talk while eating or smoking. Screen out any extra noise either in the room itself or from outside. Even though the person has trouble hearing, he or she may be aware of the distracting noises of a television or radio or lawn mower outside, making it hard to concentrate on what is being said. Finally, keep in mind that a hearing aid primarily amplifies sound. A hearing-impaired person may have gotten used to the lack of any background noise. When this person first tries a hearing aid, he or she may be assaulted by a variety of sounds. The person may need some guidance in learning techniques for screening out unwanted sounds.

Keeping on Top of the Situation

With any impairment that affects the senses such as sight and hearing, maintain a habit of regular checkups. Ask the doctor whether there is any new therapy or aid available that could help the person. Do not assume that, once the powers of hearing and sight reach a certain degree of infirmity, there is nothing you can do. Stay in touch with your local association for the blind or deaf for aids and publications that may help you and the person cope. And, finally, understand that what the person wants and needs are clues and assistance, not pity and patronizing. At all times treat the person with respect and dignity, and work to maintain as much independence for that person as possible.

The Physical Illnesses

Most people take their independence of movement for granted. They go where they want; they hop in the car or on the bus with little thought about the mechanics of such a move; they dash up and down stairs. But what if you could not? What if you were crippled or blind or paralyzed? What if everywhere you turned, you found something unfamiliar? Try it for a few minutes. Blindfold yourself for a half hour. Set the kitchen timer. Do not just sit there. Try to go on with your normal routines. Or borrow your relative's wheelchair while he or she is not using it. In short, put yourself in the person's place, and deal with life for a half hour as he or she must deal with it all day every day.

Once you understand something of the pain of not being able to function at full capacity, you may find yourself being more creative about ways to maintain that person's independence and about ways to be more sensitive and supportive of the individual's efforts to live life with as little outside help as possible. When you are running full tilt for twelve to sixteen hours a day, the leisure to just sit, watch television, or read a book may seem like heaven to you. But keep in mind that if you could not see to read anymore and all you could do was look out the window or stare at a television set, such leisure might seem more like a prison sentence.

Once you have met with the health team and gathered the information about your relative's impairments, you should have a fairly clear picture of what it will take to meet his or her needs. Keep in mind that help may be needed from you in only a very *limited* way. The affected person should be encouraged to do whatever he or she can still manage to do independently.

ARTHRITIS

Anyone can get arthritis at any age. Arthritis means the inflammation of a joint according to the Arthritis Foundation. *Arthritis* can refer to more than 100 individual diseases that can attack joints and the connective tissues. Arthritis is crippling; it is not fatal. Many believe that arthritis is a disease of minor aches and pains that is not serious and for which nothing can be done. *This is not true.* You may find that your relative believes arthritis to be a normal part of the aging process, and for that reason, he or she may resist efforts to seek proper medical attention. *This is a myth.* Arthritis is *not* a normal part of the aging process.

Symptoms

The warning signs include swelling in one or more joints; early-morning stiffness; chronic or recurring pain in a particular joint; inability to flex a joint normally; obvious redness, warmth, and swelling in a joint; unexplained weight loss; and fever or weakness in combination with pain in a joint. Notify the doctor if any of these symptoms lasts longer than two weeks.

Treatment

Since there are more than a hundred possible types of arthritis, the treatment will depend on the specific diagnosis, and for that reason it is especially important to get medical attention. Treatment will also depend on such factors as the particular joints involved, the severity of the problem, and the person's age and lifestyle. Regardless of the treatment prescribed, the affected person and the caregiver must recognize that improvement comes slowly and that it will take patience and perseverance to see a treatment through to some success.

There are some medications that can help: aspirin, anti-inflammatory drugs, drugs like cortisone, and others. Some are effective in only certain types of arthritis. Others may have side effects that are unpleasant for the patient. A person with arthritis should not take any drug until it has been prescribed or suggested by a physician.

Aside from drug therapy, patients often respond to rest and exercise programs. Too much rest can lead to more stiffness though, and a proper balance between rest periods and active periods must be found, depending on the status of the disease at any given time. Exercise properly done can improve flexibility in joints and build and preserve muscle strength. A therapeutic exercise program should be prescribed by the physician and taught by a trained physical therapist. Many exercise programs involve swimming or exercises performed in the water because the warmth of the water helps relieve pain and stiffness.

Rheumatoid arthritis, gout, bursitis, and tendonitis are all types of arthritis. People who suffer from any form of arthritis need to be aware of the proper treatment routines and follow them religiously. The hardest part of dealing with arthritis is that it is a chronic (ongoing) disease. The pain can lead to other problems such as depression, anger, and frustration, making it more difficult to cope with the disease and to care for one who has it. The disease has periods of ups and downs—days when improvement seems remarkable, even miraculous, followed by weeks when the pain is excruciating and never ending.

Living with the Disease

The thing most people who suffer from arthritis must learn to live with is pain and decreased mobility. Each person feels pain differently and responds to pain differently. Some will withdraw; others pressure themselves to "work through it." Some feel guilty about taking time (sometimes days) to rest. Others may use their pain to manipulate others. For a full discussion of living with chronic pain, see pages 203-204.

The Role of the Caregiver

Provide the person with activities and people that are pleasant and that the person enjoys. Encourage your relative to talk through moods and anxieties with you, a friend, or a counselor. If the feelings include anger, try exercise as a release for positive results. If exercise is not possible, have the person try pounding a pillow, talking into a tape recorder, or writing down those angry feelings. Tell the person that it is okay to cry sometimes. Let the care recipient clear the air, and remember, if you are the person the affected individual vents his or her anger on, it probably is not a personal attack and should not be taken as such. In Part Four of this book, you will learn ways of venting your emotions. For now, concentrate on helping the affected person deal with his or her emotional highs and lows.

Finally, encourage the person with arthritis to learn to understand the limitations of the disease, set realistic goals, adjust his or her life accordingly, and ask for help when he or she cannot manage alone.

Special Needs

The person who has arthritis may find some basic daily activities more difficult to perform, such as eating, writing, and dressing. The doctor may refer the person to an occupational therapist, who can provide information about the disease, train the person to manage the disease and the emotions that accompany the illness, and suggest resources for aids that will make life easier for the person. You can choose clothing that is simple to put on and take off and does not require motions that are painful for the person. For example, your wife may find it difficult to step into a robe that zips only part way down. Choose instead a robe that opens completely down the front or one that wraps and ties.

If your father has difficulty managing eating utensils because of the pain and crippling in his hands, ask the therapist for those utensils designed to make eating more comfortable. If such instruments are unavailable in your community, use a regular utensil, but first wrap the handle with foam tubing available at hardware stores. The thicker handle makes managing the utensil easier. There are many such aids for living available. Ask your doctor or occupational therapist. (See also *The Gadget Book: Ingenious Devices for Easier Living,* edited by Dennis R. La Buda.)

Do not be afraid to change habits. If the person has always taken a bath but now finds climbing into and out of the bathtub painful, encourage a shower instead. If the house is a two-story with bedrooms on the second floor, try to redo a room on the first floor as a bedroom for the person, eliminating the need to go up and down stairs.

Getting more help.   For more information about arthritis and its effects and living with the disease, contact the local chapter of the Arthritis Foundation as well as the local Social Services Department, the state division of Vocational Rehabilitation, the Medical Society, the mental health association, and the Social Security Administration. The health team and the home health care agencies in your community can provide the affected person with a great deal of information and resource materials for a more comfortable and independent life.

CANCER

Perhaps no word currently in the English language can strike immediate fear and despair the way the word *cancer* can; yet every day strides are being made toward controlling and, in some cases, curing the various forms of this disease known to medical science. It is interesting that in the case of this disease, it is often someone other than the patient who gets the diagnosis first. Then the big questions become, Should we tell? Whom should we tell? In most cases the answers are respectively "Yes" and "Everyone." Remind those you tell that research has been going on for years and that the medical profession is having much success in treating and curing many forms of cancer that used to be life-threatening.

If death is a possibility, allowing the person the time and the opportunity to attend to personal matters is very important. In most situations the affected individual should be allowed to decide who will be told and when and how.

Not all cancers are fatal, and the affected person and the caregiver should get thorough and careful answers to that list of questions posed for the medical staff on page 172. At any stage, cancer is a frightening illness with which to deal. It is still shrouded in mystery and misinformation. Not much has been written about coping with the illness or about how family members and caregivers cope with the person who is affected. Subsequently, as is often the case for caregivers in any role, there is a feeling of isolation. All the stories in the newspapers seem to focus on families who are coping magnificently. No one seems to talk about how difficult it is.

The Role of the Caregiver

When a diagnosis of cancer is made, the caregiver suddenly may be faced with a flood of details to attend to. These include getting a correct prognosis, making financial arrangements for care, making arrangements for transporting the person for care procedures, making arrangements for special equipment and services needed in the home, and communicating with the affected person and the rest of the family as well as with the medical community. Where do you find help? You might consider the following:

- Consult the medical staff, the health team.
- Call the American Cancer Society (1-800-ACS-2345). It offers a variety of services for both the affected person and the caregiver, including informational literature, home care items, transportation, and rehabilitation programs. In addition, call your local home health care agency for help.
- Write for information about new treatments before spending money to try the newest "miracle."
- Encourage the person to be open and frank with you about his or her feelings, wishes, and fears. Try to be open in return. Seek the assistance of a trained counselor or clergyperson to help in these discussions.
- Read everything you can about the disease. Become an "expert" on terminology, research, side effects, and so on.
- Do not withdraw from family and friends. If they withdraw, pull them back. Call and ask for simple help: "Please pick up a quart of milk." "Can you come over while I run an errand?"
- Join a support group with others who are dealing with a similar problem. If one is not available, start one. The American Cancer Society offers a free program (I Can Cope) for the person who has the disease.
- If the person will be bedfast, see page 155 for a discussion on setting up his or her room.
- *Encourage and allow the person to do as much as he or she can.* Do not treat the person as an invalid if he or she is capable

of maintaining a fairly normal routine. Take your lead from the affected person. Allow him or her the dignity to decide in what way the disease will be handled.

• If the time comes when the person needs more skilled care than you can provide at home, investigate the possibility of placing the person in a hospice care program. Under such a program the person receives supervised care at home or on an outpatient basis for as long as possible.

For more information. Contact or write the following:

> The Cancer Information Service
> 1-800-4-CANCER

> Office of Cancer Communications
> National Cancer Institute
> 9000 Rockville Pike
> Bethesda, MD 20205

> Make Today Count
> PO Box 303
> Burlington, IA 52601

> United Cancer Council, Inc.
> 1803 North Meridian Street
> Indianapolis, IN 46202

> American Cancer Society, Inc.
> 777 Third Avenue
> New York, NY 10017

DIABETES

Like arthritis, diabetes is a name for a group of chronic diseases. At this writing these afflictions can be controlled but not cured. In general terms, diabetes is either Type I (insulin dependent) or Type II (non-insulin dependent). Type I is a diabetes that most often affects children and young adults. Type II usually occurs in adults over the age of forty and accounts for approximately 80 to 85 percent of the diabetes cases. Often Type II diabetes can be controlled through proper diet and exercise. In some cases diet and exercise are supplemented by medication or insulin. The onset of Type II diabetes is gradual and can go undetected for several years. The disease may first become apparent following some acute illness such as a heart attack or a serious problem with the individual's vision or kidneys.

Symptoms

Type II diabetes may be present in cases where the person is overweight (obesity is a major factor in the development of the disease), over age forty, experiencing drowsiness or blurred vision, or complaining of some numbness or tingling in hands or feet. Sometimes there are skin infections or a slow healing process for cuts. A person who has a family history of diabetes is also at risk.

Because diabetics can continue to live full and productive lives, the disease is not always seen by the general public as a serious health problem. However, one in every forty persons has been diagnosed as having diabetes. An estimated five million people have Type II diabetes and *do not know it*. Being a diabetic increases by twenty-five times the chances of going blind, by seventeen times the chances of developing kidney disease, and by two times the chance of developing heart disease or suffering a stroke as the nondiabetic. Diabetes with its associated complications is the third leading cause of death due to disease in the United States today, according to information available from the American Diabetes Association.

As with any chronic disease, the problem is not only physical. People who must live their lives with the problems of illness affecting everything they do have the equally difficult task of recognizing and dealing with the emotional pain of the disease. Diabetes can cause shifts in mood, and it can affect mental alertness. The discipline needed to control the disease can mean changes in lifestyle that are inconvenient. Caregivers for diabetics must understand that blood sugar levels can be perfectly under control one day and out of control the next with no apparent change in diet, exercise, or lifestyle taking place. Why? Because stress and emotional crises can also affect the sugar level. Caregivers need to talk to the diabetic and the doctor to get advice on what to do in a crisis situation.

Diet

The diabetic's eating habits can be vital to the containment of his or her illness. There are six basic food groups from which the diabetic chooses some food each day: dairy products; fruits; vegetables; grain products; meat, fish, and poultry products; and fats. Diabetics need three *balanced* meals every day; they may also have snacks if these are prescribed by a doctor. It is not necessary to buy special foods; in fact many foods labeled "dietetic" are not always suitable for the diabetic. The size of the portions is as important as what is served. The doctor or dietician will provide the diabetic with a diet plan. That plan has been tailored to the age, condition, and lifestyle of the patient and should not be traded for someone else's diet plan.

It is possible for the diabetic to live a productive and interesting life—to go to work, to enjoy good food, to eat out in a restaurant, and to take part in a normal routine of activity. But both the caregiver and the diabetic need to make it clear to anyone who will be serving the diabetic that the disease *prohibits* certain food items, and the server is doing the diabetic no favor by telling him or her that "a little piece can't hurt."

The American Diabetes Association publishes a number of aids for helping the diabetic control the disease. Perhaps one of the most useful tools for the caregiver of the diabetic is *The American Diabetes Association / The American Dietetic Association Family Cookbook, Volume I and Volume II*, which helps the meal planner prepare meals without guesswork. The books are available through your local affiliate of the American Diabetes Association at a cost of $12.95 for Volume I and $15.95 for Volume II (which deals extensively with fiber in the diet of the diabetic). You can also order the books by writing to The American Diabetes Association, Two Park Avenue, New York, NY 10016. *Recipes for Diabetics* by Billie Little is another cookbook for persons who have diabetes.

Special Precautions

As the caregiver for a diabetic, what should you know? First of all, you need to know whether there are other medical conditions present and how they will be affected by the fact that the person is a diabetic. In addition obtain answers to the following questions.

1. Is the person taking medication? If so, what is the name of the drug, when and how often is it to be taken, and how should the medication be related to meals?
2. What supplies does the person need for blood testing (this is the preferred way for the individual and you to monitor the disease and ensure that it is being properly controlled)? How do you read the results of the blood test?
3. What are the dietary requirements for the diabetic? Are there foods that can be substituted or exchanged for those denied the affected person? (Ask your local affiliate of the American Diabetes Association for a list of exchange foods.)
4. What exercise plan is recommended?

You should get an identification bracelet for the person that will tell any medical personnel who may attend him or her in an emergency that diabetes is present.

If the diabetic becomes ill with something even as simple as a cold or virus, he or she should be monitored carefully, and the doctor should be alerted if the condition persists beyond a day or so.

Because diabetes can affect the circulation of blood to the feet and legs of the diabetic, you will have to be particularly concerned about the care of the person's feet. If there is any break in the surface of the skin or any sign of irritation, contact the person's doctor immediately. Such seemingly minor symptoms can lead to serious infections and, in some cases, to amputation. Follow a rigid routine of daily foot care as described below. In addition, see a podiatrist on a regular basis.

1. Check the person's feet thoroughly every day for any sign of redness, swelling, or cracks or breaks in the skin.
2. Wash the person's feet every day. Do not soak the feet or use hot water. Do not use lotion unless the doctor

recommends its use, and do not use powder on feet that perspire.
3. Dry the feet thoroughly, especially between the toes.
4. Be especially careful in pedicures not to clip the nail too close or nick the skin. Never cut or tear away dead skin around a callus, blister, or corn.
5. Protect the feet at all times with stockings and shoes that fit.

HEART DISEASE

Even after the victim of a heart attack is on his or her way to recovery, the dominant emotions may be shock and fear. Shock comes with the realization that life has been threatened in a very tangible way. Fear comes from the knowledge that the same thing might happen again.

A heart attack is the sudden manifestation of a disease that has been developing over a much longer period of time. Over a period of months or years the coronary arteries (those that supply blood to the heart) collect deposits of cholesterol and other substances on the inner walls. The passage through which the blood travels narrows and eventually blocks, producing the "heart attack." The medical term is *coronary thrombosis* or *coronary occlusion*. Once the attack has been launched, the heart muscle will sustain some injury, and this is called a *myocardial infarction*.

Be aware that an older person may not experience the symptomatic chest pain often associated with a heart attack. Instead there may be shortness of breath or extreme fatigue. Such "silent" attacks often go undetected until an electrocardiogram (EKG) is run for some other health problem. For example, a person may fall and break a hip, and later it may be discovered that the fall was caused by a silent heart attack.

Aside from the physical healing process following a heart attack, there is an emotional healing that must take place as well. It is in this process that the caregiver may play the greatest role. First, the person who has had an attack may live for some time with the fear that it will happen again. The memory of the pain and the suddenness of the attack may be fresh and may cause the person to be overly cautious in everything he or she does. These fears tend to lessen with time, and they require patience and understanding on the part of the caregiver.

Older persons who experience heart attacks may react somewhat differently than those younger persons whose fear may be replaced by anger at having been struck down. An older person may have been anticipating an attack simply because of his or her age and, having had a heart attack, may be greatly relieved to have lived through it. The person may have an attitude of being lucky to be alive. Of course, each individual will respond to having a heart attack based on his or her personality and the circumstances of the recovery.

Some persons will become depressed. They feel damaged. They feel crippled. They fear they will not be the person they have always been. They especially may fear that they cannot be a proper spouse—sexually and emotionally. Some victims may become morose as they start to catalog all the things not finished in their lives.

These emotional attacks, which are part of the healing process, should go away by six months following the attack. If they persist, or if after a few months they do not seem any better, encourage counseling. The warnings will include such behaviors as these: the person cannot sleep or sleeps all the time, will not eat, has no energy or interest, and is either tense or irritable or totally apathetic. The person may repeatedly make statements about his or her worthlessness or about dying. Inform the doctor if such feelings are present and persist.

Treatment

The doctor will probably prescribe a regimen of diet, exercise, and medication following a heart attack. It is imperative that this routine be observed even after the person begins to feel better. Ask the doctor for information about any hospital in your community that offers a teaching program for heart patients that helps the person and his or her family cope by providing educational materials and resource information.

Risk Factors

Because the onset of a heart attack is often sudden or silent (see page 166) and there is little time to assess symptoms, it helps if the caregiver is aware of the risk factors that may lead to subsequent heart attacks. These include the following:

- high blood pressure
- high cholesterol levels in the blood
- smoking cigarettes
- a family history of heart disease
- the age of the person (Men at any age are at risk, but women who have passed menopause are more at risk than those who have not.)
- diabetes
- stress (specifically, how the individual copes with it)

You should assess your relative's situation and determine which risk factors are present and how these factors may be controlled.

Angina

What is angina? Actually the correct term is *angina pectoris,* and it is a *temporary* pain or discomfort in the chest caused by a *temporary* reduction of oxygen to the heart muscle. Such pain may occur with exertion, emotional stress, eating, or exposure to the cold. Angina is *not* a heart attack but can resemble one. Angina causes temporary shortness of breath and pain, while a heart attack may be more prolonged. With angina the pain can usually be controlled within five minutes with rest and/or medications (specifically nitroglycerin tablets). If the pain is not relieved quickly, get immediate medical attention—the person may be having a heart attack.

For more information. Contact the local chapter of the American Heart Association or write the American Heart Association, National Center, 7320 Greenville Avenue, Dallas, TX 75231.

LUNG DISEASES

While many diseases are caused at least in part by a heredity factor, lung diseases are much more influenced by the environment. Almost everyone suffers from some lung infection at one time or another; colds, flus, and other viruses are common ailments. But when those simple respiratory ailments become complicated, such serious problems as pneumonia, bronchitis, or emphysema may develop. While lung disease can be life-threatening, it is important that the caregiver and the affected person be aware that strict adherence to rehabilitation routines can pay off in improved health.

Pneumonia

People who are exhausted or very old are at risk for this infection, in which the lungs become filled with fluid. The symptoms include coughing, chills, fever, chest pain, and perhaps spitting up some blood. The disease is life-threatening—particularly for those who suffer from chronic conditions such as heart, lung, or kidney disease and diabetes and for those who are recovering from a serious acute illness (especially frail older persons). When too much fluid prevents oxygen from getting into the bloodstream, the disease becomes a killer. If you suspect that the person has pneumonia, call the doctor, and if instructed to do so, take the person to the hospital.

If the person is diagnosed as having pneumonia, he or she will be treated in the hospital and perhaps later at home with antibiotics. It is imperative not to rush the recovery period. Recovering patients are prime candidates for relapse unless they follow doctor's orders to the letter.

Prevention of pneumonia is possible for some high-risk candidates due to the development of a vaccine similar to the vaccine against influenza that has been available for several years. Ask the doctor if the person should have the vaccine as a preventive measure.

Chronic Obstructive Lung Diseases

Chronic bronchitis and emphysema are the two most

common chronic obstructive lung diseases. In both cases the person may suffer through a pattern that begins with difficulty in breathing that leads to a lack of energy that leads to decreased activity that leads to depression and anxiety that leads full circle back to difficulty in breathing. In these particular lung diseases it is important to remember that the less the person does, the less he or she will be able to do. Patients should be encouraged to be active to the limits of their capacities.

Chronic bronchitis.   This disease is an inflammation and swelling of the lining of the bronchial tubes caused by ongoing and repeated irritation of the tubes due to such things as smoking and pollution. Those who are most affected are people who have been longtime smokers and/or who have lived in large metropolitan areas. The disease takes a long time to develop, and it may be years before the person begins to develop the symptoms of shortness of breath and persistent coughing and spitting. Chronic bronchitis, if untreated, can lead to heart failure and is a serious disease.

Emphysema.   This condition is an actual breakdown of the lung sacs (the alveoli). The sacs lose their elasticity, resulting in an inability to empty the lungs completely and a residue of stale, oxygen-poor air. Again, smoking and air pollution are the suspected causes of the disease, and long-term smokers are the most at risk. The disease is incurable, though some relief is possible through medication and physical therapy. This condition can also lead to heart failure.

Precautions.   Anyone who has either of these chronic obstructive diseases should not smoke or be around others who smoke. The person should eat a balanced diet; keep fit with a prescribed program of regular, mild exercise; and avoid polluted air and exposure to persons with cold or flu symptoms. Have the person ask his or her doctor about being vaccinated against influenza and pneumonia.

Of course, there are other lung diseases such as tuberculosis, asthma, and lung cancer, but those discussed above are the most common for older persons.

Prevention of Lung Diseases

There are five simple steps to preventing lung disease: (1) do not smoke; (2) avoid secondhand smoke (from other smokers); (3) stay away from air pollution; (4) take care to get the right food, rest, and exercise; and (5) have regular checkups.

Distress Signals

If you are a caregiver for someone who has a chronic lung infection or is at high risk to get pneumonia, it may be a little late for prevention. Still, you can improve your relative's ease of breathing by responding in the following ways to the conditions listed below:

Breathlessness. The person is often short of breath and becomes more so because he or she panics at the condition and tries to breathe faster, usually through the mouth. Encourage the person to relax by letting his or her head fall forward with shoulders drooping. Then instruct the person to breathe in slowly through his or her nose. Talk softly and calmly as you encourage the procedure. Next, tell the person to purse his or her lips and blow out the air slowly. Repeat until the person feels better. (By having the person breathe in through his or her nose, you are ensuring that the air is warmed and properly humidified before it reaches the lungs.)

Coughing. The individual has coughing spells that leave him or her exhausted and frightened. When the person feels the cough coming, have him or her breathe deeply and then hold the breath for a few seconds. Next, have the person cough twice—to loosen mucus and then bring it up (that is what a cough is for). Have the person breathe in by sniffing gently. If possible, when coughing starts, have the individual sit down with head forward and both feet on the ground. Force fluids. They help thin the secretions and make them easier to discharge.

Mucus. A feeling of fluid in the airways makes breathing difficult. There are prescribed procedures for draining the mucus from a person's lungs. If the doctor prescribes that the person's lungs be cleared once or twice a day, do not try to learn the procedure from a book alone.

Get a demonstration from a trained nurse or physical therapist by contacting your doctor, hospital, or home health care agency.

Exhaustion.   The individual may be tired constantly. You can help the person to build strength by teaching him or her proper breathing techniques and by starting and maintaining a daily exercise program. If possible, the exercise program should include a steady regimen of walking. Before any exercise program is established, however, seek the advice of the individual's doctor. Once the program is started, stick to it.

Breathing Aids

Breathing aids are available to ease the pain and difficulty of chronic lung disease. Most such devices are for the purpose of helping to get oxygen deep into the lungs or to clear mucus from the airways. Your relative's doctor may prescribe one or more of the following:

Nebulizer.   This is a sprayer that delivers medicine to the lungs to ease breathing. Get instructions on proper use from the nurse or therapist.

Oxygen.   If the doctor prescribes oxygen use at home, have a nurse or therapist show you how to use the equipment properly. Oxygen is medicine, and as such there are proper dosages.

Humidifiers and vaporizers.   These are machines for the purpose of putting moisture into the air. Particularly in very cold climates, added moisture can ease breathing because it will help soften and loosen mucus.

IPPB (Intermittent Positive-Pressure Breathing) breathing machine.   This is an expensive device that uses pressure to deliver medicine and/or moisture with air deep into the lungs. The device should be prescribed by a doctor, and instructions on proper use are vital.

There are other breath-saver devices on the market, but before buying or using any of them, get the advice of your doctor or home health care professional. The hazard here is with germ cultivation in the unit, and the caregiver will have to be sure that all respiratory equipment used in the home is cleaned often and thoroughly.

Cold-air mask. Be aware that perhaps the most common and least expensive breathing aid is the cold-air mask available at your local pharmacy. Caregivers for those with chronic lung disease should purchase a mask and call the air pollution control information service often for details of air quality and ozone alerts. The mask should be worn whenever there is an alert or whenever the weather is either very hot and humid or very cold.

For more information. The local chapter of the American Lung Association can supply you with literature and information about lung diseases and their prevention and treatment. You can also write to the American Lung Association, 1740 Broadway, New York, NY 10019.

MULTIPLE SCLEROSIS

The central nervous system consists of the brain, the spinal cord, and the various nerves that connect the brain and spinal cord to the sensory organs, glands, and muscles of the body. Multiple sclerosis (MS) is an inflammatory disorder of the myelin (the insulation) sheath that is wrapped in thick protective rings around the nerve fibers that send messages to the various parts of the body. The inflammation occurs in unpredictable patterns that may vary in size from a pin point to a pea or greater.

Symptoms

One of the reasons MS is so difficult to diagnose is that symptoms vary from one person to another, and there is no conclusive diagnostic test at the present time. Some common signs may include a numbness or tingling in the limbs, dragging of the feet, slurring of words, loss of balance or coordination, blurred vision, and dizziness or a spinning sensation. More serious symptoms may occur in some cases, including partial or complete paralysis of the arms or legs, loss of bladder or bowel control, and more serious problems with vision. Taken one by one, these symptoms could be indicative of any number of problems, but if several symptoms are present, a physician should be contacted.

The Patient

Most commonly, MS will affect people between the ages of twenty and forty, but it can affect anyone at any age. The disease is not contagious and will affect individuals in different ways and with differing rates of disability interrupted by periods of remission.

Treatment

The exact cause of MS is unknown, so there is no cure, but there are treatments that seem to be effective in the containment of the disease in some cases. These include a well-balanced diet; plenty of rest; and avoidance of overexertion, fatigue, or extreme emotional stress. Some available drugs can be prescribed by the person's doctor, and rehabilitation services including physical, occupational, speech, and recreational therapy may be effective.

The Role of the Caregiver

A caregiver for a person with MS needs to be aware of features of daily living that can help the affected person maintain independence and quality of life.

1. Is the person with MS balancing rest with activity?
2. Has a home exercise program been prescribed by the doctor and/or rehabilitation service?
3. Has the home been checked for both safety and accessibility?
4. Have friends and family members been instructed in ways of helping the person to maintain his or her independence?
5. Are social contacts being maintained?
6. Have you and the person with MS learned to focus on those skills that remain rather than on those that have been lost in the process of the disease?
7. Has the local MS Society been contacted for advice and support for both the person and the caregiver?

For more help.   The local Multiple Sclerosis Society can provide a number of helpful programs and information services for the MS client and the caregiver. Two very good publications are *MS Is a Family Affair* and *MS— Grounds for Hope.* Both are available from your local MS Society office. Ask your local library or bookstore for *The Pursuit of Hope* by Miriam Ottenberg. Finally, an excellent exercise program, *Maximizing Your Health*, by Debra Frankel and Robert Buxbaum, is available by writing the Massachusetts Chapter, National MS Society, 400-1 Totten Pond Road, Waltham, MA 02154.

OSTEOPOROSIS

This disease is another of those slow, gradual illnesses that take years to develop and often go undetected until considerable damage has been done. Osteoporosis is the gradual thinning and weakening of the bone mass. The bones of the spine are one area that is affected, and the result may be a condition that has become known as dowager's hump or humpback. Another common effect of the disease is broken bones, due to the increased brittleness of the bones. Hip fractures are one of the most devastating results of this weakened condition.

Causes

Although little is known about the disease, researchers have found that with women there may be a definite correlation between the illness and the drop in estrogen produced by the body during and after menopause. It is also believed that improper diet and exercise can play a role. There may even be a relation between the disease and drinking lots of coffee and/or smoking cigarettes, though research is still being done in these areas, and there are no conclusive findings.

Treatment

Most treatment programs are geared toward arresting the disease rather than trying to replace lost bone mass. Estrogen therapy is often prescribed for those women who are most at risk—fair-skinned, white, postmenopausal females with small bone structures. Such treatment has gotten some positive results, but the side effects—such as fluid retention, breakthrough bleeding, abdominal cramping, and nausea—can be significant. In some cases patients have developed cancer of the uterus.

The most common treatment is a calcium supplement sometimes prescribed in combination with a vitamin D supplement. (Some believe the vitamin D improves the absorption of the calcium.) An exercise program may also be recommended for increasing bone mass.

The Role of the Caregiver

If your relative is at high risk for osteoporosis and the resultant dangers of broken bones, talk to his or her physician and start a program of diet, exercise, and calcium supplements that may arrest the progress of the bone loss. If the person uses a wheelchair or bed for long periods of time, ask for ideas to increase the mobility of that person. Then make sure that the home is safe for the person and that safety is a key consideration before going out. Do not take unnecessary risks. For example, if it snows the day your relative is scheduled for a doctor's appointment, it is a good idea to postpone the appointment if possible until the weather is better.

PARKINSON'S DISEASE

Parkinson's disease is a progressive neurological disorder of adults. It is characterized by rigidity of the muscles, slowness of movements, and a unique tremor that is a key factor in the diagnosis. If a physician suspects the person has Parkinson's disease, he or she should refer the patient to a neurologist. Both men and women in the older age group can be candidates for the illness.

Symptoms

Parkinson's syndrome is characterized by muscle rigidity. The affected person may experience difficulty when it comes to initiating a simple movement such as getting up from a chair, walking across the room, or reaching for some object. The tremor (or shaking) that is an obvious sign of the illness may be evident when the person attempts to hold a fork or when the hand is at rest at the person's side. The person's senses of hearing, seeing, and feeling are unaffected, and if speech is affected, it is because stiffness of the muscles produces a low volume or inability to speak plainly. The person may also appear to register no expression. This again is the result of muscle rigidity and should not be taken to mean that the individual has no emotional reactions to events. The person may also experience difficulty in eating because the process is tedious and the affected person has difficulty chewing and swallowing. In the later stages the affected person may become immobilized due to inactivity and the increasing muscle rigidity.

Treatment

Many effective developments in medications and therapy for treating the person with parkinsonism have occurred in recent years. Those affected by the illness are able to live more active and independent lives. The person should see a neurologist, who will develop a program of medications, therapy, and exercises to retain muscle movement. Family members can join a support group with the affected person. Such groups are organized to provide education, self-help ideas, and an opportunity to meet with others and share experiences in coping with the emotional stress of the illness.

The Role of the Caregiver

As the muscle rigidity increases and activity becomes more restricted, the affected person may experience bouts of depression. The caregiver can help by encouraging the person to continue to perform as many routine tasks as possible for as long as possible. Remember, it takes more time and a great deal of concentration for the person with Parkinson's disease to perform a seemingly simple action. Your support and positive attitude can be instrumental in helping the person fight depression. As the caregiver, you should understand and remind others that the disease affects the body. The person's mind and feelings are very much intact.

For more help.   These voluntary organizations can help you and the care recipient.

> American Parkinson Disease Association
> 116 John Street
> New York, NY 10038
>
> National Parkinson Foundation, Inc.
> 1501 N.W. Ninth Avenue
> Miami, FL 33136
>
> Parkinson's Disease Foundation
> William Black Medical Research Building
> 640 West 168th Street
> New York, NY 10032
>
> United Parkinson Foundation
> 360 West Superior Street
> Chicago, IL 60610
>
> Parkinson Support Groups of America
> 11376 Cherry Hill Road, Apt. 204
> Beltsville, MD 20705

Each of these agencies publishes brochures and pamphlets that can help the affected person and the caregiver cope with the disease.

Robert C. Duvoisin has written *Parkinson's Disease: A Guide for Patient and Family*, which should prove helpful.

STROKES

A stroke is a sudden onset of weakness or other neurological symptom as a result of some injury to a blood vessel in the brain. The injury can be caused by a thrombus (blood clot) or by a hemorrhage (bleeding) from a ruptured blood vessel. The injury produces a lack of oxygen to one part of the brain, and the tissue in that area is damaged. The location of the damage will determine how the victim will ultimately be affected by a stroke. Different portions of the brain control highly specialized functions of the body. It is important to remember that a stroke is *not* the same as a heart attack. Stroke may cause paralysis on one side of the body. In some cases there may be no paralysis, or there may be temporary paralysis. Some people are affected in their ability to speak or understand language. This condition is known as aphasia. A person may also experience difficulty in reading, in writing, and/or in making judgments. Physical, occupational, and speech therapy can help the person who has experienced stroke regain some function and/or adapt to performing activities using the unaffected side.

Symptoms

The three major warning signs of an impending stroke are (1) numbness or weakness in one leg, arm, or side of the face; (2) temporary blurred vision or blindness; and (3) temporary speech problems. Symptoms may last for a few seconds or minutes and may occur once or several times during a day. These symptoms are caused by TIA's, transient ischemic attacks, meaning a lack of sufficient blood. Some other symptoms are harder to recognize, including a sudden headache, loss of balance, and sleepiness. Any symptom, no matter how short the duration, needs to be taken seriously and reported to a physician. Most doctors consider TIA's to be medical emergencies and like to see the affected person as soon as possible after the incident has occurred. Prompt treatment is vital if a stroke is to be prevented.

Relationship to Other Conditions

Some conditions can be related to stroke in that they increase the chance a stroke may occur. Arteriosclerosis (hardening of the arteries) is such a condition. Research has shown that high levels of cholesterol in the diet can result in the accumulation of plaque on the walls of arteries that carry the blood to all parts of the body. This accumulation can prevent an adequate flow of blood, increasing the chance for a stroke.

Hypertension (high blood pressure) is another condition that is associated with stroke. The measure of blood pressure indicates the amount of force necessary for the heart to pump blood throughout the body. When blood pressure is too high, an undue force is exerted, which may weaken an artery in the brain. If that artery ruptures, the result is known as a cerebral hemorrhage, a type of stroke. Hypertension can also be a factor in the acceleration of hardening of the arteries. Most people mistakenly believe that they will know when they have high blood pressure because they will experience certain symptoms. This misleading notion could result in death—or a stroke. Hypertension is a silent disease with few noticeable symptoms; it can strike anyone, no matter what his or her personality makeup may be. The only way to know whether a person has hypertension is to have his or her blood pressure checked regularly.

Some people believe that a stroke will be brought on by stress or exercise. While stress can be a contributing factor, it is unlikely that stress that is temporary will bring on a stroke. Exercise is not going to cause a stroke as long as the exercise program is pursued in moderation and with a doctor's approval. Research has shown that those who lead sedentary lives are more apt to experience problems than those who are active.

Prevention

The U.S. Department of Health and Human Services has published a booklet entitled *What You Should Know About Stroke and Stroke Prevention*. In this publication the department lists the "Ten Commandments" for preventing strokes:

1. Report any warning symptoms to your doctor promptly.
2. Have your blood pressure checked regularly.
3. Follow a healthy diet.
4. Stop smoking, and stay away from secondhand smoke.
5. Exercise regularly and moderately.
6. Decrease intake of salt.
7. Have regular checkups.
8. Drink alcohol only in moderation.
9. Watch your weight, and lose weight if necessary.
10. Avoid stress. Relax and enjoy life.

The Role of the Caregiver

With stroke there can be some permanent as well as temporary loss of a wide variety of abilities—and often a combination involving muscular and communication skills and response of the nervous system. Special techniques that help a caregiver whose relative is affected deal with the situation are given below.

1. Begin any activity by explaining what you are going to do, how you are going to do it, and what the care recipient should do.
2. Allow the person time to think about what you have said and time to respond and cooperate.
3. Be patient. Take time to perform the task and to allow the person to adjust and react.
4. Establish a routine, step-by-step sequence for performing any routine task. Do not change the sequence or the tempo without going back to step one.
5. Give praise for successes. Acknowledge how much time and effort it has taken for the person to attain each success.

Although it is necessary to approach each task in a step-by-step, slow, simple pattern, remember that the person is an adult. Whatever brain damage has occurred does not change that. Your relative deserves your respect and acknowledgment of age and past position. Do not talk to the person as though he or she is a child. Do not talk about the person in his or her presence as though the person cannot understand you. And do not let others do that either. Even when the person cannot speak, he or she may understand very well everything that is being said.

Occupational and speech therapists should meet with you before the care recipient is discharged from the hospital or rehabilitation program. At that time these experts will define the particular needs of the person for routine daily activities such as eating and dressing.

Therapy and rehabilitative exercises can be tedious and, if no noticeable progress is attained, discouraging. The person can become depressed and irritable. Especially if aphasia is part of the problem, the person does not even have the relief of being able to express those feelings. There can be dramatic shifts in mood and personality.

Sometimes these are the result of the illness and are not the person's choice. For example, initially there may be uncontrolled crying (or to a lesser degree inappropriate swearing or laughter) unrelated to what is happening around the person.

In many communities there are stroke clubs for those who are living with a stroke or for the family members. Such meetings can include opportunities for social contacts that can be very important to both the affected person and the caregiver.

For more information.   Additional material about stroke and how to cope with stroke is available from the following sources.

> National Institute of Neurological and Communicative
>   Disorders and Stroke
> National Institutes of Health
> 9000 Rockville Pike
> Bethesda, MD 20205

> Sister Kenny Foundation
> 800 East 28th Street
> Minneapolis, MN 55407

> Council on Stroke
> American Heart Association
> 7320 Greenville Avenue
> Dallas, TX 75231

> The National Easter Seal Society, Inc.
> 2023 West Ogden Avenue
> Chicago, IL 60612

> Stroke Foundation
> 898 Park Avenue
> New York, NY 10021

> The Dwight D. Eisenhower Institute for Stroke Research
> 785 Mamaroneck Avenue
> White Plains, NY 10605

> American Speech-Language-Hearing Association (ASHA)
> 10801 Rockville Pike
> Rockville, MD 20852
> (for persons with aphasia)

The following are books for those who care for stroke patients:

Care of the Patient with a Stroke by Genevieve W. Smith.

Stroke: The New Help and The New Life by Arthur S. Freese.

PAIN

Chronic pain is a very special area of disability. Many people have chronic pain without knowing the reason. Others, like those who suffer with the chronic pain of arthritis, understand their diagnosis but still have to deal with the pain.

Your relative's doctor may be able to advise the person of ways in which pain can be controlled or can perhaps recommend a physician who specializes in treatment for chronic pain. Many hospitals across the country are beginning to introduce special clinics and programs that will help those who live daily with pain. There are some techniques for relieving pain that you can try at home *with the doctor's approval*. Consider the following:

- Hot or cold applications to the painful area may help.
- Rest and exercise may also relieve some types of chronic pain.
- Some mild forms of medication may be helpful, *but any medication—even if sold over the counter, such as aspirin—should be given only with the doctor's approval*.
- Encourage the affected person to pay attention to the messages his or her body is sending. When there is pain, the body may be sending a message that says the person should rest and slow down.
- Work with the person to prepare for those occasions that he or she wants to attend or participate in without pain. For example, if the person knows that on Monday he or she wants to take part in a special program, the weekend may have to be spent in rest and relaxation in preparation for that event.
- If the person constantly apologizes for pain that stands in the way of normal activity, encourage that per-

son to speak as positively as possible about the disability: "I cannot manage that today, but I really would like for you to ask me again."

• One suggested method for working through pain is to concentrate on something else. Many pain sufferers find that when their minds are occupied by some meaningful and interesting activity, the pain seems to lessen.

• Plan activities that take into consideration the painful areas of the body. For example, if the person's hands are in pain, the activity should be something that does not involve the hands, such as listening to music, watching a movie, or taking a ride. Sometimes the doctor will recommend that the painful areas be used in spite of pain in order to exercise those areas. Discuss activities with your doctor or home health care professional.

• Be aware that the person who has pain will also have a range of emotions accompanying that pain, including anger, depression, and fear. A person who has chronic pain may also find excuses for giving in to the pain and withdrawing from life. Your support and encouragement may help the person seek counseling for his or her emotional despondency to find new ways to cope.

Pain is a very real physical disability that affects many people daily. Pain is not visible, and trying to translate these sensations into words is nearly impossible. Think of the embarrassment and frustration of always having to explain to others that you cannot do this or that because of pain when you look perfectly fine. It is little wonder that some chronic pain sufferers may adopt a "What's the use?" attitude and abandon their regular treatment. If your relative's disability involves chronic pain—whether or not the cause of that pain has been diagnosed—it is your job to help that person find therapy, counseling, treatment, and/or rehabilitation that will help him or her live with the disability.

11 &. Understanding Mental Incapacities

Mental disabilities can cover a range of symptoms including memory loss, failing attention, loss of orientation to time and place, and interrupted thought-speech patterns. The illnesses, while very different, are related in that the symptoms for each are similar. For this reason the mental illnesses discussed in this chapter are sometimes categorized as varying forms of the illness *dementia.* As you learned earlier, such illnesses may be wrongly identified as types of senility. Keep in mind that someone who is senile is old or aging—not going through a second childhood or crazy.

In fact, there are many possible causes of such symptoms including Alzheimer's disease, multi-infarct dementia, thyroid problems, nutritional deficiencies, drug intoxication, brain tumor, degenerative diseases of the central nervous system, and depression. None of these afflictions is inevitable, and while millions of Americans do suffer from Alzheimer's disease and multi-infarct dementia, tens of millions do not.

A few years ago the media began to print information about the "discovery" of Alzheimer's disease, correcting the impression that senility was a normal factor in the aging process but in its place creating perhaps another monster. With all the publicity Alzheimer's disease has been receiving in recent years, it may be becoming the new catchall diagnosis for any symptom of confusion or mental impairment.

Alzheimer's disease is extremely hard to diagnose

and has often been referred to as the "rule out" disease because the only possible diagnosis on a living patient is by eliminating the possibility of any of the other diseases mentioned above. The only sure diagnosis is an autopsy. In many ways Alzheimer's is the most frightening of all diseases. The good news, according to the National Institute of Mental Health, is that only about 5 to 6 percent of older adults develop Alzheimer's. Before examining Alzheimer's disease in more detail, consider the other possible causes of symptoms that have been associated with "senility."

Multi-Infarct Dementia

In lay terms this is a series of small strokes—not the stroke where the person is incapacitated by becoming paralyzed and/or losing speech powers, but rather the smaller episode when the patient may experience a short-term mild weakness of the leg or arm, slurred speech, or even dizziness. During this episode brain tissue is destroyed, but because the patient recovers rapidly—indeed, the entire episode may be dismissed as "a little light-headedness"—little attention may be given to these cerebral vascular accidents.

Before the person begins to show any noticeable intellectual decline, there may be one or several such incidents. Such small strokes often occur in people with untreated hypertension or diabetes. Such persons are often overweight and have evidence of heart disease and arteriosclerosis (hardening of the arteries). About 10 to 20 percent of those people who suffer some form of dementia, according to the National Alzheimer's Disease and Related Disorders Association, suffer from multi-infarct dementia. Their illness is treatable if caught in the early stages. While destroyed brain tissue cannot be revived, drugs that control hypertension and/or thin the blood are often helpful. Occasionally surgery on the carotid artery (the main artery carrying blood to the brain) may be indicated.

Brain Tumors

Brain tumors are of two types—those that originate in the brain and those that begin elsewhere and travel to the brain via the bloodstream. They share the common trait that both are expanding masses that compress the brain and may result in impaired memory. A tumor may carry with it such symptoms as epileptic seizures, headaches, and/or weakness. If a tumor grows slowly enough, detection may be difficult until it reaches a large enough size to exhibit symptoms or until it affects the intellect in some significant way. Benign *or* malignant, some tumors—not all—can be removed.

Another type of mass that may collect on the brain is the subdural hematoma that usually appears following an injury to the head such as might be sustained in a bad fall or an automobile accident. In this case, over a period of time, blood leaks from small torn veins into the spaces between the outermost coverings of the brain. The person may complain of headaches and be drowsy. There may be some weakness in an arm or leg and a loss of intellectual capacity. Subdural hematomas are treatable by surgery and may be detected by the use of a CT scan.

Drug Reactions

This common cause of confusion in older persons is also treatable. Older people often take a variety of medications prescribed by several doctors. In this age of specialization, a person may be seeing three or more doctors for treatment of various complaints, and there may be no one doctor or person coordinating care. Some drugs that are perfectly safe by themselves can be toxic when combined with certain other drugs.

Another problem that may occur when a person is taking several drugs is confusion over amounts and times. Aging persons maintain a drug in their systems longer than younger persons, so drug combinations that are safe for one generation may produce confusion and symptoms of intellectual decline in another.

The key to avoiding this situation is to be sure that the care recipient and the caregiver keep an accurate record of medications and that all medications are reviewed by the family doctor and/or pharmacist for possible side effects.

Nutritional Deficiencies

The diet of older persons, particularly if they live alone, often suffers. There is a tendency to "not bother" with normal mealtime amenities such as setting the table. The person will eat directly from a carton or pan rather than set a place for one. Or the person will snack on easily reached foods all day and not be interested in a regular balanced meal. Many older people skip meals, breakfast in particular. Others eat nutritionally unbalanced meals high in fats and starches because foods that contain those elements are filling, cheap, and easy to prepare. It is amazing how many of the same people who admonished their children to eat their vegetables or they wouldn't "grow up to be strong and healthy" fail to consider their own advice in their later years. Failure to eat a balanced diet can cause an imbalance in the body's chemistry that may cause symptoms of mental confusion.

Thyroid Problems

Patients with hypothyroidism may exhibit all the symptoms of dementia. They may appear apathetic and dull, their mental skills can slow down, and their balance may be affected. Other symptoms common to a thyroid problem may include hoarseness and dry skin. A blood test can diagnose a thyroid problem, and proper treatment can bring dramatic improvement.

Degenerative Diseases

Diseases of the central nervous system such as Parkinson's disease and multiple sclerosis have already been discussed in the chapter on physical incapacities. However they need to be mentioned here because sometimes symptoms of dementia can be a part of the physical problem. Although statistics would put such diseases at the remote end of the scale in diagnosing symptoms of dementia, they must be considered and ruled out along with the other remote possibilities.

Depression

In older persons depression may be called the "false senility." In an article for the September/October 1983 issue of *Perspective on Aging*, George S. Trotter and Muir Gray discuss this false senility as the "King Lear syndrome."

In their work they refer to the Shakespearean tragedy as one of the "clearest cases yet written of mental illness allied with the other problems of old age." They cite Lear's several mistakes in judgment as well as the fact that two of his daughters withdrew their support and encouragement. Gradually Lear was left with only his court fool. Trotter and Gray parallel Lear's end to the sad state of many of today's older persons, who, having been deserted by family and friends, without employment or purpose, become "the sad joke, the modern day fool; the television set bellowing forth an empty world is their impersonal [court jester]."

Lear's mental incapacity came about as a result of a combination of losses—loss of position, loss of family love, loss of support and companionship. He became isolated, withdrawing into himself and away from others. In older people these losses combine with sensory losses of hearing and sight in some cases to produce all the textbook symptoms of dementia from anxiety to paranoia. The older person may, because of his or her decreased mental ability and physical capacity, become overly cautious. This worsens the depression, which in turn exacerbates feelings of apathy and/or anger.

Symptoms

At any age the symptoms of mental depression may include a range of problems. Some of the more common symptoms that may occur are listed below. Your relative will not experience every single symptom, but if you become aware of the presence of several (three or more) of the symptoms listed, seek help for the person or encourage the person to seek help as soon as possible.

Psychological symptoms
    reduced pleasure in favorite pastimes
    loss of concentration
    fatigue and/or insomnia
    remorse or guilt
    indecisiveness
    increased anxiety
    suicidal thoughts
Physical symptoms
    overeating or loss of appetite
    complaints of aches and pains, headaches, pressure
      in the head or ears or eyes
    tearfulness or crying jags
    sleep disturbances
Verbal symptoms
    "No one cares about me."
    "I'm just in the way now."
    "All my friends are dead."

The American Journal of Psychiatry estimates that between 8 and 10 percent of those cases diagnosed as Alzheimer's disease turned out to be depression that was treatable and in some cases completely reversible. What do you look for? Ask yourself whether the symptoms have appeared after a significant event in the older person's life. Did Dad start to be up all night pacing from the time Mom died? Did Mom lose interest in eating after moving from her beloved home? Did the person seem to lose interest in things normally pursued as pleasant tasks—gardening, craftwork, or sports?

A depressed person may have bouts of inappropriate guilt and even speak of suicide or not wanting to live. Frequently the most common signal that the problem may be one of depression, especially in older people, is chronic complaining about physical ailments for which no medical support can be found. Depression is often overlooked in older persons because they are expected to slow down and not be as interested in the world around them. As with senility, the public may falsely assume that depression is a normal stage of growing older.

One sign that may help in recognizing depression, as opposed to dementia like Alzheimer's, is that often older persons who are depressed express concern about failing memory. They will wonder about feelings of worthlessness and their decreased appetite and energy level.

Often depression and dementia coexist—especially in the early stages of dementia, when the patient is aware that something is wrong.

Treatment

A person who has no dementia but only depression might be treated with great success by careful prescriptions of antidepressant medications or psychotherapy. Electroconvulsive therapy has been successful in treating some patients who suffer from severe depression.

Senile Dementia of the Alzheimer's Type

This is the biggie—the most frightening, the most frustrating. The onset is usually slow and gradual, and only in looking back do family members recall symptoms that may have gone unnoticed for years. Alzheimer's has struck someone as young as thirty-eight and is the leading cause of severe mental impairment in older people. It is an organic brain disease that destroys brain cells. It is *not* a normal stage of the aging process.

Approximately 5 percent of people over sixty-five and 20 percent of people over eighty are affected by Alzheimer's. *That means 95 and 80 percent respectively are not affected.* One-quarter of all persons confined in nursing homes today are there because of this disease. It is the fourth leading cause of death in persons over sixty-five (though frequently something else is listed as the cause of death, such as pneumonia).

The disease costs taxpayers billions of dollars and costs the victim and his or her family far more. It is next to impossible to describe the pain and problems of caring for someone afflicted with Alzheimer's. The need for care is constant, and sometimes the victim is not agreeable to that care. At times there are struggles between caregiver and care recipient because the affected person cannot be reasoned with, and the caregiver is reluctant to use white lies and tricks to cope with the person's outbursts. But caring for someone with Alzheimer's can be simpler if you can grasp what is happening to the person and can make use of community resources available to make your task easier.

The disease was first diagnosed in 1906 by a German neurologist, Alois Alzheimer, and it is currently recognized as the most common cause of severe intellectual loss in older persons. Simply put, the brain, when magnified, shows a combination of plaques (patches) and tangles (snarls)—the more plaques and tangles, the greater loss of memory and mental powers.

Initially the disease may appear in the form of problems with short-term memory. Short-term memory differs from immediate memory. Immediate memory is just that—memory of something that happened within the last few minutes. Short-term memory is memory of events that took place between a few minutes ago and a few days ago. Long-term memory is memory of events from childhood to years ago.

Symptoms

In the early stages the Alzheimer's victim may forget which medicines were taken in the morning or may forget to turn off the stove. There may be some disorientation as to time and place. There may be a mild personality change. The person may become more apathetic and less spontaneous. There may be a tendency to withdraw from others. Part of this withdrawal may be because the person recognizes in these early stages that all is not as it should be. The victim may be terrified at his or her inability to remember. Imagine someone asking about your son's wedding, which you cannot remember attending.

Later the person may develop repetitive behaviors such as pacing, rubbing the hands together, or folding and unfolding paper or cloth. Memory loss will continue while physical movements and strength may remain purposeful and coordinated; this frequently makes it harder to contain and handle the person. Many caregivers find that night or darkness will stimulate agitation and anxiety, often resulting in sleeplessness and/or wandering.

For many families one of the most tragic symptoms of the disease in the later stages is when the person does not recognize a close family member. A husband may be told, "I don't know you. Get out of my house or my husband will have you thrown out." A wife may become a mother. A daughter may become a total stranger. Nothing is quite so devastating for the caregiver as this loss of recognition. However, it is important for the caregiver to keep in mind that although a person with Alzheimer's may misidentify someone momentarily, his or her emotional attachment and responses to that person often remain intact. In some cases the misidentification is an important, symbolic communication such as when a husband misidentifies his wife as "Mother."

In the final stages of the disease, the dependency of the person on the caregiver will be complete, disorientation to time and place will be total, and recognition of even themselves in a mirror may be completely lost. It is, in short, a devastating disease for both the victim and the family.

And yet there are moments. A flicker of recognition, the retention of a dry sense of humor, a shared moment— forgotten at once by the person, but for that moment shared nonetheless. For some families these moments are heartbreaking reminders of who and what the individual once was, but for others they are tiny moments of relief in the unrelenting progress of the disease.

It is impossible to give you a finite list of symptoms. Some of those listed above will appear; others will not.

Some persons will have long periods of what appears to be a remission. Others will fail very quickly and die within a couple of years. The cause of Alzheimer's is unknown, and at this writing there are no cures or treatments, though a great deal of research is being done to find answers. The key for the caregiver is to be sure to get a careful diagnosis. Do not accept a diagnosis of Alzheimer's unless every other possibility has been ruled out. Call the local chapter of ADRDA (Alzheimer's Disease and Related Disorders Association). It can provide you with a list of tests to request from your doctor before a final diagnosis is made.

Caring for a person who has a mental disability will be discussed in the following chapter. It is important that you as the caregiver for this person seek an accurate diagnosis of the person's incapacity. Especially before you accept a diagnosis of Alzheimer's disease, be satisfied that other possible mental incapacities have been ruled out.

Whatever the person's illness may be, the chances are that you will be acting as the spokesperson for your mentally ill relative. Continue to treat the person as a functioning, thinking adult, and insist that others extend that respect and courtesy to the person as well. Fight for the best medical and support services you can get for the person and for yourself as the caregiver of that person. Let the care recipient know of your love, concern, and willingness to demand that he or she be treated with dignity. Keep in mind that even though a person can no longer express clear ideas or complete thoughts, neither you nor the medical community at this point has any idea of what may be going on inside that person's mind. Give care for the mentally incapacitated from this viewpoint: if you were the one who could not speak for yourself, what would you want the caregiver to do?

12 ✿ Caring for the Mentally Impaired

Helping someone who has some mental impairment cope with daily living is often an unpredictable job. If the person is forgetful or has permanent memory damage, reasoning with the individual or giving instructions can become tedious and time-consuming. If the person is disoriented because of drug intoxication, depression, and/or mental disease, communication can be very difficult. In fact, communicating with someone who is mentally disabled can be a full-time and exhausting job all by itself. Frequently the caregiver will be faced with unusual behavior from the person in mild cases of mental illness and perhaps with totally inappropriate behavior in cases where the person has moved into the advanced stages of Alzheimer's.

The needs of the mentally impaired person must be met in these areas: communication, forgetfulness, and disorientation. Most of the information in this chapter is aimed at the caregiver for the person with Alzheimer's disease, for it is this caregiver who will have the fewest benefits of medical and therapeutic tools to rely on. Some mental incapacities are treatable and, in some cases, reversible. Alzheimer's has no known treatment or cure, and the disease is so unique in each person that each caregiver must deal with individual symptoms and progressions of the disease in his or her care recipient.

Communication

When trying to communicate with a person who has some mental incapacity, it is important to understand that the key to your success may be your ability to convey feelings of reassurance and security to the individual. Body language is far more important than you may suspect. And the body language of the affected person may speak far louder than the confused sentences he or she is speaking.

Remember that the person will reflect his or her need to maintain control. If that control is threatened, the person may reflect panic through overzealous worry over trivial things, or the panic may be expressed in aggression and even physical abuse. If the individual is experiencing memory loss and is aware of that loss, he or she may fear that something important to the security and welfare of loved ones will be forgotten or overlooked. For example, a man may think he should be at work. A woman may be waiting for someone to return at a specific time, even a husband who has died but who used to walk through the door at a given time every day. She may have forgotten he is dead.

Be alert for sensory signals. If the person becomes agitated at the same time every day or after seeing a certain person or hearing a certain sound, that is a clue, and the caregiver needs to try to interpret that clue in order to communicate with the person. Not all mentally disabled persons become agitated. Some become quite apathetic for no apparent reason. Again, there will be clues. Look for them. Record them in your notebook until you can make some sense of them.

Following are some tips for communicating with the mentally disabled.

1. Sit next to the person rather than across from him or her. Sitting across from a person places you in a position of authority or power that may be threatening to the individual.
2. Be sure the person can see and hear you properly.
3. If the person agrees, touch him or her from time to time. Hold the person's hand, or put your arm around his or her shoulder.
4. Speak to the person as you would to any adult, keeping instructions clear and simple but not demeaning.

5. Keep your voice and mannerisms calm. Be aware of your facial expressions and hand motions. Motions should be smooth, not jerky. They should be intended to reassure, not threaten.

6. Give the person time to respond to questions.

7. If you are having trouble getting through to the person observe your own posture and vocal tone. Your words may be calm, but your face may be frowning and your posture filled with stress and tension.

8. Do not argue with the person. If possible, give credence to his or her fears and anxieties. Say, "I know you are worried about going to the doctor today. Remember, I'll be right there with you. Would you like me to go with you into the examining room?"

9. Occasionally an Alzheimer's victim will lose the power to speak coherently and will be unable to put together thoughts and sentences that make sense to the caregiver. This can be very frustrating when the person is obviously upset but you can only get him or her to say something like, "Well, I came and then it was over there and if I don't . . ." Read the body and facial language of the person. Try to determine whether the person is in pain. Note the significance of the time of day or the activity just completed or about to begin. Remain calm and get the person to sit down next to you if possible.

10. Include the mentally impaired person in conversations taking place in his or her presence, and make sure others are aware that they should also include the person and not talk about that person as if he or she were not in the same room.

11. Be aware that anxiety will always be heightened when the person is out of a secure and familiar environment.

12. Finally, understand that a part of communicating is to give the individual the opportunity to feel needed. Occasionally, express your own feelings and seek comfort from the person. "I'm feeling a little down today," or "I'd really appreciate it if you could help me decide which of these outfits to wear tonight."

Dealing with Forgetfulness

Everyone forgets. Late for work, you dash out of the house, slam the door, and then remember that your keys are on the kitchen counter. You start to introduce two people and suddenly cannot recall one person's name. Do you have Alzheimer's? Are you losing your memory?

Forgetfulness can stem from any number of causes: fatigue, overmedication, stress, depression, tumors, strokes. If the forgetfulness is persistent and frequent, if it seems to get worse instead of better, or if it seems to increase at certain times of the day or under certain conditions, you should seek medical attention. But before you panic, keep in mind that forgetting someone's name under the pressure of a social introduction and recalling it two minutes later does not mean you are demented. It simply means you are human.

Caregivers for those with mental impairments are prime candidates for anxiety that they themselves may suffer from the disease. While there may be some evidence that certain mental impairments may be inherited (or the tendency to experience them may be inherited), it is important to keep in mind that in the case of Alzheimer's, for example, 80 percent of the population will never experience the disease.

Reality Orientation

Some people who are confused or suffering from some form of dementia are forgetful and have limited ability to retain information. They may, however, retain reading abilities well into the disease or, failing that, may be able to relate to pictures and/or colors. By following the suggestions given below, you may be able to jog your relative's memory to perform the tasks of daily living.

- Place labels that indicate what can be found inside on drawers, cabinets, and closets.
- Mark the hot-water faucets and the stove dials in red nail polish to warn the person of danger.
- Hang clothing according to outfit and color. Lay

clothing out for your relative and limit choices to two or three ensembles rather than an entire closet filled with clothes.

• Make sure that throughout the house there are reminders that the person can use as clues to function by. Use items such as calendars, clocks, warnings, and signs on doors—Mom's Room, Bathroom, Stan's Office, Keep Away.

• Be certain there is a clear list of emergency numbers next to every telephone, a night-light in every bathroom and hallway, and a flashlight by both your bed and the affected person's.

• To encourage the care recipient to eat without help, use some subtle clues. Some confused persons may have memory lapses that involve food and meals. They may forget to eat or what a fork is to be used for. Say, "Enjoy your lunch, Dad," as you set the plate in front of him. Sight clues such as placing the fork on the plate of food can help. And so can touching. Lightly touch the person's hand when he or she is holding a fork filled with food in midair as if unsure of what to do next.

• For giving medications, try some of the ideas listed on page 126.

• Stimulate the memory with games such as trivia questions about current events, card games, and board games. Do not assume that the person can manage only children's games (one person was able to play a very challenging game of chess well into his illness).

• Encourage the person to hold on to memory skills by drilling him or her with flash cards. Use pictures of the family and familiar situations to make personal flash cards.

• Encourage the person to stimulate memory by recording a family or personal history.

The Importance of Maintaining Independence

Keep in mind that any individual, whether physically or mentally impaired, is fighting to hang on to his or her dignity. Remind the person that even people who consider their memories to be flawless rely heavily on memory aids such as lists, calendars, notes, notebooks, and calculators.

It may be important that you allow the person to control the memory aid. Have the person fill in the day's events on the calendar, set the timer for the next medication, and make up the labels for the cabinets. Avoid patronizing. Saying to the person, "I forgot to tell you there will be just the two of us tonight," is far better than ridiculing the person for setting the table for five when there have only been two at home for years.

One caregiver told the story of her husband, a man who suffered from chronic and deep depression to the point where he was unable to function. The caregiver wanted to relieve her husband of every possible avenue for anxiety, so she began to handle the family finances without consulting him at all. The result was that the man became overly concerned about what was happening to their money behind his back. He felt that the money was being used up, and he felt powerless to do anything about that. In her efforts to alleviate his concern, his wife had actually magnified it.

Handling Disorientation

Aside from forgetfulness, one of the most common side effects of any mental impairment is disorientation. Sometimes the person will appear to be in control and aware of the immediate surroundings. At other times the person may become agitated and confused and appear to be totally unaware of his or her surroundings. If the care recipient has shown a tendency toward disorientation, you may want to consider getting an identification bracelet for the person to wear. There are many attractive bracelets that hold the person's name, address, and emergency phone number as well as any medical information that may be useful to the person trying to assist the wearer.

Sometimes forgetfulness and disorientation can go hand in hand. For example, if the person likes to go out for a walk in the neighborhood, he or she may become disoriented and forget the way home. You can prepare for such an eventuality in several ways besides the use of the identification bracelet.

Neighbors can be alerted as well as the local police to the person's condition and what to do if the individual is seemingly lost. Provide the police with a recent photograph of the person to keep on file. Put a note in the person's wallet with directions and information about what to do should he or she become lost. Try to get the person to allow someone to walk with him or her, and if you do not have the time or if you need the time for other chores, hire a neighbor's teenager to take a daily walk with your relative. Be sure the younger person knows what to do in the event the person becomes disoriented and agitated. It does not *have* to be a younger person. There may be someone who is retired or alone who would look forward to the companionship of a daily walk.

Restraints

The idea of restraining someone, either by chemical or physical means, is distasteful. As objectionable as such an idea may be, there are situations in which some type of restraint may be necessary. For example, if a person uses a wheelchair, a restraint may become necessary to support the upper body and prevent the person from toppling forward out of the chair.

If the person is physically healthy but mentally disabled, there are still situations in which restraints may be necessary. If the person is given to wandering and there is no one to help watch over the person, such a restraint as triple locks on the doors and windows may be used. If the person is in danger of falling down a flight of stairs because the bedrooms are all on the second floor, light restraints may be needed to keep the person in bed until the caregiver can get to him or her. If the person is a danger to others or himself or herself, chemical restraints in the form of tranquilizers and/or sedatives may be indicated.

If any sort of restraint is to be used, use it only for

short periods of time and only when absolutely necessary. Physical restraints that are attached to the person need to be checked for tightness. The person's position needs to be shifted every so often to prevent the person's being held in the same position for too long. Chemical restraints should be used only under a doctor's supervision, and the caregiver needs to watch the person carefully for any side effects.

Some restraints do not incapacitate the person. For example, you can have alarms installed on doors and windows to prevent the person from leaving without your knowing it. There are sensory devices that can be attached to clothing that will signal a person's movement from one place to another.

If you think some form of restraint is needed for your care recipient, talk first to your home health care professional or the physician before taking matters into your own hands. Ask what types of restraints will be best for your particular need and where to obtain such restraints. Some resources may include sickroom supply rental houses, your local pharmacy, or home security companies listed in the Yellow Pages. Of course, you would never use a chemical restraint (tranquilizers or sedatives) without your doctor's authorization.

Caring for the Depressed Person

Each case of depression is different. The depression may last for days or weeks or even months. There is no medical evidence as to the exact cause, though some depression may be inherited, or a person can have a natural chemical imbalance that leads to bouts with depression. Still, the illness is treatable. The problem is that while most people do not hesitate to seek medical attention for a physical illness, many will not acknowledge a need for help with a mental health problem. It is important that the caregiver encourage the person to seek that help as soon as possible.

Depression is most often treated with medication and psychotherapy. Sometimes medication alone is enough, and sometimes just being able to talk to someone helps; but what works in one case may not work in another. It may not even work the second time around. It is important that the depressed person, the caregiver, and the medical team be flexible and unafraid to try new techniques to relieve the symptoms.

In severe cases depression can almost completely immobilize the person. The person is unable to act on his or her own and needs help with the simplest decision or task. The person must depend on you, the caregiver, to get help for severe depression. If you are unsure of where to turn, start by calling the local mental health center.

There is no magic cure for depression. There also is no guarantee that it will not recur. But with your encouragement, the person who is able to face the illness and seek help will often emerge happier and stronger than before.

The Role of the Caregiver

Living with a depressed person can be difficult. The person's anger, lack of trust, and apathy can be very frustrating for someone who is trying to help. At times you may feel that you are working harder at fighting the disease than the affected person is. And that may be true. The caregiver needs to beware of playing the role of a rescuer, someone who works harder at a solution than the person. If you take away the need for the person to do any of the work, he or she may never get better.

A depressed person's tendency to withdraw also makes your job tough. Try to avoid such phrases as "Everything will be okay" or "Snap out of it." This just confirms the depressed person's notion that no one understands the problem. A person who is depressed is living in a state of distorted reality. Keep that in mind. Trying to point out the good things in life can be nonproductive because the person does not see much that is good about his or her life.

Caregiving for a depressed person can be exhausting work, and it is not uncommon to find the caregiver fighting a personal case of depression while trying to encourage and be supportive of his or her relative. The care recipient may unconsciously test the caregiver by making unreasonable demands or picking fights. When the caregiver responds in frustration or anger, the depressed person may think he or she has been proven right in thinking that no one likes him or her.

How then can you help without becoming a victim? Keep in mind that your primary role is to be supportive and to listen. The depressed person must arrive at his or her own solutions. You are not there to make everything all right again; only the depressed person can do that. Encourage the person to talk about feelings. Try to understand without making any value judgments. Respond by pointing out past successes and encouraging the person to look toward future possibilities. Encourage the person to seek some professional help. Older persons seem to respond well to psychotherapy as a treatment for depression. If the person refuses professional help, you, the caregiver, should seek help in how to continue to support and encourage this person. If no formal diagnosis of depression has been made, get the person to have a thorough physical examination so that you and the doctor can rule out any physical causes for the symptoms.

For more help.   Call your local mental health association or write the U.S. Department of Health and Human Services, Alcohol, Drug and Mental Health, 5600 Fishers Lane, Rockville, MD 20857.

Three excellent self-help books on depression are listed below. Ask your librarian for others.

A New Beginning by Gary Emery

Control Your Depression by Peter Lewinsohn

Feeling Good by David Burns

Caring for the Person with Alzheimer's Disease

While there are no magic pills or therapies for improving the condition and prognosis of the Alzheimer's victim, there are things the caregiver can try that may help. The person with Alzheimer's will be most comfortable in a secure and familiar environment. Remember, he or she is sometimes aware that things are not as they should be, and for the victim the fight is to remain in control for as much of the time as possible.

The home setting should be well organized, and there should be a consistent routine. You may find that it is important for the person always to sit in the same place and to maintain the same routine through each day. Anxiety may be greatest when there is a change of plans—when the person is unprepared and out of control.

Labels, both with words and pictures, can be very helpful for the person in that they allow the individual to function without having to request information constantly. Particularly in the early stages, such labels can reduce anger and frustration. A calendar and a listing of each day's activities in order can also be important. If the person repeats the same question again and again, sometimes giving the person a note with the answer will help. For example, the individual may ask when dinner will be served. If the caregiver writes a note saying, "Dinner will be served at six o'clock. Tonight we are having chicken and peas and potatoes, with ice cream for dessert," the care recipient can be referred to the note. In general the caregiver needs to keep in mind that Alzheimer's victims who are involved and moderately stimulated to participate in life seem to do better than those who are allowed to vegetate.

Inappropriate Behavior

If you are caregiver for a person who is afflicted with Alzheimer's disease, you may find the person exhibiting some bizarre behavior from time to time. Other mental disorders can result in unusual behavior patterns at times, but none so consistently as Alzheimer's. Caregivers have told stories of relatives who have insisted on packing and unpacking a suitcase several times a day. Others told of Alzheimer's victims who were constantly into drawers and cabinets, rearranging contents and moving them to inappropriate places (putting the ice cream under the bathroom sink, for example).

Following are some of the more common behavioral situations of Alzheimer's victims and some suggested solutions for each problem. The important thing to remember is that *your relative may not exhibit any of these unusual behavior patterns. Do not start looking for the person to behave in a certain way just because someone else does.* If your relative does not have any of these behavioral patterns, count yourself lucky. If he or she does, take support from other caregivers who have been there and know what you are facing.

Packing.   If the person packs a suitcase frequently, he or she may be disoriented in time and place. Many persons with Alzheimer's who do this think they still live at "home" with Mom and Dad even though the parents may have been dead for years and the person's childhood home may no longer exist. It is not unusual for an Alzheimer's victim to seek the shelter and security of a time he or she can still recall with some clarity. The caregiver can try a number of tactics to persuade the person to unpack or to stay at home. The one tactic the caregiver should *not* try is arguing or reasoning with the individual. That childhood home and those parents are real to the person, and trying to explain that this is fifty years later and neither the home nor the parents still exist will only increase anxiety.

Try distracting the person. Ignore the packing or give credence to it. "I know you're really in a hurry, but could you help me do this? I can't do it by myself, and if you leave, I won't be able to have anyone help me." Or focus on the individual: "When you finish that, let's have lunch. I made soup today, and you have to be sure to take your medication before you go." The key is to remember that often a person with Alzheimer's will forget something in minutes, especially if he or she is distracted with some other activity. While the person is having lunch, remove the suitcase and later unpack it.

Problems with food.   Caregivers for Alzheimer's victims may face several common problems when it comes to food and meals and kitchens. Some persons with the disease eat or drink inappropriate items such as urine. Others may pick up food, even mashed potatoes, with their fingers when a fork is right next to the plate. Sometimes the person will have a voracious appetite and will rummage through cabinets seeking food and disrupting everything in sight.

If eating inappropriate items is the problem, go through the house with an eye to anything that might resemble food and remove it. Pay particular attention to plants and plastic fruits and brightly colored small objects such as soap or children's toys. If the person is eating with his or her fingers rather than with utensils, perhaps the individual has forgotten what the fork or spoon is for. Place the utensil on the plate or even in the person's hand. Sit next to the person at mealtimes and encourage self-feeding by example. If the person still insists on eating without a fork or spoon, serve as many finger-food items as possible: chicken parts, fish sticks or patties, sandwiches, soup in a mug, fruit slices, cheese, and gelatin cubes.

To keep prying hands out of cabinets and drawers, many caregivers have found that large rubber bands or a dog collar tied through the handles will solve the problem. Sliding a yardstick through all of the handles of a line of drawers can prevent opening of the drawers. Bicycle locks are a good way to protect poisons and medications. Or keep medications in a locked box in the refrigerator.

Clinging.   Clinging may be a manifestation of fear and anxiety. You are the care recipient's anchor in this strange world he or she has trouble remembering. Without you your relative cannot function. Rejecting the clinging will only increase the anxiety that someday you may go away and not return. There are several ways you can try to reassure the person of your care:

1. Touch and caress the person often, building assurance that he or she is loved and attractive.
2. When you must go away by yourself, avoid putting on your coat in front of your relative. Leave the person

busy with the substitute caregiver or aide, say good-bye, tell the person that you will return, and then leave.

3. Make a large sign that says when you will return, or give the person a note to hold on to.

4. If you simply need to leave the room or if you have found that you can leave the house for a short time (a matter of minutes), make a tape recording of your voice and leave it playing while you go.

5. If you work and your relative is staying with someone else, call your relative during the day and mention the time of your return.

Wandering.   One of the biggest problems caregivers for Alzheimer's victims have is wandering. Some mention of this has already been made in the discussion of disorientation (pages 220-222), but the habit of wandering is so prevalent among Alzheimer's victims that a more detailed discussion of the problem and what to do about it is included here.

The afflicted person may decide to leave—quite suddenly sometimes, perhaps in the middle of the night. When you try to stop him or her, the person becomes quite belligerent. Sometimes during the day the caregiver will turn his or her back for one minute, and the person will be out the door and halfway down the block. In winter the person may not bother with such things as coats and gloves. Many persons with Alzheimer's can move quite quickly and can be completely out of sight before the caregivers miss them and have a chance to react.

Locking the doors and windows is a recourse many caregivers have tried with some success, but some precautions are necessary:

1. Equip all doors with locks that open from both sides.

2. Install a slide or chain lock at the top and/or bottom of each door to the outside and use a dead-bolt lock that requires a key. (Be sure to keep extra keys in case of an emergency.) You can also purchase keyless traveling locks that attach inside or outside the door.

3. Purchase baby safety knobs to slip over the regular doorknobs. The plastic safety knob simply spins around, making it impossible to operate the regular doorknob.
4. Use the sensory devices and alarm systems mentioned on page 222.

Whatever steps you take, from locks to alarm systems, take into consideration the safety of the person and yourself in the event of emergencies such as a fire.

If the person does wander away, do not panic. Go after him or her and approach with a calm, reassuring attitude. Tell the person that there is a telephone call or that it is time for medications or that you have a gift for him or her (and then have some small item wrapped to give the person). This type of deception is very difficult for some caregivers, and it is certainly regrettable. But when someone you love is outside in freezing weather with no coat and you are seeking a way to bring that person inside, you will find that a small deception can sometimes accomplish what all the reasoning and pleading in the world cannot.

Night wandering.   Those who care for Alzheimer's victims frequently are called upon to deal with the problem of night wandering. The key to understanding why this problem may occur is to remember that the primary emotion most confused people feel is anxiety. Darkness can increase anxiety because, in addition to being disoriented, the person is also frightened by darkness. Sometimes doctors can prescribe medication that will help in controlling the insomnia and night agitation, but the caregiver will need to monitor such medications carefully.

If possible, try to discover the reason behind the wandering. Is the individual bored? looking for something? sleeping during the day? If you can discover the cause, you may be able to distract the person and gain some sleep for both of you. Do not insist that the care recipient return to his or her room if that seems to be the source of the agitation. Try old-time remedies of warm milk or herbal tea. It may be that the person is going to be up all night but is perfectly capable of being left alone in a well-lighted room with something to do such as folding laundry, looking at colorful magazines, or working a puzzle. If nothing works, you may need to consider hiring someone to stay overnight to be up with your relative while you sleep. Sometimes a college student is willing to take such a job.

Inappropriate sexual activity. This is an area of care that can be very trying and embarrassing for the caregiver. Do not anticipate that it will be a problem unless there are symptoms. Most Alzheimer's victims go through life with no instance of inappropriate sexual behavior at all. But in a few cases caregivers have suddenly had to face the problem of a mother who thinks her son is her husband or lover, a father or husband who will masturbate in a room filled with people, or a wife who may quite suddenly start to disrobe in a public place.

Such instances of inappropriate behavior are not deliberate on the part of the affected person, and no amount of berating or reasoning will solve the problem. Your anger and embarrassment may simply aggravate the situation. The person may be trying to express a need. For example, the woman who unbuttons her blouse may be doing so only because she is warm and the only concept she recalls is that less clothing makes her cooler. She is not trying to be provocative deliberately and should not be treated as if she were.

Masturbation and exposure of the genital areas are very difficult for many caregivers to deal with. The caregiver needs to examine his or her own feelings about sexuality before trying to handle the situation. Whatever those feelings may be, it is important to keep reminding oneself that what is happening with the affected person is only overt to the caregiver and others in the room. The person has no concept that the action is wrong. Inappropriate sexual actions may be totally unrelated to sex. A person who pulls off clothing of the lower body may need to use a toilet and may have forgotten where the bathroom is located.

The key for the caregiver in any situation of this type is not to overreact. Handle the problem as quietly and discreetly as possible. Be aware of your body language and facial expression, for they will convey far more than any words you may say. If the behavior persists or becomes worse, consult with a counselor and the person's doctor. The counselor will help you deal with your aversion to the behavior, and the doctor may be able to prescribe some medication or therapy that will limit the behavior.

Aggressive behavior.   A person who is no longer feeling in control of his or her own life and actions may occasionally lash out physically at whoever is nearest. As the primary caregiver, you may become a target. In such a potentially volatile situation try to approach the person in a calm and reassuring manner. Speak softly, and avoid sudden moves that may startle or frighten the person further. This is not the time to try and reason with the individual. If possible, agree with some of what he or she is saying, or at least express some positive support: "I know you're feeling really angry right now. What can I do to help?"

If the person becomes aggressive often and there is frequent danger of physical violence, get professional help. Protect yourself by removing anything that might be used as a weapon, and if you cannot isolate the person, isolate yourself until help arrives. It may be possible to have medication prescribed, but be very careful with any type of drug therapy.

Keep in mind that a person who is combative and aggressive can seemingly be inviting abuse. It is hard to convince yourself to think rationally about the person's inability to understand his or her actions when that person is striking you across the face. Sometimes you will find yourself fantasizing about or in actuality striking back. The abuse of older persons is a growing problem in our society. If you have such incidents of abuse fantasy or if you actually ever strike back verbally or physically, seek help at once for yourself as well as for the person you are caring for.

Accusations.   Like acts of aggression and inappropriate sexual behavior, accusations may mask a fear the person is unable to express. Some caregivers are unjustly accused of stealing by those for whom they are giving care. Others are accused of posing as someone else, such as a spouse or child. When such accusations come from a person who is mentally impaired, the caregiver needs to be aware that in the following moment the person may forget that the words were ever said.

If possible, try to pass over the accusation and avoid a fight. If the accusations become constant or impossible to ignore, get some professional advice by calling the local mental health center or the person's doctor or social worker for a referral to a psychologist or psychiatrist.

Outings

Many caregivers are apprehensive about taking their relatives out into the world to such places as restaurants, places of worship, or shopping centers. The caregiver may be afraid that the person will embarrass both himself or herself and the caregiver. Or, if the caregiver is having problems with wandering, he or she may fear that to take the person away from the home would be the worst possible idea.

The truth is that most Alzheimer's victims are very social beings and maintain far into the illness the ability to interact on a social level. In fact some caregivers have discovered that by taking the person out in controlled situations, the problems of wandering and the agitation associated with wandering are reduced. There are unique problems though, and the caregiver needs to think through the outing in advance and be prepared for any unusual circumstance.

Shopping. Shopping for anything is generally time-consuming under the best of circumstances. Stores are often crowded and noisy. Help is sometimes in short supply, necessitating waiting in line. Shopping with a person who has Alzheimer's can be especially frustrating unless the trip is well planned in advance. To simplify outings, you might do the following:

1. Get to know local merchants and make them aware of the person's illness. Enlist their help by asking when

the shop is least busy and whether they offer special services such as delivery.

2. Keep the person interested and busy. Give him or her a list to mark off for you in the grocery store. Ask for opinions about selections and brands and freshness.

3. A few caregivers have experienced the embarrassing problem of the person's shoplifting while in a store. If this situation should occur, stay calm. The person may have forgotten the details of shopping and may not understand that items on the shelf must be purchased. If possible, take the article from the person and replace it on the shelf or pay for it. If you are unaware that shoplifting has taken place until the store detective comes, quietly request a private place to meet with the detective and store officials. Explain the nature of the illness and offer to pay for any goods. Try to work out some understanding for future visits.

If shopping is really impossible, consider a shopping spree at home through the use of pictures and catalogs. Include your relative by having him or her make the shopping list or check off the items when they are delivered.

Dining out.   A meal at a restaurant could be a nice respite for both you and the person you are caring for, or it might turn into a nightmare. Again, the key is prior planning. If the restaurant is one that requires reservations, ask about the rest room facilities when you call. Explain that your relative has an illness that can cause him or her to become confused. Ask whether you will be able to go into the rest room with the person (if the person is of the opposite sex). If not, you can ask whether an employee might be able to attend the person and be sure he or she returns safely to the table.

When you arrive at the restaurant (any restaurant, from a hamburger takeout place to the finest place in town), find a moment to speak with the help alone. Explain that you will do the ordering and that the bill should be given to you. If the person you are caring for becomes upset about bills or money, make arrangements to pay in advance with a credit card. You do not have to give detailed explanations about the illness; just let the help know that you are in charge of the meal, and the other person is your guest.

When the waiter or waitress comes to take your order, announce to both that person and your relative that tonight is your treat and that you will take care of everything. Some caregivers order an extra plate and dish out the other meal because the person with Alzheimer's does not eat very much or has trouble dealing with several food selections on one plate or several selections placed in front of him or her at the same time. Avoid this if possible. Remember, the person's autonomy needs protection.

If the person needs to go to the rest room, accompany him or her if possible, and if not, ask for the maître d' for assistance. If the person is sometimes incontinent, carry some extra clothing for security, but also make sure you have prepared for the eventuality of an accident by clothing the individual in adult pads before leaving the home.

Occasionally a person with Alzheimer's will become agitated when taken into a strange environment where there is noise and a great deal of activity. Be careful in your selection of restaurants and go at quieter times. If you find your relative cannot manage a meal out, consider takeout food and having a special evening at home.

Programs Outside the Home

Some caregivers make use of programs outside the home to aid in caring for the mentally disabled person. These programs may include a church volunteer service, a day hospital or nursing home program, or an adult day-care program (see chapter 14). If you decide to enroll your relative in such an activity, where he or she will be away from home without you for several hours, you should think of ways to make the transition from home to new environment as simple as possible.

If the person carries a purse or wallet, put a note inside that reminds the person that you are at work or shopping and will pick him or her up at a specific time.

Enclose some small change and a couple of dollars. Sometimes it is hard for Alzheimer's victims to understand that the programs they are attending have been paid for and that even meals are included. If the person sits down for lunch at a strange place, he or she may assume that payment will be expected. If the wallet is empty, the person may panic and either refuse the lunch (rather than suffer the embarrassment of not being able to pay) or try to leave (again because he or she cannot pay). Tell the staff at the center what they may encounter with the care recipient and what activities or techniques you have found effective in dealing with the person at home.

Problems with Automobiles

If your relative no longer can safely operate a motor vehicle, the safest thing to do is take away the keys. But what if you still need to use that car and the person still believes he or she can drive? There are a number of things you might try in order to prevent constant battles over the car. See whether a neighbor has an extra parking space where you can keep the car so that it is not a constant reminder of the person's inability to drive. Tell the person that his or her doctor has "prescribed" no driving. If necessary, have the doctor back you up.

The Role of the Caregiver

Alzheimer's can be embarrassing to some families, and they will try to hide or excuse any unusual behavior of the care recipient by isolating that person at home and not allowing him or her to interact with the community. Such actions lead only to loneliness and depression for both the relative and the caregiver. Alzheimer's is no one's fault. It is nothing to be ashamed of and says nothing derogatory about your family history.

Your best bet is to be open about the illness. You will find that people are willing to help and that there are numerous community agencies ready to provide support. Also, do not anticipate symptoms. Your relative may never pace, may never become unmanageable, may never have to be fed. Do not assume that skills are gone. Are you sure the person can no longer read? He or she may not remember what has been read in two minutes, but the reading skill is still there. Finally, treat the person with respect, and allow him or her the dignity of maintaining independence for as long as possible in every way possible. The victim of Alzheimer's disease is an adult. He or she has the right to be spoken to as an adult, to be included in conversations and activities taking place in the same room, and to be touched and held by those who love this person.

For more information.   The following books have been written specifically for the caregiver of an Alzheimer's victim.

The 36 Hour Day by Nancy L. Mace and Peter V. Rabins.

Alzheimer's Disease: A Guide for Families by Lenore S. Powell and Katie Courtice.

Handle with Care: A Question of Alzheimer's by Dorothy S. Brown.

The Hidden Victims of Alzheimer's Disease by Steven H. Zarit, Nancy K. Orr, and Judy M. Zarit.

Two other books that are more technical but still of interest to those dealing with Alzheimer's disease are these:

Dementia: A Practical Guide to Alzheimer's and Related Illnesses by Leonard L. Heston and June A. White.

The Myth of Senility: The Truth About the Brain and Aging by Robin Marantz Henig.

A Guide to Alzheimer's Disease by Barry Reisberg.

Another Name for Madness by Marion Roach.

In addition the following publications are available at no charge or at nominal charges.

U.S. Department of Health and Human Services, NIH Publications #81-2252, 1982, and #80-1646, 1981 (Both are available from the national ADRDA office, 360 North Michigan Avenue, Chicago, IL 60601, or call toll-free 1-800-621-0379.)

Managing the Patient with Intellectual Loss at Home, Burke Rehabilitation Center, 785 Mamaroneck Avenue, White Plains, NY 10605 ($2.00)

Family Handbook on Alzheimer's Disease, Health Advancement Services, 444 East 86th Street, Room 19B, New York, NY 10028 ($4.00)

Your first step as the caregiver for an Alzheimer's victim should be to contact the local chapter of ADRDA and ask for their help and support. If there is no local chapter, start one. You are not alone, and you are going to need some help.

Hospitalization—A Special Situation

Hospital stays can be frightening and stressful for people in the best of mental health. When one is frequently confused and disoriented, hospitalization can be very threatening. To make a necessary (overnight or longer) stay in the hospital less difficult, try some of the following caregiver techniques.

• Take along a couple of familiar items such as family photos or a favorite quilt, but not too many because there is not much extra space in hospital rooms.
• Be sure there is a night-light in the bathroom and in the room itself. If not, install one yourself.
• Ask the hospital staff to avoid restraints unless they first check with you.
• Make certain that there is someone with the person as often as possible, even if that means requesting to stay overnight in the room yourself.
• If possible, request that the same people on the same shift care for the patient each day. It is frustrating for a person who is coherent to meet a new face with each new shift and each new day.
• Limit visitors to two at a time.
• Discourage the patient's napping during the day unless it is necessary for recovery.

• Share information with the staff about the person's mental condition and how to handle the confusion and disorientation.

If the person is to be admitted to a psychiatric ward or hospital, there may be more resistance on the part of the person to accept that hospitalization. There are several concrete steps the caregiver can take to make the transition easier.

1. Learn to recognize the symptoms that might explode into a full-blown crisis, and seek help for the person before that crisis occurs. The earlier you can seek treatment, the less likely a long hospitalization will be necessary.
2. If possible, before the hospitalization talk to the person's doctor and the hospital's psychiatric social worker and seek advice about making the hospitalization easier for your relative.
3. Create a sense of security and reassurance for the person.
4. Keep in mind that active involvement with the patient throughout the hospitalization will facilitate an earlier discharge. Visit and call often. Have others do the same.
5. Be open to becoming involved in family therapy, where you will have the opportunity to ventilate your own feelings.

Promoting the quality of life for someone who is mentally impaired is a challenge for any caregiver. The normal tools of cheering someone up or bolstering someone's self-esteem may not be available because of the confusion and forgetfulness of the person. The caregiver may experience more success and less frustration if he or she remembers two things:

1. The person, regardless of mental impairment, is still a human being with the same needs and anxieties as any other human being.

2. It is not a sign of failure to accept the services of support groups, home health care agencies, and community activity programs.

Keep in mind that the ultimate goal with any mentally disabled person is to keep the person enjoying whatever he or she can enjoy for as long as possible.

In Part Three you have become more familiar with the care recipient's illness(es) and special needs. This should have been helpful to you and the person in establishing a daily routine of living that allows each of you to have some time for yourself and for each other. When you are caring for someone who is ill or impaired in some way, you have to look beyond the disease and care also for the basic needs of the person in those areas where he or she may no longer be able to manage alone. *There may be no catastrophic illness at all.* Some older persons simply need help with the basic routines of hygiene, medications, diet, exercise, and safety. Others can manage personal grooming and hygiene quite well but are totally incapable of finding ways to fill their time constructively. Answer those questions from the list below that apply to your relative. They will serve as a review of those subjects you have studied in this part of the book. If you can answer yes to the questions below that apply to you and your caregiving situation and if you have already answered yes to those questions posed on pages 108-109, you are already established as an excellent caregiver. You are then ready to go on to Part Four, where you will see how good you are at caring for yourself.

1. Have you determined the basic needs for help the person has in the areas of hygiene (bathing, showering, cleaning teeth, shaving), dressing (dressing and undressing self, choosing appropriate clothing), and

grooming (hair care, makeup, nail care)?

2. Does the person need a special diet? If so, has the doctor advised you on that diet? If not, are you making certain that the person eats well-balanced, nutritious meals throughout the week?

3. Have you and the person (if possible) worked out a daily routine of exercise? Are you sticking to it? If the person is bedfast, have you learned the range-of-motion exercises from your home health care professional? Have you gotten the doctor's approval before beginning any exercise program?

4. Is the house safe for the person? inside and out? Have you taken whatever extra steps may have been necessary to ensure the safety of your relative (installed grab bars in the bathroom, installed smoke alarms, registered with a telephone reassurance system)?

5. Does your relative have meaningful activities to occupy his or her time? Have you explored the possibility of activities outside the home if the person is capable of being away from the house?

6. Does your relative have a social life even though he or she may be confined to the house? Have you encouraged visitors to call? Have you contacted the person's clergyperson? Do visitors know what to expect, and have you told them frequently how much their visits mean to both of you?

7. Do you have a clear diagnosis of what the person's physical impairments are? Do you know how to treat them? what the prognosis is?

8. Have you interviewed the person's doctor and gotten satisfactory answers to those questions posed on page 172.

9. What special needs does your relative have because of his or her physical impairment(s)? Do you know what your role as caregiver will be in dealing with these impairments?

10. Has the doctor or home health care professional instructed you about special equipment that may make dealing with the person's impairment easier, such as a Hoyer lift?

11. Have you researched basic care aids available through community services even if you are not making use of such services at this time?

12. Is your relative's illness represented through one of the national organizations for research and support? Is there a local chapter? Have you contacted them for help?

13. Have you talked with both the pharmacist and the prescribing physician about any medications your relative takes? Do you understand what the medicine is for, how to administer it, what the side effects may be, and when *not* to give the person the medication? Have you alerted both the doctor and the pharmacist to any over-the-counter medications the person takes? Are you keeping an accurate record of each medication taken?

14. Is the person in a wheelchair or bedfast? Do you understand the special requirements of such persons?

15. Have you gotten professional training in the proper techniques for lifting a person who is physically impaired?

16. Do you know what to do and what *not* to do about a bedsore?

17. Is the person having a problem with incontinence? If so, have you spoken to his or her doctor? Can the problem be treated or cured? If it cannot, are you prepared to deal with the person's needs? Have the two of you discussed (if possible) the problem? Have you assured the person that you understand the problem is common and not controlled by the person and that there is no malice or forethought on his or her part?

18. Have you learned those nursing skills mentioned on pages 151-152 by attending a Red Cross training program or in another manner through the assistance of your home health care agent?

19. Do you know how to handle a variety of emergencies? Do you know what to do if you suspect that your relative is having a heart attack? a stroke?

20. Has a clear diagnosis been made in the event your

relative's illness is mental? If the person has been diagnosed as having Alzheimer's disease, are you satisfied that an exhaustive testing has been done to rule out any other possible illness?

21. Do you understand the special needs of the mentally impaired person as they are now? will be in the future? Do you understand the role you will play in seeing this person through the mental impairment?

22. Have you sought advice on communicating with your mentally impaired relative? Have you found ways to reach him or her even when that person is incoherent? Do you know what reality orientation is, and have you established patterns for using such therapy in your daily routine?

23. Is the person frequently disoriented? Can you expect that he or she will be in the future? Are you prepared to deal with any accompanying problems such as wandering, increased agitation, or anxiety?

24. Does your relative exhibit any signs of inappropriate behavior—sexual, aggressive, or accusatory? Have you planned for that possibility?

25. In the event the mentally impaired person has to be hospitalized, are you ready to make that hospitalization as free of anxiety as possible for the person and for yourself?

Part Four

❧

Meeting the Caregiver's Needs

While I knew that I was overdoing, I could not believe anyone could manage as efficiently as I.
                                   —Diane Rubin

13 ∾ Dealing with Difficult Feelings

How does one keep going? How can you, the caregiver, deal with the emotions that pile up in the course of the caregiving process? How do you cope when there is no end in sight?

First of all, recognize that there are no rules of etiquette for coping with feelings. Feelings exist, and they cannot be labeled as proper or improper. You will start to cope by admitting your feelings, no matter how unattractive they may seem to you. Write down your feelings in your notebook. Use complete sentences. Do not just write, "I am angry." Write, "I am angry at _____ _____ because _____ _____ ." Write, "I am depressed because _____ _____ ."

Take a minute now and write down some of the feelings you have experienced since taking on the role of caregiver.

Were you honest enough to list anger as one emotion you may have felt? How about guilt? fear? loss? insecurity? entrapment? loneliness? depression? None of these feelings is uncommon for the primary caregiver. How then do you cope when the job seems to be never ending, your own life seems to have been placed on hold, and there does not seem to be anyone who can help you?

The first step toward coping with your feelings is to realize that you, and everyone else, have feelings that are sometimes difficult to deal with and that you are living in a situation that generates those particular difficult emotions. Do not try to place a value system on your feelings. They are neither good nor bad, negative nor positive. They just are. You need to be aware of them, think about what may have caused them, and find ways to treat them in the same way you might a headache or a strained muscle.

Occasionally the best thing you can do may be to ignore the emotion for a time until you have done whatever it is you must do for the care recipient. Some caregivers find that by the time they get back to thinking about it, the difficult emotion is gone. In that case, no harm has been done, so do not try to recreate the emotion. Sometimes you will feel the need of immediate relief, and unfortunately some caregivers find that immediate relief in a bottle, pill, or candy bowl. Be aware that you may overuse these chemical releases—liquor, drugs, and sugar.

Whatever the emotion and whatever the need for relief may be, you need not ever feel guilty for having been emotional. You are not helpless or a failure because you broke down and cried when your relative used your living room carpet for a bathroom. If you try to hold in your emotions until the other person no longer needs you to be strong and caring for him or her, you will probably end up needing a caregiver of your own.

Sense of Isolation

Start with that sense of aloneness, that feeling that you are in over your head and there is no one out there to help you get back to shore. Once the person has moved in with you (or is settled into the living arrangement the two of you have selected) and you have begun your daily routine of caregiving, you may learn that the job is far more demanding than you had thought.

Barbara Keyes, executive director of the Milwaukee Alzheimer's Disease and Related Disorders Association (ADRDA), has offered caregivers this list of ideas for "making the load of caregivers a little lighter."

1. Meet with other caregivers and share your life's happenings with one another. (See pages 270-273 for information on support groups.)
2. Encourage and accept offers of help from family, neighbors, and friends regularly. When help is available, maintain contacts *outside* of your home to give you some diversion.
3. Exercise frequently. It helps you relax.
4. Do not allow others to add to your burden by criticizing the care you are giving. You alone know how difficult your job is.
5. Share with caring family and friends your feelings, and do not be afraid to shed some tears.
6. Some spiritual advice: pray frequently.

There is nothing wrong with seeking out some recognition and praise for the job you are doing. Although your parents may have taught you that it is wrong to do so, from time to time every person needs to know that the job he or she is doing is worthwhile and that its worth is noticed by others. On the other hand, you do not want to become a burden yourself. If you are fortunate enough to have a spouse, friend, or neighbor willing to lend you a shoulder to cry on and an ear to bend, do not abuse the privilege. From time to time, ask yourself if in the last three times you have talked to this other person, he or she has heard more than doom and gloom from you. If not, put down this book and call the person right now with some cheery or good news. Share a funny moment, and let your supporter hear the sound of your laughter. Now and then be sure to say aloud to that person how much his or her support means to you.

Caregivers have to work from the beginning to protect their *own* lives. Some things will have to go, but long-standing friendships are a vital part of the caregiver's ability to perform the job. For that matter, maintaining the friendships of the person you are caring for with others can be helpful to the caregiver.

You will be most successful at maintaining friendships for both you and your relative if, from the beginning, you make it clear to those who care what you and the person are facing, what you can give to a friendship, and what you need back. Your relative's friends should be made aware of the fact that regardless of that person's illnesses and infirmities, he or she still needs human companionship. Encourage the friends to take an active role in the maintenance of the physical and mental health of the person. Do not let embarrassment keep you from including others in the caregiving picture. Sometimes caregivers complain that everyone has gone away, that no one visits or calls. Occasionally it becomes clear that friends may have left because the caregiver has shut them out, refusing any offers of support and/or help.

When caregivers are spouses, there is often a problem of isolation if all the children live out of town, friends are dead or infirm themselves, or the neighbors are younger and not well known to either the cared-for spouse or the caregiver. If you are a caregiver who is caring for a spouse and the two of you can get out of the home, you may want to try some of these ideas for relieving isolation and loneliness.

• Remain active in religious and community affairs for as long as possible.
• Register for classes for seniors at the local college.
• Participate in programs for seniors at senior centers and day-care centers, and join support groups.
• Take a daily walk through the local shopping mall. Sit down for a cup of coffee. Window-shop. Get to know the shopkeepers.

If leaving home is difficult or impossible, try these ideas.

• Use your telephone to stay in touch with relatives, neighbors, and friends.
• Take advantage of every service you can that will bring another human being into the home to deliver that service.
• Invite others to come to you and your spouse—

neighbors, clergypersons, community groups that could meet in your home.

- Write frequently to distant relatives and friends, and let them know how much their letters mean to both of you.
  - Listen to and participate in radio call-in programs.
  - Get a pet, and talk to it.

Anger

As the caregiving process goes on, anger may become a more prevalent emotion. The anger may be directed at any number of people or circumstances. There may be anger directed at family members and friends because they seem free to pursue their own lives. Anger may be directed at the person's illness and, through that, at the person. You may also become angry with yourself for imagined failings as a caregiver.

You need to understand that anger is a normal reaction. At the same time, you need to be aware that anger can lead to other emotions that, if allowed to go on unchecked, can be destructive. For example, sometimes if anger is directed at the person who is ill, the caregiver will feel guilty for feeling angry. Guilt can escalate into depression, and depression can affect the caregiver's ability to function in his or her own life, much less care for the ill person.

Accept that there will be times when you will be angry. Accept that there may even come a time when you entertain thoughts of striking out at the care recipient. If that happens, do not wallow in remorse or guilt. Take action and seek help. Most likely you need respite from the care routine and counseling in a setting where you can express these aggressive feelings aloud without being judged. The key is to learn not to repress your anger. Discuss those feelings with someone not directly involved. Discussing the feelings aloud allows you to put those feelings into perspective and discover underlying causes for any anger that is being repressed.

Another healthy release is exercise, especially when no one is around to hear the caregiver's feelings. Exercise—some vigorous physical exertion—can be a safe release for the if-I-have-to-stand-this-one-more-second-I-will-scream syndrome. Even if the anger is directed at the illness and the care recipient, allowing the person to join with you in the exercise (if possible) can be healthy for both of you.

A third idea for dealing with feelings of anger (as well as feelings of sadness and depression) is to isolate yourself briefly. Go into your room, shut the door, and have a good cry or listen to music or pound a pillow. But set a time limit; do not wallow in your pain. Every caregiver should have a place of his or her own—some small corner of the world that is his or hers alone, someplace that the caregiver knows is waiting if he or she can get there for a brief respite. For one it might be at a piano where the strains of favorite selections can take over. For another it may be on a chair next to a window overlooking the garden. Yours might be in the bathroom or the kitchen or the basement. Wherever you have your special place, schedule some brief times there every day. Make it as much a part of your routine as caring for your relative.

Anger is a natural emotion in everyone's life. Do not be afraid of it. Instead find ways to deal with it that will not leave you feeling guilty afterward. Whether your method of burning out your anger is to take a walk, bake bread, or relax in a hot tub or shower, plan for it. You *will* be angry at times.

Do not always try to conceal your anger from your relative. You are both human, and that person needs to see that sometimes you have needs also. If your anger is directed at someone or something other than the person or the illness or incapacity—the repairperson who does not come, the neighbor who promises to and then cancels—let your relative share in that. He or she has feelings of anger too and must be allowed to vent them. It is important for both you and the cared-for person to feel a part of the life around you and to be full participants if at all possible.

Depression

Every caregiver is going to have times of depression—times when the whole lifestyle seems overwhelming. There are coping mechanisms that give momentary relief and others that will relieve for the long term. First, you must give yourself permission to be miserable *for a short time*. You have the right to feel sorry for yourself occasionally and to acknowledge your feelings of sadness and loneliness. Some of the release mentioned above in the discussion on anger may provide some short-term relief.

Over the long term, the hour-by-hour, day-by-day labor of the job may sometimes get to be too much. That is the time to seek some solutions that will offer more substantial respite that you can look forward to each week. Health care services in the home, day-care centers, and caregiver co-ops (where a group of caregivers band together to provide relief for one another) are some possibilities for long-term, ongoing relief. Ask another family member to assume responsibility for care one afternoon a week or one weekend a month. Attend support group meetings (many offer aide services for the persons who need care). Find respite programs that will work for you and the care recipient and use them.

Guilt

Guilt is a common malady for the caregiver. It can take over your life if you let it. Am I doing everything I can? Have we been to enough doctors? Have I spent enough money? Am I being selfish? How could I have yelled at him like that? What will other people think?

Do not allow yourself to become the shadow of your loved one's impairments. Many caregivers feel that they are not doing an effective job if they are not living with the illness or incapacities twenty-four hours a day. They feel guilty if they allow themselves respite, happiness, or enjoyment of anything that the person receiving care is being denied. The truth is that the caregiver who understands the need for rest and relaxation is a far more effective caregiver than the one who feels obliged to live through the impairments along with the relative.

Do not expect perfection of yourself. You are going to make mistakes in caregiving as you would in any activity of life. You are going to have some bad days, but recognize that most of the time you are doing the best that you can, and take the time to pat yourself on the back. When you start feeling guilty, consider the following as you try to climb out of that guilt:

1. Assuming you are doing the best job you can to balance *all* of your roles, is it reasonable to expect more of yourself?
2. Will spending more money make the person any better, or will it simply make you feel better?
3. Are all the doctors telling you the same thing? If so, you have been to enough doctors.
4. You are human. Humans get upset. They even unleash their anger by yelling, sometimes at innocent bystanders. The recipient of your care is not going to die because you yelled.
5. You have a right to be selfish sometimes. After all, by nature a caregiver is unselfish *most* of the time.

Jealousy

Just like other emotions, jealousy is a normal reaction to the caregiving situation. Jealousy may be the cause of the anger directed at others who blithely go on about their own lives while yours is in limbo. It may also be directed at the person who is receiving all of this care and attention; at times you may actually wish that you were the sick or incapacitated one.

One way to combat jealousy is to save those moments that are positive, that make you feel great about what you are doing, and bring them to mind when you are jealous of someone else. Another tactic is to talk about feelings of jealousy with the person who makes you jealous—not in anger, but calmly and frankly. And finally, try talking to yourself. Who knows better than you what you are doing and how well you are doing it?

Fear and Frustration

Giving care—whether that care is limited or total—to another person can cause the caregiver to have times when he or she must deal with his or her own fears and frustrations. The person may experience fear that the illness is hereditary—for example, for the adult child caring for a parent or in-law with Alzheimer's disease, the fear that what that person is witnessing in the parent or in-law as the illness progresses may someday happen to the caregiver and/or the spouse.

Many illnesses are suspected or proven to be hereditary. A woman whose husband suffers a stroke at a fairly young age may develop an unreasonable fear that their son will also become disabled when he is in his prime. A daughter who watches her mother's battle with diabetes and its many side effects (visual impairments, problems with her feet, and so on) may imagine that the slightest sign of abnormality in her own health is in fact the onset of her mother's illness.

Caregivers need to understand that such fears are not unusual, especially in the first weeks of caregiving. If the fears increase as time goes by, the caregiver may want to consider seeing a trained counselor, talking with his or her clergyperson, or joining a support group. The support group may be particularly helpful because the caregiver will be with several others who perhaps have experienced similar fears.

Frustration is another emotion caregivers deal with, and it can arise from many different situations. For example, if the person being cared for refuses to accept help or care from anyone other than the caregiver, that can be very frustrating for the caregiver. Or if the caregiver attempts to arrange for support and care for the person through existing community programs and those programs fall short of their promises, the caregiver may become frustrated and begin to feel that he or she will never be able to get any relief or help for the person.

Again, talking with other caregivers in the environment of the support group can be very helpful. First, such a group forum will allow the caregiver to vent his or her feelings in an atmosphere of sympathy and understanding, and second, other members of the support group who may have faced exactly the same problem may be able to offer concrete suggestions for a solution.

Joy

Yes, there is joy in caregiving. Sometimes it is bittersweet, and sometimes it is pure and rich and very exhilarating. It can come in a moment of unique closeness when you realize that your mother is more than your parent— she is your friend and sister. It can occur in a flash of insight when you see in the eyes of your spouse how truly he or she loves you for what you are doing. Joy can come through memories lived and relived. It can come through laughter at an impossible situation.

In a normal lifestyle joy often goes unnoticed. It is taken for granted. People think of being happy as a right rather than a privilege. In the lives of an aging person and his or her caregiver, joy and happiness sometimes get buried under that pain, fear, and anxiety that accompany illness. Where do you look for joy? Attitude is a good starting point. Expect to find happy times. Enter the caregiving role with an attitude of loving and giving. Touch the person often, and express your need to have your hand held or to receive a hug in return. Talk through feelings of fear and anxiety. Support each other, and if possible, share the experience of depending upon each other.

Recognize that you are doing something quite out of the ordinary experience of most people, and take pride in that. Life spent caring for another adult can be difficult. The person may be demanding and constantly finding fault. If that is the case, you can still feel good about yourself and the difference you are making in that person's life. Set as your goal the bringing out of the positive traits in your own and your relative's personalities.

Coping Mechanisms

Whatever feelings you are trying to cope with during the course of giving care for another person, realize now that it is common to experience such feelings. Understand that rather than allow the feelings to overpower you and lessen your effectiveness as a caregiver, you should meet them head-on and be prepared to handle them. Try some of the following ideas for coping.

1. Focus on what *is* rather than on what *is not*.
2. Give yourself a present of time for you.
3. Make time to participate in activities other than caregiving.
4. Maintain your personal appearance.
5. Make a list of all the new skills you have developed since becoming a caregiver.
6. Keep a diary.
7. Practice some form of meditation.
8. If you are depressed, do the hardest tasks early in the day and get them over with.
9. Be good to yourself. When you shop for groceries, buy something just for you to enjoy alone.
10. Train yourself to recognize your emotional signals. Stop what you are doing and attend to those emotional needs. It may mean just thirty seconds for some deep breathing.

14 ✿ Getting Support and Finding Respite

Exhaustion, stress, a sense of isolation—these are symptoms of caregiver overload. Where do you find relief? What will that relief cost? And perhaps most important, will the person you are caring for accept care from anyone but you?

Many caregivers answer no to the last question and cease the search for any type of support or respite to keep them going in a job that is demanding and filled with stress. If the caregiver allows the care recipient to dictate how others will live their lives, the caregiver may never find a way of having time off from the job. Consider the following caregivers and their particular needs.

NANCY AND JIM: "My father-in-law is coming to live with us," Nancy says. "I work, and we really need two incomes. How am I going to continue to work full-time *and* be a primary caregiver?"

Being a full-time caregiver and having a successful career is a lot like being a full-time mother and maintaining a career with one large difference: children grow up and (one hopes) become independent. Parents and in-laws grow older and often become more dependent. What are Nancy and Jim, her husband, going to do?

First, they need to get organized and research every resource that is available in their community that will allow Nancy to maintain her career and the two of them to provide excellent care for Jim's father. Nancy and Jim need to call every home care agency and volunteer group, and, even if one or more of them seem unsuitable for the present, they need to record the information for future use.

Nancy and Jim also need to take a good look at the rest of the family. Does Jim have siblings who might share in the job of caregiving? Does Nancy have siblings or parents who might be able to help? Do they have children old enough to help? Could a daughter or son take over the task of preparing dinner? Could Nancy's mother stay with her father-in-law in the afternoon?

Is there any possibility either Nancy or Jim could work at home or adjust her or his working hours to fit more conveniently the dual role of caregiver–working person? Could Nancy and Jim talk to their employers about a more flexible work schedule? The two of them need to reassess their finances, their careers, and their total family obligations. Then they can begin to work at the job of fulfilling those obligations within the restraints and limitations imposed upon them.

Finally, once Nancy and Jim have lined up as much help as possible from the community and the family, they need to seek possible help from friends and neighbors. They should then set up a schedule with Jim's father and stick to it. And they should encourage Jim's father to take an active role in his own care wherever possible.

If you are working and at the same time about to become someone's primary caregiver, get organized by taking the following actions.

1. Research as much information as possible about the person you will be caring for and his or her infirmities.
2. Find out what services are available in your community that can assist you in providing care.
3. Meet with other family members (and neighbors and friends if they are willing to help) and determine what their roles in the caregiving process will be.
4. Determine which caregiving tasks will be purchased from community agencies and who will pay for those services.

5. Recognize that your role as primary caregiver, however limited that role may be, will take time. Realistically look at the hours you have to give to the role, and think through your routine to find out where that time will come from and what will have to be curtailed or sacrificed.

BARBARA: "My children are becoming angry and withdrawn since Mother came to live here. They were a part of the decision to have her come, but now they seem bitter and resentful, and they treat her badly."

Barbara needs support not only for herself but for her children as well. Even when each child is given the opportunity to voice concerns before the decision is made to have Grandma come into the home, children rarely understand the full meaning of such a move until the new living arrangement is established. Children play a role in the caregiving process when the person is living in their home, and, as secondary caregivers, these children are entitled to respite and support.

Barbara might try sitting down with each of her children individually or with all of them in a group and having them talk through their feelings. Perhaps they need to hear that they are helping and that their sacrifices are appreciated. Every caregiver needs to know this occasionally. Barbara and her husband should examine in what ways each child's life has been affected. Perhaps one child is sharing a room with Grandma, and another child feels that Grandma disapproves of his or her friends. Some children may be frightened by the older person's illness or impairments.

If the children continue to be upset and behave badly, Barbara's stress will increase dramatically, and she could be a candidate for serious illness herself. In a house where there are more people involved in the caregiving relationship than just the care recipient and the primary caregiver, adjustments need to be made to care for the needs of all.

Barbara might enroll her mother in a day-care program a couple of days a week. That would allow the children to have friends in after school while giving Grandma an outing to a different and interesting environment. Many families find that when the members of the family, including the care recipient, go their own ways during the day and come together at night, life is more tranquil and interesting for all the generations.

Occasionally Barbara might arrange for her mother to stay a weekend or even a week in a nursing home so that she and her family could enjoy time together without her mother. Finally, if her mother's impairment is one for which there is some national organization, Barbara might encourage her children to educate themselves about the illness and attend support group meetings to learn how other families cope with the disease.

When another adult comes to live permanently in an already established household, there can be problems. Prior planning can help the family anticipate those problems and seek possible solutions. Consider the following:

1. Present a realistic picture of what changes and sacrifices will have to be made to family members before the person moves in.
2. Continue to hold periodic family meetings to air feelings and consider ideas for solutions of any problems.
3. Actively plan for the privacy and independence of each person who lives in the house to pursue a life outside of the family unit.
4. Occasionally give members of the family the opportunity to be together without the care recipient. Caregiving is a job, and no matter how much you and your family love the person who is in need of your care, you deserve time off.

HARVEY: "Anything I have her do is twice the work for me. I have enough trouble being organized and getting everything done without worrying about her trying to help."

Harvey's wife has Alzheimer's disease, and he has not only taken on the role of primary caregiver but also that of househusband. He is struggling to learn to do the tasks his wife mastered over all the years of their marriage and has now forgotten how to do—the laundry, the cooking, the housecleaning. Harvey can do a number of things to relieve himself of the strain of his multiple duties without excluding his wife.

Harvey's first job is to organize the house so that everything he needs for daily and weekly chores is together in one place. Many caregivers load plastic caddy trays with supplies and store them in the area they will be needed (for example, under the bathroom sink, in the hall closet, and next to the washer and dryer). If this means buying duplicates of cleaners and other products, Harvey should do that.

Next, he should determine what chores his wife can still do with some skill. Some Alzheimer's victims retain their ability to peel vegetables and dry dishes well into the disease. Others are very good at repetitive tasks such as vacuuming, raking leaves, and folding laundry. Harvey needs to note those chores his wife can do and allow her to do them while he accomplishes those tasks she can no longer manage. If his wife insists on helping with those other chores, Harvey might work on those jobs when his wife is sleeping or otherwise occupied. One caregiver suggested rising an hour earlier in the morning and accomplishing the most difficult tasks before the person is up.

Harvey and his wife may be eligible for a homemaker service in their community. He may also find that having his wife join a co-op care group or become a client of a volunteer respite organization would allow him the time to accomplish the chores while his wife is cared for by a substitute caregiver.

When a person becomes the primary caregiver for a spouse, it is not unusual for that person to begin to feel that he or she is expected to be superhuman. The caregiver may need to continue working in order to support the household. If you find yourself assuming all the roles of the marriage that were formerly divided between two people—cooking, cleaning, chauffeuring, and so on—it is time to take stock by asking yourself these questions.

1. What needs to be done today? What can wait until the weekend or next week or next month? Can I plan a week in advance? Can some things be done simultaneously (a load of wash while I prepare dinner)?
2. What tasks can my spouse still manage? Who else can help? Are there children, grandchildren, neighbors, or friends who are willing to help?
3. Are there community services that my spouse and I are eligible to receive or can take advantage of—meals at a nutrition site or a day for my spouse at an adult day-care center? Am I taking advantage of such services whenever possible?

Remember, refusing to accept help from secondary caregivers or outside agencies will not make you a better caregiver. It will only make you an exhausted caregiver.

DON: "My mother is up several times at night. I need my rest."

Don's first job is to determine whether his mother is sleeping during the day. If he works and leaves her alone all day, she may spend the day sleeping. One caregiver noticed that her relative ran out of steam around two in the afternoon and slept until six in the evening every day. That caregiver solved the problem by locking her relative's bedroom until it was time for bed and finding activities to keep the person occupied until then.

There may be other causes of insomnia, of course—fear of the dark, anticipation of a coming event, pain. But many caregivers find that the most common cause is boredom and a lack of purpose during the day. If Don can find meaningful activity for his mother during the day, he may solve his problem of sleepless nights for both of them. He could investigate a number of options, depending on his mother's health. Adult day-care programs, activities at senior centers, college classes for seniors, and community-run activity programs for seniors are just a few of the ideas he might try. If his mother is housebound, he could consider services that would come to the house, such as respite volunteers, library services, or volunteers from the church or synagogue.

By finding the source of his mother's sleeplessness, Don will achieve his own goal of getting some rest. If he can find no solution for her insomnia, Don may want to consider the idea of hiring an aide to stay in the home at night to assist with the caregiving role while he gets some sleep.

Sometimes the caregiver is handling the job splendidly except for one particular problem. In Don's case, it is his mother's insomnia. For someone else it might be the care recipient who wanders or the one who becomes combative without warning. If you are managing well in the caregiver role with the exception of one or two problems, consult the following sources for help.

• For any unusual recurring behavior, seek the advice of the person's physician. There may be some treatable cause for the behavior such as a chemical or drug imbalance.

• If the doctor tells you that the behavior is not uncommon in connection with the person's particular condition or illness, ask your social worker or home health care agent for ideas for coping. Or, you might join a support group and ask your fellow caregivers what they have done to handle the problem.

• Continue to try different remedies until you find one that works or at least offers some relief from the problem.

MARY: "Since my husband's stroke, I am the sole financial support for our family. At times I also feel as if I am the sole emotional support as well. I feel guilty that I am not capable of being Superwoman all the time."

Many caregivers suffer needlessly because they believe themselves to be alone. Mary may operate under the assumption that there is no one else or at least no one she knows who is having to manage all the roles she is. At times she recognizes that her husband is equally frustrated. No one else they know is going through what they are. It is hard to explain to friends. It is embarrassing to ask for help. They do not want to bother their relatives.

But Mary and her husband are hardly alone. In many communities there are stroke victims' clubs that meet on a regular basis to allow both the victims and the caregivers to vent their frustrations and share their successes. In fact, for almost every major impairment affecting older people in the United States, there is a support organization at some level. Such organizations are created to provide information, references, and support for both care recipients and caregivers (see pages 270-273).

If your care recipient has an illness for which there is a national support and information organization, get in touch with the local chapter of that organization as early in the caregiving process as possible. Such organizations can help by providing the caregiver with the following resources.

- pamphlets and other informational materials about the illness
- classes for you and/or the affected person to learn coping techniques
- support groups

ELLEN: "My parents live several hundred miles away. I am their only daughter. Now that they are aging, I worry about what I can do to help them adjust to the health problems they are beginning to experience. It is so hard to know the truth. When I call or visit, they claim everything is fine. But I see signs that they are not managing, and their neighbors tell me stories that verify these signs. I am a nervous wreck over this. I can't keep running back and forth to check on them."

Long-distance caregiving is becoming more prevalent in America's scattered families. But the strain of the primary caregiver's role is not lessened by distance; it may be an even more difficult position in some ways. In addition to the problems of dealing with the medical community, community health agencies, and legal and financial considerations, the long-distance caregiver often must deal with large expenditures for travel and telephone calls. There is often confusion in getting medical information, and handling a medical emergency from across the country can be exasperating. Laws and services vary from state to state, and many long-distance caregivers find it impossible to get clear information about their relatives' rights unless they personally meet with the local professionals who are assisting their relatives with medical and legal matters.

If caregiving help is needed in the home, the long-distance caregiver generally has the task of hiring such help without a lot of time or information. In addition many long-distance caregivers suffer feelings of enormous guilt that they are unable or unwilling to change their own lives to go and become full-time caregivers for their relatives.

In many cases absentee caregivers worry unnecessarily. Often their relatives are capable of managing for some time without extraordinary support measures. Many older persons are independent and do not wish their children or other relatives to take over their lives.

In the event of medical emergencies or failing health, the long-distance caregiver can get help without spending a fortune on needless trips back and forth to attend to the needs of the care recipient by taking the following precautions before an emergency arises.

• Research services and agencies available in the person's area in the event of an emergency. Talk to social workers; make contacts; keep names. In short, become known as a caring potential caregiver.

• Meet with the person's doctor. Provide him or her with information about how to reach you in the event of an emergency. Encourage the doctor to contact you also if there is any reason for concern.

• Talk to the potential care recipient and find out what he or she wants in the event of an emergency. Ask what should happen legally and financially in the unlikely event the person becomes incapacitated.

• Investigate the religious resources close to your relative's home. Protestants can call 1-212-777-4800 for the Federation of Protestant Welfare Agencies. Catholics can contact the National Conference of Catholic Charities at 1-202-785-2757. Those who are Jewish can call the Jewish Information and Referral Service in New York, 1-212-753-2288, for information about local agencies around the country.

• Finally, there is a nonprofit agency that will help long-distance caregivers locate services for their relatives. For information send a self-addressed, stamped envelope to Family Service America, 44 East 23rd Street, New York, NY 10010.

Respite Options

Respite is a time of rest and relaxation. It can be a few moments, hours, or even days. Day-care programs can provide respite for caregivers as can co-ops, foster homes, board-and-care group homes, and substitute caregivers. Caring for another person all the time can be very stressful, and caregivers deserve breaks. Respite care may take place in or out of the home. The purpose of respite care is to provide a substitute caregiver while the primary caregiver has some time off. What can you expect from these respite services? And how do you know which are the right services for your relative?

Adult Day-Care Programs

Day-care programs for adults can offer a wide range of services in a wide range of settings. Regardless of the particulars, day-care programs aim to provide older people with the opportunity to be involved in the community, and they aim to provide caregivers with respite and support. The programs differ from senior centers; in a day-care setting there is health support—personal care and surveillance—in addition to social support for the client.

A day-care center may be privately owned, publicly owned, supported by a religious organization, or supported by a private foundation. The program setting may be a church or synagogue, a nursing home, a school, or a freestanding building. The program may include everything from meals to activities to physical and occupational therapy to medical checkups. The staff may be made up of nursing assistants, activity personnel, social workers, therapists, registered nurses, and physicians. In many states programs must be approved and certified or licensed by some state agency.

Some day-care centers are open five days a week from early morning until late afternoon. Others are open only a few days a week and for limited hours. (The hours are especially important for those caregivers who work and need to have full-time care for their relatives during the working hours.) Charges are per day, per week, or per month, and clients can usually choose to attend every day of the week or less frequently. Weekend and holiday service, if available, may be more expensive.

Sometimes there are public monies available to aid those who could benefit from day-care programs but who cannot afford to attend. Call your local Office on Aging or hospital social worker to find out if such public funds are available in your relative's community. Fees usually include all services offered, though there may be additional charges for transportation, therapy, and medical services. Also the Internal Revenue Service will credit the caregiver's income taxes for some of the expenses incurred for the out-of-home, noninstitutional care of a disabled spouse or other qualified care recipient if such care is necessary in order to allow the caregiver to be employed. The person cared for must be in the taxpayer's home for at least eight hours a day, and the adult day-care center must meet any state or local regulations that apply. For further information call the IRS twenty-four-hour hotline at 1-800-242-9699 or call the local IRS office and request Publication 503.

If you are considering adult day care for your relative, you will need to decide whether to look for a program that offers rehabilitation or one that offers simple social interaction. Some centers offer new clients a trial day, but if those in your area do not, at least visit the center with the individual before the first day. Ask questions. Look around. And visit several centers before you choose. The concept of adult day care is relatively new in the United States; therefore centers are often small with a limited and sometimes untrained staff. The following checklist may help you assess each center and its program as you visit.

1. Call your local Office on Aging and/or physician or social worker and ask whether the center is recommended. In some communities and states centers must adhere to regulations for certification. Is that true in your community or state?

2. What are your impressions as you approach the center? Are there ramps for wheelchairs? Is the entrance well lighted and attractive?

3. How are you received by the staff? What is your first impression as you enter the activity and social areas of the center? How is your relative reacting?

4. Is there enough light? Is the center warm enough or cool enough? Are there any unpleasant noises or odors?

5. Are there safety features such as call bells in the bathrooms and handrails along the passageways if the center encompasses more than one room? Are the furnishings sturdy and clean? Are there designated smoking areas? What evacuation plan is there in the event of an emergency?

6. Can you have a copy of the menu for the last week or month? Can you tour the kitchen? What precautions are taken to ensure that a diabetic stays on his or her diet and does not indulge in improper snacks or sweets?

7. Are there any medical or therapy services available (eye examinations, blood pressure checks, speech and/or physical therapy)? What procedures does the staff follow if a person has a medical emergency while at the center?

8. What is the staff ratio to clients? What do you notice about staff interaction with clients?

9. Do the clients appear to enjoy being at the center?

Are they active? Ask to see a calendar of planned activities for the month. Note what is scheduled on the calendar during the time you are visiting and observe whether that activity is being done.

10. What does everything cost? What is the billing procedure? What about refunds or credits for days missed due to illness?

Co-ops

Some caregivers have found that by banding together in a cooperative group, they are able to give one another respite by sitting with one another's relatives in groups on a regular basis. A caregiver would be scheduled to "sit" with another caregiver's relative at regular intervals, allowing that caregiver time for errands and respite.

Foster Homes

In England there is a program in which host families take a person for a weekend or week while the caregiving family has time off. The host family is paid a stipend (very low, so that there is no chance the family will be doing this for the money) and is instructed on the basics of caregiving. Such programs exist in the United States, though at this writing there is no government support of them at the federal level. Again, contact your Area Agency on Aging to locate a program in your area.

Board-and-Care Group Homes

A board-and-care group home is a residence where a few persons in need of some care or support live together with the help of a day manager and/or a night supervisor. Group homes may take persons for a short respite period if they have a vacancy at the time. The person will have a room and meals and social interaction with the other residents. Look for homes that have been licensed by the state. Call your Area Agency on Aging for information about such homes in your area. Keep in mind that, in general, group homes are for people who can manage with a minimum of supervision and care.

Substitute Caregivers

The National Council of Catholic Women sponsors a substitute caregiver program in several communities around the country. The program, called Respite, sends a trained volunteer to the home to watch over the care recipient for specific and limited periods of time. The volunteer is not there to cook meals or clean the house. Volunteers attend a training session for one day and are then matched with those in need through the local parishes.

In other communities similar volunteer and public programs are available. Contact the local Area Agency on Aging to find out what services are available in your community.

Hired Companions

If there is enough money, you might consider the idea of hiring a nurse or companion to stay in the home with the person. Such companions should stay for several hours at a time, and the caregiver should leave the companion alone with the person needing care so that the person gets used to the idea of care that comes from sources other than the primary caregiver. Occasionally there should even be an extended stay of several days.

Making the Correct Choice

How do you know which respite service to choose? Look at the affiliation of the program first. Does it have public funding? Is it privately operated? Are there people on staff who have professional training in the needs of older persons? If not, are there advisors for those workers who may not have formal training in working with older care recipients? Is there a program coordinator and an established method of providing services and getting help in emergency situations? Can the agency or program provide references? Does your social worker, clergyperson, or physician know anything about the program? If the services are offered by a privately held, for-profit agency, have you contacted the Better Business Bureau for a reference?

Self-Help Through Support Groups

Sometimes the first step toward gaining respite and relief for the caregiver comes through a support group. In support groups caregivers are able to learn coping skills that prepare them to make choices based on both the care recipients' needs and their own. Most support groups meet on a regular basis at a time most convenient to the participants. Generally there is a facilitator or group leader who may be a professional in the health care field. This person conducts the business of the group. He or she calls meetings, arranges for a meeting place, arranges for relief caregivers to keep the care recipients content during the time of the meeting, and schedules special programs and discussions at the request of the group.

The most successful support groups are those in which the members direct their own programs and choose their own topics for discussion. Most groups encourage sharing of experiences and techniques, occasionally scheduling an expert who can contribute to the education of the group. Although most meetings last only a couple of hours and often caregivers must exert tremendous efforts and considerable inconvenience to manage attendance, the caregiver will benefit from the emotional support he or she receives from the knowledge that caregiving is not an isolated experience. Caregivers often gain new and useful insights into the feelings and needs of their relatives and learn of new options for caring that may have been unavailable in the community. They receive encouragement and sympathy. They share laughter about circumstances no one else would see as funny at all. They find friends and receive positive feedback for the work they are doing.

Many support groups are organized by the local chapters of organizations for a particular illness. Meetings are held in public buildings in various locations. Call the local chapter for your relative's illness and ask for the support group nearest you. Sometimes your need for support does not fit into any neat category such as Alzheimer's disease or multiple sclerosis, but that does not mean you could not benefit from meeting with others who share your concerns and situation. Three national organizations may be able to advise you of a support group in your area:

> National Support Center for Families of the Aging
> PO Box 245
> Swarthmore, PA 19081
>
> Children of Ageing Parents
> 2761 Trenton Road
> Levittown, PA 19056
>
> Family Caregivers Program
> National Council on the Aging
> 600 Maryland Avenue, SW, West Wing 100
> Washington, DC 20024

Sometimes a caregiver will say, "I don't have time to attend a meeting. I can barely get through the day now. Besides, why should I listen to others talk about their problems?" Support groups are not crying sessions. They are opportunities—opportunities to learn more about giving care, to gain important information about services, and to socialize with people who understand and need no explanation.

What if there is no support group to meet your needs? Start one. It is not as difficult as you might think. Follow this procedure.

1. Make a list of people you know or others tell you about who are dealing with a caregiving situation similar to yours.
2. Call those people and ask whether they would be interested in getting together informally for two hours in the near future. Set a date, and ask them to invite others.

3. Once you have decided on the time and place that will be most convenient for everyone, ask a few people to bring along some light refreshments. (Banks, libraries, and religious institutions often will provide meeting space at no charge.)
4. At the first meeting make sure there are name tags available, and, if possible, have volunteers to stay with care recipients who attend but who are unable to participate.
5. Start the meeting by asking each caregiver to introduce himself or herself and briefly describe the caregiving situation.
6. Establish the working details of the group. How often will you meet? When? Where? What time and for how long? Establish program topics, and designate leaders for the next three meetings.
7. Be sure each member signs a mailing list, with phone numbers, so you can send notices for the next meeting.
8. Establish dues if they seem necessary to cover refreshments and mailings.
9. Keep the business part of the meeting brief, allowing most of the time for members to share in the program and socialize.

Materials on starting support groups are available from some local libraries or Area Offices on Aging. Or you might write for the following:

How to Organize a Self-Help Group by Andy Humm, National Self-Help Clearing House, Graduate Center, 33 West 42nd Street, New York, NY 10036

Starting a Self-Help Group, Milwaukee Area Self-Help Alliance, Family Services, 2819 West Highland Avenue, Milwaukee, WI 53208

Starting a Self-Help Support Group, CAPS (Children of Ageing Parents), 2761 Trenton Road, Levittown, PA 19056

Hand in Hand, Crisis Support Program, AARP, 1909 K Street NW, Washington, DC 20049

In addition, you might contact CARERS (Caregivers Assistance and Resources for the Elderly's Relatives

Series), Center for the Study of Aging, State University of New York at Buffalo, Buffalo, NY 14214.

In Support of Caregivers and *Something for the Families* by Dr. Marilyn J. Bonjean are filmstrips, cassettes, and guidebooks for professionals and others interested in training for conducting family support workshops. They are available for sale at the Vocational Studies Center, University of Wisconsin Publications Unit, 265 Educational Sciences Building, 1025 West Johnson Street, Madison, WI 53706.

Supplementary Services from the Community

These services have been discussed in Part Two of this book. Ask whether the following are operating through your local Area Agency on Aging or some other resource.

- chore services in the home
- homemaker services
- home health services
- telephone reassurance programs
- visits from volunteers
- home-delivered meals or nutrition sites

Such services, though intended for the benefit of the care recipient, provide indirect respite for the caregiver by lightening the load of the daily routine.

Whatever resource or combination of resources you choose, the first step toward finding time for respite and support is to convince yourself you need it, you deserve it, and you have earned it. Many caregivers keep putting off time for themselves in favor of doing something else for the care recipient. "I'll take time off as soon as . . ." or "I'd really like to come to the meeting, but I have to . . ." Of course, the job of caregiving being what it is (sometimes twenty-four hours a day, seven days a week), the work is never done, and the time a caregiver gives to taking care of self gets short shrift.

15 ⚭ Working for Better Conditions

The present health care system in the United States is aimed at caring for those who are acutely ill rather than those who are chronically ill. Medicare and Medicaid are government programs that help pay for health care.

As the American population ages and more citizens become involved in caregiving relationships, the need for expanded and/or reorganized services for both chronically ill persons and their caregivers will increase. Government agencies at the federal, state, and local levels must begin to examine current programs in light of increased future demands. The need will expand as Americans continue to live longer.

Consider one typical caregiver case study: She is a wife caring for her disabled husband. Her doctor gives her the diagnosis and sends her on her way to care for this man with little information and even less public financial support. No government agency recognizes this woman as someone who is giving society the benefit of her twenty-four-hour-a-day caring at no charge. If she raises an issue and asks for help, she is often regarded as a troublemaker who wants only to bankrupt an already faltering system. She is poor and made poorer as she uses every private financial resource to support her husband's need for care. When she is thoroughly exhausted, she may choose with a great deal of guilt and sadness to place her husband in a nursing home. At this point, assuming she has also exhausted their savings and assets, the system will take over and care for her husband in a skilled facility. But there is no safety net to catch this caregiver. As long as she maintains some semblance of health and independence, she will not be a part of the plan to provide care for her husband. She has done her job as an unpaid caregiver, and she has few, if any rights, once she ends that job.

What must be done? How can you, a caregiver, who is already working all day every day, make a difference? Who do you go to for help? How do you get a law passed, changed, or revoked? Industries pay lobbyists to live and work in Washington, D.C., and state capitals throughout the country in order to advocate new legislation that will benefit a particular group or industry. Millions of dollars are spent every year to support these efforts to influence the lawmakers of the land. How can one caregiver or a small group of caregivers out in Iowa or Idaho effect any change?

Because the majority of caregivers in the United States are women, rights for caregivers must be viewed as a feminist issue. Eighty percent of those older persons who live alone are women, and in this society it is women who can least afford the services of unsupported private agencies. Caregivers for these older persons are primarily women, who themselves may be single, widowed, or divorced. On top of this, for the first time in history, perhaps one-fifth of the total population—men and women—is retired or out of active society. The world has no historical model for such a phenomenon. Caregivers and their relatives have a unique opportunity to break new ground as the government at every level seeks to deal with the changing population.

What Changes Are Needed?

Most of the change that is needed for caregivers and their relatives affects the long-range planning for health care in this country. The needs of the caregiver as well as the person he or she cares for must be addressed. Funding for programs should be based on need and realistic definitions of disability. Caregivers need not only community support networks but also financial incentives to continue the services they are performing. In short, change is needed that will establish a long-term health care program that will address the physical, emotional, and financial needs of both the acutely ill person and the chronically ill person and will in the process support and sustain the caregiver who maintains that person at home.

The Older Women's League (OWL) based in Oakland, California, is one advocacy group concerned with the needs of the caregiver as well as those of the care recipient. In a recent paper highlighting issues in need of action, OWL revealed that of those functionally disabled persons who need long-term care, only one-third receive that care through public programs. Most are cared for at home, and well over half the care given in the home is provided by a caregiver.

In some countries programs are being developed to encourage temporary foster care for care recipients, giving caregivers some opportunity for respite. Such placements are short-term, not permanent. Where it exists, the program is getting good marks, but the foster families are not paid very well, and demand is far outstripping supply.

Another trend in some countries is toward allowing more flexible work arrangements for full-time caregivers. Group support through self-help seminars and support groups is on the rise around the world. In Britain there is the National Council for Carers and Their Elderly Dependents.

There is universally a trend toward shifting away from government support. The current U.S. health policy is rooted in two things: trying to relieve the pressure on the family and trying to relieve the pressure on the national pocketbook. The second item tends to win out. As of this writing, some programs actually penalize familial support (Social Security I and Medicaid) and reward institutionalization. The current trend is toward laws that would legislate familial responsibility—demand that families care for their own. Such ideas are based on a false picture of the typical caregiver as a middle-aged woman whose husband is at the peak of his earning power, who is healthy, and who can provide care for an older person in need of support because she is at home. The picture is wrong. Most caregivers in the United States today are young-old who themselves are bordering on retirement. Most are female, and many hold full-time jobs that they need for survival because they themselves are alone or because they are a necessary income producer.

Other countries have tried mandating care by family members with almost no success. The program that will succeed in providing proper care for our aging society is the one that starts with a picture of most older people as functioning independent individuals. Why? Because that is the way older persons *want* to see themselves. And their caregivers will not need rewards or rebates but rather support in the form of programs and services that will directly address the problems of full-time caregiving.

In the current political climate, Congress acknowledges the need for long-term care and at the same time fears paying for any services that are currently being provided by families without government involvement. However, Congress and the state governments are aware of the demographics; they know that over the next decades the number of people in need of caregiving will increase while the numbers of those available to provide caregiving in the home will decrease. Congress wants to deinstitutionalize the nation. There are far too many people in nursing homes today who are there simply because they have no families to provide the care they need at home. To succeed, Congress will have to join forces with caregivers in initiating realistic programs to deal with the problem.

How to Advocate for Change

The potential advocate must understand that Congress and state legislatures are *political* bodies. They are not receptive to proposals that appeal totally on the basis of need. Taking a care recipient or two or three to address the body will certainly generate some response, but lobbyists understand that to succeed one must address the audience. And in this case the audience is a man or woman who is as concerned about being elected next year as he or she is about the care recipient before the committee.

It is no longer enough to build an issue on the basis of "desperate need." That need must be translated into arguments to which a legislator can relate:

1. How will the proposal affect tax revenues and losses?
2. How can the proposal save the government money in the long run?
3. How will the proposal eventually, if ever, become self-supporting?
4. How will the proposal win votes for the legislator in the coming election?

Advocates for change in the programs that currently serve the aging population must demonstrate that unless programs are enacted that will prevent the collapse of the family structure for support and caregiving, more and more citizens will have to depend on total government care in their older years. There will simply be no one else to care for them. In Seattle a research and demonstration project to seek ideas for future health care programs has been undertaken by the Pacific Northwest Long Term Care Center at the University of Washington. The project, which is funded by the Administration on Aging and the Health Care Financing Administration, is called the Family Support Project.

Five different demonstration services are being tested by the project. These include family seminars for caregiving (six two-hour training and informational seminars for caregivers), caregiver support groups (organized by those who have completed the seminars and wish to continue meeting), family coordination services (provided by a social worker to help families locate and utilize community services), volunteer respite services (volunteers who go into the home for a two- to three-hour period to relieve the caregiver), and paid respite services (families in the project are allotted Medicare funds equal to the cost of fourteen days of care for the care recipient in an institutional setting; the funds can be used all at one time or can be used over a period of time for several short-term respite periods).

It *is* possible for one or a few caregivers and their relatives to make effective changes in the current climate of health care in the United States. These efforts will take time and organization, but successful change can be achieved if the caregiver works through existing networks, such as support groups, and national advocacy groups, such as OWL. Whenever possible, the care recipient can be encouraged to participate in developing strategies for change. The idea that he or she is doing something positive not only stimulates self-esteem but also adds to a feeling of personal independence.

There are a number of consumer interest groups and groups whose primary function is to lobby for better living conditions for the aging population in America. For more information about how to get organized and get your ideas written into law, write Ralph Nader's Public Citizen Network. This group has a number of splinter organizations that tackle change for specialized groups:

Health Research Group, 2000 P Street, NW, Room 708, Washington, DC 20036

Congress Watch, 215 Pennsylvania Avenue, SE, Washington, DC 20003 (also the Tax Reform Research Group at the same address)

National Insurance Consumer Organization, 344 Commerce Street, Alexandria, VA 22314

(These are national organizations. There are also state Public Interest Research Groups, which are nonprofit and nonpartisan organizations directed by students with a staff of professional advisors including attorneys, scientists, and organizers. Write any of the above groups for information about a state group in your area.)

In addition, the following organizations specialize in

issues for older Americans and can advise you about lobbying for change in your community.

American Association of Retired Persons, 1909 K Street, NW, Washington, DC 20049

Gray Panthers, 3700 Chestnut Street, Philadelphia, PA 10904

National Council on the Aging, Inc., 600 Maryland Avenue, SW, Washington, DC 20024

If you are interested in becoming involved in lobbying or advocating for better care and support for yourself and your care recipient within your own community, these books will help you get organized.

How You Can Influence Congress by George Alderson and Everett Sentman.

In Our Own Interest by Dorothy Smith.

Ask your librarian for other books and information on the subject.

16 ❧ Letting Go

In most caregiving relationships there comes a time when to maintain the relative in the home is more harmful than it is beneficial. The caregiver is trying to do more than reasonably can be expected and in the process may be causing irreparable harm to everyone involved.

There is a time to let go. There is a time, in some cases, for long-term institutionalization. Neither is an indication of failure. On the contrary, making the decision to institutionalize a loved one takes real courage.

What are the signs that the time has come to seek another solution? If a nursing home seems to be the answer, how does one choose a good one? Finally, once the person has moved into an institution or died, how does the caregiver deal with the aftershock?

A person who has in effect been living for two people for several months (or even years) may find that adjusting to being on his or her own again is very difficult. Friends and family who have seen the caregiver's strength for such a long period of time may be unable to comprehend the depression and sense of isolation that may begin once the caregiving role has ended. Indeed, others may think this will be a time of great relief for the caregiver. But, perhaps more than at any other time in the process, this is the time when the caregiver needs emotional support and should be encouraged to get the help that will see him or her through this period of transition.

Moving On

When is it time to stop being the primary caregiver, not in the sense of giving up but rather in the sense of moving on? The signs are fairly simple, but often the caregiver cannot see the forest for the trees. Fatigue, depression, withdrawal from the rest of the family and the world— these are just a few of the reasons you, as caregiver, should consider finding someone else to take over the role. Another consideration is that, as the condition of your relative worsens, you may be overextending yourself, thinking you can continue to give full-time care. Whether the disability is physical or mental, there may come a time when care at home is not only improper but downright detrimental.

Some caregivers keep going because they think that to stop after all this time would be to admit failure. Nothing could be further from the truth. It takes genuine courage to seek help and to admit you can no longer give as much care as necessary to maintain both your health and your relative's.

It is not necessary to turn the job over to an institution cold turkey. You have already considered ways of finding temporary, short-term respite. These temporary solutions can make the step of placing a loved one in a nursing home or hospice easier for both the caregiver and the care recipient. For example, regular attendance at a day-care center introduces the person to the idea that others can provide good care, even in a setting where there are many to be cared for.

Another way of testing the idea of long-term care is for the caregiver to find nursing homes that will allow short-term stays, for a few days or a weekend, while the caregiver takes a short break or vacation.

After a long period of time, during which you have created and refined the procedures of care that work best for your relative, it is very hard to imagine that anyone else, even a skilled nursing facility, could do as good a job. And, in fact, they may not do it as well in that there will not be the constant one-on-one attention the person is receiving at home. But you also need to consider yourself and the rest of the family.

If you are a caregiver, and have been for some time, ask yourself these questions.

1. In the last several weeks or months, have I had more illnesses or symptoms of possible illness than before?
2. Has my relative's illness become more complex?
3. Are there things happening with my relative that I no longer know how to handle?
4. Does my relative's illness now require that I have more physical strength for lifting, turning, and moving the person?
5. Do I no longer have the energy and time to pursue other tasks and interests besides caregiving?
6. Am I often depressed, irritable, and exhausted? Is my relative?
7. Do I resent the job, worry constantly about what might happen to my relative if something happens to me, or feel there will never be an end?

If your answer to any of these questions is yes, you should consider seeking some extended respite care or even skilled nursing care for your relative. Getting help is not a sign of weakness. It is a sign that you are continuing to do the best job you can in caring for another human being by having the courage to recognize your own limitations.

Choosing a Nursing Home

What do you really know about nursing homes? Do you know anyone who lives in a nursing home now? Have you ever visited a home? If not, what are your expectations?

Many people have several mistaken ideas about nursing homes. A nursing home is not a hospital. Even though many people enter a nursing home after a hospital stay, nursing home care is not an extension of hospital care. Nor is everyone who lives in a nursing home demented or frightening. Contrary to many popular ideas, a nursing home is not a warehouse where people are numbered and piled in rooms and forgotten. Nursing home personnel are not bad guys who delight in giving the minimum care for the maximum money.

What is a nursing home? Nursing homes are places of residence that provide nursing care. If the individual's condition lends itself to rehabilitation, they provide that rehabilitation in an effort to get the resident back into the community, and in some rare cases that happens. Most often, however, it is the job of the skilled nursing home to maintain a level of health against the ravages of disease and age and attempt to prevent further or unnecessary problems whenever possible. Nursing homes also try to sustain families emotionally by providing opportunities for counseling and family activities.

Many people who have never had any experience with nursing homes are unaware that homes must pass stringent inspections and live up to strict codes of operation. Something as seemingly insignificant as not keeping an extra chair available for each resident can be considered a violation—inspection teams are strict. The staff is professional, and many of the members must pass examinations for licensing. Staff members are expected to create plans for care for each person who resides in the home. Trained dieticians are expected to plan nutritious meals for all residents and to plan special meals for those residents with particular dietary needs.

Of course, someone always has a story about poor care, poor food, and the disappearance of personal belongings; certainly these things may happen even in the best of homes. But that does not mean the failure was deliberate. Many times these are isolated incidents that can be remedied quickly when brought to the attention of the nursing supervisor, dietician, or home administrator. Sometimes the home may be short-staffed, or there may be a problem elsewhere in the building that temporarily makes proper service impossible.

Still, many caregivers are constantly frustrated by the state in which they find their relatives when they visit at the nursing home. The person may be unshaven or not properly dressed for the day. Clothing, done in a central laundry for all residents, is constantly being lost. The caregiver, who took pride in the quality of care he or she gave this person for years, may feel a mixture of emotions ranging from anger to guilt when the person is not being cared for in the same personal way in the nursing home. When this happens, the caregiver should seek an appointment with the home administrator and/or the staff that provides care for the person. At that meeting the caregiver should cover the following points.

1. When the caregiver and care recipient toured the home, what services were presented as normal care? Are those services being provided every day as promised? If not, why not?
2. Has something changed about the person's condition that makes providing those services difficult or impossible? If so, why wasn't the caregiver advised of the change?
3. Can the caregiver ask that particular attention be paid to certain services that seemingly are being overlooked with the person (for example, bathing, shaving, and dressing properly)?
4. Will the administrator and/or staff agree to investigate the caregiver's concerns and report back to the caregiver within a definite period of time?

If, after supervisory personnel have been alerted, your relative receives no better care or you receive an unsatisfactory explanation, you might consider looking at other homes. The nursing home business is a competitive one, and other homes are available. As stated earlier, a move is never easy, but the person will adapt, especially if care improves in the new setting.

What about costs? The cost of care is high whether you are caring for the person yourself or hiring others to do it. Unfortunately, at this writing most insurance companies as well as the federal and state governments see long-term care for the chronically ill as *custodial care,* and there is little financial support available. It is important then that you find out exactly what the costs at each home you visit will be. For example, some homes may charge an additional fee for hand-feeding a resident or doing personal laundry. Before you choose a home, sit down with the administrator and get *in writing* what the basic charges will be and exactly what will be included for that amount.

If the person is eligible for Medicare, what will Medicare cover? If the person has been in the hospital for at least three full days and is admitted to the nursing home within thirty days of leaving the hospital, Medicare will cover the costs of the nursing home for up to twenty-one days as long as the care needed is skilled nursing care and *not* custodial care. Another instance where Medicare will cover costs is when the person is transferred to a skilled nursing facility because he or she requires care for a specific condition that was treated in the hospital—bedsores or a fractured hip, for example. In these cases Medicare may pay for up to 100 days of care.

What happens when Medicare coverage runs out? When you meet the nursing home staff before your relative moves into the home, someone will probably ask what financial arrangements are being made to cover care once Medicare coverage runs out. You have two options: (1) pay privately for as long as you and/or the relative can or (2) apply for Medicaid Title 19 benefits. Eligibility for such benefits will vary from state to state, but generally speaking the person's assets (and in some cases the spouse's assets) must have already been depleted to a minimal level. (Caregiving children and their assets are not affected.)

Anyone who has ever placed a loved one in a nursing home has wondered about the decision. It is a moment that is filled with the threat of guilt and anxiety for both the caregiver and the rest of the family. It is an emotionally charged time in any person's life. In the first place, the person must deal with not only frailty and illness but also the additional sense of loss and separation. The caregiver's feelings include guilt and a sense of failure and inadequacy. A caregiver often feels that he or she is deserting his or her relative just when that person seems the most in need. There is a grieving process that accompanies the move.

Even some of the language associated with nursing homes is negative: "I had to put my father in a home." "My aunt had to give up her apartment and go into a nursing home." "She'll have to go to a home." There is that sense of putting someone away and the unspoken thought that this is an act of sentencing the person to death. People do die in nursing homes—many more than reenter the community. But that is not because of the nursing homes. People die because they age and get sicker and their bodies can no longer fight their illnesses. Try rephrasing the language: "Mom is living at Glenview now. It's a good skilled nursing home," or "Dad will be taking a room at Forest Manor next week." Correcting the false images of nursing homes as dumping grounds would alleviate some of that sense of guilt. Often that guilt stems from your fear of what others will think when they hear that your loved one is moving into a nursing home.

Elaine M. Brody of the Philadelphia Geriatric Center had this to say about most families and their reluctance to place a loved one in a nursing home: "The romantic view admires those who continue to care for an impaired older person under conditions of such severe strain that there is deprivation and suffering for the entire family. Such families may be psychologically unable to place the older person in a nursing home, or, as every service worker knows, may be unable to use the formal support services that are badly needed. Whatever dynamics are at work—symbiotic ties, the gratification of being the 'burden bearer,' a fruitless search for parental approval that has never been received, or expiation of guilt for having been the favored child—excessive caregiving may represent not emotional health or heroism or love, but pathology."

In short, the idea of placing someone you love in a nursing home should not be dismissed as impossible. Before making your choice, see several homes and get the following information.

1. Is the home certified? Does it have its current license or certification?

2. Does the nursing home have experience with or perhaps specialize in the disease or condition of your relative?

3. Are there special services such as physical therapy, dental care, eye examinations, and hearing tests?

4. What services are offered by the social services department to both the resident and the family? What is the ratio of staff to residents?

5. What was your impression of the staff? the other residents? the general atmosphere of the home?

6. Again, what is the ratio of staff to residents? As you walk the halls, what are your observations about staff rapport with residents?

7. Do residents appear well groomed and cared for? Are they out of their rooms and active whenever possible?

8. Use your senses: Is there enough light? Are rooms well insulated to sound? Are there any unreasonable odor problems? Is the food served tasty (try to have your visit include a meal)? Is the place pleasant and inviting and comfortable?

9. Look carefully at the common areas of the building. Is there a place where residents can occasionally be outdoors? Are there lounges and other places where residents are encouraged to gather for cards, television, or reading?

10. What about safety? Are there call bells in the rooms and bathrooms? Are there grab bars in the bathrooms and handrails in the hallways? Are there ramps for wheelchairs? Is furniture sturdy and clean? Are there No Smoking areas? Is there a clear evacuation plan in the event of fire or an emergency?

11. What is the procedure for transferring the resident to the hospital in an emergency?

12. Ask for a copy of the menus for the month. Ask to tour the kitchen. Ask when meals are served and how much time is allowed for each meal. Ask about snacks and eating in the resident's room.

13. Ask for a copy of last month's activity schedule. Check the calendar for events that are scheduled the day you visit; then ask to see that activity in progress.

What is scheduled for evenings and weekends?
14. Are there religious services? Are there fringe ser-
    vices such as a beauty or barber shop?
15. What does everything cost? What are the billing
    procedures? What about refunds? What about per-
    sonal money for the resident to use for incidentals?

Again, you should look at a number of homes and
evaluate each according to those features that are most
important to you and your relative. If you visit homes
with your loved one, watch for his or her reactions to each
place.

For more information.   The following pamphlets can be
obtained free of charge by writing the American Health
Care Association, 1200 15th Street, NW, Washington,
DC 20005.

> *Facts in Brief on Long Term Health Care*
> *Thinking About a Nursing Home*
> *Reactions to Nursing Home Admission*
> *Myths and Realities of Living in a Nursing Home*
> *Resident Councils*

How to Select a Nursing Home is available from the U.S. Department
of Health and Human Services, Public Health Service, Office
of Nursing Home Affairs, 5600 Fishers Lane, Rockville, MD
20857.

Living in a Nursing Home by Sarah Burger is a handbook for
residents, family members, and friends.

Following Up

Your role as caregiver has not ended just because your
loved one is now living in a skilled care facility. You will
need to make frequent visits and keep the relative abreast
of activities within the family. In the beginning your
relative may be depressed and complain about the care,
the food, and the staff. You should listen and then talk to
the staff about the resident's concerns. This will show the
staff that you intend to be a concerned supporter of the

person, and it will show your relative that he or she is not being abandoned.

Your caregiving role now includes making sure that the person adjusts to the new environment, makes new friends, and takes part in activities whenever possible. Your visits should be positive and frequent, not mere duty calls. Popping in unexpectedly is a good idea for seeing the type of care being given and for keeping your relative's spirits raised. If possible, occasionally take the person out for an afternoon. Take an interest in the person's room and surroundings and make sure that as the months go by, you find ways to make the room as personal as possible. Providing small treats for your relative to share with the staff (if allowed) will not only raise the self-esteem of your relative but also almost guarantee more interest from the staff—not because those people are mercenary, but because they are human and appreciate any sign that they are seen as individuals rather than as so many uniforms. For that same reason you should call each staff person by name.

Coping with the Death

The caregiver's role can change suddenly when the loved one dies. All at once the job is finished. There may have been warnings—the lingering illness, hospitalization, even coma. But the end still comes as a shock, for to the end the caregiver is still necessary—still there to handle the details, hold the hand, and take care. With death the role ends. It is the final loss for the person cared for, but it may be only the beginning of many losses for the caregiver.

Some diseases of aging, such as Alzheimer's, have themselves been described as "never ending funerals." When death finally comes, it is sometimes hard for those outside the relationship to understand why the caregiver does not feel relief that almost borders on the euphoric. In their eyes the caregiver has been freed of what had appeared to be a life sentence. They fail to understand that however difficult the job may have been, at times it was incredibly rewarding. Friends and family may have grown so used to your ability to cope and overcome any obstacle that they fail to realize that what has been done has called for enormous growth, creativity, and inner strength. Your role as caregiver has been a primary focus in your life for a long period of time, and now it has ended. You may be entering your own later years, and the thought of starting again to find some new focus for your life may be terrifying.

In addition there may be that unspoken feeling, "What did it all mean? I just gave six years of my life to caring for that person, and now he is dead. What was the point? At the end he didn't even know me. I gave this my best shot, and it wasn't enough."

Of course, there is little if any truth to that, but feelings are not true or false—they are. Neither the caregiver nor those around him or her should ignore this. On the day of the funeral and for days immediately after, there will be many people eager to help you. Friends and family will fill the house with food and comfort. But gradually they will go away with admonitions to "Live for yourself now" and "Take time to do for you—enjoy your freedom." There is always at least one in the crowd who comes up with, "Actually, it's for the best. It's a blessing he died." Not for the survivor. In spite of every rational, practical, logical examination of the person and his or her illness, sometimes in the final analysis the caregiver finds it hard to do more than mouth the words, "Yes, it was a blessing." But inside there may be the gnawing afterthought, "But what do I do now? I'm going to miss him so much."

Each caregiver will handle the death of his or her relative in his or her own way. Factors that will play a role will include whether the death was lingering or sudden, whether the caregiver feels guilt connected with the death, and whether the relationship with the person was one of two alert adults who shared and had the time to express feelings and love.

Whatever your feelings are following the death of

your relative, permit yourself to have them. As you have already discovered during the caregiving process, there will be difficult feelings, including guilt, at some point in the process. Letting those feelings surface is the right thing to do. Be prepared for the fact that it might be several days or weeks after the funeral before the reality of your new life fully sinks in. Find some people you can talk to honestly and openly. Express your natural anger at having been left behind by the one who died. Seek help for the depression you almost surely will have to face. If you feel that you need professional counseling, obtain it. If not, talk with a clergyperson, family member, or close friend who will help you find ways to examine and deal with your feelings and then move on with your life.

Just as when the caregiving role first began, the end of that role is the time when people are most available to help. Let them. If someone asks you to come for lunch, go. If someone offers to take you shopping, go. If someone offers to drive you to church, go. You will have plenty of time to be alone—let people in now. If you do not, later, when you need them, they may not be there.

Aftershock and Rebuilding

Caregivers need to be aware that the first year following the placement of a relative in a nursing home or the death of the person will be a high-risk health time for the caregiver. Doctors report that during this time of stress and change they often see an increase in depression, eating disorders, sleep problems, chest pains, dizziness, vision problems, and general aches and pains.

Your eating habits may change, especially if there were no others in the household. No longer responsible for preparing meals for the other person, you may neglect your own eating routine. Your sleep may be disturbed. Your vulnerability to colds and flu as well as other physical ailments may increase dramatically. You even may begin to exhibit signs of serious illness yourself, such as high blood pressure or heart palpitations.

Whether through death or long-term care placement, separation is painful. It is not possible to be totally prepared, but you can make things easier for yourself by doing the following:

1. Accept the loss or change, and recognize that you will survive it.
2. Allow yourself to feel the pain. It hurts, and that is what is supposed to happen.
3. Remind yourself, if you are feeling guilty and punishing yourself with a thousand if-onlys, that you have given for a long time and that you made a more comfortable life for your loved one.
4. Give yourself time to rest and take care of yourself during this vulnerable time. Do not try to fill the void right away. Do not make any major decisions that you do not have to make. Allow yourself some time off from responsibility.
5. Maintain a routine and a schedule. Go to work, or, if you had been able to do so prior to the nursing home placement or death, keep up with clubs and other groups.
6. Put together a support system of friends and relatives. Give them the opportunity to help. Remember that helping you helps them deal with the loss or absence of this person.
7. As you begin to feel better, look forward to the future, and plan for your life without the full-time responsibility of caregiving.
8. If one day you do not think of the person who is now in a nursing home or has died, do not feel guilty. It is not necessary to spend the rest of your days mourning a loved one's death or feeling guilty about your own good health just to prove your love.
9. Use the new skills and character traits you have built during the years of caregiving. You are an exceptional person—strong, creative, and capable of growth.
10. Invite others into your life. If you were unable to accept the help of friends and relatives immediately after the person went to live in the nursing home or

died, seek those people out now. Stop by for coffee. Invite someone to share potluck with you. Giving—as you have already learned—is a great healer.

11. Comfort yourself with the memories of times shared with the person you cared for. Know that for many those special moments never come.

12. Give yourself credit for the sacrifices you made for the person, and do not play games of wishful thinking: "I wish I had told her I loved her," or "If only we could have had one more day . . ."

13. Finally, do not set a timetable for when you should expect to "get over" your grief or loneliness or allow anyone else to set one for you. If you have been married to a person for over fifty years and giving total care to that person for the last ten, even if that person is still living and in a nursing home, that is a lot to get over.

You may now be alone. Perhaps your caregiving role has not entirely ended. Perhaps there are still some visits to the nursing home. Perhaps you are still acting as the person's legal and financial representative. But, generally speaking, you are finding yourself with blocks of time to concentrate on yourself. You may be at a loss to know where to start.

If you have worked during the caregiving process or just before and can go back to work, do so. The routine and discipline will be good for you until you can make some planned decisions about your new future. Many caregivers are older and past the working years. If that is your case, reinvolve yourself in those activities you tried to maintain through the caregiving years—church or synagogue, civic organizations, political groups. During these first few months anything you can do to get yourself into a routine will be helpful.

Do not forget to schedule a thorough checkup for yourself. The chances are that throughout the caregiving years your focus has been on the health of the care recipient. Now is the time to see your own doctor. Schedule eye, ear, and dental examinations as well. Keep a food diary to monitor your eating.

If there were others in the household (spouse or children) during the caregiving process, keep in mind that life has also changed for them. Depending on their relationships with the person, they may run the gamut of emotions from relief to depression. Take the time to encourage them to express their feelings honestly and openly. By listening and discussing, each of you will work through the period of transition with less friction than if everyone is trying to play a guessing game about the others' feelings.

Children, in particular, should be allowed to express their thoughts, especially following the death of the loved one. They may have trouble dealing with the enormous anger that they feel at the one who has died if the two were very close. They may be alarmed at their inability to cry. They may see you trying to be strong and not break down in front of them as a negative rather than a positive.

In whatever way you and your family choose to deal with the aftershock, keep in mind one thing: it will go away. You will feel better. You will be able to smile and laugh and enjoy life again. Several weeks or months after your relative moves into the nursing home or dies, you will start to rebuild your life after caregiving. Many caregivers find that this is the time they become most interested in advocating for the rights of other caregivers and those who need care. Others choose lifestyles as far removed from illness and pain as possible. The key is in remembering that you have completed a job and are ready to move on. You have not failed. On the contrary, by giving care to another person, you have allowed that person to live a more fulfilling life. Many caregivers would say they themselves have been fulfilled by the experience of caregiving.

The caregiver who cares for himself or herself as well as he or she cares for another person is likely to be the most successful at the job. Check yourself by answering the following questions. If your answers are consistently yes, you are doing a good job of caring for yourself and probably a better job of caring for your loved one.

1. Have you been able to identify your feelings about the role of caregiving?
2. Have you recognized that you will probably sometimes feel isolated? Have you planned what you will do to combat that feeling? Can you say the same for anger? depression? guilt? jealousy?
3. Have you felt proud of your ability to provide good care for another person? Have you learned to savor those moments of tenderness and companionship you and the care recipient have shared? Do you remember to laugh at yourself and the situation?
4. Are you familiar with those services in your community that could offer you respite and support such as adult day-care centers, co-ops, board-and-care homes, foster homes, and support groups?
5. If you are a long-distance caregiver, have you researched your area and found those resources that will best meet your needs and those of the care recipient? Have you found one person who can act as your agent in dealing with these services in your absence?
6. Have you joined a support group? If none is available in your area, have you started to organize one?
7. If you have an interest in fighting for rights for your relative and yourself, do you have ideas about what is needed to achieve more effective caregiving and what steps need to be taken to meet those needs?
8. Have you thought about when it might be necessary for you to stop being a full-time caregiver? Are you prepared to do that? Have you thought about what would happen to you if the person went into a nursing home? died?
9. Do you know how to go about choosing a nursing home for your relative?
10. Have you thought about what you will do with your time after the person goes to live in a nursing home or dies?

11. Have you planned for your life after caregiving—your social needs, your emotional needs, your practical needs?

12. Have you realized that the work you are doing in caring for your relative is vital to that person's well being? And do you take pride in your ability to offer that care?

✍ A Caregiver's Bill of Rights

Caregivers and the persons who receive care are equal members of a society that guarantees the right to the pursuit of individuality, quality of life, and personal fulfillment. If there is one theme that runs through this book, it is that at any step along the way, you, the caregiver, have the right to say, "I cannot do this," or, at least, "I cannot do this forever." You are responsible for another human being, but you are not responsible for that person's disease or impairments. You did not cause the condition, and the situation in which you and your loved one find yourselves is not one either of you would have chosen—if, indeed, there had been a choice. No matter what you do or how well you do it, the chances are that your relative will not get better.

Across the country caregivers are beginning to realize that society's focus has for some time been totally on the problems and needs of the care recipient. In support groups and national and state organizations, caregivers are beginning to take a stand by banding together and stating that they too have certain needs that must be met. To this end many groups are composing a caregiver's bill of rights.

As your final exercise in this book, add to the list on the following page your own statements of the inalienable rights that you as a primary caregiver for an aging loved one have earned.

A Caregiver's Bill of Rights

I have the right

— to take care of myself. This is not an act of self-ishness. It will give me the capability of taking better care of my relative.

— to seek help from others even though my relative may object. I recognize the limits of my own endurance and strength.

— to maintain facets of my own life that do not include the person I care for, just as I would if he or she were healthy. I know that I do everything that I reasonably can for this person, and I have the right to do some things just for myself.

— to get angry, be depressed, and express other difficult feelings occasionally.

— to reject any attempt by my relative (either conscious or unconscious) to manipulate me through guilt, anger, or depression.

— to receive consideration, affection, forgiveness, and acceptance for what I do from my loved one for as long as I offer these qualities in return.

— to take pride in what I am accomplishing and to applaud the courage it has sometimes taken to meet the needs of my relative.

— to protect my individuality and my right to make a life for myself that will sustain me in the time when my relative no longer needs my full-time help.

— to expect and demand that as new strides are made in finding resources to aid physically and mentally impaired older persons in our country, similar strides will be made toward aiding and supporting caregivers.

— to _____

_____

_____ .

Add your own statements of rights to this list. Read the list to yourself every day.

✄ Appendix

State Agencies on the Aging

Many state agencies on the aging provide free information about state, county, and city services for the elderly and give information on private agencies that offer assistance.

Alabama
Commission on Aging
State Capitol
Montgomery, AL 36130
205-261-5743

Alaska
Older Alaskans Commission
Department of Administration
Pouch C–Mail Station 0209
Juneau, AK 99811
907-465-3250

Arizona
Aging and Adult
   Administration
Department of Economic
   Security
1400 West Washington Street
Phoenix, AZ 85007
602-255-4446

Arkansas
Office of Aging and Adult
   Services
Department of Social and
   Rehabilitative Services
Donaghey Building, Suite 1428
7th and Main Streets
Little Rock, AR 72201
501-371-2441

California
Department of Aging
1020 19th Street
Sacramento, CA 95814
916-322-5290

Colorado
Aging and Adult Services
   Division
Department of Social Services
1575 Sherman Street,
   Room 503
Denver, CO 80203
303-866-3672

Connecticut
Department on Aging
175 Main Street
Hartford, CT 06106
203-566-3238

Delaware
Division on Aging
Department of Health and
    Social Services
1901 North DuPont Highway
New Castle, DE 19720
302-421-6791

District of Columbia
Office on Aging
1424 K Street, NW—2nd Floor
Washington, DC 20011
202-724-5626

Florida
Program Office of Aging and
    Adult Services
Department of Health and
    Rehabilitation Services
1317 Winewood Boulevard
Tallahassee, FL 32301
904-488-8922

Georgia
Office of Aging
878 Peachtree Street, NE,
    Room 632
Atlanta, GA 30309
404-894-5333

Guam
Public Health and Social
    Services
Government of Guam
Agana, GU 96910

Hawaii
Executive Office on Aging
Office of the Governor
1149 Bethel Street, Room 307
Honolulu, HI 96813
808-548-2593

Idaho
Office on Aging
Statehouse, Room 114
Boise, ID 83720
208-334-3833

Illinois
Department on Aging
421 East Capitol Avenue
Springfield, IL 62701
217-785-3356

Indiana
Department of Aging and
    Community Services
Consolidated Building,
    Suite 1350
115 North Pennsylvania Street
Indianapolis, IN 46204
317-232-7006

Iowa
Commission on Aging
Jewett Building, Suite 236
914 Grand Avenue
Des Moines, IA 50319
515-281-5187

Kansas
Department on Aging
610 West 10th Street
Topeka, KS 66612
913-296-4986

Kentucky
Division for Aging Services
Department of Human
    Resources
DHR Building—6th Floor
275 East Main Street
Frankfort, KY 40601
502-564-6930

Louisiana
Office of Elderly Affairs
PO Box 80374
Baton Rouge, LA 70898
504-925-1700

Maine

Bureau of Maine's Elderly
Department of Human Services
State House, Station #11
Augusta, ME 04333
207-289-2561

Maryland

Office on Aging
State Office Building,
    Room 1004
301 West Preston Street
Baltimore, MD 21201
301-383-5064

Massachusetts

Department of Elder Affairs
38 Chauncy Street
Boston, MA 02111
617-727-7750

Michigan

Office of Services to the Aging
PO Box 30026
Lansing, MI 48909
517-373-8230

Minnesota

Board on Aging
Metro Square Building,
    Room 204
Seventh and Robert Streets
St. Paul, MN 55101
612-296-2544

Mississippi

Council on Aging
Executive Building, Suite 301
802 North State Street
Jackson, MS 39201
601-354-6590

Missouri

Division on Aging
Department of Social Services
Broadway State Office
PO Box 570
Jefferson City, MO 65101
314-751-3082

Montana

Community Services Division
PO Box 4210
Helena, MT 59604
406-444-3865

Nebraska

Department on Aging
301 Centennial Mall South
PO Box 95044
Lincoln, NE 68509
402-471-2306

Nevada

Division on Aging
Department of Human
    Resources
Kinkead Building, Room 101
505 East King Street
Carson City, NV 89710
702-885-4210

New Hampshire

Council on Aging
14 Depot Street
Concord, NH 03301
603-271-2751

New Jersey

Division on Aging
Department of Community
    Affairs
363 West State Street
PO Box 2768
Trenton, NJ 08625
609-292-4833

New Mexico

State Agency on Aging
La Villa Rivera Building,
    4th Floor
224 East Palace Avenue
Santa Fe, NM 87501
505-827-7640

New York

Office for the Aging
New York State Plaza
Agency Building 2
Albany, NY 12223
518-474-4425

North Carolina

Division on Aging
708 Hillsborough Street,
    Suite 200
Raleigh, NC 27603
919-733-3983

North Dakota

Aging Services
Department of Human Services
State Capitol Building
Bismarck, ND 58505
701-224-2577

Northern Mariana Islands

Office of Aging
Department of Community and
    Cultural Affairs
Civic Center
Susupe, Saipan, Northern
    Mariana Islands 96950
Telephone Numbers 9411 or
    9732

Ohio

Department on Aging
50 West Broad Street—
    9th Floor
Columbus, OH 43215
614-466-5500

Oklahoma

Special Unit on Aging
Department of Human Services
PO Box 25352
Oklahoma City, OK 73125
405-521-2281

Oregon

Senior Services Division
313 Public Service Building
Salem, OR 97310
503-378-4728

Pennsylvania

Department of Aging
231 State Street
Harrisburg, PA 17101-1195
717-783-1550

Puerto Rico

Gericulture Commission
Department of Social Services
PO Box 11398
Santurce, PR 00910
809-724-7400 or 725-8015

Rhode Island

Department of Elderly Affairs
79 Washington Street
Providence, RI 02903
401-277-2858

(American) Samoa

Territorial Administration on
    Aging
Office of the Governor
Pago Pago, AS 96799
011-684-633-1252

South Carolina

Commission on Aging
915 Main Street
Columbia, SC 29201
803-758-2576

South Dakota

Office of Adult Services and
    Aging
Kneip Building
700 North Illinois Street
Pierre, SD 57501
605-773-3656

Tennessee

Commission on Aging
715 Tennessee Building
535 Church Street
Nashville, TN 37219
615-741-2056

Texas

Department on Aging
210 Barton Springs Road—
    5th Floor
PO Box 12768 Capitol Station
Austin, TX 78704
512-475-2717

Trust Territory of the Pacific

Office of Elderly Programs
Community Development
    Division
Government of TTPI
Saipan, Mariana Islands 96950
Telephone Numbers 9335 or
    9336

Utah

Division of Aging and Adult
    Services
Department of Social Services
150 West North Temple
Box 2500
Salt Lake City, UT 84102
801-533-6422

Vermont

Office on Aging
103 South Main Street
Waterbury, VT 05676
802-241-2400

Virginia

Department on Aging
James Monroe Building—
    18th Floor
101 North 14th Street
Richmond, VA 23219
804-225-2271

Virgin Islands

Commission on Aging
6F Havensight Mall
Charlotte Amalie, St. Thomas,
    VI 00801
809-774-5884

Washington

Bureau of Aging and Adult
    Services
Department of Social and
    Health Services
OB-43G
Olympia, WA 98504
206-753-2502

West Virginia

Commission on Aging
Holly Grove–State Capitol
Charleston, WV 25305
304-348-3317

Wisconsin

Bureau of Aging
Division of Community
    Services
One West Wilson Street,
    Room 663
PO Box 7850
Madison, WI 53702
608-266-2536

Wyoming

Commission on Aging
Hathaway Building, Room 139
Cheyenne, WY 82002-0710
307-777-7986

∾ Notes

1. Pages 1–2, "A Slow Death of the Mind," *Newsweek*, 3 December 1984, 56.
2. Page 9, Ellie King and Deborah Harkins, "Old Folks at Home," *New York*, 8 August 1983, 36.
3. Page 26, Alan L. Otten, "The Oldest Old," *Wall Street Journal*, Monday, 30 July 1984, 1.
4. Page 55, Ruth Seegrist, "Caregivers of the Aged: Part 2— Beth Initiates Action," *Springfield Press*, Wednesday, 23 November 1983, 1.
5. Page 57, David Gelman, "Growing Old, Feeling Young," *Newsweek*, 1 November 1982, 60.
6. Page 72, Betty Risteen Hasselkus, "Relocation Stress and the Elderly," *American Journal of Occupational Therapy* 31(Nov.-Dec. 1978): 631.
7. Page 74, Elaine M. Brody, "'Women in the Middle' and Family Help to Older People," *The Gerontologist* 21, no. 5(1981): 474.
8. Page 83, Diane Rubin, *Caring—A Daughter's Story* (New York: Holt, Rinehart and Winston, 1982), 106.
9. Page 111, Brody, "'Women in the Middle,'" 472.
10. Pages 141–142, Adapted from Maggie Strong's "The Best Medicine Can Be You!" in *Woman's Day*, 11 December 1984, pp. 102–106.
11. Page 243, Rubin, *Caring*, 43.
12. Pages 246–247, Barbara Keyes, "A Word from Our President," *ADRDA Milwaukee Newsletter* 3, no. 2 (Winter 1984), 2.
13. Page 287, Elaine M. Brody, "Parent Care as a Normative Family Stress." The Donald P. Kent Memorial Lecture presented at the 37th Annual Scientific Meeting of The Gerontological Society of America, San Antonio, Texas, 18 November 1984, 17.

◆ Reading List

Throughout the text are recommendations for further reading on specific aspects of caring for another adult. Here is a complete list of books that may contain information helpful to the primary caregiver.

Alderson, George, and Everett Sentman. *How You Can Influence Congress.* New York: E. P. Dutton, 1979.

American Diabetes Association. *The American Diabetes Association/ The American Dietetic Association Family Cookbook.* Vols. I and II. Englewood Cliffs, N.J.: Prentice-Hall, 1980 and 1984.

American Genealogical Research Institute Staff. *How to Trace Your Family Tree.* Garden City, N.Y.: Dolphin Books, 1973.

American Society of Hospital Pharmacists. *Consumer Drug Digest.* New York: Facts on File, Inc., 1982.

Anderson, Margaret. *Your Aging Parents.* St. Louis: Concordia Publishing House, 1979.

Berland, Theodore. *Fitness for Life: Exercises for People Over 50.* Washington, D.C.: AARP, Glenview, Ill.: Scott, Foresman & Co., 1986. (An AARP Book)

Brown, Dorothy S. *Handle with Care: A Question of Alzheimer's.* Buffalo, N.Y.: Prometheus Books, 1985.

Bumagin, Victoria. *Aging Is a Family Affair.* New York: Thomas Y. Crowell Pub., 1979.

Burger, Sarah. *Living in a Nursing Home.* New York: Continuum Publishing Co., 1976.

Burns, David. *Feeling Good.* New York: William Morrow & Co., 1980.

Butler, Robert N., M.D. *Why Survive? Being Old in America.* San Francisco: Harper & Row, Pubs., 1981.

Cadmus, Robert R. *Caring for Your Aging Parents.* Englewood Cliffs, N.J.: Prentice-Hall, 1984.

Caine, Lynn. *Widow.* New York: Bantam Books, 1975.

Chasen, Nancy H. *Policy Wise.* Washington, D.C.: AARP; Glenview, Ill.: Scott, Foresman & Co., 1983. (An AARP Book)

Cohen, Steven Z., and Bruce Michael Gans. *The Other Generation Gap: Middle-Aged Children and Their Aging Parents.* Piscataway, N.J.: New Century, 1978.

Covell, Mara Brand. *The Home Alternative to Hospitals and Nursing Homes.* New York: Rawson, Wade Pubs., 1983.

Duvoisin, Robert C. *Parkinson's Disease: A Guide for Patient and Family.* New York: Raven Press, 1978.

Emery, Gary. *A New Beginning.* New York: Touchstone Books, 1984.

Freese, Arthur S. *Stroke: The New Help and the New Life.* New York: Random House, 1980.

Galton, Laurence. *Don't Give Up on Your Aging Parents.* New York: Crown Pubs., 1975.

Gaumnitz, Jack E. *The Social Security Book.* New York: Arco Publishing, 1984.

Graedon, Joe. *Joe Graedon's The New People's Pharmacy.* New York: Bantam Books, 1985.

Heston, Leonard, and June A. White. *Dementia: A Practical Guide to Alzheimer's and Related Illnesses.* New York: W. H. Freeman and Co., 1983.

Hoffman, Adeline. *Clothing for the Handicapped, the Aged, and Other People with Special Needs.* Springfield, Ill.: Charles C. Thomas, 1979.

King, Eunice M. et al. *The Illustrated Manual of Nursing Techniques.* 2nd ed. Philadelphia: J. B. Lippincott Co., 1981.

La Buda, Dennis R. *The Gadget Book: Ingenious Devices for Easier Living.* Washington, D.C.: AARP; Glenview, Ill.: Scott, Foresman & Co., 1985. (An AARP Book)

Lewinsohn, Peter et al. *Control Your Depression.* Englewood Cliffs, N.J.: Prentice-Hall, 1979.

Little, Billie. *Recipes for Diabetics.* New York: Grosset & Dunlap, 1981.

Long, James W., M.D. *The Essential Guide to Prescription Drugs.* 4th ed. New York: Harper & Row, Pubs., 1985.

Mace, Nancy L., and Peter V. Rabins. *The 36 Hour Day.* Baltimore: Johns Hopkins University Press, 1981.

May, Elizabeth Eckhart. *Independent Living for the Handicapped and the Elderly.* Boston: Houghton Mifflin, 1974.

Murphy, Lois Barclay. *The Home Hospital.* New York: Basic Books, 1982.

Nelson, Thomas C. *It's Your Choice: The Practical Guide to Planning a Funeral.* Washington, D.C.: AARP; Glenview, Ill.: Scott, Foresman & Co., 1983. (An AARP Book)

Otten, Jane, and Florence Shelley. *When Your Parents Grow Old.* New York: Funk & Wagnalls, 1976.

Ottenberg, Miriam. *The Pursuit of Hope.* New York: Rawson, Wade Pubs., 1978.

Percy, Charles H. *Growing Old in the Country of the Young.* New York: McGraw-Hill Book Co., 1974.

Persico, J. E. with George Sunderland. *Keeping Out of Crime's Way: The Practical Guide for People Over Fifty.* Washington, D.C.: AARP; Glenview, Ill.: Scott, Foresman & Co., 1984. (An AARP Book)

Powell, Lenore S., and Katie Courtice. *Alzheimer's Disease: A Guide for Families.* Reading, Mass.: Addison-Wesley Publishing Co., 1983.

Raper, Ann Trueblood, ed. *National Continuing Care Directory.* Washington, D.C.: AARP; Glenview, Ill.: Scott, Foresman & Co., 1984. (An AARP Book)

Reisberg, Barry. *A Guide to Alzheimer's Disease.* New York: Free Press, 1981.

Roach, Marion. *Another Name for Madness.* Boston: Houghton Mifflin, 1985.

Rubin, Diane. *Caring—A Daughter's Story.* New York: Holt, Rinehart & Winston, 1982.

Schwartz, Arthur. *Survival Handbook for Children of Aging Parents.* Chicago: Follett Publishing Co., 1977.

Selye, Hans. *Stress Without Distress.* New York: New American Library, 1974.

Shepherd, Martin. *Someone You Love Is Dying.* New York: Harmony Books, 1975.

Silverman, Harold M., and Gilbert I. Simon. *The Pill Book.* New York: Bantam Books, 1982.

Silverstone, Barbara. *You and Your Aging Parents.* New York: Pantheon Books, 1976.

Smith, Dorothy. *In Our Own Interest.* Seattle: Madonna Pubs., 1978.

Smith, Genevieve W. *Care of the Patient with a Stroke.* New York: Springer, 1976.

Soled, Alex J. *The Essential Guide to Wills, Estates, Trusts, and Death Taxes.* Washington, D.C.: AARP; Glenview, Ill.: Scott, Foresman & Co., 1984. (An AARP Book)

Tomb, David A. *Growing Old, A Complete Guide to the Physical, Emotional and Financial Problems of Aging.* New York: Viking Press, 1984.

Weaver, Peter, and Annette Buchanan. *What to Do with What You've Got.* Washington, D.C.: AARP; Glenview, Ill.: Scott, Foresman & Co., 1984. (An AARP Book)

Weiner, Marcella Baker, and Jeanne Teresi. *Old People Are a Burden But Not My Parents.* Englewood Cliffs, N.J.: Prentice-Hall, 1983.

Zarit, Steven H., Nancy K. Orr, and Judy M. Zarit. *The Hidden Victims of Alzheimer's Disease.* New York: New York University Press, 1985.

Index

✄ About the Author

Jo Horne is a Wisconsin writer whose interest in caregiving is twofold. She and her husband, Larry Schmidt, are the administrators of an adult day-care center in Milwaukee. Through her contact with clients and their families, she became aware that many caregivers had little idea where to turn for help or information. When she sought answers to questions these caregivers raised, she found that often she had to make numerous phone calls or check several references before she could properly answer a specific question. Most caregivers she knew did not have that kind of time.

The other reason Ms. Horne became interested in caregiving is that she began to understand that at some future time she might be called upon to act as a long-distance caregiver for her own parents, who live in Virginia. Looking ahead to that time, she began to investigate what resources might be available for her parents should they need support and care from someone outside the family.

Ms. Horne has a master's degree in Communication from the University of Cincinnati. She has been writing for the last five years. Currently she is producing a monthly newsletter for the adult day-care center that goes to the professional health care community in Milwaukee. In 1983 she was awarded a grant by the Wisconsin Arts Board in association with the National Endowment for the Arts to write a play about the Holocaust entitled *Bridges*.

319

810. **Alone – Not Lonely:** Independent Living for Women Over Fifty.
$6.95/AARP member price $4.95

811. **Travel Easy:** The Practical Guide for People Over 50. *$8.95/AARP
member price $6.50*

812. **Keeping Out of Crime's Way:** The Practical Guide for People Over 50
$6.95/AARP member price $4.95

815. **Cataracts:** The Complete Guide From Diagnosis to Recovery for Patient
and Families. *$7.95/AARP member price $5.80*

817. **Looking Ahead:** How to Plan Your Successful Retirement. *$9.95/AARP
member price $6.95*

181. **Your Vital Papers Logbook.** *$4.95/AARP member price $2.95*

ORDER INFORMATION ━━━━━━━━━━

To order state book name and number, quantity, and price (AARP
members: be sure to include your membership no. for discount) and
add $1.75 *per order* for shipping and handling. *All orders must be
prepaid.* For your convenience we accept checks, money orders,
VISA and MasterCard (credit card orders must include card no., exp.
date and cardholder signature). *Please allow 4 weeks for delivery.*

Send your order today to:
AARP Books, Dept. CBI, Scott, Foresman and Co., 400 S. Edward St., Mt. Prospect, IL 6005

AARP Books are co-published by AARP and Scott, Foresman and Co., sold by Scott, Foresman
and Co., and distributed to bookstores by Farrar, Straus and Giroux.

NO POSTAGE
NECESSARY
IF MAILED
IN THE
UNITED STATES

BUSINESS REPLY CARD

FIRST CLASS   PERMIT NO. 3132   LONG BEACH, CA.

POSTAGE WILL BE PAID BY ADDRESSEE

American Association of Retired Persons
Membership Processing Center
215 Long Beach Boulevard
Long Beach, CA 90801-9989